Virtus Game
Virtus Saga Book 2
The Game: Author's Cut

By

Laura Tolomei

When Prince Duncan Caldwell has to enter Cecilia Hurst's Game of Masters and Slaves, he already knows he'll have to play Master if he intends to retrieve the pyramid Cecilia stole from the sacred Nephis Valley. And his choice for a slave can only be Ylianor Meyer, however fiercely Lord Christopher Templeton resents her and her overpowering erotic intrusion in a trip that should've been his and Duncan's alone.

No, make that in a love that should've been his and Duncan's alone!

Then, things precipitate into chaos, and Duncan's new responsibilities will inevitably change everything forever, their inner balance included.

Such is the new setting of the Virtus Saga, where nothing is as it seems. Not the world, since its all-pervading sex drive hides a scary lack of violence. Not the people, since soul mates Prince Duncan Caldwell and Lord Christopher Templeton burn from a love that is unrivaled until that fateful knock on Ylianor Meyer's dilapidated shack.

This book picks up right where Virtus Sex, Book 1, leaves off and explodes lust and leadership into estrangement and chaos. It's a unique connection, laced with such jealousy and violence that are unknown to their world. Not just another erotic dark fantasy series, this is the making of a trio. Of three remarkable characters that must overcome their uncontrollable lust to face the truth about themselves and their planet if they want to defeat the darkness about to devour them. To be as one whilst three! To share power and love in equal measures. That's their real challenge, the lesson they must learn. Otherwise, how will their world survive?

Virtus Game
Copyright © 2020 Laura Tolomei
ISBN: 978-1-4874-3080-1
Cover art by Angela Waters

Published by eXtasy Books Inc or
Devine Destinies, an imprint of eXtasy Books Inc

Look for us online at:
www.eXtasybooks.com or www.devinedestinies.com

CHAPTER ONE

"Who is Cecilia Hurst?" *And why don't I give a damn about her, only about Prince Duncan Caldwell and his phase mate, Lord Christopher Templeton?*

Oh, fuck!

If she could just concentrate on piecing together the sketchy information gathered at the Nephis Valley and find the stolen heart, she would be the happiest woman alive. Instead, Ylianor Meyer's attention kept shifting on the two gorgeous men riding by her side, which made it unproductive to focus on anything besides the scorching memories of their stay in the pledge's sacred valley and their consequent hurried escape from it.

If it had been a spell, which she hoped it had not, it could not have happened with two more breathtaking creatures than the one she had loved all her life, and the one she was coming to appreciate after weeks spent traveling together.

Under her eyelashes, she stole a peek at *her prince.* Slightly older than his shiny blond phase mate, the very masculine Duncan Caldwell had raven black hair, falling to his shoulders, dancing black eyes, a chiseled face with a square jaw over a tall, powerful, well-built frame with muscles rippling at every movement. Yes, he was impossibly gorgeous and impossibly taken, given how much he loved the very striking and very smug Lord Christopher Templeton.

Who was a real demon, no question about it, had been ever since he had walked into Black Rose with a load of rage and fury so staggering it would have demolished anyone except him—the eight-year-old boy who looked like an angel and had the core of a demon.

Goddamn him and his regular features with that aristocratic nose, the short thick hair flashing brighter than Stella's rays and those intriguing blue-gray eyes she found hard to read at times. As if it were not enough, he was also tall, and his less muscular build spoke of natural grace, elegance and sensuality that were impossible to resist. Goddamn him twice for having her fall all over him, as if she did not know he had despised her from the moment he had set eyes on her.

There was no way around it.

Not just around his arresting appearance. Mostly around his preferences, since he was even more unreachable than the man whom he loved above and beyond his own life—Duncan Caldwell.

To think that, however different they were, both had the same erotic charge, the undeniable allure to beguile men and women alike. Which made it all the stranger they would ever end up in the Nephis Valley, the spot where couples tied the knot that allowed them to have children. *Hardly the place for two such attractive men and me in the middle to look for clues and end up in heated, passionate sex that still burns me all over simply remembering about it.*

Then again, she would have never been there, had David Smith, Duncan's supposedly faithful valet, not insisted that the prince take her along on his trip. He and his concern that Lady Sophia Caldwell might harm her had been her undoing. Or perhaps, it was all Duncan's fault for believing David and his insinuations about how evil his mother could become.

Which was no fabrication, considering how much Ylianor had already suffered from the dreadful woman ever since she was born. That there was no end to her cruelty had become kind of palpable when she had thrown out her little nine-year-old self from Black Rose, her native home, banning her from ever returning. Just her bad luck, her son had found her again and brought her back to stay as Black Rose's new stable keeper, despite all the impediments blocking their way during the ten years they had not seen each other.

Or so she had hoped until David had got it into his head Sophia Caldwell might put her in danger and packed her off to follow the two stunning men, one of which would have gladly reduced her to cinders, rather than have her intrude in his alone time with his adored prince.

Having an agenda to keep had not improved matters any.

Thing was that the High Council Leader, Lord Arthur Fairchild, had summoned them to find the missing piece of the sacred valley's symbolic structure. Not just Chris and Duncan. Ylianor, too, as it turned out, for the High Council Leader had made it very clear the three of them were to work as one. Duncan was the leader and mind of this small group, Chris the body, and she was the spirit of it all. *Hey, who would have ever imagined that?*

Now, she had a prolonged sitting in front of the mysterious tower of three-sided pyramids to prove she belonged with them. Their bond sealed by the unexpected after-effects that had kept all of them chained to a bed for days on end, prey to unforeseeable sexual cravings that refused to let her go now that she was miles away from the wretched place.

"The real question is, what was that all about?" Chris blurted.

No, the real question was, why could she not suppress the torrid images that had already started a furious throbbing between her legs?

"Wasn't it clear enough, Angel?" Duncan grinned.

However mocking the tone, she could not help feeling stung by the prince's sheer love for the blond, beautiful demon, knotted in the throaty endearment.

"At least now we know why pledges take place there." The prince chuckled. "The way it influences people . . ." His grin widened as he gazed at Chris. "It would make it easy to commit to a woman, even for someone like you."

"That was just madness," the demon spat hotly. "A trick of the damn pyramid! Something that would never happen under normal circumstances."

Yeah, sure, as if he could dismiss his odd reactions that easily, him, Christopher Templeton, who had never stooped as low as to touch a woman before in his life, except to stick his cock in her ass or mouth. Well, guess what?

He had not just sampled her all over, using the most seductive stroking ever. He had also played with his fiery energy as if she were his beloved. Unreal to say the least, yet never in her life had she felt warmer and safer than inside the same flames that had tried to burn her alive just days before. One mere touch from him and her blood had raced. Her heart had thumped so loudly that she was still giddy from his passionate kisses and rough sex. Uh, how she had begged for more, yielding to his demands the way she had with her prince alone. And how she would do it again in a heartbeat, regardless of how much he hated her guts.

"Whatever the reason, I never thought I'd see my angel kiss a woman so passionately," Duncan sniggered, his black eyes sparkling in amusement.

"Not funny, lover." Chris turned red. "I was under a spell, remember?"

"Yes, I'll be sure to mention that when I spoil your immaculate reputation at the Hall." Prince Caldwell laughed out loud.

The Hall being the seat of the High Council, the top ruling body of their lands, it was also where Chris had chosen to live after Duncan had ended their phase. Or to hide, depending on the point of view.

"You wouldn't dare!" Chris hissed, his blue-gray eyes sending blazing darts in Duncan's direction. "I'll deny everything."

"If you can." Tightening his knees around Fuzeon, his black horse, the prince flanked Chris. "I'm not sure about what we did with that pyramid, but pledges are notorious at reproducing their own living side effects."

Meaning that no pledge, no children, for no amount of sex between men and women ever produced any life.

"It couldn't . . ." This time, Chris paled all together, his face draining of all blood as the implication of what Prince Caldwell said sank in. "We didn't . . ." With an enquiring gaze, he spun to her, quickly imitated by Duncan.

"Hem . . ." Now, it was her turn to redden under their scrutiny." If the structure's primary purpose is to help couples have babies, it's unlikely to work since it's missing the heart." Catching their looks of relief, she was quick to add in a naughty tone, "Or so I think."

"That's what we hope, Princess." Duncan's tone confirmed he also was not looking for heirs, not at the moment anyway. "But if things should work out the more traditional way, you'll have to do the honorable thing, Angel, since I can't possibly pledge to her."

"What?" Chris's face turned even paler. "That's ridiculous!" Licking his lips nervously, he narrowed an icy cold stare on her. "Are you pregnant?"

Now, funny he should ask.

Among other things, Christopher Templeton was a healer, and that was just for starters. Like the rest of them, he had powers or Virts as Arthur Fairchild had told them the ancients called it. Like her, Chris had discovered the ability to wield nature's forces to his bidding from the earliest years possible. As far back as childhood, for he and Ylianor alone had been aware of what most adults knew nothing about or would learn only later in life.

That was why she was an aura tracer. Seeing people's ethereal bodies in their million combinations of colored lights that shifted according to their moods was one of her specialties. Best of all, she had managed to awaken Prince Caldwell's sleeping potential. Something, not even his phase mate had been able to do, however overpowering he was.

Eat your heart out, Lord Templeton!

Now, Duncan's incredibly strong Virt coursed through his every fiber. More formidable than anything her world had ever seen, it was a boundless pool of cool, deep and potent energy that had lain dormant for the better part of his twenty-one years, as confirmed by Arthur himself.

Next, there was nineteen-year-old Chris. So very powerful, he was fire through and through, a pyre so strong it could disintegrate just as quickly as heal, erasing the memory of it if necessary. Not that he was always so merciful. Not so cruel, either. Like when he had decided to show his rare talents in front of the prince, no less.

While carving her to bits in the process.

Appalling, if not downright monstrous! Her people did not kill animals, not even to eat them. You could just imagine how utterly shocking the sight of someone slashing live flesh could be.

And getting a kick out of it, too!

No, she would not have thought it possible had it come from any other person. The way of her people had never included any form of adult violence as far back as time itself, at least until Christopher Templeton had the lousy idea to show his face around. Being the black-hearted demon he was, she had not allowed the utter shock of it all get to her.

No, she had fought back, refusing to give in to his sadistic knife play, when not going as far as feeling a twisted sense of pleasure at some very particular incisions of his.

"It's too early to tell." An amused snarl curved Duncan's lips.

"Not necessarily." She shifted position on Starlet's saddle. "Whoever is the father . . ." She deliberately spun her gaze from one to the other to make sure they understood she included both. "Any offspring of yours would have so much Virt it couldn't possibly hide its presence, even at an early stage."

"Great." Chris took a deep breath of relief. "This means there's no foreseeable danger of—"

"But the first stages are always tricky," she cut him off, pressing a palm over her flat belly. "And I've been feeling kind of queasy since we left the valley."

"Hey, they might be the warning signs." A dazzling smile split the prince's handsome face.

Her heart stopped dead.

Literally.

Yes, she knew it. She was a fool simply to hold on to her love for him, given how his lights went crazy whenever around the horrible demon. For there was no way he could hide his deep feelings for his angel, not to her, not to her aura reading Virt. But to be fair, she had been there first. At a time when Duncan had not even known Chris existed, she had fallen in love with him beyond any hope of recovery. Just three years younger and barely old enough to stand, she had allowed her dark, handsome hero to chase her on Black Rose's many hills, relishing the feel of being with him in the place that was his home, too. He had always been there for her until something had gone terribly wrong and caused a ten-year separation.

All the demon's fault for sure, what with the prince unexplainable forgetting all about her during the ten-year-estrangement. Too bad, his plan to become Prince Caldwell's sole suitor had backfired most deliciously, and she had returned to be at Duncan's side, stronger than ever.

More in love than ever, too, particularly now that sex had complicated everything, to the point she had not bothered hiding it from him. What would have been the point anyway?

Prince Caldwell would have sensed it eventually. Better to come clean about it, even if she had no guarantees things would change any time soon. He had told her as much at the Hall, admitting straight up he could not return her feelings. Still, he had not cut her out entirely, asking for more time instead. If time was the only obstacle in the way to her prince's heart, she would give him as much as he needed. And Lord Christopher Templeton be damned.

"Who knows?" Duncan's gaze dropped to her belly. "We might have to—"

"Will you two cut it out?" Irritated, Chris pursed his lips. "Don't you think I suffered enough as it is in that damn valley with its fucking side effects?"

What do you say, Princess? The amused glance he exchanged with her was nothing if compared to his deep voice booming in her head. *Shall we let him off the hook?*

That Duncan Caldwell owned his father's gift to share thoughts and emotions had been the most exciting twist of all. For too long, she had missed Prince Charles talking in her head, something that had started as far back as her memory would go. Attuned to his words and feelings, she had drowned in his sensations, as close to him as no daughter could ever be to a father.

Which he was not since he had never pledged to her mother, Mary Jane Elspeth. So, she shared no single drop of blood with the Caldwells, however similar to her appearance was Duncan's. She looked so much like him that she could have easily passed for a twin, which infuriated Chris every time his blue-gray gaze chanced to glance her way. It made no difference as far as family ties went.

Charles's only children were Duncan and his sister, Elizabeth, no matter how hard little Ylianor had tried convincing him of the contrary during the nine wonderful years she had spent with him. Only natural, she would mistake Virt for a non-existent family connection and call Prince Charles, Father, while Duncan had nearly lost it when learning about it. About the will, too, and his father's intention to adopt her into the Caldwell fold. Which would not just give her a name and a station, but outright acknowledge what she had meant to him. Now, she could not wait to know if Duncan would honor it despite all the obstacles standing in the way, like his inner reservations when not his mother's downright fierce objections.

Then again, if it never came about, she would not complain. Not since she had managed to re-establish a link that Prince Charles's death had severed most atrociously. She still reeled from the agonizing silence and the unbearable emptiness suffocating her when he had closed his eyes forever, unable to stand either.

Then, his son had knocked at her shack, and she had known she could have it all back again.

You decide, my love. All sweet and yielding, she pretended to go along with him. Were it up to her, Christopher Templeton would be dangling from that hook for the rest of the day and possibly the night.

"Oh, come on." Not for Duncan, though. "We were just talking—"

"No, you were being a pain in the ass." Chris glared at her as if he had picked up her intention.

Fine!

Nothing in their long ride over had changed the demon to the point he had become the angel Duncan claimed he was. The gods forbid! Christopher Templeton's nature continued to swing from one extreme to another. But then, what else could you expect from someone made of fire?

Unpredictable and uncontrollable, such was his essence, and no amount of incredibly sweet sex or heart-to-heart talk could alter it in the least.

Yet, against her better judgment, she was coming around to the idea of liking him more than she had alleged so far. It was probably the reason for her slip in front of the multi-pyramids structure, which had not failed to catch the prince's attention. Not that it surprised him any.

Oh, all right, maybe he had guessed her change of heart before she did herself, and now she wished she could ask for his support or some sensible advice.

Ha! If only she was not falling for him harder than she had initially assessed. So hard, she could never quell her heart from jumping to her throat every time his arresting gaze traveled in blatant appraisal all over her body. For nothing had prepared her for the storm of the senses that he unleashed so effortlessly—

Oh, crap, she was back to square one, unable to think things through because both men blinded her to the point all she wanted was to be their special toy and nothing else.

"When we should turn our attention to serious matters," Chris reminded.

"As you wish, but I'll never forget how you and the princess looked on that bed." Prince Caldwell cocked his head. "Kissing and fucking like you had no tomorrow—"

"Cut it out, lover." His tense tone revealed just how upset the demon was at the memory. "I can't forget it either if that's any consolation."

"Hey, there's no need to get uptight about it." Duncan seemed bent to make Chris relive the experience, whether he wanted to or not. "You were damn arousing." The images running through his head made her flush. "Not just 'cause you did it with a woman for a change. 'Cause you even went as far as using your fire without hurting her." His black eyes brimmed with glee, as they fixed on Chris with a love so powerful she felt embarrassed merely to see it. "I'm very proud of you, Angel." He changed register, "If I were you, I'd never forget this experience 'cause pledges need happy memories."

"My dear prince, let me remind you that you're in dire need of an heir worse than I'll ever be." Shoulders thrown back, Chris flashed blue-gray eyes in challenge. "If worse comes to worst, perhaps you'd be the one to profit more from all this."

"Yeah, right." The velvety black eyes twinkled maliciously. "I can just imagine my mother's reactions if she thought the princess carried my child," he retorted sarcastically. "She'd be so thrilled she'd probably get a heart attack."

"Only after she kills Ylianor." Chris burst out laughing, obviously imagining Sophia Caldwell's hate for what she considered an unwanted meddler in her family's affairs. "And maybe, you, too."

She worked hard at keeping a straight face. If they could joke about something that had caused her insufferable pain for the past eighteen years of her life, it was only thanks to Duncan and his resolve to break down the barriers that had stood in the way of their true unity. For sure, she had some pretty heavy load of her own to get rid of, all beginning and ending with Duncan's mother, at least until her sharing it with the demon and the prince had not lightened it somehow.

"Would you two get over yourselves?" Ylianor snapped in mock exasperation. "What makes you so sure I'd pledge to either of you?"

"Why wouldn't you?" Offended, Chris swung his gaze to the prince. "Can you believe it? She wouldn't even want us."

"Aren't we good enough for you, Princess?" Half teasing, half-serious, Duncan studied her face.

"I might have other plans for my life." She giggled mischievously. "Which may include someone else entirely like David," she taunted until the prince's scowl made her quickly change the subject. "But this is beside the point." She had almost forgotten Duncan telling her how jealous he had felt of the man. "We should concentrate on finding who stole the pyramid from the tower in the Nephis Valley, and Cecilia Hurst seems the most likely candidate."

David, too, or why else would she have glimpsed his aura during the long night spent sitting in front of the multi-pyramids tower?

Out of respect to Duncan, she preferred to concentrate on the woman.

The man was no ordinary one, after all. Not just Prince Caldwell's personal valet since forever, he was also a close and trusted friend of Duncan's, something she hoped would not change given this recent discovery.

"So, who is Cecilia Hurst?" Her gaze swung from Chris to Duncan.

"She was one of the prince's flames." The blue-gray eyes blazed, probably under the influence of memory.

"That's hardly significant," she scoffed. "From what I can tell, there's a long list of them." Which had all been part of Duncan Caldwell's search for a suitable pledge mate after he had ended his phase with Chris.

An unsuccessful attempt, she was glad to report.

"The girl is bright, not to mention highly perceptive." Ignoring her, Chris's focus trained on Duncan alone. "Too bad, she doesn't want to pledge, or I might just have proposed."

"It happened some time ago, Princess," he was quick to block Chris's sarcasm. "After I broke off with the angel."

"A wise choice you should've stuck to." Oh, boy! Was she glad for the chance to get back at the demon. "But you can still reconsider it."

"No way can he live without me, dearie." Spitting fire from every pore, Chris raised himself on the saddle. "I'd have gotten him back no matter what."

"I wouldn't be so sure," she bit back. "Had Arthur himself not interfered in getting the two of you just to meet again, you'd be history by now." The High Council Leader loving the demon with such desperation, made his gesture all the nobler.

Chris growled, "Why, you presumptuous witch—"

"Cecilia has nothing to do with what happened between the angel and me." Duncan's tone was firm as though to dispel any doubts.

One thing she was noticing about him was that he was getting a kick out of her quarrels with Chris, which she was not sure was such a good thing.

"She was my first experience with women and an odd one at that." The prince paused as if to recapture some of the old memories. "Sex obsesses her." Given her people's propensity to do it as much and as often as they could, she was not sure how Duncan meant this. "I've never seen anyone do it with so much effort yet get so little out of it." He frowned in puzzlement. "It's like her mind works overtime to undermine what her body should know by instinct."

"Hey, since you're such an expert, tell us what sex is," Chris provoked in mock dare.

"Well, my dear angel, sex is your beautiful body language." The prince's attention was all on his blond lover. "The way you react to my every touch is what tells me how much you want me to claim you, possess you in all ways possible." His voice lowered, "Then, you swing your ass, and I can't take it anymore. I just gotta have you, gotta melt in that irresistible fire of yours until nothing matters except my erection stuck up your ass or down your throat until we both shatter in pleasure."

There was a comprehensible momentary suspension as she felt the vibrations travel from one to the other.

"Great! You convinced me." Eyes glowing with lust, Chris seemed ready to jump off his horse. "Let's stop and do it here."

"I was merely answering your question." Duncan smiled regretfully. "It's a shame Cecilia can't even come close to understanding any of this. Her mind always prevents her body from joining in the fun. 'Cause she uses a cold and rational approach to what's hot and fiery by default."

"Cecilia is just a bitch out to make any man pay for her lack of sexual satisfaction," Chris snickered. "At the Hall, she always goes around with that stern expression of hers, like she wants to chastise everyone for taking pleasure in sex. Which is something so beyond her that she's got no hope of ever getting it." Kind of obvious, the demon knew her well enough and couldn't stand her.

"I bet she doesn't approve of the Arthur boys either," Duncan offered.

Now, who were the Arthur boys, she had no idea.

If she had to take a wild guess, it would have to involve Chris and Lord Fairchild's need to find a way to control what no one could except for the dark-haired prince. Knowing Chris, this way would have had to do with sex.

"That's an understatement," Chris snarled. "As a high and mighty council member, she abhors our innocent orgies and harmless parties, to the point she'd erase them from the Hall's life if she could." He gripped his reins harder. "If it wasn't enough, she's a permanent member, too, which means I'll have to put up with her forever."

Right. Had Cecilia only been a temporary one, she would have had to leave the Hall after three years. How long they stayed in office, this was the difference between the twelve permanent members and their twelve temporary counterparts.

"I bet she already can't stand you." Ironic yet to the point, she had no doubt Duncan was correct.

"Hates my guts is more like it." Never one to ignore demeaning people he detested, Chris was only too happy to tear the poor woman apart. "She's a jealous bitch who hasn't taken it kindly that I rose higher than she ever will in the Hall's hierarchy."

Had she mentioned how vain Christopher Templeton was?

"'Cause I got the looks she never will." The demon licked his lips like a satisfied feline. "And a rank she can just reach in her dreams."

"At least, she's an official council member." Just for the heck of it, she loved to ruffle his feathers the wrong way. "While your title is what exactly? Besides being the leader's sex toy, I mean."

"That's a whole lot more than Cecilia will ever be." Scornful, Chris threw back his shoulders as though getting ready for a fight. "Being the leader's lover and the son of the vice-leader is all you need to get to the top of that place."

Yes, Christopher Templeton had such a high sense of self nothing could bring it down.

"All in all, she's one of the worst women at the Hall." Smirking, he glanced at Duncan. "I'm not surprised that, in the end, you dropped her for her phase mate."

"Her phase mate?" *Uh, do tell, Prince.*

Not that she shared this thought. She just tried to keep her extreme curiosity in check, knowing how little Duncan cared for her unwanted invasion of privacy.

The sad thing was that Prince Duncan Caldwell had not accepted his Virt of head-talking all that readily. To put it mildly, he still had a world of reservations about it, most stemming from her and her constant presence in his mind.

"Rowena Sentry." At the name, Duncan flooded her with the woman's face.

Quite different from Cecilia's hard cut features, Rowena had a lovely warm smile, dazzling blue eyes, blond hair falling softly around her perfect oval face with a straight nose and tempting lips.

"She's beautiful." Ylianor had to suck in her breath.

"At least she's feminine." Chris grinned. "While the other one . . ." Meaning Cecilia. "Looks like an ugly man."

"They were phase mates until Rowena decided she wanted men in her bed." Duncan intercepted her gaze. "Cecilia never got over the break-up."

Nothing strange there. Phases often ended abruptly. It was an adolescent thing, after all. Her people's unique way of discovering and exploring sex with a friend of the same age and gender. Just her bad luck, not everybody had one. Not having had it herself, simply watching Chris and Duncan's easygoing relationship, had made her realize how much she had missed out in her life.

"What you have to understand is that Cecilia was an orphan." The prince sat up straighter to tighten his hold on Fuzeon. "She lost both her parents when she was but a baby. An aunt took care of her, but then she died when Cecilia was only ten. It's hardly surprising she fell in love with Rowena and believed her phase would last forever."

"Didn't Lord Templeton have the same insane notion?" Oh, she was asking for it.

She knew it!

Only could not resist provoking the detestable demon to his face.

"We lasted, dearie." Of course, Chris would strike back. "They didn't."

"That's because Rowena was very interested in men." Prince Caldwell lifted a shoulder. "She thinks they're more fun in and out of bed, at least until she got the urge to pledge."

"Don't tell me she had the nerve to ask you!" That this was new information for Chris was evident from his shocked expression.

"She did." Duncan made it sound like he was sorry he had not accepted her offer.

Just to make fun of his blond lover.

"I refuse to believe you regret it!" Which got Chris flying off his horses.

"She wasn't a bad lay," the prince kept taunting. "I could've lived with her, had I been ready to commit to a woman."

For her, it was not a question of being ready, instead of being too choosy. Duncan Caldwell had such an impossible aristocratic taste people seldom met his extremely high standards. This was why he had few friends, no mate and no stable keeper, as Anne Peacock, Black Rose's cook, had so aptly put it.

"What's happened to her now?" She pushed some loose strands off her face.

"She's happily pledged to an older man who stays at home and looks after their son while she goes around, screwing any available male." The demon beamed. "In other words, she's got the perfect pledge."

Small wonder Chris should know. His love for gossip had become clear from her first day on the road with him. Something told her he had used it abundantly in his rise to the top of the Hall, taking advantage of all his influence and information to become its number one.

"Theirs works perfectly." The prince nodded in agreement. "Also 'cause Oliver prefers to dedicate his time to farming. He has such a gift for it and uses such innovative techniques no one else dares put into practice. To the point, he has managed to turn parts of Cecilia's desert lands into green and fertile areas."

"The man is nothing short of a genius." There was a note of healthy respect in Chris's tone she had never heard before, if not connected to the prince. "My brother, Steve, says so, and he should know 'cause he was Oliver's phase mate."

"I've no doubt he is." There was no hiding Duncan's

admiration, either. "Anyone who could make plants sprout from a wasteland is."

"But Rowena cares nothing for this," Chris remarked. "Even if he's a good man, he's too boring for her taste. That's why she's always after every pair of pants passing her way."

"Completely unlike her phase mate, who cares little for men and has way too many responsibilities as it is." The black eyes sparkled in obvious arousal. "Besides her council duties, Cecilia is also the heir of the Blandry District, a desert land west of the Nephis Valley."

"Yeah, and a neighbor of ours, unfortunately." Chris hung his head in mock despair. "Our district, Dartmouth, is just south of the Nephis Valley and borders with Blandry."

"Please, don't tell me we have to cross another desert." After how stressful travel through the Wadirum Desert had been, the last thing she wanted was another go at those steeply rising temperatures and Stella's rays blazing all day on her head.

"I'm afraid so." Duncan shrugged apologetically. "It's right there." He indicated the vast emptiness just a few miles away. "She probably keeps the missing pyramid at Blue Oasis, her home, which is where we're going now."

"I see." Now, she understood why Duncan had seemed to follow a definite direction, despite his rush to leave that enchanted shelter in the Nephis Valley. "But how do you suppose we look for it without arousing suspicions?"

"That's easy." Prince Caldwell seemed certain of it. "By entering her Game, which starts in about ten days."

"You received her invitation?" Chris sounded surprised.

"I most certainly did." A flash and the image of a red carton slip with an emblem engraved on it filled her mind. "I think she invited me to all the editions, all four of them."

"She must really like you." Chris seemed impressed. "I know for a fact she has never asked the same person twice and only after a very rigid selection."

"I guess she must think I'd be particularly good at playing her Game." Duncan chuckled.

"Her Game?" Now, why did she have the sneaky suspicion she would not like this new twist? "What game?"

"Well . . ." Duncan exchanged a knowing glance with Chris.

"Oh, no, lover, I'm not going to help you." The demon held up a hand as though to block the prince's unspoken request. "It's your idea, so you tell her."

"I see." Prince Caldwell cleared his throat. "As I said, Cecilia is obsessed with sex. After I met her, she devised a game for it, with strict rules about how to play. Like the one about participants having to be at least two but no more than three at a time. That's because there are only three roles available — master, guest or slave."

"Slave?" She knew she would not like where this was going.

Even more, she knew she should have stayed at Black Rose instead of following them around like a lovesick puppy.

"Yes." Duncan spurred Fuzeon to get closer to Starlet, her beautiful gray mare, a gift from Prince Caldwell himself. "On entering the Game, you have to choose who plays what and follow every rule for that particular role." His piercing black eyes bore into hers as though wanting her to have no misunderstandings about what would happen. "Take the slaves, for instance. They have no rights. They're forbidden to do anything, including speak or eat, without express permission. Their only purpose is to serve, and they can't refuse to have sex. Or to obey their master's every order, however outrageous it might be. They can starve to death. They're not allowed to ask for food or drinks. Only they can provide these things, and sometimes masters aren't so merciful."

"So, masters have total control over their slave's body and

mind, right?" This was not too difficult to get.

"Right." He rewarded her with a luminous smile splitting his handsome face. "They dominate the slaves completely, and nothing but total surrender is accepted."

That's where you got your idea of turning me into your slave. Dots connected fast. *Isn't it?*

It was practically what she had been doing with Duncan ever since leaving Black Rose, enslaved to him body and mind, at least as far as the bed went. Only difference, she had no one to blame except herself for having surrendered everything to him. True, he had asked her to do it. She had to spoil it all by accepting.

Partly, he confirmed. *Though Cecilia is still an amateur at this.*

"What's the guest supposed to do?" Whatever it was, she suspected it would fit Chris's needs perfectly.

"Guests are a step up from slaves, so a master cannot order them around." *Yes, my angel would have no problems playing guest.* "They're free to do pretty much what they want, but only if their masters consent to it."

"Sounds a lot like our present arrangement." Which was a sort of relief. At least it would prove no hardship to enter this game of Cecilia's. "There's no need to guess what role I'll be playing."

"Actually, Princess, there's also an age limit for each role." It was kind of obvious Duncan was ill at ease.

Not because she would play the slave.

Because she seemed to have no choice in the matter, yet choice was all her handsome dark-haired prince believed in wholeheartedly.

"Masters must be twenty-one or older, guests nineteen and slaves at least eighteen." Duncan took a deep breath. "I've played guest once, but for obvious reasons, I've never played with the angel—"

"'Cause I could never play the slave." The demon threw back his head defiantly.

"While I have a natural talent for it, don't I, Lord Templeton?" Ylianor challenged.

Nah, whom was she kidding?

Truth was—she loved being Prince Duncan Caldwell's slave.

Not because she got to service him.

Because she got the other one in the bargain.

There could be no greater pleasure than being at their complete mercy.

If the prince seduced her every time he got his hands on her, the demon laced his sex with that extra veneer of cruelty she was coming to appreciate every day more. No, crave was the operative word, particularly after he had revealed the extent of his fiendishness. As though that knife of his had awakened something buried inside her, to the point she sometimes fantasized they could repeat it . . . just to see how far this intriguing game might get.

Yes, she was a slave through and through and would have gladly dropped to the ground to obey their every whim, had they only ordered it right there and then.

"You said it, dearie, not I." From his noncommittal tone, there could be no doubt he thought her nothing better than a slave.

That sent a thrilling shiver down her spine.

Because no matter what he said, she would get him in the end. Nothing would work better or faster than playing it like she had no will of her own.

"No one's born slave," Prince Caldwell was quick to rectify. "It's simply a question of balances. Like you said, Princess, this seems to fit our present arrangement, at least when we're in bed." No surprise he would underline this particular detail.

Things had slid so far down when he had been angry with her and had treated her like she was a slave *for real*, which was the farthest thing from the man he was and the principles he had upheld ever since his childhood.

"Our age doesn't help, either, 'cause it determines our roles." Again, he seemed sad she would get the short end of the stick. "Neither you nor the angel could play master, nor can you be a guest, so . . ." He hesitated. "But we'll do it only if you agree to it." This improved his mood. "I don't want to force you into anything, Princess." The caring gaze he sent her way melted her heart. "Like we agreed at the Hall, you are no slave. You are an equal partner of this arrangement of ours, so I'll understand if you'd rather not play this game."

Oh, could she love him more than she already did?

"Should such be the case, all we've got to worry about is finding another way into Blue Oasis." A most enchanting smile was his reassurance that he would not consider this as a setback at all.

"Sure, losing a whole lot of time in the process." The blue-gray eyes blazed in annoyance.

"Oh, I'm sure we can be inventive enough." The long, black hair fluttered as Duncan spun to confront Chris. "Even if this game is the best opportunity for us." His gaze locked on her. *Not to mention the most exciting.*

She swallowed hard, her face growing hot with the images he was sending her.

"What's important in this Game is the interplay between a master and his slave." His voice became husky, "'Cause it tests their limits and determines how far they can both go. The master in submitting his slave, the slave in obeying her master's every order." The picture he painted was so arousing her clit throbbed furiously, "Most people don't understand this. They think that any slave would do, so they bring someone who's inconsequential. They are such fools." He snorted contemptuously. "They don't realize that, without a connection between the two, the Game becomes a sterile repetition of heated fucks." Glancing fondly at the demon, he beamed. *I know you understand why the angel could never be a suitable candidate for playing slave.*

Yeah, she got that. The difference in Duncan's treatment of her as opposed to that of the demon would be the key to spin this particular game out of its rigid structure.

Yeah, you get it. Duncan's broad smile, splitting his beautiful face, was her special reward for being on his same wavelength. "The fact slaves can't talk will be an extra turn-on for us." *'Cause we don't need limited words, do we, Princess?*

"That would be cheating!" The demon flared.

Sometimes Chris was too perceptive for her taste. Like at the moment, when he seemed to have heard his lover's silent musing.

"Since when have you followed the rules, Angel?" Duncan raised the stakes. "Just for the record, don't think I'll make it easy for her only 'cause I know what she likes —"

"You'd choose the exact opposite." She could practically count on it. "Wouldn't you?"

"Sure, just to spite you," Duncan joked.

"As if I didn't know it already," she scoffed. "That you'll use our connection to . . ." *Get a real kick out of what they'll do to me.*

Exactly. His full lips curved in a most attractive grin. *The angel was right. You are a bright girl, after all.*

How devious. She stuck out her tongue at him.

How delicious! "But we'll do it only if you agree to it." Sober once more, it was apparent her consent was essential to him.

What you're proposing is a game within the Game. She still could not believe he was cutting the demon out of this, wanting her to be his playmate in a way Chris could never be.

Right again, Princess. The velvety black eyes shone with barely suppressed arousal. *It'll be loads of fun. You'll see.*

Damn him!

She could not wait for that to happen, though she acted like she had not heard. "Has Cecilia set up a special place in Blue

Oasis to play this Game of hers?"

"Yes." The prince nodded. "She has devoted an entire hall to it."

Unbidden, the images came to her of a large rectangular chamber. Lit by torches hanging on the walls, it was full of nooks with comfortable leather couches around low black tables. Everywhere she looked, people had sex with just about anything that moved. Smoke, sweat and sex oozed from the stonewalls, hazing the naked people sitting on the tables and the more dressed ones hovering over them.

"What an odd setting." She sifted through Duncan's pictures. "The dress code is weird, as well."

"Masters wear robes." The projection he sent her was of a man dressed in a dark blue tunic that fell to his ankles. "Guests have bare chests and wear either pants or skirts. Slaves are naked."

Only natural, she wondered how she would look on one such low table.

"Oh, you'd make a most erotic addition to that chamber." Duncan smacked his lips in evident anticipation.

"If I decide to participate." No, she would not give him the satisfaction of an easy surrender, no matter how fiercely her body stung. Why should she?

He had taken too much for granted already, also using her foolish love against her. If she were to accept anything, it would have to be on her own time!

No point in sharing this, she straightened her shoulders. "I'll think about it while we get there." Fixing her gaze on the long road ahead, she pretended nothing else mattered.

CHAPTER TWO

"Cecilia's desert is hotter than the Wadirum ever will be."
Have I mentioned how much I hate it?

Hated it since he was a child. Glancing at the vast and very empty sandy wasteland Chris would have to cross in the coming days, he scowled.

"It gets so damn hot in this season my family avoids it whenever we have to come this way." Not all the desert's fault, though. Mostly Cecilia's and her none too friendly attitude. He, for one, did not particularly relish Duncan's agenda, nor the thought of having to confront the odious woman any time soon.

What about the way his lover planned to play her goddamn game? Using the one person he should have never brought along in this trip and confirming her status as his official slave? In front of everybody, no less?

The mere idea made his blood boil, and the fucking heat had nothing to do with it. All to do with his mounting rage, considering how long the detestable witch had been intruding in his alone time with his beloved prince.

"I know." Full of understanding, the black eyes sparked his way. "But it takes more time to go all the way around it, and that's something we don't have." The long silky hair fluttered around Duncan's shoulders as he spun to sweep the horizon. "But you shouldn't have any problems." He grinned as he turned again to him. "Not with all that fire you have inside."

"Hey, in case you haven't noticed, I'm still made of flesh and blood." Annoyed, he threw back his head.

25

Today, his lover seemed bent on irking him, and after what happened at the blasted valley, it was the last thing he needed.

"I haven't been noticing anything else all day long." A mischievous twinkle brightened the velvety gaze.

"That's it! Let's stop for the night." *And have some real fun finally!*

"I don't know." Dubious, Duncan glanced upward. "It's just the twentieth hour, and Stella is still kind of high."

"So what?" He needed to stop so badly he could not stand it anymore. He just had to wipe out of his system Ylianor's taste and feel.

Not to mention punishing and giving her a lesson she would never forget.

Ever!

For being the perfect slave, though that was just for starters.

Never, ever, in his life had he wanted a woman as fiercely as he had her, and it still grated on his nerves. Not because she was a woman. Because it was *her*, the pesky nuisance he had found at Duncan's side when he had first met the dark-haired handsome prince, the only one stupid enough to challenge him outright.

The only one with the power to do it, something he could never forget, even if he had sent her packing almost ten years ago. Just another top item on his long list of grievances against this witch who looked like a twin of his adored prince, all of which were reasons enough to skin her alive, had his unqualifiable behavior at the Nephis Valley not been more pressing at the moment.

"I need the rest." Spotting a log cabin just a little bit off the road, he maneuvered Black toward the intended track.

"Yeah, now it's called rest," his phase mate teased, spurring Fuzeon to follow.

"You're right, lover, it isn't." Reaching his destination, he jumped off his horse and tossed the reins aside. "It's called *let's have fun just the two of us*." Grabbing Duncan upon dismounting, he wrenched him toward the threshold. "Let your stable keeper earn her keep for once."

If such had been the excuse Prince Caldwell had used to get her back into his life, he was more than justified to hold it against him. *Right?*

"Can't wait to punish her for your loss of control, eh?" Chuckling, Duncan resisted his pull.

"Can't wait to have you all by myself, after the gods only know how long we've spent in that godforsaken shelter in the Nephis Valley." Just his luck that flashes of the sex with the witch rushed at him upon perusing inside the refuge.

All the damn place's fault, since they all looked alike. Built by the Shelter System, they all had the same characteristics to offer travelers a providential roof over their heads and adequate food during their journey. None knew it better than he did since he had worked as a Shelter Boy during his early years, making the rounds of his district to clean up and bring supplies.

"She can keep to the stables until we're done." Not that Duncan would allow it for real.

If he said it at all, it was to prove to himself nothing had changed. That he still craved the masculine feel of one man alone, and that his lifetime convictions had not just gone down the drain.

"Without my slave watching, where would the fun be?" As expected, Duncan objected.

The man was getting far too deep into her for his taste, and that asking her to give him more time promised nothing good.

"What sort of lesson could you teach her if she isn't burning in her skin to have the very cocks you'll deny her?" Whispered seductively in his ear, this sounded like a very reasonable argument.

"Fine, she can come inside," Chris relented. "But she isn't to move or talk." *Not breathe either,* he would have added, was it not a physical impossibility. "Not even in your head."

"Heard that, Princess?" Handing her the bridles, Duncan peered at her intently.

Which gave him the impression he was saying much more in her head.

"Take care of the horses. Then, come straight here." Letting the reins go, his phase mate turned to him. "All right, Angel, I'm all yours."

"Damn right, you are!" Gripping him harder, he tugged him inside. "And she better never forget it." Spotting the couch, he drove Duncan to it, pushing him down on the fluffy cushions.

Too hungry to waste time, he bent until his head rested on Duncan's lap. Breathing hot air on the prize already stiffening, he freed it from its confining clothes and gobbled it to his throat. Just opening his mouth, the twitching piece was a good way to his stomach, where he would have loved to imprison it if that trifle about choking did not prevent it.

Still, he would not let such insignificant details spoil it for him. Not since the most amazing stick of all had become so rigid, it was increasingly difficult to hold it all in his mouth. To think he had an extremely spacious cavity when it came to cocks. Yet, it never applied to that fabulous equipment, since it was always far bigger than anything he had ever savored in his life.

Now, as massive and as unmanageable as a veritable monster, it slipped past his tongue's blocking effect and aimed straight for his guts. It made no difference that throat and stomach stood in the way. From the forceful blows hitting his wide-open mouth, he had no doubt his lover would reach it eventually. Which was absolutely fine. When it came to sex, Prince Caldwell was the unrivaled master, and he would do whatever it took to satisfy his every whim.

Except perhaps suffocate.

At the renewed attack on his throat, he increased the pressure of his cheeks around the very long and very thick length of the shaft, impaling his oral cavity. Sucking was also the way to prevent it from taking too many initiatives that were sure to preclude him from finishing up his skillful blowjob. With his own shaft throbbing from arousal and anticipation, he was just about to dive further down on the fat crown shoving to require more space when he went slab of marble all together.

Not just him.

Duncan, too.

Since his rhythm had not changed any, he could only guess the damn witch had entered the room. It fucking galled him that his body should react so strongly to her presence. It so pissed him off he could just wonder if maybe what had happened at the Nephis Valley had nothing to do with spells or witchcraft. What if it was just sheer raw craving of her?

Furious, he assaulted the unwavering erection more viciously. If sadly Duncan had become too partial to women since the end of their phase, he would do his best to make him forget all about it. His licks and laps more scorching, his intakes were so violent he almost carried the balls through, and suffocation be damned!

"Hey, Angel." Yanking his hair, Duncan snapped his head back. "What do you say we make it more difficult for her?"

"For her?" Seemed to him, he and Duncan were in serious trouble just because she was there. "What do you have in mind?" Resigned to have the fastidious woman torment him also during his favorite activity, he groaned.

"Just a more fitting attire." A broad grin split the prince's handsome face before he spun his gaze on her. "Strip," his tone became colder. "And kneel."

That she scrambled to obey, he guessed from the frantic movement he caught with the corner of an eye. Not that he bothered to look. He much rather preferred keeping his gaze trained on the black one now locked on his.

"This way, she won't be able to hide how badly she wants us." Duncan chuckled.

"If you really want her to suffer, there are more efficient means to do it," he blurted the words before he had the chance to think.

"Like tying her down?" For someone who had never loved any kind of bondage, the prince seemed to have a surprising ability to be one step ahead of him.

"Exactly." Well, maybe this might just turn out not so bad, after all.

"Very well." Letting go of his hair, Duncan reclined on the couch. "Can't wait to see what your fertile imagination will come up with."

If this was not a dare, he did not know what was. Straightening, he went to a small chest next to the couch. Opening the lid, he spotted several pieces of ropes and took them all. Then, he whirled around and saw her.

Body slightly trembling, she studied him coldly, almost defiantly. Like she had the night he had carved her to bits, she seemed to be expecting the worst from him, ready to sustain whatever cruelty he would inflict. Goddamn it, he just loved it!

So much, his equipment had a quite visible jerk, something she had no trouble noticing and counting as a measure of victory over him.

Ha! He would just have to show her worse than he had planned, and nothing would work better than the low table beside her.

"Get up there and kneel," he snapped.

If she obeyed, she was not as prompt as she had been with

Duncan, which was just as well. She was giving him one more excuse to be a vicious bastard.

Going around her, he clamped her wrists and tugged them backward. Hard and ruthless, he wrenched both arms until her hands almost touched the floor, and she had to arch her back if she did not want to break it. Absolutely perfect this way, he crossed over her arms, fastening just above the left elbow to the right ankle, the right elbow to the left ankle. Buttressing the bondage, he tied more rope around both ankles and elbows until she could not budge an inch.

"By the gods!" Rising from the couch, Duncan approached her. "I suspected you were good at this but never thought you could be such a master."

"Had a lot of practice while playing my . . . games." Unwilling to dwell on just how many of his victims he had tied down to torture more efficiently, he got up and reached his phase mate.

"Only thing, Angel . . ." The prince was eating her up with mere glances alone. "I'm not sure you achieved the desired effect."

He looked.

And he could have kicked himself for having done such a splendid job of it, for she was so tasty with her cunt pushed up and out that he would have taken her himself.

"The important thing is that she's at our complete mercy." Annoyed, he tried downplaying it. "So that, whatever you want to do to her, you'll have plenty of chances to do it later — "

"I'm not sure I can wait that long." In front of her, Duncan brushed the defenseless cunt. "She's just too inviting." Which was so wet, honeydew stuck all around his fingers.

"But I haven't finished sucking you." Irritated by now, he clutched what he considered his beast possessively.

"Oh, you will." Detaching his paw, the prince straddled the

low table. "Don't worry."

One thrust was all it took for him to sink into her velvety pussy.

"Lover, I thought we had agreed this was going to be a lesson for her." Unable to tear his gaze away, he watched the swollen rod disappearing inside of her before pulling out, slick and drenched on all sides.

"That's exactly what it is." Keeping a steady tempo, Duncan penetrated to the hilt once more and out again. "So, you better make sure she doesn't come."

"Easier said than done." He smirked.

One thing he had fast learned about her. She was a slut worse than he would ever be. Not just because she loved cocks, his and Duncan's in particular. She seemed built to give and receive pleasure. A mere touch and she could easily climax. That was how immediate her response was. No wonder she came as many times as she did during a single fuck.

Which so fucking turned him on that he could not stand it!

Now that Duncan's erection was so deep inside her, she was losing it already. He could bet on it, so again it was more of a challenge on Duncan's part.

"But I'll try." Bending over, he reached for her taut nipples and twisted them brutally.

If she did not jump from the pain, it was only because she could not. No way could she move, not even if in excruciating pain, which was a further turn-on that made his cock leap from inside his pants. He took it out and jerked it while pinching her most sensitive spots, loving the way her skin cringed, torn between pain and pleasure.

Duncan had stepped up his dance and was now slamming inside her. She was so liking it that her clit throbbed wildly from the need to burst.

Which was not an option, so he became more ruthless in hurting her.

But the only way to make her suffer for real was removing the fantastic cock splitting her apart at just the precise moment. Since he could feel her orgasm as it built from her pussy upward, he snatched the marble monster the second before she exploded and gulped it to his stomach.

"Fuck, Angel." Of course, Prince Caldwell was coming all inside his mouth.

While he was trying to hold it together somehow. Because between the heavy jets shooting down his throat and her bitter lemony taste exploding all inside him, he was losing it himself.

"No, no coming for you now." Blocking his hand, Duncan drew back. "I want you to come inside her."

"Again?" Like in a nightmare, he could not seem to be free of her. "Lover, in case you've forgotten, I haven't done anything else in ages besides coming inside her."

"This time, it'll be different." After tearing off his pants, Duncan dragged him to the low table, placing him in front of her curved-up slit. "This time, it'll be your choice." Driving Chris's cock forward, he screwed it inside the yielding opening.

Boy, talk about wet and tight!

So fucking tight, he was about to spill what was pressing on the tip of his erection.

Amazing how her pussy felt in this position. Like a narrow strip of burning flesh he enlarged beyond its capacity with each blow. Best of all, the sensation of tightness never diminished. Just too constricted, her slit could not accommodate him without an effort.

With Duncan shoving in his ass, it was the beginning of the end.

It was simply too good to last. To have his lover ramming his rear ring was always a treat in itself. To have it combined with her crushing effect on his shaft was too much, also because his pumping coordinated with Duncan's beautifully.

"Now, to teach her the real lesson," Prince Caldwell whispered.

"What lesson?" He spat, "She's loving this too much for any lesson to be effective."

"Wrong." Hot breath tickling, Duncan bit his earlobe. "The way to teach her a lesson is to show her who is in control." Grasping his hand, he brought it on her cunt. "You'll be in charge of her orgasm simply by stroking this very hungry clit of hers." Using both their fingers, he dipped and circled the pounding knot. "While if you don't want her to come, simply pinch it, and it'll stop whatever surge of pleasure she's building inside." He let his hand fall. "Again, the choice is yours, Angel." Bending him slightly, he heightened his beat. "Just be quick about it 'cause I'm not going to last any in this delicious behind of yours."

Neither was he, for that matter.

Already the scorching waves had coiled around the long gland and were pushing the sperm to the exit. She was right along with them, would have probably beaten both him and Duncan to the finish line, if he did not hurry to put a stop to it.

But when he went to squeeze her clit in a way that would prevent it from bursting in pleasure, he found that he much rather wanted her to come.

Yeah, as strange as it sounded, he craved her come more than her pain. Which was puzzling, to say the least, yet so very exciting that he could not waste time wondering about it. He merely tightened his touch and dived into her honeydew as though his life depended on it.

She froze, probably not expecting this turn of his.

Soon, his slow, forceful rubs won her over, and she tensed to get more. Astonishing to say the least, considering how impossible it was for her to budge. Still, her body bent further as though wanting to gobble him up—cock and fingers together.

Only natural, she screamed and shattered under his touch.

Oh, boy! Had Duncan been right!

There was no describing the feeling of having complete charge over her, knowing that one twist of his fingers could prolong or end her exquisite pleasure. It was all up to him!

Just for the fun of it, he made her come again and again. At her fourth climax, he could not keep it together anymore.

Opening his ass wide to receive his lover's furious slams, he lowered on her, and his load swamped her dripping slit, just like Duncan was doing in his butt.

Had everything stopped right there and then, it would have been great sex. What made it extraordinary was Ylianor's energy blending inside his and driving away the dark cloud of rage he had been nursing since leaving the Nephis Valley. Then, she pulled Duncan into this seductively immaterial embrace, and it was like they were one.

At least for a moment.

A long moment.

The moment she stayed coiled around them both, trapped like when they fucked her together before her energy dispersed, and he was back in the shelter.

CHAPTER THREE

"I'm sorry, Ylianor." Scrambling to his feet, Chris began untying her. "I didn't mean to be so angry with you." Ankles and elbows now free, he massaged the wrinkled flesh while flooding her with healing Virt. "Too much is happening too fast. Like that thing at the Nephis Valley, which I'm not sure was a spell at all." He tightened his grip on her. "Not since I craved you like crazy and burned for your every touch." Gently cradling her against his chest, he sat on the floor and stretched her out on his legs. "That's why I cannot think it was only a spell. I wanted you with all my body, mind and energy. And it wasn't the first time, either." He pushed out a heavy breath, for this was the tricky part. "I thought I'd hate to be with a woman for so long, but I like you more than I care to admit even to myself. The worst thing is I keep thinking I might also miss you when our task is over." Averting his gaze from her, he fixed it on his phase mate. "To think I prided myself on hating her gender." His attention was all back on her as he raked his fingers through her long thick hair. "Maybe, I need to reconsider some of my beliefs about women—"

"You need to consider people as human beings, not as genders or categories." Clasping his hand, Duncan squeezed it forcefully. "'Cause people aren't just men or women. They are individuals first and foremost, like I already told you. That's why I don't find it strange you should like the princess." Still holding on to his hand, he ran it down her back. "For she isn't just another woman. She's the one person who is open-minded enough to accept us as we are, including our love and passionate sex."

"If I admit I like women . . ." He shifted uncomfortably. "Where would that leave you, lover?" The thought was so unbearable he had to swallow hard simply to keep talking. "Would I still love you?" Anguished, he could not even bear to look at the prince.

"I'd rather you asked yourself those questions than love me because I'm a man." Duncan cupped his face. "Did you choose me because I was in the right category?" Narrowing a penetrating gaze on him, the prince focused on his face. "I'd give up this love in a heartbeat if this were the case." An anguished flicker crossed the velvety black eyes. "I dare hope I mean much more than just my sex, and that you chose me, not drifted my way 'cause I was of the right gender for you."

"Like you chose me that night at Arthur's party?" That had been their new beginning. Their reconnection after the very shattering two-year separation Duncan had enforced between them at the end of their phase.

And he still wondered how he had managed to survive them.

"Exactly." His lover bent forward, his forehead practically touching his. "I didn't do it for sex. I wanted you back 'cause you are the most important person in my life. Lover, brother, best friend, phase mate and more. You are my everything."

The tender kiss that followed took his breath away. Not because the avid tongue plunged to his throat. Because the voraciousness of his claim threw him off balance, crushing her between their two bodies.

"I love you, Angel." Drawing back, Duncan seemed out of breath, too. "For so many different reasons, I couldn't possibly list them all." Not breaking their proximity, he settled her so that he could stroke her more comfortably. "If I look back, I can't believe how much we've grown together, which is nothing if compared to what I glimpse ahead of us." A wide grin split his beautiful face. "Together, you and I can only get better and reach heights other people only dream about, some of which are happening right now. But the only way we can keep growing is by questioning our convictions every day, testing them against the persons we were yesterday. For if we take them for granted, how can we be sure we still believe in them?"

Yeah, this made sense, however much he was still reeling from his lover's most powerful declaration to date.

"I know it isn't easy to admit we were wrong. It takes a lot of guts, and that's why I'm so proud of you, Angel." The full lips crushed his one more time.

His senses began swimming.

"'Cause you aren't afraid to take a chance and change if necessary. That's what I most love about you, for I get too bored to hang around people who stay the same year after year." The black eyes sank into his. "So, keep growing and changing, my beautiful angel. Then, I'll recognize the person I chose that night at the Hall."

"Lover, I . . ." What was there to say? What was there to do besides attack his mouth and drown in his intoxicating flavor?

For he did not just *love* the man.

He adored him.

Literally!

He would die for him.

Literally.

The way he felt about the dark-haired prince was unlike anything he had ever felt for anyone in his entire life. What better way to prove it than opening and giving up everything to the man entitled to have it all?

While heat rose rapidly, Duncan flattened him to the carpet. With Ylianor still trapped between them, he shifted her to lie on top of him, her buttocks pressing on the stirring shaft.

Which at once perked up his interest to stone-like consistency.

Yeah, nothing like her ass to make him lose the last of his perspective, particularly now that his cock throbbed from the need to stuff that deliciously tight ring of hers.

"Impatient, Angel?" Evidently having no trouble picking up his unspoken request, Duncan circled her waist and raised her.

"Extremely." His erection jerked so hard he thought it would go after her butt, however unreachable it was at the moment.

"Relax." Thanks to a perfect aim, her slam-down flung open that intoxicating narrow hole of hers.

With the most hurtful impact possible, he was happy to report.

"Her ass is all yours." Duncan laughed as he screwed her to the hilt.

Too good for words, he sank in her constricted channel, pumping upward to crack it hard and fast. If anything, he hoped to reach her throat going through her guts. Which explained the necessity to ram her behind to bits.

"Hey, not so fast." Halting his rush, Prince Caldwell grabbed her hips to steady her. "Only her ass is yours." On his knees, his rigid gland targeted her pussy. "The rest of her is *mine*." Given the possessive note, it was only natural he would impale her with a single thrust that almost carried his balls along with the long length.

Not that he could blame him any.

She was Duncan's slave, after all. That had made all the difference for him, too. He had been authorized to treat her as a mere toy, an object of his pleasure.

Or so he liked to play it while ravaging her rear.

When out of bed, he had kind of vowed he would not treat her as a slave, which was sort of impossible considering what a slut she really was.

Which was her best trait so far!

Now, stretching that once tight ass of hers was making him lose it faster than ever. Partially Duncan's fault, his claiming her cunt had reduced the available space to a minimum that squeezed his beast to perfection. Mostly her fault, the way she rotated those hips of hers to suck more cock was simply indecent.

She did not just slip more thickness inside. She gorged on it, probably wanting to explode from her voracity to have them both stuffing her to her ears.

If that was what she craved, he was more than ready to give it to her.

Duncan was right along with him, considering how his rhythmical pounding of her front was juggling her good and proper.

In perfect sync, they coordinated their beats to obtain the most significant impact possible. Since she wanted to burst, he accelerated, loving how his shaft embedded deeper and deeper inside her. So far up, he wondered whether he would ever manage to retrieve it.

Just thinking this made him aware of the burning point at the tip of his erection.

Then, his lover had the lousy idea of devouring her in a hungry kiss, and the tide rolled on its own. She was the first to surrender to it, coming the second after the prince stuck his tongue to her throat. Lying beneath her, he felt every one of the swells convulsing her body in repeated throes. Not one climax alone. She came over and over while they fucked her harder and harder.

It was always like that for her. Something about her body was just amazing when it came to sex. No, when it came to pleasure and pain to be exact, for he could not forget her reactions during his brutal torture.

Thinking of that was a mistake.

Nothing like pain set him off like crazy, his sadistic side always getting more than one kick out of cutting up real live human beings. Since no one had given him more pleasure than she had during his vicious ritual, he lost it for good at the same time Duncan swamped her slit with a full load of his powerful jets.

CHAPTER FOUR

"Now, Angel, where were we?" Grinning, Duncan reclined on his heels, carrying her along.

Chris straightened and pressed close to her, strangely reluctant to let her go. "I believe I was about to promise that I'll keep changing." To emphasize his point, he wrapped her in his fiery energy, teasing her in an almost loving caress. "That's one of the reasons I want to have that talk with my father."

"I can't wait for that to happen." The prince's vote of confidence was a surge of emotions that invested him with the power of his support and love.

"It will and sooner than you think." He had to pause to catch his breath.

When he was with Duncan, it was always like that, his senses spinning so fast nothing mattered except the striking prince and the depth of his emotions for him.

"I'll sit down with him and have a heart to heart talk he's never going to forget." He could just imagine how surprised his father would be. He had been asking for one ever since he had moved to the Hall, the same place where James Templeton lived and worked as Vice-Leader of the High Council. Dodging him for the past two years and a half had been his main preoccupation.

"I hope you convince him to leave you his seat at the High Council." She smiled brightly.

Yeah, sure! That'll be the day! "Aren't you running a bit?"

His father had kind of made it clear that his firstborn, Steve, was to take over the important task of council duty. Should Steve fail for any reason, there was a second-born, Bran, ready to take over. As the third in line, Chris had no chance to get to that council seat. Not that he gave a damn about it! Did not look too hot of a deal for him, not after all he had seen and heard from Arthur's own lips.

"No, I'm sure it's going to be sometime soon." The way she said it sounded like she knew it for a fact. "Even Arthur said so, remember?"

"I doubt he was serious," Chris retorted, rolling his eyes.

Sure, the leader had mentioned it often enough. Not just during his last lecture, but while pumping his behind in every position known to man. Still, it had always struck him as wishful thinking, when not an excuse to fuck his brains out in an official capacity for once.

He could just picture what would happen, were he to become one of the twelve permanent council members with a leader so hot for him to grant him just about anything he requested.

"I know too many of his secrets." His lips twisted in an ironic snarl.

Not just because he had lived in Arthur's room, in his bed actually, for the past two years and a half. Because he had been his eyes and ears, a regular spy the leader used to keep up with all the gossip running around the Hall.

"I don't think he'll have a choice in the matter." She sighed sadly.

"Why not?" Something about her tone went straight to his heart and crushed it painfully.

Despite how hard he had tried denying it in the past, Arthur meant more to him than he cared to admit, far more than he had played it out to Duncan. Not that the handsome prince had fallen for it. He had seen right through Chris's act and called his bluff, forcing him to come clean about it. Had gone as far as accepting it, which did not lessen his sense of betraying his true love by merely feeling something profound for someone else.

Then again, such was Prince Duncan Caldwell. Not just his lover, his best friend, too, the one-man he could tell just about anything that came to his mind.

"Lord Fairchild is dying." She pushed out a heavy breath as though the words were strangling her.

"What?" The prince was the first to react. "How do you know?"

"I read it in his lights." Right, how to forget the woman was a witch whose aura reading Virt gave her access to what people usually kept hidden?

It was the reason she pissed him off so fucking bad! She was a spy worse than he could ever be, and these tricks of hers were making her slip beneath his skin faster than he could block her.

And that was simply unforgivable!

"But he doesn't want you to know." Her gaze shifted on him.

"Why not?" However hard he tried, he could not suppress his aggressive tone. "Whatever it is, I could heal him."

This did not make too much sense. If Arthur loved him as much as he claimed he did, he would do anything to stay with him. *Right?*

"That's exactly what he doesn't want you to do," her voice was very soft, almost apologetic. "If it's any consolation, he didn't tell me what was wrong." Lightly, she pressed a hand on his chest. "But it's not something that has to do with his body, rather with his spirit." Her arresting green eyes fixed on a point in midair. "It's like he's tired of living and wants to quit."

No, not for one minute would he believe Arthur could die.

Not even if he had glimpsed the same dark cloud, hanging

like a cloak about to snuff the life out of Arthur. He had commented it with Duncan on their first night from Black Rose to the Hall, in front of the damn witch no less.

Which meant he had to be ready for anything. "Who will replace him?"

"I don't know." She shrugged as though it made no difference to her. "Nor did Lord Fairchild say. What I do know is that this mission has something to do with it somehow."

"Or maybe you're wrong." This sort of talk was giving him the creeps. "So, let's just drop it, shall we?" To avoid misunderstandings, he got up and went to the kitchen to look for something to eat.

"Sure, Angel." But Duncan exchanging a glance with her told him how much credit he gave her words.

Which was enough to make his heart sink way below his feet.

CHAPTER FIVE

"Cecilia takes good care of those who pass through her district." Duncan pointed at the long line of log cabins in the distance. "Considering how inhospitable her land is, I think we'll take advantage of her excellent Shelter System."

So, this is Blandry's desert! Dejectedly, Ylianor glanced around. *Talk about empty and desolate!*

"Like we did in the Wadirum Desert, we'll have to use our day wisely, all thirty-six hours of it." Prince Caldwell swung his gaze first on her, then on Chris. "To beat these godforsaken temperatures . . ." He meant the torrid midday heat and the freezing nighttime spells. "We can ride from dawn until the fourteenth hour, break midday, then resume after the twentieth until we reach Blue Oasis."

As she checked once more the sandy flatland, she wondered whether Lady Cecilia Hurst would turn out to be as bare and as bleak as her homeland was. For sure, she missed the Nephis Valley's breathtaking beauty and the less stunning but still welcoming passageway that connected northern to southern districts. No, this dry and arid lifelessness was not the place for her, nor was seeing everything becoming grayer the further west she went.

"You should just hear how loudly she bitches with Richard Ellis to get more shelters built on her lands," Chris snickered, evidently recalling some of the funniest scenes at the Hall. "He's in charge of the Shelter System now and has been since—"

"My father died," Duncan's grave tone cut off the demon.

46

"I know." Quite clear, he missed Prince Charles deeply.

Almost as much as she did.

"My father loved that responsibility." A warm smile lit his beautiful face. "He always said it was the most important of his council duties. 'Cause hospitality was sacred to him. That's why he made travelers' needs his top priority."

"I'm not sure Richard takes it as seriously." From the wild waves in Chris's lights, she guessed there was more to this Richard than he was telling. "Or that Arthur has the same faith in him he had in your father." Suddenly softer, his tone became husky, "I know he valued him a lot and misses him greatly, even if he never said it in so many words."

"Yeah, I know." Duncan shook his head as though to clear it from the sadness that she perceived closing in on him. "He told me as much when I came to the Hall on the night of our reunion."

She saw it, Arthur standing on the threshold to embrace the prince while commenting on how similar he looked to Charles.

She flashed Duncan a grateful smile for having shared this small detail about himself.

Just thought I need to open up more to you, Princess. His deep voice booming in her head melted her senses all together, all at once. *After everything we've talked about, I realize I haven't given this Virt of ours enough credit.* Averting his gaze, he stared at an invisible point in the distance. *Just blamed you for being in my head all the time, which isn't all bad. Sometimes it could be a real advantage.*

Like in Cecilia's Game? No need for special powers to know exactly where he was going with this.

To her doom, since his masterful use of sex had shrunk her perceptions to mere sensations. His sharing everything he felt while in bed only spun everything out of any control. One-touch from him and she would be trembling all over, ready to submit to whatever took his fancy. No way around it, she loved the enslavement so much she could not wait to see how far he could take her.

Right, and it's precisely the reason I want to see you fucked by as many cocks as possible. There was an undeniable shiver of anticipation running down her back at the mere idea. *To test your limits and see how far I can push you.*

How to doubt him?

After his great speech to Chris, she had learned how important tests were to him, so being able to prove she could make it was all that mattered. Better yet, she would have given anything to see him as proud of her as he was of Chris.

What do you say, Princess? His black eyes locked on hers. *Will you do me the honor of playing with me, of being my chosen playmate in Cecilia's game?*

Yes, yes, take me, use me, do whatever you want with me.

If she did not blurt it out as it came, it was because she had lost herself in the arousal of it all. She would have never thought Virts could have such inebriating side effects on sex while the prince did. To think he was a newcomer at this. Imagine that!

She and Chris had been the only ones to acquire higher skills over something no one knew how to train, yet Duncan was proving to be a fast learner. Increasingly confident in his grasp of what had been a mystery until recently, he would soon outrun both she and the demon. Not just in knowledge. In Virt, mostly.

Before you answer, remember that you are mine. There was no denying the erotic undertone lacing his words. *Whether you like it or not.*

She swallowed hard, her clit pounding in furious excitement. *I . . .*

"What do you say if we stop for the day?" Indicating a log cabin just a short distance away, Chris steered Black toward it. "I'm sure you'll have much better luck convincing her in a horizontal position, lover, rather than in this vertical one."

"How do you know, Angel?" Duncan provoked him on purpose.

"'Cause it's the only thing that explains her deep blush," Chris snickered, his gaze fixing on her face. "Like you've been describing one torrid sex scene after another."

"That's exactly what I've been doing." Duncan grinned amusedly. "But she hasn't relented yet."

"Take my advice and try when you're in bed." Laughing, Chris spurred his horse forward.

Prince Caldwell went right next to him while she brought up the rear.

Upon their arrival, the two men discarded their horses and rushed inside the shelter. Not bothering to attend to their mounds, naturally, since it was her task. Something the demon never failed to underline both in words and actions, particularly now that he had hurried away to have Duncan all to himself.

No, his sincere apology and his stunning admission she might mean more to him than he had led on had not changed the fundamental balance between them.

Which was fine with her.

Lord Christopher Templeton remained a bastard, however earnest his attempts at changing were. Too bad for him, she was slipping deeper below his skin. And there was not a damn thing he could do about it!

He could borrow the handsome prince all he liked. She had no problems lending him!

What Chris could not fathom was that she was just content to watch their tantalizing bodies making love. Whatever their position, they were so seductive it scorched her flesh merely looking at them. Following that incredibly shiny head bobbing up and down to swallow Duncan's erect beast always whetted her mouth, not to mention her cunt.

And that was just for starters.

Shaking her head free from the erotic visions clogging it, she grabbed Fuzeon and Black's bridles. No rush to be with them. Since she had not obviously received any invitation, she took them along with Starlet to the stable annexed to every shelter. She remembered Prince Charles sharing bits of information about the Shelter System, some about the hardships horses sometimes had to endure to reach the most faraway places. To think that her people had an organized Shelter Assistant workforce, but they had no specific horses to carry out the duties of supplying and repairing the many shelters available on the roads!

Stepping through the threshold, she settled the horses together, Fuzeon and Black flanking either side of Starlet, full trough and freshwater in front of their muzzles. The three of them were getting used to being together. Even Fuzeon, one of the most challenging horses she knew, did not complain of the company, liked it in fact. He had confirmed as much through his silent sharing, something she had no trouble picking up given her close connection to animals.

This was another side of her Virt, the one she liked best because it did not involve having to deal with obnoxious demons or their enthralled lovers. Or to put it more mildly, with people in general, which had too many complications for her taste if compared with animals.

Patting Fuzeon's stiff neck, she wondered whether it would not be better for her to stay right where she was rather than disturbing Chris at his favorite game. The first days on the road together, the odious beast had even suggested she sleep in the stables. If he had not said as much in a good while, she could not suppress the feeling he still thought about it whenever a particular icy glitter sparked his amazing blue-gray eyes and made them look so very cold and menacing. On those occasions, it would have been sheer luxury to sleep in the stable instead of putting up with his insufferable temper that —

Princess, get your ass in here! The court order exploding in her mind jolted her. *Now!*

Yes, Master. How had he managed to catch her intention? *Immediately, Master.* Was he not too busy with Chris to mind her?

Scrambling outside, she ran to the shelter. Maybe, Chris was in the knotting mood, wanting her as helpless as the other time. When he had lost it for real, making her come instead of punishing her like his lights had promised before Duncan intervened. Which had so taken her by surprise she had loved every second of it, particularly the part about being at the demon's mercy, completely spellbound by his mastery and refinery in the bondage art.

Uh, he had been so good! She hoped he would repeat it soon enough, maybe even now, if possible!

The door slightly ajar, it made no noise as she hesitated on the threshold, catching sight of them next to the fireplace.

Predictably, they had not gone too far. They were both in too much of an urgency to make it anywhere near a bedroom. Then again, couches worked just fine when all you needed was a place to lean on while sucking your lover's cock to the hilt. Precisely what Chris was doing to Duncan's monstrous piece. Gulping it so far down, she could only wonder how he managed to breathe at all. Or maybe he just did not care, since nothing had to interfere with his enjoyment of good, hard male equipment.

For the demon, cock sucking was pure art. That he excelled at it, she knew it for a fact, given the providential lesson delivered on the shores of that lake during their first days on the road. Thanks also to Duncan sharing his sensations whenever stuck deep inside that wet cavity gobbling him up, she had proof enough that he had learned from the best of them. Now, he had surpassed that faraway master, seeing how completely the shaft disappeared inside the capacious cavity, drawn to the balls if not beyond.

The way they were so deep into one another, the prince's rush to call her seemed unjustified until she caught the leap in their lights and their cocks. Just like the other time, she could not shake the feeling they not only noticed her entering. They wanted her right there, where she could watch them.

Which was pure ridiculous! Despite the frantic flashes of their auras, it was next to impossible they had seen her.

Duncan could not because his shoulders fronted the door. The other one because he would go through hoops before acknowledging her any. Then again, it was kind of impossible now that the prince pinned the demon to the carpet and went for his ass.

One decisive thrust and she could swear she heard the ring crack.

Ouch!

That would have hurt her for sure.

Not Christopher Templeton and his extremely well-trained ass. Or one made of butter, given how effortlessly it was swallowing Duncan's imperious stick to the root. Not content and from the way he swung his butt upward, she guessed he was asking for more as though the forceful possession had not disturbed him any.

Duncan had no problem delivering. The gods only knew he had enough length and thickness to satisfy the most voracious appetite of all — Christopher Templeton's.

Inside and out, the gigantic erection slammed to the demon's guts.

No, beyond if she was any judge of it.

Which, damn them, started a dull throbbing in both her cunt and ass, an ache so strong she wished she had a fraction of that very beefy rod stuffing Chris's behind to the fullest.

Not that the demon would consent to it. He usually was in a no-sharing mood whenever it came to his lover's cock, particularly now that it had stretched that once tight hole of his to an unbelievable size.

Hard and rough, the prince rammed Chris as though he had to split him apart. Not a show at all, she was learning this was how they both liked to play it. If they toned it down a notch when she was with them, it was only because the prince saw to it that Chris did not overdo it.

Their breaths short, she guessed their race was about to come to an abrupt halt. She wished she could link to Duncan to get all the second-by-second sensations leading up to the climax, but he was too deep into Chris. She could just watch as his speed increased, and the blows became fiercer. Then, Chris gasped and unloaded all over the carpet.

With one final effort, Duncan pulled out of the snug confinement, straddled Chris and sprayed his back with fat ropes of whitish juice staining his fair skin.

Still dripping, he turned and caught sight of her. *About time you got here.* Fixing his gaze on her, the prince sounded more annoyed than he was in reality.

"Lover, don't tell me the witch is here." If Duncan's was an act, Chris's irritation was for real, even if there was no surprise in his tone.

Could it be that both men had been aware of her watching them like she had initially perceived?

"She is, and she saw everything," the prince snickered. *Now, strip and get here.*

At the new order, she obeyed promptly, tearing off her worn pants and shirt, both of which had belonged to her father, John Meyer.

"Ah, fuck!" Still lying on the carpet, with Duncan perched on his back, Chris pressed his forehead to the ground. "I bet you called her, even if we don't need her—"

"Wrong, Angel." Straightening, Prince Caldwell gestured for her to approach. "You certainly need some good cleaning, and I can't think of anyone else who could do it on such short notice."

"You're right!" This perked up the fiendish creature's interest.

While hers sagged way below her feet, for she had just understood what her task was, and she did not like it one bit.

No one asked for your opinion. Brusquely, Duncan forced her down on her knees. *Now, shut up and lick him clean.* Clamping her neck, he pressed her face over Chris's back, right on top of the pools covering his skin.

Darting out her tongue, she gave her first tentative flick.

"Harder." He crushed her face on a gluey splotch. "My angel doesn't have all day."

In her haste to obey, she had to guzzle up everything as her tongue slid on the demon's smooth skin. Her long, lavish laps removed the sticky fluid in avid gulps trickling down to her stomach until none remained.

"Good." Yanking her long hair, he snapped her neck as far back as it could go. "Now, his cock." He waited until Chris flipped around, then pressured her head over the giant tip staring her in the face.

"Great thinking, lover." As smug as a cat, the demon raised his hips and centered her mouth.

Now, why was she not surprised he should be as swollen as when Duncan had screwed him?

Between the two of them, they had such fast recoveries they could go on an entire night having sex without failing a single blow.

"Now, while you relax, I'll try something I get too little of." Chuckling mischievously, he knelt behind her.

Her ass melted at the mere thought it would soon be his.

"That's because it's the only place worth a damn of her," Chris retorted piqued.

No need to get so uptight, Lord Templeton.

Not that she had the chance to utter it. His massive rigidity going for her stomach cut off her words along with any air she had managed to save in her lungs.

Spurting frantically, she tried to recover enough to keep living, at least until the damn blowjob was over. Too bad, His Highness Lord Christopher Templeton seemed determined to cut it short, and her life along with it. How else to explain the repeated lurches that got past her tongue's attempt to block them?

The scorching sensation in her butt diverted her attention to a whole different problem—Prince Duncan Caldwell and his rear-splitting penetration.

Ouch!

This would have been for real, had she only allowed herself to think it. Instead, she opened as much as she could and hoped her ass would become as buttery as Chris's had just minutes before.

It's no use, Princess. Sardonic, Duncan taunted, *Your ass will never be like his.*

"Can't believe you're going to crack her in two." Impressed by the show, Chris's piece went slab of marble in five seconds flat.

Or rather, the thought she was in pain was what caused the shift, though the gods only knew how he always managed to understand what she felt with such precision.

Whatever it was, now her problems had just doubled. If one would eventually crack her open like a nut, the other would cramp her to the point of choking. Either way, she was doomed.

Come on, Princess. Slowing down his beat, Duncan seemed concerned. *I thought you wanted a fraction of what I was giving the angel.*

But I wanted to live to tell, she blurted out. And since when did he pluck her thoughts without her noticing it?

Just because I pretended to ignore you doesn't mean I wasn't paying attention. Relentless in the rhythm, Prince Caldwell pumped all his engorged rod inside her ass, balls included if considering how enlarged her rear hole now felt. *And your body's reactions were among the greatest turn-on of that particular fuck.* "Hey, Angel, you didn't tell me her ass had become so mouthwatering."

"It's just passable." Of course, Chris would take advantage of any occasion to demean her. "Nothing exceptional as far as I can tell."

"Nothing like her mouth, right?" Ironic, Duncan's tone was vaguely mocking, "Is that why you're digging so hard in it our cocks will meet in the middle sooner or later?"

"Just having fun, lover." To mark his point, Chris lifted his hips in a particularly vicious impact that had the tip of his erection slipping past her throat.

"By suffocating her?" At her coughs, Duncan yanked back her head to give her space to breathe.

Not a moment too soon!

"Yes, if that's what it takes." Undaunted, Chris snatched her back down. "At least it makes for a more exciting blow-job."

"Not to mention more exclusive," Duncan observed. "Since it would be a one-time deal."

"Works for me." Sure it would!

Or how else would the despicable fiend get rid of her?

"Not for me, since we still need her to get into Cecilia's Game." Screwing more of his length inside, Prince Caldwell spread her buttocks apart. "Unless you'd be willing to take her place and play the slave—"

"She's breathing! She's breathing!" Suddenly easing all the pressure, Chris's cock almost fell out of her mouth. "See?" That was how far back he had pulled in his rush to avoid any harm from happening to her.

"Your concern is touching, Lord Templeton." She could not help the heavy sarcasm lacing her words. "Though I would like to see you play the slave."

"Not my call, dearie." Chris sat up straighter. "Since you

can't wait to do it yourself."

"Me?" Defiant, she challenged him. "I still haven't de-cided—"

"Oh, drop the act!" Tugging her by the hair, he twisted her neck until his mouth pressed on her ear. "You can't wait to be his goddamn slave and get rid of me! To be alone with him and play that fucking game without having me around, just the two of you."

Damn it!

How could he know her so well to have guessed it?

"Now, say that you'll be his slave." His hot breath tickled her. "So, we can get on with our sex without any more inter-ruptions."

If it sounded like an order, she did not notice it, too taken by the surge of pleasure shooting up her ass by the realization he could be as commanding as the prince could, only in his own cruel way.

"Yes, yes, I'll be your slave." The way it came out, she meant it for both. "I'll play the slave in Cecilia's Game." Which was the reason she corrected herself.

"See, lover?" Raising a sarcastic gaze, he fixed it on Dun-can. "I told you you'd convince her in a horizontal position." He adjusted her wet cavity over the tip of his erection. "Now, be a good girl and drink me up before you come all over the place. And the more you gag, the better."

That did it!

She could not arrest the tide over flooding her. What with Duncan's monster embedded in her guts now advancing to her throat and Chris's beast trying to reach it from above, she burst all over the place like the demon had guessed. So con-vulsive her orgasm, she practically swallowed both cocks to-gether with their balls. If not entirely true, it was close enough for breathing to become hard all of a sudden while her ass was about to explode from the attempts to hold something far too big for it.

The mere thought made her climax again.

No screams, of course. Chris had seen to it her mouth's sole task was to pamper his stick. Grown so stiff and ruthless, it was fucking her face as though it were her pussy.

Not that she minded any. No, she welcomed it, since it made her convulse again and again over both pieces stuffing her to the hilt.

She would have continued ad infinitum, had they both not decided to end it with a tremendous climax of their own. Both simultaneously flooding her front and back and staying inside her until she had drunk all their juices down.

That was how she agreed to play the slave in Cecilia Hurst's fantasy of domination and submission.

Chapter Six

"We made it." On glimpsing the familiar blueish walls glistening under the last of Stella's rays, Duncan felt kind of sorry his traveling was at an end. "Way ahead of time, too, since Cecilia's Game isn't due to start until a few days."

If the journey had been long, he had hardly noticed, too absorbed with the developments in his three-sided entanglement. The sex's fault at first, blowing his mind away ever since leaving Black Rose. The Virt's fault for second, shaking a balance he had taken for granted, invading his perceptions and forcing him to re-evaluate his priorities.

Something profound was responsible for it all. Something more intimate that went far beyond anything he had ever shared with Chris. Whatever it was, it had grown stronger with each step nearer to Blue Oasis.

But that was just skimming the surface.

What had most distracted his attention had been them, his two splendid yet unruly lovers. His need to understand the mechanisms at work between them had no equals.

Safe to say, both had come a long way toward one another, considering they had started as bitter enemies when just kids.

Not that he remembered any of it.

She was nowhere present in his usually good memory up to the moment he had knocked on her rundown shack in the village near Black Rose, and it still bugged the living daylights out of him. Why should something have erased her, and her alone, out of all his recollections?

He had not the faintest clue!

Even so, he had seen enough during the trip to have no doubt Chris and Ylianor had indeed begun on opposite ends until that shocking knife play of his angel's had changed everything.

Not because of her lack of disgust or outrage. Which would have been justified, given how inconceivable and out of his world such a monstrous act was. Dreadful, to say the least, Duncan had been stunned, incapable of processing the horror of it all, while she . . .

She had seemed to accept it.

Like with Chris, her reactions had been so implausible that he was still trying to analyze them in all their ramifications.

For sure, this had changed something between them, as though they had discovered some sort of common ground they did not know they had before. Funny, though, something at gut level had told him straight up the two shared a link of their own. Maybe, the fact that they, alone in the whole world, had been aware of their Virts from childhood had something to do with it, and this was no small feat, according to the leader himself. Or perhaps, the fact that she had antagonized the angel from the start had been his undoing. However loud he protested, something about her made his blood boil and his cock stiffen. She totally fascinated him, and to no avail did he play it like she was a worthless slave.

Then again, Chris could never resist provocations, and that was probably her secret for keeping him hooked.

Now, their fumbling attempts to establish some connection of their own made him proud of them. Just too bad, he could not breathe any of it, lest he endangered the fragile balance he had managed to establish. For the same reason, he had to avoid any interference between them, however curious or amused he was by their fumbling approaches.

As if it were easy to do!

Truth was—they were so intriguing he would have

continued their journey forever. Not an option, alas, still he would not pass up the chance to spend one last night alone with them despite the mission he had to accomplish.

"That's Blue Oasis." He pointed at it for Ylianor's sake. "Now, find us an empty shelter, Princess."

Why?

If the question hovered in her lovely green eyes, she had more sense than to ask it. Instead, she glanced at the area around Cecilia's home, surrounded by countless log cabins.

"Why are there so many shelters around here?" As she checked them over, Duncan had no doubt she was picking up the aura traces from the occupied ones. "Isn't Blue Oasis big enough to give hospitality to everyone?"

"It is, but Cecilia keeps them for players in need of rest before the excitement begins." He licked his lips, imagining how feverish his and Ylianor's would soon get. "Or for those who don't want to stay at Blue Oasis."

"Which isn't our case. Right, lover?" Chris smirked. "Since this is my first time here, I don't want to miss a single thing of it."

"Let's find a place to rest first." He perused the wooden lodges lit up by glowing candles in their windows to fend off dusk's darkness. "But let's not forget why we're here."

"Of course not!" Chris scoffed in mock annoyance. "How could you possibly think that an inconsequential sexual game could make me forget my duties?"

"Not just forget." He laughed. "Ignore them outright."

"Hey, give me some credit." Blue-gray eyes flashing, the angel looked ready to flare up for real. "I'm not that —"

"I found an empty place over there." Ylianor gestured at a spot on the far-left side, steering her mare toward it.

"Great." He hurried Fuzeon after her. "Now, the angel can forget all he likes for the next few days."

"I heard that." Spurring Black forward, Chris reached him. "And I have every intention of forgetting anything not related to your cock from now on."

"Including her ass?" Eyeing Ylianor's backside, he made a show of smacking his lips.

Not a show. He loved that magnificent ass of hers, the shape as much as the reactions. Both drove him crazy, and he would have taken more advantage of it had his angel not monopolized it so often. Which was another pretense, an attempt to deny her femininity if not the hold she was having on him.

Ha! Highly doubtful Chris's refusal to touch or use her cunt would stop the craving that had started at the Nephis Valley. For she and that shaven pussy of hers had sent his senses reeling to a place they had no business going for someone claiming to lust after male equipment alone.

And there was no turning back.

"Well . . ." Her ass remained the piece Chris most adored about her.

It had been what had seduced him into accepting her along a trip originally intended for the two of them alone, and she had been intelligent enough to use it to her full advantage.

"I might just remember it from time to time." Chris beamed enchantingly. "But it'll never beat your cock." Having reached the shelter's front yard, he slowed down.

"Liar." Daring him outright, Duncan jumped off Fuzeon. "As if I didn't know that's all you crave lately."

"Not true!" Getting off Black, Chris headed to the door. "I'll prove it—"

"I don't need proof." If he did not rush to follow Chris to the door, it was because he wanted to take her with him.

He did not particularly relish Chris's habit of leaving her out in the cold or of having her just watch. Even if she liked to be a mere spectator while they fucked, it was no excuse to keep her on the sideline as much as the angel demanded. If he had not challenged it so far, it was because both he and Chris were discovering just how truly arousing this new twist was.

Which was no reason to allow it to get out of hand.

This time, like it or not, she would play with them no matter what.

Since she had rushed to take care of both Fuzeon and Black, he waited for her.

"I know." Catching her arm as she appeared from the stables, he dragged her to the inside of the shelter. "Just as I know that one look at this mouthwatering ass and your cock goes crazy."

Crushing her face against his chest, he unbuttoned her pants, dropped them to her ankles along with her underwear and spread her buttocks wide apart.

"Now, tell me I'm wrong." For good measure, he stuck a couple of fingers in the tight back ring that sucked them up immediately.

"I . . ." Swallowing hard, Chris glued his gaze onto her butt, rotating to screw more fingers inside.

No, there was no way he could deny the effect it was having on him. Absolutely no way he could hide his cock's yelp of craving that stiffened it all at once.

"You were saying?" Deliberate in his taunting, Duncan increased the number of fingers to four and twisted them to enlarge her hole.

"Give me her ass." If it came out as a low growl, it was because Chris could not take the pressure anymore.

It was always like that with his angel. Resistance had never been his strong suit. Nor would it ever be when it came to sex.

"Sure." Jabbing a knee between her legs, Duncan pushed them far apart. Then, he pressed her back until she had to flatten both palms on the floor to keep her balance, raising her ass in the process. "But what do I get?"

This was just provocation. Truth was — he would be happy with whatever piece of her he got. Cunt, ass or mouth, it made no difference to him as long as he got to drown in her very feminine essence.

Unlike his angel, he liked women far more than men. Ever since the end of the phase, he had devoted his time and attention to them alone, often getting lost in their seductive allure and their *treacherous curves*, as Chris loved to scorn them. They had the power to excite him, which men did not with the exclusion of his angel naturally. Nothing was more arousing than pressing his nose, chin and mouth on a dripping wet cunt while lapping all its juice down to his belly. That bittersweet taste always thickened his shaft to a spasm. With Ylianor, this effect seemed twice as potent.

Partly because of her pungent lemony flavor that was an aphrodisiac in itself. Partly because her cunt was clean-shaven, so very smooth and silky, so very unlike any of his other women. Mostly because she was like a fever in his blood. Nothing he did could quell this insatiable need to have her over and over. Since it combined with the feeling that she belonged to him like no other person in the world ever would, not even Christopher Templeton, the mix became so highly intoxicating he could never resist it.

As if it were not enough, he had further complicated everything by latching his sensations to hers whenever on a bed, also when she was just watching. In hindsight, it had been a mistake and the beginning of her enslavement.

Not that he ever considered her to be a slave for real!

Between her Virt, her intelligence and her fantastic personality, there was not a slave's bone in her body. Nor could he ever think so of someone who could pass as his twin.

No, he did not want to dwell on this or on any of the other aspects of her resembling him so much. She shared no single drop of blood with him. So, why bother?

He would have left it there, were it not for that bit about his father treating her like his best-loved child, favored over his two rightful offspring. It still fucking galled him, along with that bit about Prince Charles's will and the unconventional clause to adopt her into the Caldwell family.

Not just the will!

The damn letter had done most of the damage, touching as it was and proclaiming his love for her.

All things Duncan had yet to digest, so preferred to suppress at the moment.

Much better to focus on this using her as a slave. Which had turned out to be the most erotic of his games. In bed, nothing beat exploiting her as an object of his and Chris's pleasure, acting as though she were no better than a toy they used to spice up their sex. The fact she loved it — came on it actually — had made him cross more than one line until it had spilled over into reality, and he had treated her like a worthless nothing *for real*.

Which was unforgivable!

He was still very sorry he had allowed things to slide so downward he had lost his sense of fairness and balance when it came to her.

Or maybe, it was just a matter of Virt. The way it worked, it required them to be as close as no two people could ever be. So close, he picked up just about all her feelings without any trouble, including her love for him. Amazing, she would have hung to it for so long. Since she was a little girl, he had been her chosen one. Now, eighteen years older and not a day wiser, she loved him like that first time, and it made him uncomfortable he could not return even a fraction of it.

"Her cunt and mouth." Quick to come up behind her, Chris took out his beefy cock and slid it over the crack of her ass cheeks. "Or whatever else you want of this contemptible hide of hers." That he was getting in the game's full swing was evident from his shaft's visible jerking. "After all, women have always satisfied you one way or another." He scowled. "Except if they were servants, of course."

"Never bothered with the likes of them." Duncan just did not like having sex with someone he did not consider his equal.

"'Cause that aristocratic sense of yours always gets in the way." At Chris's chortle, his slides became more decisive. "So, what went wrong with this one?"

"She's not a servant." At least, she had never felt like one, though technically she was.

As the daughter of John Meyer, Black Rose's stable keeper, and Mary Jane Elspeth, a maid to all effects and purposes, her status seemed kind of clear.

No, the fact Prince Charles had been in love with Mary Jane did not improve Ylianor's social standing any.

"She's a slave." Clasping Chris's firm length, he drove the tip to the tiny entrance. "Our slave, to be precise." He rammed it open with a forceful tug of the fathead.

The angel gasped at the sudden plunge into her rear.

"Since I want a piece of her ass, too, why don't you tie her up so that we can share it?" Still holding on to Chris's gland, he screwed it deeper.

"Knew you'd like that!" The angel beamed in satisfaction as his stick disappeared inside her.

"Liked it?" He had been goddamn impressed! "Loved it, you mean." This newly discovered skill could have so many implications his shaft twitched at the scenarios he imagined. "I can't wait for you to repeat it."

"Right now?" Chris seemed way too cozy inside her ass to get moving any time soon.

"Yes, right now." Retaking charge of his beast, Duncan withdrew it from its snug confinement.

"All right." With a resigned look, the angel glanced round the room. "I have just the position in mind." He went to a chest next to the fireplace to dig out the ropes.

Will it hurt her? Duncan knew he should not ask.

Of course, it will, Master, she was quick to set his mind at ease.

That his angel loved pain as much as pleasure, if not more, was something he had long suspected, and nothing like this trip had confirmed it to its extreme consequences.

For the angel cutting her to bits was something he would never forget, however dazed his perception had been at the time.

She shifted on her feet as though she was reliving the same scene. *You know that's the only way he tolerates to have me.*

Not entirely the truth.

Still, close enough to expect something not too pleasant when Chris grabbed her.

"The way she'll be, we'll be able to use whatever we like of her." Having sprawled her on the dining table, he raised both her arms and legs. Spreading them wide, he fastened wrists and ankles together, before binding her waist to the wooden surface with another piece of rope.

He had to hand it to his angel. His princess did not just lay wide-open and defenseless. She had no way of moving from the constricted pose Chris had placed her. She made for such an erotic picture that his erection had to tweak in response.

"Like it?" Gaze slipping to his crotch, Chris's smug expression said he had caught the sign of appreciation.

"A lot." *But if it's too much for you, Princess, I'll tell him to —*

I can take it. Something about her interaction with Chris always pushed her to the limit, sometimes even beyond what was safe. It was uncanny, as though she could not resist any of the angel's dares. No, worse, as if she anticipated them and plunged into danger headfirst.

Which was baffling, and he was still trying to figure out why.

Don't worry about me. To be honest, she did not look too comfortable wrapped up like she was.

"Best part of all, we have free and unlimited access to the whole of her." None too gently, Chris pushed her head until it hung down the edge of the table. "Don't feel too guilty if she doesn't look too comfy." Removing all the chairs scattered around, he set them aside. "She loves it." Halting midway, the angel locked gazes with him. "Trust me."

How could he be so sure?

Duncan only knew it because she had told him. In such terms, he had no doubt she did.

"Don't overrate yourself, Lord Templeton." However tied, bound and helpless, she fought back, even if with words alone. "The day I'll ever love something you do has yet to dawn."

"While the day your master tells you to shut that trap will never come too soon." His cock going slab of stone at her goading, Chris bent his knees. "But I'll take care of it." Centering her throat, he shoved.

So fiercely, she would have fallen off the table, had the fastening not seen to it she remained glued to it.

"And get the traces of your worthless ass off my cock." Slamming again, Duncan was kind of sure he had reached her stomach.

No, he's gone further down. Sarcastic despite her uncontrollable coughs and spurts, she refused to let Chris have the upper hand. *Almost reached my ass.*

Can't wait to see if that's true. Chris was right. Time to quit worrying about her and take full advantage of the situation. "Not that worthless if you were about to lose it just a second ago." Nearing her backside, he aimed his stiff equipment at the narrow ring.

The way Chris had spread her, she was such an easy screw that it took no sweat to impale his meaty monster to her guts.

"That was just for show." Chris shrugged dismissively. "How could you possibly think her insignificant hide holds any excitement for me?"

'Cause you're so deep in her throat, you're about to spill it all for the second time today. "Silly me." Adjusting his fit, he penetrated to the hilt. "I forgot you only liked men."

"Exactly." A malicious gleam sparked the intriguing blue-gray eyes. "As far as women go, this is the worst one you ever forced me to share."

This was such a blatant lie Duncan almost burst out laughing. "Is that right?" Barely holding it together, he concentrated on stretching her narrow backspace to accommodate his vast dimensions.

"You know it is." Stubborn, Chris banged her mouth with another of his merciless blows. "At least, I had fun with the other ones."

"The only fun you had was denying them that splendid cock of yours." Caught between the playful banter and the ass squeeze, he tried to keep his attention on the former rather than the latter. "Same cock, you're feeding her so eagerly."

"Only because her ass is unavailable," Chris quipped, rolling his eyes.

"Let's switch then." It was the purpose of this arrangement of hers, after all.

"Hem . . ." Truth was — whether ravaging her ass or mouth, Chris could never get enough of her. "Sure." Pulling away, not without a visible effort, he went around the table.

While Duncan had to leave the constrained confinement he had just enlarged to his convenience.

Regretfully, alas.

"It's better like this, anyway." Without wasting time, Chris sank in her behind. "If we linger too much, she'll come and spoil our fun."

"So, you don't want her to come, either?" Now, why was he not surprised at Chris's new dictate?

"I say you make it a rule that she doesn't unless you say so." Deliberately cruel, Chris licked his lips in anticipation.

"While we get to come as much as we like."

Somehow, Duncan did not think it would be the same without her climax, giving them the extra shot of energy that made it always so special. Yet, there was no fighting the extreme arousal of this new proposal.

"Did you hear that?" He lowered his head to catch her gaze. "No coming for you —"

"What if I disobey?" Defiant, her green eyes blazed in protest. "Sometimes, I can't control —"

"If you do, I'll make sure to treat you like a real slave at Cecilia's Game." It was just an empty threat, of course. Still, he worked hard to make it sound credible. "And leave you to starve or —"

"All right, all right." Arching her back, she slipped more of Chris's monster up her butt. "I won't come." Her gaze was vaguely apologetic. "Promise."

"Good." Straightening, he glanced at Chris. "Happy?"

"Ecstatic." The wicked creature celebrated with a ruthless thrust in that yielding rear of hers. "Or I'll be when you gag her good and proper."

No, there was no limit to Chris's fiendishness.

"You mean like this?" It was all so damn exciting he could not resist.

He went for her ass going through her throat, relishing the feel of the moistness suddenly enveloping him on every side.

Which made her cough like crazy, jolting and tightening her body in the most lustful way.

"Oh, yes, do that again." Going for her throat, Chris rammed harder. "I love the way she clenches around my cock whenever she's suffocating."

"Insatiable angel." Chuckling, he pumped faster. "You just won't rest until we —"

"Split her open." To emphasize his point, Chris stepped up the tempo in her ass.

Which forced Duncan to accelerate, too. Oh, boy, did he just love it! Sliding past her tongue's frantic blocking and having the tip of his erection squeezed by her cheeks was just about unbeatable. Since Chris did not pause one second, her body shaking added an extra thrill that made him go over the edge in no time at all.

The pressure at the large crown was too much to handle anyway. So, Duncan wrenched his cock out of her wet cavity and sprayed his load all over her body. Same as Chris, who was inundating her after having pulled out, their jets mixing on her belly and breasts.

With all the juice dripping to the table, she made such an enchanting sight that both cocks became stone-like in a matter of instants.

Good thing, there was no need to coax a new response from his princess. She was so hungry she would have jumped out of her skin.

Master, please, she implored with a raspy voice. *I —*

Shut up! His tone harsher than he intended, he softened it, *Just be patient.* "Now, give me her ass." Moving away from her head, he went toward her backside. "You've had it far too long already."

"Party pooper," Chris snarled amused. "I know all you want to do is make her come, but I won't let you."

Frankly surprising how the angel always managed to guess what his intentions were, and it was something he had noticed way before any Virt business had altered his perceptions about what people were capable of doing.

"Aren't you forgetting who the master is?" Raising an eyebrow, Duncan looked him up and down in fake annoyance.

"No." Chris's legs tightened around her head. "And neither should she." He stuck his shaft to her throat. "Which is why you shouldn't allow her to come." He pounded her senseless. "Not yet, anyway."

Master, I beg you to be merciful. Her voice sounded strained. *Since your insufferable lover will never let me come if it's up to him.*

Can't say I blame him.

Nah, who was he kidding?

Her sheer need was enough to throw his resolve to the wind. *You can —*

"Lover, tell her she isn't supposed to talk with her mouth full." Inflexible, the angel seemed bent to make her pay for her disobedience. "And that you aren't considering giving in to her pitiful pleas."

"Of course not, Angel." The lie slipped out easily. "Just as long as you don't choke her to death."

"Me?" A shove and Duncan could have sworn he saw the tip of Chris's erection coming out of her butt ring. "Whatever gave you that idea?"

"Mmm . . ." To push him back, Duncan drowned his piece to the balls with one nudge alone. "Not sure . . ."

She was nice and large after Chris's ride, ready to lodge ten more the size of him and the angel combined. Her flesh wrapped so fiercely around him as though it wanted to sever the rod from the rest of him, imprisoning it forever.

Which was not what spun round two out of any control.

No, what did it for him was narrowing his gaze on her throbbing clit and getting the irresistible urge to stroke it. To dip his fingers in her moist wetness was more like it. That exposed cunt of hers was an invitation he could not ignore. It was no use telling himself that this would only get her overboard.

There was no fighting it. He already felt the tight knot hammering as though it were a part of him. Aching so loudly, he could not stand it.

Knowing that she must be the one sending these sensations did not assuage his urge.

Not one bit.

His hand moved as if with a mind of its own. Running to

her pussy, he glided over the dripping honeydew, relishing the stickiness clinging to his fingers. The hard bud slid between his thumb and forefinger, and there was no halting his luscious rubs on what was about to burst.

"No, lover, wait!" Chris's alarmed blue-gray eyes flashed at him.

Too late.

Everything was already happening. Ylianor was convulsing under his brushes. Her body arched despite the bindings. Her scream piercing his mind, he was swamping her ass with a full load of unstoppable sperm.

At the same time, Chris was exploding all over her face.

Then, the energy kicked in, and his barriers went down. So much, Chris and Ylianor became one with him. Their energy fusing together, he and the angel trapped her between them. Like when they screwed, only this was so much better at so many different levels. This was so right, so *them*, which made it impossible for him to analyze any of it, except for the tide taking him away, while everything else faded in the background.

CHAPTER SEVEN

"Hey, lover, are we late or something?" The angel glanced at the long line of people and horses waiting to enter Blue Oasis.

"No, we're right on time." The sky had just gone dark, after all. "'Cause judging from the light, it must be the twenty-fourth hour."

Since he, Chris and Ylianor were the last ones to arrive, Duncan had all the time and space to admire Blue Oasis from afar. With the shape of a pentagon, the large stone building rose from the brownish floury desert sand. Pale torches hanging from strategic heights enhanced the characteristic blueish gleam and gave it a trembling image that made for quite an effect. Like the place was a mirage.

Which maybe it was, considering everything that happened in it.

"I didn't know there was a specific time to be here." Clouded green gaze, the princess fixed it on the groups of people chatting among them while they waited for Cecilia, the official Game Master, to welcome them.

"Like everything else about this Game, admission has its own rules." No, people were not just chatting. They were gossiping outright, given the bits and pieces that he overheard thanks to the soft desert breeze caressing his face. "And it's at dusk." He tugged Fuzeon to bring him closer. "That's why everybody is here at the same time."

"Getting high for the coming sexual frenzy." Licking his lips in anticipation, the angel focused on a circle of young men that was further up the line, nearer to the entrance. "If you'll excuse me, I think I'll go say hi to a few friends of mine." He handed Black's reins to Ylianor. "Be a dear and watch him for me." But before he left, he raised his arms in the air and stretched most luxuriously, as though to reactivate his muscles after days spent on a bed alone.

She ate him up.

Literally!

How to blame her?

He himself would have jumped on that lean body with the rippling muscles. A body he had possessed a thousand times already. A body he longed to own a thousand more times again, well knowing it would only spin his hunger out of control.

"Don't rush to get anywhere without me, lover." A malicious gleam in the naughty blue-gray eyes told him that Chris had no trouble picking up either craving. "I'll be right back."

He set off, immediately stopped by two men stepping out of the line to greet him.

A wide smile, a few words, then the angel moved on, not getting too far this time, either. More men detained him, all gesturing excitedly, all obviously wanting his attention and company.

From the crowded line Chris had to go through before he reached his intended destination, Duncan braced himself for a long wait.

The demon knows just about everybody here. Ylianor's eyes flashed in amusement. *I knew he was popular, but —*

You said it yourself. He creased his forehead, trying to recall her exact words. *How did you put it?*

Spreading his energy around. She flooded his mind with the scene of when she had said it. There, on the shores of that lake during their second day on the road to the Hall.

Couldn't have worded it better myself! He laughed. *Unlike me, he's never been too fussy about what ends up in his bed, nor will he ever be.* He stared at her ironically. *At least, if it comes with a great big cock.*

None of them ever resisted him? Her soft voice sounded vaguely challenging. *No one ever turned him down?*

That she would have in a heartbeat was not difficult to guess from her determined stance.

As though realizing she was talking to him, not to the angel, she stood down, and her tone became softer, *Not even for the fun of it?*

How could they? A rueful smile, full of love and mischief, curved his lips. *His charm is too alluring, too impossible to resist.*

Oh, boy, had he learned not to mess with it on his own skin!

Which is why I love him so damn much. He could not just say it. He had to overwhelm her with the intensity of a feeling so powerful, so strong, no words could adequately describe it.

As if I didn't know already, her soft voice scolded gently.

I know you do, Princess. She had been right there when it had started, back when they were all kids, and Chris had first set foot in Black Rose. The fact Duncan did not remember her in that particular picture did not diminish his perception that somehow she had grasped the surge of love going from him to the angel on that faraway summer day.

But it's something so unique. Sometimes I can't believe it's real. Again, he used a flow of sensations to convey his meaning, which worked far better than the limited words at his disposal. *That's why I need to share it with the one person I'm sure understands it.*

Is that why you're ignoring all the pretty women that have been staring at you since we got here? Ylianor teased.

Who says I've been ignoring them? He had noticed them the moment they had joined the line.

Whatever role they would end up playing, all of the women had turned their heads toward him. He had intercepted more than one interested gaze, though they had all played it like they were looking elsewhere.

It just confirmed that, like Chris, he also had his pick, had he only given a sign.

Which he had not.

The only woman worth a damn was standing right in front of him, and he could not wait to get his hands on her in every way possible, yet again.

Wrapping an arm around her waist, he crushed her to him and went for her nipple, stroking it hard and rough until it became very erect and visible through the thin fabric of her shirt.

A mouthwatering morsel he had sorely neglected in the days of hot sex that had kept him chained to the bed. Inebriated by his lovers' erotic pull, he had been unable to get enough of either. Whether trapping Ylianor between him and the angel or screwing Chris's ass while his phase mate was up to the hilt in her ass, he had played out all the infinite combinations offered by their number and gender. Getting rougher at times, also when he allowed his angel certain extremes in how he dealt with her. With him, too, for at times, Chris required her to watch alone, jealously seeking a privacy Duncan had promised to guarantee.

Not that he ever excluded her. Whatever he was doing, he kept up a steady sharing that always turned to be his undoing.

Hers, too, since she had not stopped coming once ever since closing the door of the shelter.

With Chris giving the impression he knew what went on in their minds, everything kind of became too hot for all of them. Strange how the angel would do his best to argue with her even if her only answer was inside Duncan's head. It was not just surprising. It was so goddamn powerful in such a way that he was beginning to understand how the two of them could have gotten to be who they were.

Because this bit about having an aware Virt had a way of

influencing people, and he was witnessing the amazing consequences firsthand with the only two who had it since they were old enough to walk.

Moaning softly, Ylianor arched her back and gave him more flesh to torment. Her curves pressed so seductively to his that there could be no mistake. She wanted him as much as he did her. His stone-like cock digging on her belly was all the proof she needed.

Best of all, every pair of eyes seemed mesmerized by his sensual show. To make it worth their watching, he bent and flicked his tongue on the taut bud about to perforate the cloth. Sucking it was another great addition, along with grazing his teeth on its uneven surface.

Having her jump in pain and pleasure was the delicious conclusion of it all, particularly since it gave him an excuse to tighten his hold on her.

"Don't move," he ordered loud enough so people could hear him. "I want everyone to see what an obedient slave you are."

"But we haven't entered the Game, yet." She could object all she liked.

She was swimming in that thick honeydew of hers that was dripping to her thighs. Even had he not possessed the Virt to pluck it out of her awareness, he would have smelled the pungent odor hitting his nostrils and shaft with the full load of her craving.

"As far as I'm concerned, the Game starts *now*." Raising an eyebrow, he regarded her coldly to emphasize his act. "So, when your master orders, you obey and shut up."

"Yes, Master." She played along beautifully, going all limp and submissive.

It was just a ruse, even if he checked to make sure her energy was not abandoning her. Good thing, he had her eat before leaving the shelter. The way Cecilia treated slaves, the stars only knew when Ylianor would be able to ingest food again.

"From now on, I'm at your complete service." The huskiness of her breath implied she was ready to do it right here.

Right now.

"Just ask." No question about it. Everyone's naked expectation and raw excitement were hitting her harder with each passing moment.

Peeking toward Blue Oasis, he caught sight of Cecilia on the threshold. The line had thinned considerably while he had been busy fondling his slave, so he dragged her forward, along with all the horses.

"I'll wait until we've officially entered the Game." He had given spectacle enough.

It had also not failed to ensnare his angel's attention, at least judging from the scowl crossing his beautiful face upon his return.

"Couldn't wait to start the damn Game, could you?" Chris hissed in a low tone only Duncan and Ylianor could hear.

"Just getting in the part, Angel." He grinned.

Of course, he had known this game between him and his princess would spark Chris's jealousy. It could not be helped. Thankfully, he had the most effective way to defuse it, even if he could not possibly do it here.

"And working up my slave." To distract Chris's rage, he squeezed her buttocks possessively.

"Ha! As if she needs the practice!" Another low growl, this one was less angry.

The blue-gray eyes glued to her backside must have had something to do with it.

"Or the attention," he added. "In case you haven't noticed, no one could tear their gaze away from what you were doing." This pissed him off considerably. "You might as well have fucked her right here and now without waiting for the start of the stupid Game."

"I would have," Duncan retorted. "But I didn't want to give them any sneak previews."

"Now, everybody is just dying to know what you'll do." There was an unmistakable note of regret in the angel's voice.

"Afraid of a little competition, Lord Templeton?" As mellifluous as a snake, Ylianor eyed Chris with the most adorable expression in her brilliant green eyes. "Or that it'll spoil your game?"

"My game, dearie, doesn't need the likes of you," Chris scoffed haughtily. "My friends and I will be so much better off without an insignificant slave that doesn't even know how to blow properly." To make sure she got the full impact of his scorn, he looked her up and down as though she were dirt.

Literally.

And this was no play.

"Unlike you, Lord Templeton, I have plenty of interesting holes beside my mouth." It was uncanny. "Something my master will take ample advantage of in and out of this Game." She simply could not resist Chris's dares.

"Don't flatter yourself," the angel spat. "Had I only agreed to it, I'd be playing his slave now, while you'd be stuck waiting for us in a shelter." Kind of apparent, he was just as ready to pick a fight with her as she was with him.

Duncan could only imagine their explosive combination were he to let them play by themselves. What with his angel going all sadistic and his princess all challenging, he could almost taste the ripples of extreme lust coursing through the Game's chamber, which intoxicated him way beyond what he already was!

"Too bad for you, I'm here," she countered with a gleeful smile. "People are already talking about him and me," she taunted. "While not a word about you or your friends over there." She tossed her head disdainfully toward the group of men about to enter Blue Oasis.

"Only 'cause they're still deciding who plays what to bother about showing off." The blue-gray eyes brightened at the prospect. "Troy wants to play master, but Patrick refuses to accept anything that isn't the master's role."

"Who'll win?" Not that Duncan cared a fig about it.

Patrick and Troy were two of the Arthur boys, so only natural Chris should know them so well. He had probably fucked with both in that renowned attic at the Hall.

Under the leader's very hungry stare no less.

Which meant that whatever combination they decided, it would make no difference to his angel.

"Technically, Patrick received the invitation." After eying the fast-dwindling line, Chris strode forward. "I hope Troy gets to play the slave. I've been wanting to—"

"Hey, aren't you forgetting the rules?" Duncan cut him off abruptly. "You have to ask for my permission before you can fuck with anyone."

One thing he had learned early on about Christopher Templeton was that he had to reach a specific limit before he could steam off thoroughly. Since the dastardly creature was nowhere near it, he knew precisely what buttons to push to get him flying off every one of his horses.

"What?" As expected, Chris flared up immediately, "You wouldn't dare deny—"

"Wouldn't I?" A sardonic snarl curled his lips. "Just try me."

"I can't believe my ears!" The blue-gray eyes widened. "You can't restrict me, not after what I've had to put up with for your sake—"

"That's a private matter." Inflexible, Duncan pursued a track of his own. "This is a game, so I can very well do what I damn please."

"That's not fair!" Chris stomped his feet. "Only 'cause you

have the age to do it—"

"And the authority, remember?" To make him feel the full weight of it, Duncan pinned him against Fuzeon, overshadowing the lithe angel body with his more massive one.

"Arthur didn't mean it this way." Not that Chris tried to get out of it. He so loved being under Duncan's spell that his cock went slab of stone all at once.

"Are you sure?" Seizing the opportunity, he clutched it with a forceful jerk that left Chris begging for more.

"No, lover, don't." The rage quickly melting into unabated desire, the angel signaled he was ready to stand down and surrender.

Too bad, there was no more time to play silly games.

Blue Oasis's grand and now empty entrance glowed in the darkness, lit from behind by high torches. With no one standing either ahead or behind, he, Chris and Ylianor would be the last ones to set foot into the building. As he hurried up the landing, he handed her Fuzeon's bridles and placed her behind him and Chris. Between the three horses trailing at her back and the human frames in front of her, she would be virtually invisible, which was exactly what he wanted.

Only thing, where was the Game Master?

CHAPTER EIGHT

"Prince Caldwell!" Stepping on the landing in front of the door, a tall, dark-haired woman, with hard-cut features that made her face resemble more that of a man, opened her arms wide. "What an honor to see you here!" An ironic grin twisting her lips, Lady Cecilia Hurst looked as though she wanted to throw herself in his arms.

Which lucky for him, she did not.

"With Lord Templeton no less." Now that he observed her better, she seemed to hold herself back on purpose. "You've finally decided to accept my invitation, dear Duncan."

From the way she was eating him up with her eyes alone, she had not changed any. Not since he had last seen her, which was roughly three years before.

"One of my many invitations, I must add." Kind of obvious, it grated on her nerves that he had ignored all her previous ones.

"Dear Ceci, you submerged me with them." Just a figure of speech for the Game had not been around that long.

When he had first known her, there had been no Game, if not the vague skeleton of it locked inside her brilliant mind.

"It was just a matter of time before I accepted one." He smiled back, well knowing he would have to take full advantage of her clear penchant for him to accomplish his mission.

"That's why I kept sending them." Her insistence was downright puzzling.

Like Chris had observed, she never invited the same

person twice nor someone too young for the role, like he had been until very recently.

"Though I'd have never thought you'd come with Lord Templeton." Shifting her gaze on him, she scrutinized the angel thoroughly. "If memory serves me right, you are nineteen years old, so I guess you'll play the slave—"

"Sorry to disappoint you, Lady Hurst." Mocking to the point of being offensive, Chris bowed slightly. "I'm here as a guest."

"You are?" Wide-eyed in surprise, she spun to Duncan. "Where's your slave?"

"Right here." Having shielded Ylianor on purpose, he stepped aside and pushed her forward.

"This is your slave?" A sarcastic gleam lighting her dark eyes, she inspected Ylianor up and down. "Where did you find her?"

Curious, eh? Since it was the same nosiness he would expect from a jealous rival, he eyed her coldly. "I believe I'm not required to answer any of your questions regarding my slave."

"Just wondering . . ." Waving a dismissive hand in the air, she played it like it did not matter one bit to her.

Which was all crap as far as he was concerned.

"Hey, Ceci, still admitting guests?" Coming up from behind, a stunning blonde woman stepped out, preceded by her husky voice.

Well, well, if it was not Lady Rowena Sentry, Cecilia's phase mate. As opposite to Cecilia as day from night, she was more of his type of woman, so nothing strange he had neglected the former for the latter.

"Yes, dear." Spinning around, a dazzling smile brightened Cecilia's masculine features. "We have the last and most honored guest of all."

"Duncan? Is it really you?" Rowena's incredibly blue eyes sparkled with barely suppressed lust. "Darling, it's a real pleasure to see you again!" Reaching over, she clasped him tightly, her body fitting seductively around his and pressing every soft curve on his strategic points.

Her lips closed on his in a passionate kiss, and he drowned in her scent.

Or something to that effect as he forced his tongue into her warm cavity like she wanted him to do.

By the gods, she had hardly changed over the years! No wonder she had been the reason he had shifted his attention away from Cecilia. Of the two phase mates, she had all the femininity Cecilia lacked. Not just a question of looks. Cecilia was as hard inside as she was on the outside, while the other was one of the most sensual women he had ever known.

Years later, she was still as beautiful as he remembered. Only grown a little softer.

Unwrapping her lips and body from him, she took a step back. "You've made poor Cecilia sweat for your presence." She glanced at her phase mate. "Frankly, I lost count of how many invitations she sent you since the start of her Game."

"Me, too." Grinning, he held her at arm's length. "But I'd have accepted sooner had I known I'd see you and in such great shape."

"Yours isn't bad, either." She winked maliciously. "It's better than I remember." Her tongue tracing her lips was all the erotic innuendo he needed to know she would love to jump in his bed again. "And with the combination of Lord Templeton, you'll be sure to be irresistible." Getting closer, she lowered her voice, "Have you brought him as your mouthwatering slave so that people won't know which gorgeous man to choose?"

"Not to worry, Lady Sentry." Kind of apparent, Chris did not have much liking for her, just as he had none for her phase mate. "We come separate, and we'll make our own choices."

"Who's the slave then?" Puzzled, she swung her gaze from

him to Chris.

"It's her, apparently." Cecilia gestured toward Ylianor.

Peering behind her shoulder, Rowena made a show like she had just seen the princess. "Her?" As though picking up her phase mate's dislike, something in her tone told him she did not have too much consideration for Ylianor. "Is she old enough to play?"

"How old is your slave?" Cecilia's dark eyes blazed in his direction.

"She's eighteen." At least he hoped so.

In all the excitement of coming here, he had forgotten to ask her exact age.

Just barely, but I'm eighteen. Her soft giggle filled his head.

"Very well, let's get on with it." Piqued that this limit could not be grounds for Ylianor's dismissal, Cecilia went all solemn. "Who stands master, and who is his slave?" Her formal tone indicated she was now acting as the official Game Master.

Ready, Princess? No need to ask or to wait for an answer.

Not since she was dripping all over the place out of sheer excitement.

"I, Duncan Caldwell, am the master." It rang out as imposing as the occasion required. "I bring this woman as my slave and Lord Christopher Templeton as my guest."

"I accept you in the Game." With a slight note of regret veining her voice, Cecilia bowed to him and Chris. "Welcome, my friends." Striding forward, she kissed him full on the lips, lingering those few seconds more than necessary.

Next, she did the same to Chris. Only it lasted a whole lot less, and she retreated hastily as though she feared he might bite her.

Which, knowing the angel, he would have, had the kiss lasted an instant longer.

"As for you . . ." Her business with the master and the

guest over, he had no doubt she would start on her humiliation of the slave.

Only natural, since this was another big part of her Game. To treat slaves as objects and depersonalize them as much as she could.

"From now on, you are a slave, therefore forbidden to speak or wear clothes." Clamping the two separate ends of Ylianor's top, she ripped it off. "You will act only under your master's instructions and obey his every command and wish."

Coming out of the shadows, two beefy servants reached their mistress, their massive bodies fully displayed by tight-fitting pants and bare chests.

"Take the horses to the stables," Cecilia addressed the smaller of the two.

Scuttling to comply, the man grabbed the reins off Ylianor's hand and disappeared from the landing with Fuzeon, Black and Starlet trailing behind him.

"While you better prepare this slave for the Game." Pushing the princess toward the remaining servant, Cecilia made sure he dragged her off to a narrow passageway that ran to the right. Then, her attention snagged back on him. "Dear Prince, what sort of accommodations do you require? Will you take one room for you and your guest? Or perhaps, you'd prefer a room each? Of course, your slave can stay by herself downstairs in the common area —"

"We need only one room." No way would he pass up this opportunity to be alone with his angel. "And the slave sleeps with *us*." His tone sounded more possessive than he had planned.

"As you command." Cecilia bowed to acknowledge his request. "If you follow me, I'll take you straight to your room." Heading for a left corridor, she led the way.

Not just for him and Chris. For Rowena, too, since she

tagged along before she accelerated to get to Cecilia's side.

"So, you care about this particular slave?" The way Cecilia blurted this out, it was clear she was fishing for just about any information. "Is she a relative, perhaps?" She peeped at him nervously. "'Cause she resembles you a whole lot . . ."

You'd just love to know, wouldn't you?

"All right." Stopping on his tracks, he smiled coldly. "Since you're so interested, what are you going to offer in exchange for my answer?"

"Already getting in the spirit of the Game?" Cecilia mocked, pretending the matter was not significant.

"Isn't that what we're here for?" Duncan sneered, her tone not fooling him one bit.

"Prince Caldwell, I'm impressed." Moving up closer, she eyed him admiringly. "You're one of the few people who understands what my Game is all about, and you've only played it once before." She frowned. "As for your proposal, I suppose I could give you the best accommodations in the house if you answer my question."

"What do you think, Angel?" He locked on the stunning blue-gray eyes. "Can it be enough?"

"I'd also ask for the best position in the chamber." Deliberately cutting her off, Chris kept a steady gaze trained on him alone.

"You drive a hard bargain for one simple answer," Cecilia scoffed impatiently.

"You seem uncommonly interested in my slave." He raised an eyebrow. "Some particular reason why?"

"We never expected you to turn up with a woman." All innocent and wide-eyed, Rowena sounded as though she and Cecilia had talked about it. "You took us by surprise."

Had Cecilia been expecting him? If so, did she already know he was looking for more than just fun and games?

"Is she another Game Master?" Ignoring Rowena on purpose, he focused on Cecilia alone.

"No, she isn't." From the way Lady Hurst snapped, it obviously irked her.

If because Rowena was no Game Master or if because she had given Cecilia away, he was not sure.

"I'm just helping Ceci straighten things out." Laughing as though nothing had happened, Rowena startling blue eyes glittered. "And I don't understand what all the fuss is about. Rules allow to question a master, don't they, Ceci?"

"Yes, dear, they do . . ." Cecilia's tone was very patient, like someone who had tried explaining the concept a thousand times to a child and failed each time. "But not from the Game Master."

"I always said you had too many rules, even if they make for an exciting play." Flashing a radiant smile, Rowena took a left turn. "See you all at the Game."

"She's never going to change." Gaze glued to the tantalizing backside disappearing down the hallway, there was so much tenderness in Cecilia's remark that it was not hard to figure out how deeply attached the woman still was to her phase mate.

Something Rowena did not return in quite the same terms.

"Nor understand the first thing about your Game." He grinned to win back Cecilia's attention.

"While you do, Prince Caldwell." She shook her head, amused. "That bargain of yours—"

"Take it or leave it." Playtime over, he became very serious. "The choice is yours."

"All right, all right." Whirling around, she raised a hand. "I'll give you the best room in the house and the best spot in the chamber if you answer a few questions. Will that be enough?"

Exchanging glances with his angel, he received a silent go ahead. "It's a deal." He squeezed her hand to make it final. "What do you want to know?"

"Who is she?" It came out in such a rush that her words sounded slurred.

"She's my stable keeper." He had to work hard to suppress a laugh.

"Your stable keeper?" *So, it's her!*

Not that she went as far as saying it outright.

He read it off the flash lighting her dark eyes, which implied she knew a great deal more than she had led on so far.

"Just a stable keeper, eh?" Her skeptical tone sounded anything but convinced.

"Yes, just a stable keeper." He suppressed the twinge of his guilty conscience.

The stars help him!

She was so much more!

Like Chris had admitted, he was not sure he would be able to let her go once his task was over.

"Angel, please . . ." Cocking his head in Chris's direction, he caught the blue-gray eyes. "Tell her I'm not lying."

"Her father happened to be Black Rose's stable keeper." Chris did not exactly scramble to give Cecilia his attention, though he managed to look at her without that supercilious air of his. "When he died about a month ago, the prince hired her in his place."

"She looks like one of your family." No, she was not buying Chris's sensible explanation.

It was like she knew the answer already. David must have said something about Black Rose's latest news. Had he also mentioned how close he had become to Ylianor? Was Cecilia acting out her jealousy or what?

Exchanging a glance with his angel, he guessed Chris was thinking along his same lines.

"It's just a coincidence." He shrugged nonchalantly. "A passing resemblance, nothing more."

"Is that so?" Clearly not fooled, she insisted, "But—"

"I think I said enough to satisfy your curiosity." This was as much as he was ready to tell her, at least until he confronted her about the stolen pyramid.

Then, he would lay all his cards on the table.

Recovering her composure, she nodded. "You're right."

Snatching her gaze to the hallway winding around Blue Oasis's central body, she resumed walking. Turning first right then left, she came to a halt in front of a dark blue door.

"Here you are, Prince Caldwell." Throwing it open, she gestured at the large room.

Very spacious, it had a giant bed, a couch in front of an impressive fireplace glowing and crackling from the heat of burning wood. On the opposite side, he noticed chairs around a dining table, with a bottle of amber liquid and glasses on top.

"As promised, this is the finest room in the house." She signaled for both him and his angel to go through the threshold. "I hope it suits you."

"It does." No question about it.

I guess it was worth it to answer her damn questions. If Chris did not say it out loud, he had no problem picking it up from his sideway glance in Cecilia's direction. "The giant bed in particular." The mesmerizing blue-gray eyes sparked in arousal when they snagged back on him.

Chris could not wait to try it. So, what else was new?

Duncan himself had half a mind to kick Cecilia out and be alone with his adored angel.

"Glad you approve, Lord Templeton." From her snicker, it was obvious she had no trouble understanding Chris's intentions, either. "The Game will begin shortly. You can reach us at any time, and your slave will be waiting for you." Brisk and practical, she was once again entirely in her role as Game Master. "If you need anything, this bell will call your servant." She pointed at a hanging chord. "Over there are your clothes." She indicated a blue robe on the bed, leather pants and skirt on the couch.

"Everything looks perfect." Satisfied, he checked around the comfortable and warm place one more time. "Thank you, Ceci."

"I'll see you later." After nodding his way, the woman left. And not a moment too soon!

CHAPTER NINE

Now, you be good while I fuck the angel's brains out.

As Duncan's husky and very aroused breath reverberated in her head, Ylianor drowned in the pool's hot water, half-hidden from the steam floating to the ceiling in a dustlike fog that misted down in a sort of drizzle.

Sure, go right ahead, she would have answered if given half a chance. Since it's the last, you'll be fucking of him for a good long while!

Soon enough, Prince Duncan Caldwell would be *hers*, while the odious demon would be history.

At least for the duration of Cecilia's Game.

"Is it too hot?" Solicitous, one of the two servants assigned to her, the one called Bilitis, bent on her.

She treated the woman with her best smile. "No, it's just perfect."

Just perfect to get her body ready for the upcoming challenge.

This would be only between her and her dark-haired master, with no annoying blond beauty to spoil it for her.

She could not wait for things to get started! To get away from this underground chamber full of soon-to-be slaves that Cecilia's servants were prepping for the upcoming task. Nor could she suppress the ferocious hammering splitting her clit in two and whetting her appetite beyond any excitement. Particularly now that she sank in her element, splashing against the edges of the pool cut into the stone and lit by trembling torches reflecting onto the glittering surface. Same light that bounced back on the brownish stonewalls, combining vapor and fire into fantastic colored designs.

"Some can't stand it." The second servant, dark-haired Francisca, glanced at the many slaves squirming uncomfortably at the heat, before refocusing on the job of folding Ylianor's clothes on the side cot of one of the cubicles. Carved inside the wall surrounding the large square basement, they broke the even surface into elegant arches that gave the place a refined look it would have lacked otherwise.

"That's too bad." She shrugged indifferent, watching other servants pushing a riotous young man back in the water. "'Cause I like it just fine."

"Yeah, we can tell," Bilitis smirked naughtily.

"All right, I think we got you cleaned up just right." Having finished arranging her things, Francisca motioned her to get out of the pool. "Now, lie here." She pointed at the cot padded with a soft-looking towel.

As soon as she stretched out belly down, both women were on her. Their trained hands applied perfumed oil on her back, and off they went, torturing her skin mercilessly with a deep, forceful rub down that had her jumping and thrashing.

This was definitely nothing pleasant!

This was torture!

The most refined kind, since she could not keep still under the onslaught of those fastidious shivers that were both a blessing and a curse.

"You don't like it?" Bilitis stopped to peer deep in her eyes.

"Not really." *Or maybe, I just like it too much.*

Actually, she was still making up her mind. Now that Duncan and Chris had discovered this weakness of hers, they had confused her even more.

"Come on." Francisca kneaded her back. "It can't be that bad."

"You're right." Suppressing the urge to bolt, she forced

herself to breathe. "It's worse!"

"Good thing, it's over, then." Bilitis slapped her ass. "You can get up."

Grateful, she scrambled to her feet, her skin tingling all over.

"Now, come, sit here." Bilitis patted a stone seat inside the cubicle that faced the wall. "We'll take care of this gorgeous hair of yours."

They first poured silky oil that made the long mass shine after repeated brushes. The next step was to braid a few strands and place them on top of her head, letting the rest hang free. The final touch was to her face, adding makeup that was a first for her.

"You look beautiful." Francisca took a step back to admire her work.

She leaned toward a small mirror hanging on the wall to check for herself.

"Who is your master?" Bilitis adjusted a stray lock.

"Prince Duncan Caldwell." Looking at a very different version of herself, she could not believe how easily they had managed to transform her into someone so alluring.

For sure, it was not just the effect of the new hairstyle, which exalted the oval of her face. The reddish powder made her cheeks glow, and the black eyeliner caused the green of her eyes to sparkle.

"He has never played master." The light-haired woman smiled warmly. "Only as a guest once."

"People couldn't stop talking about how great he was," Francisca intervened. "Or how gorgeous he was." She licked her lips as though she had stored all of Duncan's features in her memory.

"Aye, he was." Bilitis's husky tone indicated she had also taken due notice.

"He still is," Ylianor set the record straight.

Yes, the most gorgeous one and Lord Christopher Templeton could just eat his heart out, for he would never beat Duncan in that department.

"More gorgeous than ever." She sighed, shaking her head free of silly comparisons.

"He'll probably turn out a great master." Francisca removed the excess of powder on her chin.

"An unconventional one for sure." Taking a narrow brush, Bilitis dipped it in a small jar full of red cream.

"Why?" Curious to know what the woman was planning on doing, she watched her intently.

"Because masters don't usually insist on having slaves sleep in the same room," Bilitis sniggered. "They want to have nothing to do with them once the night's play is over." She shrugged as though she did not agree with such treatment. "Which is why they don't bring anybody beautiful or worthy of notice as slaves." She turned her head behind her shoulder. "Just take a look, and you can judge for yourself."

Maybe, the woman was not wrong. The specimens getting ready did seem kind of insignificant and submissive, the men as much as the women.

"Now, open your lips." After having dipped the brush a couple of times, the servant neared it to her mouth and began painting her lips red. "He must care for you or something . . ."

Ha! That'll be the day. "No, you're wrong." Her eyes flashed in the mirror. "I mean nothing to him, and this Game isn't going to change anything." *Not a damn thing, unfortunately.*

"Could be." Unconvinced, Bilitis studied her lips.

"Not a chance!" Francisca did not appear to have any doubts instead. "Most masters think slaves are only an excuse to get into the Game, so they bring people who don't mean a thing, and who won't distract attention from them." Her lips twisted in a cold snarl. "But they're fools who don't realize that sharing is the Game's objective. Your prince, instead, seems to have understood it perfectly, which is why he must've brought you. To have the others appreciate, too. That's why we think he cares for you."

"I think you've been doing this game for too long." Ylianor giggled.

"Perhaps, we've been so long with Lady Hurst we're starting to think like her." Satisfied with the final effect on her red lips, Bilitis placed both flacon and brush on a shelf.

"Does she even like this game of hers?" After everything Duncan had said about Cecilia Hurst, she had the feeling she did not.

"Well . . ." Francisca exchanged a glance with Bilitis. "It's hard to tell . . ." She swallowed hard. "She invented it, of course, but I think because she doesn't enjoy sex like the rest of us."

"But lately, she's changed." Taking a small bottle of perfume, Bilitis poured a few drops on her neck. "Since David's been coming here I mean."

"Who is David?" Looking all disinterested, she pretended to study her face in the mirror.

"We don't know exactly." Francisca adjusted her hair again. "He doesn't talk much and hasn't said much about himself. All we know is that he first came with your prince then returned to visit by himself."

"When he's here, Lady Cecilia is more cheerful, more inclined to play, so to speak," the other servant confirmed.

So, he means something to her. That much was becoming clear.

She was suddenly glad that David had someone besides Prince Caldwell to hold his interest.

"Is he here now?" She made it sound like she did not care either way.

"He is, only he's never involved with the Game." Francisca nodded. "I think he doesn't like it much —"

"I think he doesn't approve of it," Bilitis retorted.

That would figure given David's rigid class distinction.

"Then, why is he here?" Again, she said it like it was just small talk.

"Maybe, he just likes being around Cecilia, no matter what the occasion." Bilitis laughed.

"Or maybe he's coming round to it," Francisca pointed out. "Like the rest of us did with Lady Hurst's way of thinking." She examined Ylianor's hairdo with a critical eye before stepping away satisfied.

"'Cause it makes for a damn good show." Grinning broadly, Bilitis gestured her to rise. "You'll have plenty of time to understand it better once we take you there."

After wrapping transparent silk around her body, they led her out of the chamber. Through a maze of hallways, she followed the two women down the intricate passageways that twisted in what seemed like an endless circle. That it might never end crossed her mind as she went past many, too many, closed doors, most brilliantly colored in sharp contrast with the blue of the walls. At a gray door, she felt David's presence.

No, not just David.

Something else seemed to call her, something that could have been the pyramid stolen from the Nephis Valley. She wished she could stop to investigate.

Not an option, alas.

Not since it was nowhere present in the servants' agenda. She had to keep going through Cecilia's labyrinth, turning left and right until they halted in front of a white door.

CHAPTER TEN

"Here we are." Throwing open the door, Bilitis waited for Francisca to remove the silk scarf from around her body before stepping through the threshold.

Close at her heels, completely naked, Ylianor had her first glimpse of the large chamber.

Big and sparsely furnished, it did not seem particularly cunt dripping, were it not for the many nude men and women seated on the low tables in front of large couches. Their skins trembling, none of them dared move, not even to breathe. How could they?

Arousal clogged their senses so deeply it was a mystery how they managed to keep erect at all. Never had excitement felt more tangible. The smell and taste of it drowned out anything not related to sex. Affected their aura, too, to the point she began losing herself in the sensations about to over flood her until Bilitis's voice snapped her attention back to the here and now.

"Game Master." Bowing low to Cecilia, the woman's forehead touched her knees. "Here is Prince Caldwell's slave." She pushed Ylianor forward.

So hard, she practically bumped against the formidable Lady Hurst.

"What is your name?" Sidestepping the servant, Cecilia rushed to her.

"My master is Prince Duncan Caldwell." Just to spite her, she kept her head lowered.

"Slave, I asked for your name." Impatient, Cecilia tapped a

foot nervously on the floor.

"I believe I'm not supposed to answer this question." Raising her gaze, she looked straight into Cecilia's dark eyes.

Boy, was it a mistake!

Totally baffled, she could not believe what she read in that startling aura. In that disturbingly cold wall of dark blue light arranged in such a complex geometrical structure. Instead of the familiar jumble of colored flashes flickering in warm confusion, there was a sequenced pattern filled with icy voids.

That freezing emptiness of hers was reaching out to crush Ylianor and her defiant stare.

"I'm the Game Master, so I'm entitled to ask anything I damn well please!" Cecilia spat angrily.

Ylianor blinked twice to regain a measure of balance.

What she had just seen confirmed that the woman knew nothing of sex. That her disciplined and rational mind had worked overtime to fit it into a logical grid. Which was all a waste of time, since sex was nothing like she had made it out to be.

Which had not stopped the dark-haired masculine-faced lady from inventing a whole bunch of rules and regulations designed to make it as inflexible as her mind was.

"Now, tell me your name," Cecilia insisted.

"Why should I?" Stubbornly, Ylianor met her gaze without a trace of fear, for she would be damned if she allowed the woman to have the upper hand. "My master is —"

"I'm her master!" Duncan's deep manly voice rang above the background chatter, with a mix of pride and possessiveness that had her heart race several beats ahead. "Ceci, I believe you're asking the wrong question to the wrong person."

"Hem . . ." Frustrated beyond words, a now bright-red-in-the-face Cecilia spun around to confront him. "I just wanted to know —"

"The rules are very specific," he cut her off brusquely.

"You, for one, should know that since you invented them."

She had no trouble perceiving how annoyed he was with Lady Hurst. But not out of any breach in etiquette.

Impossible as it seemed, what truly galled him was having Cecilia come between him and her, as though he could not stand being apart from his slave one second longer than necessary.

This was like a sweet balm to her enflamed spirit.

"I believe the Game Master can't talk to the slaves. All questions are for their masters alone." His black eyes flashed, daring her to contradict him. "Am I correct?"

"Yes." There was no disguising how much it grated on Cecilia's nerves to admit he was right. "But—"

"There are no buts." Intransigent, he did not let Cecilia off the hook. "You already asked about this particular slave, and I satisfied your curiosity." He peered deep in her eyes. "Or is there something else you wish to know?"

"No." Obviously defeated, Cecilia hung her head. "Nothing else."

Yet, she did not budge an inch, still standing between him and Ylianor as when he had first approached.

"Then, give me *my* slave." It was an order pure and simple.

With a jolt, Cecilia stepped aside.

Clamping Ylianor's hand possessively, he tugged her toward him.

Is everything all right, Princess? He could not hold back the rush of energy as their hands touched.

Which coursed through her and gave her new vigor.

Yes. Just to be on the safe side, she clung to him as though her life depended on it. *Now that you're here.*

What about the sheer warmth of his muscular body that flattened her to him and chased away Cecilia's coldness?

Uh, she would have stayed in his embrace forever had he just allowed.

But you're icy cold. Grasping both her hands, he circled them behind her back and clashed their bodies together until every inch of her glued to his, and he would have to peel her off, literally.

What happened? Full of concern, his black eyes locked on hers.

Nothing, my prince. As fiercely as he had trapped her, she could not move, not even to shrug. *Just Cecilia's welcome, I guess.*

What did she want to know? He pulled back to search her face.

Everything. Ylianor had no doubt Cecilia wanted to know everything about a woman she considered her rival. *But mostly my name.*

You think she's jealous. There was no surprise in the prince's even tone. *Don't you?*

I do. Though she had no idea why she should.

He raised his voice in Lady Hurst's direction, "Where's my place?"

"As promised, it's the best one here." Going all appeasing, Cecilia gestured in front of her. "The one in the middle of the chamber."

Come on. Without letting her go, he dragged her away.

Who was more than happy to leave him in charge of everything. Even more, when she spotted the demon deep in conversation with a blondish master.

"In the end, you got Troy to play the slave." Leaning confidently over a couch, Chris beamed one of his most enchanting smiles. "Right, Patrick?"

"Absolutely, 'cause I wouldn't have had it any other way!" Amused, the man looked him over. "Why do you ask?" He suppressed a smug smirk. "Are you by any chance interested?" It sounded like a bait if she ever heard of one. "You know that Troy simply adores your great big cock." He fondled Chris's crotch.

Only natural for the demon to swallow it with all the hook.

"But rules are rules." Patrick's tone grew more serious, "What does your master have to say about it?"

Chris gulped hard as though he had to quell his excitement from rising too fast, too soon. "Oh, he's—"

"Not sure he'll let his guest play around." Devoid of any trace of humor, Duncan's grave note was like an icy shower over the most heated fire of all.

If Chris did not lash out at once, she guessed he was still in too much of a shock over such an icy answer.

"Oh, Prince, but he must." Patrick, instead, sounded vaguely pleading.

"Why?" Curling his palm tighter around her arm, Prince Caldwell stopped in front of the man.

"Some of us asked permission to use the underground pool area for a change." He seemed proud of himself for having thought of it. "And Lady Cecilia has agreed to it."

"You're going to play down there, rather than up here the whole night long?" Impossible to hide the demon's growing arousal.

"That's the idea." Patrick stared at Chris's eyes. "It's going to be a men-only thing." He chuckled. "There's quite a few of us already, and we can't wait to get started on the wet version of this Game." His gaze latched onto Duncan. "That's why you ought to allow your phase mate to join in—"

"Pardon me, sir." A petite servant approached, looking specifically at Patrick. "Lady Hurst requires your presence to discuss the final details about the underground pools."

"Sure." Getting up, he glanced at Chris. "I trust I'll see you downstairs later."

"I'll certainly be there." Acting as though Prince Caldwell had already given his blessing, Chris's voice held no trace of hesitation.

"Only if your master agrees to it," Patrick mocked as he

moved off to follow the servant.

As soon as he was out of the way, Chris spun around. "Lover, what's the matter with you?" Exceedingly irritated, Ylianor perceived how hard he was trying to hold the violent surge that threatened to explode. "I thought we agreed —"

"No, we didn't." Her prince was loving Chris's reactions way too much for her taste. "I told you I'd decide here."

That Duncan was baiting the demon on purpose seemed kind of obvious. That the rash man was falling for it with all his shoes was another self-evident truth. And the two of them were so good at their interplay that she had to suppress a giggle, lest she spoiled it all by bursting out laughing.

"Now, we're here," Chris retorted. "What's your decision?"

"I still don't know." Pulling her arm, Duncan turned away from Chris and headed toward his center place.

"Oh, come on!" Furious with Duncan ignoring him, Chris scrambled to follow. "It's not fair you should have all the fun!" His gaze caught hers.

And she was not quick enough to avert hers.

No, worse, she sank in the bottomless blue-gray depths that promised delight and torture in equal measure, thrilled beyond words to have him so focused on her for a change.

Being the bastard he was, he took immediate advantage of it. "You tell him, honey —"

"She can't talk," Duncan cut him off brusquely. "Remember?"

"The fuck she can't!" Wrenching her from Duncan's grasp, Chris pinned her body to his and bent to whisper in her ear, "Didn't you want to play alone with him?"

Sure, he was doing it on purpose, using his hot tongue and the scorching whiffs of breath teasing her earlobes as an unscrupulous attack on her senses.

Sure, she should know better than to fall for his devious

ways.

Then, why was she swimming in her craving to have him?

His shaft, now come to life and digging in her belly, was not helping, either.

"Didn't you want to have his great wonderful cock all to yourself?" Relentless, he continued to enflame her every fiber.

The pounding of her clit reached the stars!

"Didn't you want me out of your goddamn way to show him what an obedient little slave you can be?" Chris snapped her head back to stare into her eyes.

Where she read his certainty that he would get just about anything from her. How could he not?

All that wetness dampening her cunt was kind of messing with her priorities.

"To prove him, you can be a true slut if given half the chance?" A luscious lick to her earlobe sent shivers down her back. "To show him, you can take the biggest cocks around and still ask for more?" He glanced around the chamber. "To have them stuff your every hole, provided they aren't too tired for the likes of you."

True, most men were screwing whatever came on the tip of their erections. And those who were not were carefully watching those who were.

His mouth pressed more fiercely on her ear. "So, be a good girl and tell him to let me go." His breath tickled her. "Like everyone else, I'm entitled to my share of fun."

As if you didn't have enough already. Had the prince not told her himself, she would have smelled the sex oozing from every pore of Chris's body. From Duncan's, too, which, combined with their frantic auras, gave her the measure of just how good it had been.

"Even if my ass is still dancing to his beat, it's no reason he shouldn't allow me to give it around to whatever cock comes asking for it." Smug as a cat, Christopher Templeton seemed to have plucked her ironic come back straight from her head. "If you convince him, I may just make it worth your while." Impatient, he yanked her hair, tilting her head further back. "I'll fuck you so hard once this Game is over that you'll have to beg me to stop."

Now that qualified as a prize!

And she did not want to miss it.

Princess, don't tell me you're falling for his ruse. Black eyes blazing at her from behind Chris's shoulders, Prince Caldwell took a step forward.

Why not? Arching, she tried sliding against the demon's tense frame, loving the twitch that jerked his piece into stone. *He has a point, after all. You shouldn't deny him, not after what he gave you for it.*

Knowing Chris, she could just imagine the lengths he had gone to get Duncan's permission.

He can't trade his way out. Her prince sounded stern. *Not even if he gives me his ass a hundred times over.*

I believe he has given it much more than that. She smiled coyly. *But at least, his heart has always been in the right place.*

Yeah, in his ass. Duncan chortled before his tone became more serious and interested, *Are you getting a soft spot for my angel?*

What if I am?

No, she did not say it.

Did not even dare think it. Too afraid he would pick it up anyway.

She simply blushed violently and tried to look away.

Which he did not allow her to do, trapping her gaze for an agonizingly long moment.

"He's treating you bad, too, isn't he?" Releasing her hair, Chris glared at Duncan. "He thinks he can trample on us just because he's playing master."

"I am the *Master*." Not a joke, Duncan meant it *for real*.

There was no doubt in Ylianor's mind that he was the most

suitable man in the whole chamber for the role.

"Don't you ever forget it." Untangling her from the demon's hold, he drew her to him. "Since I'm such a great master, I'll let you go." A sparkle lit the black eyes. "But simply because the princess pleaded for you and convinced me."

"I owe you one, honey." The demon winked, flashing a dazzling smile angel-style.

The kind he reserved for his lover alone.

Too bad, it did not last nearly enough for her taste.

His attention was all for the handsome dark-haired prince once more. "Can I go now?"

Duncan nodded, and Chris sped away.

We won't have to worry about him for the rest of the night. Amused, the prince watched him disappear down the stairs to the underground pools before continuing to advance toward his place.

And that's a real pity. There was no point in sharing this.

However anxious she was of starting Cecilia's Game with her adored prince, she regretted not having Christopher Templeton's fiery brand of excitement.

I agree. Somehow catching her thought, Duncan's deep tone confirmed he would miss his blond lover as well. *But there's enough excitement here to last us the whole night long.*

He was right, of course.

Sexual tension ran so high that she ached for something vast and thick to stuff her every hole.

You feel it, Princess, don't you? Having reached his assigned place, he clasped her more tightly. *Everything here reeks of sex.* He led her toward a low table in front of the largest couch in the entire chamber. *I was sure it would affect you like crazy.* He arranged her. Legs widespread, arms behind her back. *Now, lean on your arms and push out your cunt.*

Complying meant that her very bare and very moist cunt would gleam in the semi-darkness while the juice would drip to the wooden surface.

That's exactly how I want you. He moved off to sit on the couch.

She obeyed. Shifting her weight on her arms, she arched until her cunt stuck up and out in all its splendor.

Now, stroke that delicious pussy of yours, he ordered. *But make sure you don't come.*

Ha! Easier said than done.

Not since all gazes had suddenly swung her way, their lights confusing her perception to a hazy blur that made her dizzy.

Or perhaps it was not her at all.

Perhaps, it was him, the striking prince. With his chiseled features, long dark hair to the shoulders and piercing black eyes, he had every woman and men in the chamber staring at him with unabated lust.

Come on, he snapped. *I haven't got all day.*

She dipped in her dense honeydew and brushed the tender folds, opening in hungry anticipation.

It was the end of her.

Of her control, to be precise.

As she rubbed the swollen bud about to burst on its own, she surrendered to him, giving him full charge of her mind and body. Nothing else mattered except the fulfillment of his every desire, however outrageous it would prove to be.

He was *her master,* and she would be damned if she let him down in any way!

CHAPTER ELEVEN

"Dear Duncan," Rowena Sentry's husky voice wafted like a sweet perfume.

Perched on the couch of his center-stage position, he turned. What he read on her face was enough to make him spin to Ylianor.

For the blonde woman was gawking, at his princess's shaven cunt as though she could not believe her eyes. It made her so envious that a pea-green shade flushed her face before she managed to get a hold on herself.

Pretending everything was fine and dandy, she averted her gaze from that enticing pussy that glowed in the half-light and fixed it on him.

But not without a visible effort.

"I'm so glad you're here." Acting like her usual cool self, she sat next to him on the couch. "I haven't seen you for like a lifetime, and I've missed you."

Me or my cock? He could not suppress the thought, remembering their heated fucks.

Your cock for sure, Master. Ylianor's snappy retort almost made him laugh.

Shut up. He had to restrain himself from calling her Princess. *No one asked for your opinion.*

Just trying to be helpful, she sniggered.

Sure, she was.

Point of fact, she looked so inviting with that over flooded pussy of hers, so open and defenseless that he would have gladly ditched Rowena to stick his cock in it.

Which was not the way he wanted to play this game.

He refocused on Rowena, not without a good deal of will-power. "It's been just a few years." He smiled mischievously. "I hear you pledged in the meantime."

Examining her up close, he realized she had become more artificially seductive over the years. Sure, she had always been very comfortable with her physical self. But now that he had tasted his princess's less experienced yet more natural appeal, Rowena came out as a calculated seductress. One who carefully studied pose and movements to attract men and make them lose their minds.

"Yes, and Oliver is a darling." She pouted as though she had said a half-truth. "But he's too . . ." She creased her lovely forehead evidently in search of the right word. "Homey, if you know what I mean." Her naughty smile implied he would have no trouble understanding the underlying gist of it. "I want to travel, see places—"

"People, mostly." He chuckled. "Men in particular."

"Yes, absolutely." Rowena's arresting blue eyes flashed in an appraisal. "And you're the best-looking one I ever saw." There was a note of genuine appreciation in her tone. "It's too bad we didn't match-up when we had the chance." She edged closer. "If you had been my mate, I would have never gotten around as much as I have."

There's no way I'd have ever taken you, dearie.

Careful to keep the thought to himself, he locked his gaze on hers. "I wasn't ready for commitments."

"Well, not much has changed, has it?" She was obviously up to date with the latest news.

Small wonder.

With her phase mate as one of the High Council's permanent members and all the Hall gossip Chris had told him about, it was doubtful anything would escape her notice.

"Right," he confirmed her assumption. "No pledge mate for me and no one in sight, either." It was the plain truth.

Except for the two fabulous lovers he could not get enough of, no one was even remotely interesting to spur him toward a pledge any time soon.

"Nor do I intend to start looking for one here." Suppressing the image of his mother's stern face, he silenced the guilty twinge of his conscience.

"Not that there's a lack of available candidates." Rowena made a show of checking around the chamber. "Only I get the feeling a pledge is the farthest thing from their minds." She giggled provocatively.

"Would you happen to know what they're here for?" Playing dumb on purpose, he leaned forward.

"Oh, for this and that." Deliberately vague, her hands ran to his crotch. "But mostly, for this." She stroked his stirring shape from above the master's robe.

"I can't wait to see who tonight's first lucky woman will be." He grinned, daring her to make her move.

"Oh, I could have a candidate in mind." Her fondling became a definite jerk of his now rigid piece. "Only she doesn't much like doing it here in the open." Shifting her gaze, she glanced at the princess, sitting on the table with her back to them. "Are you free to leave?"

"Not until someone takes charge of my slave." That was one of Cecilia's number one rules.

Slaves could never remain unattended.

'Cause they would just get up and leave, Ylianor chortled in his head.

However funny her pun, he worked hard to sound annoyed. *If you keep yapping that trap of yours, I'll be sure to leave you with Cecilia herself—*

I'm shutting up, she rushed to interrupt him. *I'm shutting up, and I won't open my mouth again until the end of the Game. Promise.* Half-turning her head, she caught his gaze. *See?* She pressed her lips together as though they were sealed.

As if you couldn't talk with your mouth closed, he teased.

I won't, she insisted. *I swear.*

If he allowed her lie to slip, it was just because Rowena had grabbed his arm, squeezing it forcefully.

"Where's Lord Templeton?" Rowena's head spun to search for him. "He can stay with her."

"The angel has flown away faster than lightning." He grinned. "I doubt I'll see him for the rest of the night."

"Oh, darn." In frustration, she looked around for help. "Let's call Ceci." Her expression brightened at the prospect. "She'll look after your slave."

Master, I promised I'd keep my mouth shut. Vaguely pleading, Ylianor squirmed on the table.

Then, why are you talking now? Duncan retorted, acting like she had just committed a capital offense.

That he had no wish to leave her with Cecilia was something he did not want to share, unwilling to give her the satisfaction.

Sorry, Master. Out of breath, Ylianor gulped for air. *It won't happen again —*

I know it won't 'cause one more word out of you, and you're going to regret it. Harsh to the point of being biting, he grabbed Rowena and ignored Ylianor.

Pushing the blonde woman to lay on the couch, he traced the contour of her ear with slow flicks. After bending to bite her neck, he trailed up to whisper huskily, "Actually, I'm hungry for more than one girl."

"You want us both?" That she was thrilled out of her skin by his request seemed kind of a given. "Great!" She clutched his hard cock as though wanting reassurance that he was not kidding. "Let me call her over."

Slithering from beneath him, she got to her feet and ran to find Cecilia.

"Ahem . . ." A man with a familiar face stepped forward. "Duncan, what a pleasure!" He strode to his place once Rowena vanished behind the chamber's main doors. "I didn't expect to find you here."

Well, well, if it isn't Jeff Macy. Duncan got up to meet him halfway. There was no mistaking about what he was after, considering he was eating up the princess with his eyes alone.

Good thing, the angel had split beforehand, given how little he could stand the man in his younger years.

Childhood friend and neighbor of the Caldwell's, Jeff lived in Harbor Town with his brother, Robin, and his parents. The last time he had seen him had been during his visit to Isabella Turner, which had been the reason he had found his princess again after a ten-year separation.

"Hello, Jeff." He squeezed the man's outstretched hand. "To be honest, it was a last-minute decision." Remembering David's latest news regarding Harbor Town, he gazed at him concerned. "How's your father doing?"

"Not well after that blasted fall." A sad look crossed Jeff's face. "He was riding too fast until a storm frightened his horse into throwing him off." His lips twisted downward. "Now, doctors assure us he'll make a complete recovery, but I don't know." He shrugged helplessly. "I don't see him recovering all that much."

"I'm sure he'll soon be on his feet again," Duncan offered as a measure of consolation.

"That's what I hope." Jeff licked his lips nervously, his gaze fixing on Ylianor with undisguised lust. "The Game will help me take my mind off things, especially if this slave of yours is available."

"She's yours for the asking." Not bothering to check Ylianor's reactions, he extended a hand toward her.

"I ask your permission to use her," Jeff was quick to pop the question.

He wore a master's robe, so he had every right to it.

"And to bring her to my room." The man meant serious business. "If you agree, I'll return her in an hour."

Raising his gaze, Duncan noticed Cecilia and Rowena approaching from the opposite side of the chamber.

"We're ready," Lady Sentry called out, waving at him.

No more time to waste, he wrenched Ylianor by the hand. All he had intended was to give her to Jeff. Too bad, he had not counted on the energy surge going from him to her, then back again.

Like a tide about to drown him, the sheer force of his craving took him by surprise, and he could not resist wrapping her within his arms.

Which was a mistake that had his cock flaring up from the need to bury somewhere in her.

I'd kiss you if I could, Princess. His throaty whisper could not hide the fierceness of his arousal for her. *But I can't.*

Not because the rules kind of forbade it, though not in so many words.

Because if he gave into his insane desire for her, there would be no Game worth its name.

Pulling himself together, he let her go. "She's yours." He pushed her toward Jeff. "See you in an hour."

Hard to describe the measure of the man's excitement on taking her hand and dragging her to the exit. Safe to say, his cock had grown so stiff it was visible despite the robe's loose fit.

Which was not his concern.

His was to grab both Rowena and Cecilia and tug them in the direction of the chamber's massive front doors.

"Where to, ladies?" In a second, he reached the impressive arches, decorated with gold leaves that lit the dark blue walls.

"My room, darling." Steering him to the left, Rowena accelerated her pace.

He was right next to her, with Cecilia trailing just a few paces behind.

CHAPTER TWELVE

His arousal rising fast, Duncan flung Rowena on the bed the second he stepped in her room. If she had grown sexier over the years since he had first known her, her sensual curves had nothing to do with keeping his erection going. Nor did Cecilia's attempts at swallowing his giant stick.

The real reason was *her*, his fucking slave, as goddamn irresistible at a distance as she had been while under his nose. Between his arms, too, considering the sexual fever still tensing his every muscle after the mere touch of her.

No, there was really no way he could fight her or the temptation to link their minds and live both perceptions as though they were two sides of the same awareness.

Her side was drowning from the pleasure of having Jeff's beast going for her stomach. Not that he could ever reach it from her mouth, though it did not stop him from pumping as fast as he could. She had no way of dodging him anyway. He had seen to it she lay on the bed, straddling her face and pressing his knees in such a way that her head dug on the mattress every time he pushed downward.

Clamping Cecilia's head, Duncan held her while he increased the beat in and out of her wet cavity. Like Jeff, he wanted to suffocate her. The more she gagged, the more she reminded him of his princess. Of her adorable reaction of gasping and choking whenever a cock constricted her throat. Which also tightened her entire body most deliciously.

He wished he was ramming her ass just about now.

Not an option, of course, he had to be content with Cecilia's amateur blowjob. No amount of ferocity got him past her throat's apparent limits. Bending, Jeff lapped Ylianor's wide-open cunt.

It was the end of his princess.

Arching her back, she rotated her hips to screw his tongue to her belly and shattered under the fierce throes wrecking her body.

With Jeff unloading all inside her mouth, he began losing it himself.

"Hey, darling, not fair Ceci should have all the fun." Pouting like a child, Rowena pressed her mouth to his. "I also want a piece of your fabulous cock."

"Then, take it." Yanking back Cecilia's hair, he offered his engorged piece to Rowena.

Who fell on it like it were candy, licking and lapping every side, balls included, before gulping him down.

As he pushed for greater depth, she opened wider, letting him reach her throat without pulling back too soon. The sense of drowning sped his juice up the long gland.

It was not bad.

Not as expert as Chris nor as exciting as the princess's gags, still she was a far-sight better than Cecilia. Hence the need to reward her.

"Time to get properly fucked." After hurling her down on her knees and arranging her on all fours, he addressed Cecilia, "You'll make her real wet for me."

There was no need for it, if not as a thrilling preliminary. Both women were swimming in such thick honeydew that he could have quickly taken either without the slightest problem.

This would also give Jeff time to recover from his tremendous come. That is if his princess allowed him to retrieve his cock.

Which feeling how greedy she was, she would not any time

soon.

But Jeff had other priorities. Removing his still hefty piece from her voracious cavity, he went around the bed to her feet. Picking up her legs, he aimed for the pussy.

Going behind Rowena, Duncan propped her ass to his starving cock's convenience. Below her, Cecilia's tongue was doing wonders and swamping her cunt like she was a fountain or something. His first choice was her slit, maybe because it gleamed invitingly in between her legs.

Then again, maybe the blonde woman's extreme wetness had nothing to do with it.

As he slammed into the yielding flesh, his only craving was to have a gigantic monster stuffing a slit until it exploded. Since this could come from his princess alone, he was not surprised Jeff had just impaled Ylianor's drenched pussy and was making mincemeat out of it. Pumping so damn fast, it increased the friction, to the point she was burning all over from his accelerated thrusts.

Good thing, Duncan had Cecilia's tantalizing tongue hitting his balls at times to keep him focused, or he would have lost it for sure.

Just like his princess was doing, climaxing over and over while Jeff's dance spun her senseless.

Since Rowena seemed on the verge of total bliss, it was time to change holes.

Nothing was easier given how slick his equipment was on all sides, and how her ass ring had opened up at his fingers' penetration, posing no sort of resistance whatsoever. Wrenching out of the hot confinement, he pushed into the narrow entrance. She bent her back to give him more leeway, and he plunged to her guts in a matter of seconds.

Nice, tight and overcrowded, her ass fitted his erection like a glove, like a second skin that wrapped around his long length and refused to let him go.

This was just how he liked it, so he pushed to get to her guts. Just unfortunate, his balls could not follow. Stuck on the outside, they slapped her thighs instead. But at least, she squeezed him to perfection the deeper he went, which would spell an inevitable end to his steady hammering.

To give himself more playtime, he leaned to whisper in her ear, "Now, lick your phase mate's cunt until it drips."

Since his order admitted no objections, Rowena did not hesitate. She dipped on Cecilia's cunt, spread her legs far apart and dived tongue first.

As her face buried between the open legs, Cecilia jumped in shock at the unexpected pleasure, until the luscious laps won her over. Arching her back to ask for more, she swayed at Rowena's rhythm, seeking the pleasure Duncan knew she was not easy in finding.

Despite the years and the advice he had imparted, she still had sex with her mind instead of her body.

If he analyzed it rationally, there was nothing in Cecilia's moves that made her the cock-wrenching show his princess was on a bed. Out of it, too, considering how easily she aroused him and Chris. Jeff, too, seeing how he could not get enough of her. Still ramming her front, Duncan knew the man would not wait long to claim her ass, and that was something he did not want to miss for sure. But since his perception of her was clogging his senses, he shifted his focus back on the two women.

Their synchronized movements and their perfect timing left no doubt they were phase mates. It was just too bad that Cecilia was still as hooked on Rowena as on the first day their phase had started. All that licking and lapping was not helping, either. Not for Cecilia, who drowned in her craving for the blonde woman. Not for Rowena, who had moved on from the moment her phase had ended.

He was just sorry Cecilia had no chance of replicating what

he and Chris had going for them.

Which was so unique, he doubted many people experienced it.

Then again, Cecilia now had David, even if he had no idea how and where he fitted in with all the other variables at work.

Jeff cracking Ylianor's ass snapped Duncan back to the here and now. Back to his cock, ravaging Rowena's behind and to his need to explode in it.

Same way Ylianor felt now that Jeff had stuck his monstrous beast up her guts. Her back ring so large, Duncan wondered how it had not yet split in half. Given Jeff's furious tempo, he guessed nothing could stand in the way of his getting to her throat going from her ass. Not even friction.

Not that Ylianor complained either way. She was too busy climaxing thanks also to her fingers rubbing the tender swell above her pussy.

Jeff pulled out and unloaded all over her belly and breasts.

Which was not what pushed Duncan over the edge.

What did it for him was sensing the aching void of a second cock stuffing her front. She had gotten so used to having two of them at the same time that one alone did not quite cut it anymore.

That rushed the juice to the tip of his erection. So fast that, when Rowena's tongue glazed over Cecilia's clit, he lost it. But not inside her ass. Inside her mouth actually, for he had pulled out and stuck his rigid beast in Cecilia's face, unloading the moment her cheeks enveloped him on all sides.

"Now, it's your turn, Ceci." Barely satisfied, he gagged her just to get his cock ready for the next challenge.

Oh, boy, was she surprised he should want her.

Her dark eyes widened in shock, and she would have asked whether he was sure of it, had his shaft not kept her mouth busy.

It was always like that with her. She never thought herself good enough to receive any kind of attention, which was a real pity because she had a lot to offer to anyone who would take the time to know her better.

Personally, he admired that logical mind of hers.

Except when it came to sex. For everything else, she was profoundly loyal and well organized, with a sharp sense of duty and a quick intuition that made her question some of the values people usually took for granted. That was an asset in itself. Perhaps, it was the key to understanding why she had stolen the pyramid from the Nephis Valley.

Jeff plunging to Ylianor's throat scattered the distracting thoughts. Or maybe it was Rowena joining in with her phase mate to compete for her share of his beefy rod.

Either way, his cock throbbed impatiently, ready for action once more. So, he flipped Cecilia around until her ass was in front of his stick.

"Now, Ceci, I want Rowena to come." Cradling her legs to his chest, he aimed for the constricted hole at the center of the cleft. "So, you'll lick her until she does."

If it sounded like another order, neither woman complained. Not Rowena, since she seemed more than willing to allow him to have his way with her. Certainly not Cecilia, since she put up no sort of resistance and confirmed all of Chris's assumptions.

Then again, the angel was seldom wrong when it came to sex. Rowena straddling Cecilia's face and pressing her cunt on her mouth gave him the measure of just how right Chris could be.

On his part, Duncan shoved through the narrow ass ring, uncaring if he enlarged it too fast, too soon.

His raw need escalated when Jeff shifted his aim and went for Ylianor's butt.

Again!

That was enough to melt his senses, had not Rowena bending to guzzle Cecilia's pussy already fired them up good and proper.

He drowned in Cecilia's ass squeeze. So forceful, he guessed few had used it lately, which was an extra turn-on for him. He loved to feel her cramped channel trapping him on every side, prisoner of those heated walls of flesh and prey to the uncontrollable friction that scorched his very spirit.

No way he could take it much longer, especially when Ylianor's dance became a surge or orgasmic pleasure that blew her mind away. Then, Rowena convulsed in bliss, taking Cecilia with her. Those frantic contractions jerking his cock worse than before had him spraying her ass in repeated jets.

But that was just the beginning of what turned out to be the longest hour in Cecilia's Game of Masters and Slaves.

CHAPTER THIRTEEN

*F*rom now on, nothing private between us. That Duncan was tongue deep in Ylianor's throat was an unavoidable yet unfortunate incident.

He could blame his lack of resistance all he liked. The truth was that, after he had succeeded in reclaiming her from Jeff's possessive grasp, he had been overwhelmed by the need to devour her. Since sex was not an option, he had gone for the next best thing—her sweet, yielding mouth.

An unconventional move for sure, not to mention that he was probably breaking all of Cecilia's rules on masters and slaves.

We're going to play here in the open, where I can see you with my own eyes. Having managed, not without a great effort, to break off the lustful kiss, he reached his assigned place. *I won't touch you again, even if it kills me.* Setting her down on the low table, he straightened to enforce his decision.

No matter how much you want me? Maddeningly bewitching, she taunted maliciously.

No. He grinned seductively. *No matter how much you want me.* No way would he fall for her coyness, not since the ferocious pounding in her cunt gave her away all too easily. *Which isn't going to make me change my mind.* Studying her face, he caught her disappointment, however quick she was to suppress it. *There'll be no coming for you, not unless I say so.* He made it sound final, without any grounds for an appeal. *'Cause you'll be nothing more than a mere object, a worthless toy people will use for their pleasure alone.* Simply envisioning it, made his cock twitch. *And you'll have to service them all. 'Cause I'm going to push you so far beyond your limits. You'll never be the same again.*

What if it sounded extreme?

He meant every word of it.

He would turn her into a real slut whatever the cost like he had vowed to Chris.

I won't stop until you yield to sex for the sake of sex alone. He curled his lips in a snarl. *Until they fuck you so hard, you'll have to beg me to make them stop.*

I'm no beggar. She threw back her head in defiance. *No quitter, either.* Her smoky green eyes glittered. *Test me all you must. I won't fail you, Prince.*

It's Master *to you.* Impressed in spite of himself, he leaned forward, carefully avoiding the slightest physical contact between their bodies. *And I wouldn't be so optimistic if I were you.*

"Excuse me." Cloaked like a master, a tall, dark-haired, beefy man bowed in his direction. "I'm Koren, and I want that slave of yours." For good measure, he pointed at Ylianor. "*Now!*"

If the ritual formula was not as it should have been, Duncan already knew he would not object. Not since the man's massive crotch more than made up for any lack of formalities.

"Only if you do it here," Duncan's tone was even to avoid the impression he was giving in too readily.

"No problem." Koren licked his lips, unable to avert his greedy gaze from her breasts.

"You also can't have her come," Duncan added.

"I had no intention to." This time, a malicious glint brightened the man's eyes. "As long as I can use my slave." He hesitated. "Or perhaps you'd like to join me?"

"No, not me." Duncan made it sound as though she did not tempt him at all. "I want nothing to do with her."

Goddamn it if it was not the most difficult lie he ever told in his life!

"She's all yours." Gesturing behind him, he urged Koren to take her.

The naked figure of a younger man, lighter in both skin and hair, approached from the left side.

"Get her ready for me," the master barked without as much as glancing his slave's way.

He just nodded in her direction, playing it like he had no interest whatsoever the moment the young man grabbed her.

"These slaves can be difficult if not broken in properly." His focus all on Duncan, the man pursed his lips. "I hate to spoil my pleasure with details."

Like her holes being too tight for any sort of penetration, or so it seemed to Duncan considering how the manservant was enlarging her by sticking just his fingers first in her mouth, then in her pussy.

Best part of all was having him flip her on her stomach, slamming thumb, index and forefinger in her ass and twisting them brutally in an attempt to split the narrow space in two.

Ouch!

Kind of obvious, his princess had not been ready for this.

She tensed all together, which trapped the digits and had Koren nearly exploding inside his master's robe.

Didn't you say you could take anything? Duncan jeered.

I did. She relaxed, and the pain decreased. *But —*

There's no better time than the present to prove it, he sneered.

The man raised his gaze and indicated her mouth.

"Very well, let's see how good she is at swallowing me." Koren moved toward the low table. Yanking back her hair, he took out an absolute beast and stuck it in her mouth. "You keep working on her ass until it's truly welcoming."

Finger-drilling-time over, the young man shoved his sizable erection through her back ring.

How he managed not to crack it remained a mystery.

"But don't come inside it." The warning was more than justified.

The way the cock was going for her guts Duncan guessed it would not last long. Just like the one now sliding to her throat and forcing her to gag at every lurch.

Well, both men had impressive pieces. Were his angel to see them, he would have never let either go—

He can have them both, she was quick to catch his thought. *No problem.*

Shut up and suck. The show was too exciting to have it stop any time soon.

Partly because Koren's huge fathead was proving to be a harder challenge than his princess had anticipated. Mostly because she did not let the mere impossibility of holding it in her mouth stop her from swallowing it anyway.

Or almost.

Safe to say, she opened as wide as she could and even managed to glide her lips to the hilt. Which was just touch and go, or she would have suffocated for sure.

Not that Koren gave a damn whether she would still be breathing by the end of the blowjob. Holding her head steady, he rammed her mouth worse than if it had been her pussy. Giving her no respite, he always aimed for her throat.

Good thing, the slave's shaft pushed it back every time. He had so enlarged her that the rod rammed her constricted space as if it encountered no friction whatsoever. Which would have certainly been a first.

"Now, move her to the couch." Letting go of her hair, Koren motioned the slave to get on his new task. "I want to be comfortable."

Quick to comply, the man had no trouble picking up her small frame and carrying it to the intended destination. Once there, he arranged her on all fours, positioning himself behind her ass.

Once his master perched on the couch, he pressed her head over the swollen crown. One thrust and the man reached her stomach.

Or something to that effect considering how far back she jumped to avoid choking.

Which was not an option.

Rather, it worsened her situation considerably, allowing the slave to reclaim the crammed channel he had just vacated.

Now, both men had trapped her, so there was no escape possible. No way out for her. She could only give in to the massive beasts perforating her mouth and butt, all at once.

Not a problem at all!

His princess was loving their enslavement so much she was floating on her arousal. Her senses were high on the mere notion that she was an object. A thing men would use for their pleasure alone without any regard to her feelings. Such was the purpose of his lesson, and she had gotten it right from the beginning.

What else was new?

As Chris had said countless times already, she was a fast learner. Nothing like this new awareness of hers proved it more than adequately.

Without the slightest pity, the slave rushed to expand the narrow space with a shaft turned monster.

"Yeah, like that," Koren growled appreciatively. "Open her fucking ass wide 'cause I want it nice and large."

No need for instructions.

The slave was already doing a splendid job of it on his own. The shine of her firm round buns revealed all the splitting effect of the huge piece slamming to the balls each time he shoved. It would get Koren to spill his guts sooner rather than later.

The slave as well, given his plain inability to hold it together for much longer.

"Hey, I told you not to come!" Koren raised his voice, having evidently determined his slave's actual state. Next, he intercepted Duncan's gaze. "Ah, you trained your slave's mouth admirably."

"Her ass, too." Duncan laughed, his focus shifting on the slave's fierce hammering. "I've had it broken in and overworked to fit any shape and size."

"Really?" Tugging her long hair, he stopped her head bob. "Then, it's time I try it for myself." After flopping out of her mouth, he got to his feet and neared his slave. "That's enough." Impatiently, he pushed the young man away. "Now, go suck her master." Taking position behind her, he spread the ass cheeks wide apart and aimed. "He needs your services." Uncaring about any other concern, he flung the hole to the maximum dilation possible with just the first thrust.

If his princess did not curl on herself to escape, it was because his vicious clutch did not allow her to budge. Nowhere for her to run. Ravaged by a beast so gigantic, even his angel would have needed extra adjustments.

Duncan's heart went out to her, and he would have brushed that inviting clit of hers had not the slave's hot breath on his crotch stopped him on his tracks.

Only then did he realized his cock was throbbing uncontrollably and had been for some time. Too taken by the heated interplay, he had ignored it. But the expert fingers pulling it out of the robe's confinement and jerking it at a delicious rhythm brought the sensation to the fore. The swallowing was not helping matters, not since the need to burst took precedence over everything else.

Not all the slave's merit.

His princess was the main cause of it all. Her magnificent ass rammed to bits by a very demanding monster, to be precise.

Too fucking hot the show for him to hope to last any longer. Too fucking good the sucks that suffocated the slave every time he shoved to get to the stomach without impediments. He intensified the beat, accelerating in the hopes the balls would follow. Or that at least he could get to the ass, no matter the distance from the throat.

"Shit!" Koren's exclamation distracted him. "She's divine." His taut pole cracking her open with every slam, it was kind of plain the man was having the time of his life. "You weren't kidding when you said you had her ass trained."

"By the best of them," Duncan assured, for his angel could definitely qualify as such.

Just saying it brought a fresh wave of desire that made his sperm rise dangerously to the tip of the erection. Which was not what made him lose it.

What made the difference was perceiving how the earlier pain had turned into extreme bliss for her. However scorched by Koren's vigorous blows to her asshole, she was having a hard time holding off on the pleasure coiling up from her cunt. He blocked her cold.

I said no coming for you, he snarled. "Master Koren, remember that I don't want my slave to come under any circumstances."

"What?" Taken off guard, Koren blinked at him as though he had not heard. But then, he must have realized, for he leaned down and pinched her clit so hard that she jolted. "Right."

This was the last straw.

With one final thrust, Koren's piece burst into a flood of pearly jets, which sprayed not just her ass. Her hair and back, mostly.

It was the end of the line for Duncan, too.

Holding the slave's head to keep him still, he shoved twice and unloaded everything down his throat.

CHAPTER FOURTEEN

*D*amn you! Alone again, Duncan peered at her intently. *You made him come after only a few shoves.*

Wasn't that what you wanted? Her body screaming in dissatisfaction, Ylianor tensed as though she was about to undertake a new challenge.

Yeah, but I didn't expect you to do it so fast. He could not help chuckling at how sheer incredible she had been. *Or so well.*

Then, I deserve a prize. All hopeful, her huge green eyes flashed at him.

Only if I so decide, he was quick to intercept her sneaky trail, making it sound stern and inflexible on purpose. But I wouldn't get my hopes up just yet. *Nothing you've done so far has earned you permission to come.*

I can do more. Recoiling on herself, she looked ready to jump on him. *I can do better if only I wasn't so . . .*

Extremely frustrated, she licked her lips, mouth ajar as though she wanted to convince him to use it.

Hungry, she concluded, charging the word with all the erotic connotation she could muster. Jabbing her cunt confirmed she was telling no lie.

Not to mention a sure way to get him hard again.

On spotting his latest erection, she could not suppress a satisfied glee. *Since we're alone, I could service you for a change —*

"Ahem . . ." Clearing her throat, a woman in a mistress robe came to stand in front of him. "I couldn't help noticing you, Master." She bowed formally, quickly raising her gaze to train determined bright blue eyes on him. "'Cause you're the sexiest man on this whole damn floor, and I want you."

"Do you now?" Playing it cool, he reclined on the seat as though he could care less about her and her requests.

"I absolutely do." Unaffected by his icy appraisal, she slid out of her mistress's robe.

Stark naked, she made a pretty picture. Even if she lacked Ylianor's blatant sensuality, she could still help in curbing his maddening instinct to throw all pretense to the wind and go for his princess in the most public way.

"What about my slave?" Just pure provocation on his part.

"I want her, too." Inching forward, she pressed her lips to his ear. "But not for the reasons you think," her hot husky breath tried to seduce him.

"Why then?" Since the little vixen was asking for it, he clamped her waist and began fondling her cunt with slow brushes on her clit.

Damn!

She was soaking wet.

"'Cause she seems in love with you." To make his task easier, she flayed her legs wide apart. "And I want to take away her illusions."

Good luck with that. Ylianor giggled, unable to resist the ironic comment.

I wouldn't be so elated if I were you, he was quick to retort. *'Cause I just decided to help this pretty little mistress get her wish.*

Accurately avoiding crossing Ylianor's gaze, he intensified the rub on what had become a swollen knot about to explode from pleasure. "What's your name, Mistress?"

"Lydyen." Lowering her head, she traced the contour of his lips with an avid tongue tip.

Catching it, he first bit it then chased it back in her mouth.

It was time to show her who the master was, so he broke off their kiss.

"I've got a better place where you can stick that tongue of yours." Giving her no time to react, he tugged her head on his lap. "Make it good." His free hand uncovered his colossal equipment. "Or you won't get anything else from me."

A vigorous suck told him that the woman's competitive nature had picked up his dare and would work her ass off to prove him wrong.

She was not half bad. Not as skilled as his angel. Still, she must have done her share of blowjobs and liked them a whole lot. It was probably the reason she took the gagging with such ease, not always jumping back even if he went for greater depth with consecutive lurches that were sure to cut off her breath. Had he still some doubts, the way she drew the fathead to her throat without any hesitation was proof enough, along with the tantalizing squeeze of her cheeks. With both her palms curled around his engrossed stem, she jerked in sync with her mouth. Up and down, up and down, the effect was near complete.

Naturally, he suppressed all reservations while dumping all his sensations on Ylianor, relishing her extreme discomfort at the sudden rise in the heat department.

For which she could do nothing except burn in her skin and hope he would take pity on her.

Not gonna happen. Duncan baited her. *So, don't count on it.*

I won't. Going all slave-like, Ylianor made a visible effort to silence the tempest hammering her clit wild. *Since it's obvious she can satisfy your every need.*

That sounded like a taunt to him. He hoisted Lydyen on her knees to catch her gaze. What he read in them was the confirmation that the damnable witch had managed to pick up the slight dissatisfaction he had tried to suppress and was throwing it back at him.

To reply would have meant acknowledging she was right. To ignore her was his best course of action. Nothing would work better than fucking the woman.

"Enough of this." Grabbing her by the armpits, he pulled her up on the couch. "Time to get to serious business."

Sprawling her, he pinned her down under his weight.

"Thought you'd never ask." A smug smile curving her lips, she flattened on the plush cushions and spread her legs.

He took immediate advantage of her offer and nailed her to the spot with a huge cock burying in her pussy. She was so drenched that he had no problem sinking to her belly and setting a frenzied beat to his pumping.

Too bad, his shaft had a mind of its own.

It would have much preferred impaling the princess instead of any other woman in the world.

"Was this what you had in mind?" To defy his body and increase his excitement to an acceptable level, he bent to graze her nipples with an impatient mouth.

"Almost." She wrapped her legs around his waist. "What I want is for your slave to lick me while you take your time to ram my holes." Her eyes gleamed maliciously. "All of them."

"Why didn't you say so from the start?" Out of her slit in the bat of an eye, he flipped her around on all fours. "Hey, slave." He avoided looking at Ylianor. "Get your ass here. The mistress gave you a direct order."

Without any great hurry, the princess got her butt moving enough to reach his couch. Slipping underneath Lydyen, her back pressed to the cushions.

"Now, lick!" The woman thrust her dripping cunt in the slave's face.

That Ylianor was none too pleased by the new twist seemed kind of obvious from her lack of an enthusiastic response. Her tongue darting out to lap the moist folds did a halfhearted job of it.

No great passion. No great effort, either.

No matter how intense or how clogging the woman's flavor was. Regardless of how furiously Lydyen's clit throbbed in impatience, Ylianor did not plunge into her assigned task, rather hurried all the way through, like she could not wait for it to end.

Well, how about that?

She did not like women much.

That was a juicy piece of information he was sure would come in handy during the long night ahead.

For now, though, his priority was scorching her to the bone — something he could not accomplish if she did not get off on what she was doing.

"Don't forget her ass." If nothing else worked, this might perk up his princess's interest. "'Cause I plan to use it real soon."

He figured this would do the trick.

Somehow, despite any analysis, she was more similar to his angel than he had given her credit for, so far.

"I knew you wouldn't resist it." Thrilled out of her skin, Lydyen arched her back as though wanting him to take it immediately.

"Gotta admit it's irresistible." If his princess had a much better rear than poor Lydyen ever would, he kept silent about it. "It'll be my pleasure to crack it once my slave has made it nice and wet."

"Heard that, slut?" Pinching Ylianor's clit, Lydyen made her jump back.

Now, her head was just at the right height for a thorough pampering of the tiny butt ring in between the cleft.

"And be quick about it." Rotating her hips, she crushed her behind on Ylianor's mouth.

This time, his princess did not hesitate. Her tongue licks gustier. She insinuated the tip in the narrow entrance before flattening her tongue and covering the entire space.

Hardly surprised, he repressed a grin as he rimmed the hole to spread the moisture and play with her tongue. Sometimes catching it, he held it to increase her appetite out of any boundaries. Other times, he deliberately ignored it to dip three fingers and twist them to enlarge what was still narrow.

When the butt gave in, he made his move.

"Enough of her ass, slave." Pressing on Lydyen's back, he had her bending over and sticking out her backside. "Now, lick her cunt."

"As long as you order her to do a better job than she did before," Lydyen snarled.

"Oh, she will." *Or I won't allow you to come ever again.* "Trust me."

Having perceived his threat was not an idle one. His princess stopped fidgeting and devoured the woman's clit.

Literally.

Sucking it hard and deep, she lavished all the attention she had not previously.

Slamming in Lydyen's behind proved quite easy thanks to her relaxing everything at his first nudge. Definitely, Ylianor's repeated brushes on the puffed clit and pussy were driving Lydyen wild.

As a bonus, she also tried following his rhythm, which drove his cock to penetrate more ruthlessly than before. Or was it because Ylianor managed to lick his balls at his every shove?

Too good to stop or scold her, he kept going. The woman's backswings invited him to split her open, and he would be damned if he stopped before he achieved it. His beefy stiffness embedded to the hilt, he stepped up the pounding and stretched what had once been a tight sheath into an outrageous size.

The woman was so close to the edge that he was sure she hardly noticed. At this point, all she craved was to come. Grinding her pelvis on Ylianor's mouth got her right what she needed.

At her gasp, Lydyen clenched around his thick monster. So hard, it felt like it wanted to sever it from the root.

Her climax barely over, she unglued from his cock and

grabbed Ylianor's head. "Now, lick off my taste from your master's cock."

Before he could react, Ylianor's tongue touched his fat crown, and it was the end for him. Hot, unstoppable juice sprayed all over the slave's face and body until not one drop remained.

"Come on, slut." Smugly triumphant, she dragged Ylianor's head forward. "Get to work on the cleaning." With a new shove, she maneuvered Ylianor close enough to puff hot breath on his piece.

Which went from soft to stone-hard in seconds.

"Hold it." Clutching Lydyen's wrist, he detained her. "I don't allow slaves to touch me." He pushed the princess away, breaking off his dangerous proximity to her.

For it would mean throwing his resolve to the wind and having sex with her alone, to the exclusion of the infinite varieties available on the damn floor.

"But you're welcome to it," he teased, having understood what kind of woman she was.

Lydyen pulled back, scrambling to her feet.

"Not worth my time." Rounding the couch, she bent on his ear. "'Cause you can't help being in love with her," she sneered. "Can you?"

She whirled around and was gone.

CHAPTER FIFTEEN

"*Sex is physical, Ceci.*" No question about it, Prince Duncan Caldwell's *words seemed more valid today than they had been when he had first uttered them, at the beginning of their relationship, more than three years before. "You have to switch off your mind if you want to enjoy it."*

Sure, as if anybody can just turn it on or off at will. *If anybody could, Cecilia indeed could not. Her mind always replayed what most hurt her, like what had happened with Rowena. So way back, it seemed like a lifetime before.*

"*Hey, Ceci.*" Shaking her, Duncan pulled her out of the past.

The attractive eighteen-year-old prince had stumbled entirely by accident on Blue Oasis's doorsteps some years after her phase had ended, looking for better accommodations and food than what he could have found on the road. She had not been able to resist the impressive sight of him, and not only on account of his good looks.

"*Did you hear me?*" His deep tone returned her to the glorious *afternoon full of sex with the most gorgeous body she had ever eyeballed.*

But what had mesmerized her about Duncan Caldwell had been his brilliant intelligence, the great mind she perceived behind the black piercing eyes.

To think she had prided herself on having the most unique mind of all when his own was far superior. Though younger than her, she had felt him as the wiser of the two. It had shattered her diffidence toward men.

She had not just opened her home.

She had opened all of herself to him. How could she not?

For one thing and quite unlike other men, he was interested in

136

her as a person. Which set him in a category all his own, had his warm-heartedness, sardonic humor and unobtrusive caring not placed him there already.

It had been her downfall.

Feeling the physical attraction on top of the mental one, she had quickly gone from friends to bedmates.

Oh, boy!

Had she not expected how that would unfold!

Duncan was different in bed, no question about it. He requested and sometimes obtained a passion she usually lacked. He seemed to know what she craved and gave it to her, revealing secrets about her body unknown even to herself.

Truth was — he really liked having sex with her, and that was certainly a first.

"Is that possible?" She could not even come close to fathoming it.

"Of course, it is." Duncan chuckled. "And it's real easy to do." *Spectacularly naked, stretched out on the bed they had been in for the whole afternoon, he reached for her breast and pinched the erect tip. "If you're not scared of your body like you are."*

"I'm not!" And that nipple squeeze had no business starting a new dull throb between her legs. At least, not when it comes to women.

"You are." Duncan was quick to press his fingers on her half-open lips. "But probably, only with a man."

How can he possibly know what has taken me an eternity to figure out myself?

Ever since the end of her phase, sex had not been the same. It was one thing to do it with her chosen woman, quite another to do it with a man.

They were just too different and too hard for her taste. Plus, that bit about penetration had not excited her all that much.

If her first time with a man had been a disaster, her second had not gone any better. So bad, in fact, she had erased the memory just as quickly as she had washed away the man's smell and juice.

No, she had not liked men.

At least, she had not back when her phase had just ended and in that horrible way.

Something about those straight, clear-cut lines with the hard bulge in the middle had not impressed her. Designed to hurt the delicate feminine opening – that was how she used to see them. Like an invading army, men attacked, conquered their position, retreated once satisfied and left all their waste behind.

Women had been more of her thing. Warm and curvy, their soft round bodies had aroused her far beyond any man she had known. And what about their wetness?

It was always enough to drown her senses like no stiff male equipment ever could, except for that of the very striking Prince Duncan Caldwell. He alone was changing the way she lived sex, and she still wondered how he was managing to drive out the loneliness of a lifetime in just a few touches.

With her parents dying when she was only two years old and leaving Aunt Susan to look after her, solitude had been her refuge. Good thing, Aunt Susan had also trained her mind to reason and logic. Something Cecilia could never thank her enough, not even now that her aunt had been dead for more than fifteen years.

Then, what Susan must have glimpsed locked up in her mind had taken control over everything, her body included. How could it not?

It had been the only way for ten-year-old Cecilia to deal with her aunt's sudden death. The only way to dry the unstoppable flood of tears while cooped up in her room, in forced solitary confinement that she would have never ended had it been up to her. Too cold, empty and desolate, she had been unable to do anything besides crying for days and weeks. Despite all the servants' efforts, the bluest funk ever had swallowed her whole.

"You'd rather be a prisoner of your mind than deal with it." When Prince Caldwell shook his head, she watched fascinated the long, dark strands fluttering around his shoulders. "You should find a way to break free of its control."

Ha! Easier said than done!

She had tried it as soon as the servants had lured her out of her room. Playing games with the many children, who had filled Blue

Oasis back then, had been her way to escape the great sorrow for her loss.

If it had not proved quite so effective, it had to do with the other children's reactions. Or maybe, the fact she had begun inventing her own games had something to do with it.

Either way, her fate was to be alone.

As her games had become more complex, the other children had abandoned her to the intricate mazes her mind had created so effortlessly. Not that it had saddened her any. She had been getting used to loneliness, and this new one had quickly become an excuse to trap herself inside her creations.

Lost!

That's how far estranged I got from everything and everyone, losing touch little by little with reality altogether. *Then again, who cared about insignificant company, anyway?*

Always the quiet one, she knew her mind was superior to that of the stupid children refusing to share her world. She did not need them nor anybody else, would have continued on her solitude, had she not fallen head over heels in love with the most intriguing creature of all.

"I had a way . . ." *She swallowed hard, unwilling to reopen the wounds still fresh in spite of the years that had already passed.* *"But apparently, it couldn't last . . ."* *Not her fault if her voice broke. The lump at the back of her throat would not let her continue.*

Why, oh, why is it so difficult just mentioning it? Why, oh, why am I still hooked on her big time, like I was the first day I met her?

CHAPTER SIXTEEN

W hen Rowena Paulen crashed into her life, Cecilia became suddenly aware of all she had missed out on experiences.

On people, especially.

The blonde, blue-eyed goddess made her live for the first time. Ever!

She made her love, too. A love so strong and powerful, Cecilia still reeled from it.

Just gazing into those brilliant eyes awakened a burning hunger for more. Those deep crystal blue eyes of hers were the same shade as a mountain lake where Aunt Susan had brought her once.

But that was only skimming the surface.

A straight nose on an exquisite oval face framed by short blonde hair, tantalizing figure and a dazzling smile — such stunning combinations justified Cecilia's breath always falling short at the mere sight of her.

All Rowena's fault, she and her very feminine curves drove Cecilia crazy, what with that smooth alabaster skin of hers begging for a touch.

She would have been quite happy simply to adore this goddess from afar. Instead, the fantastic creature took a liking to her!

To Cecilia Hurst!

To the same lonely child, no one had bothered with in the first place!

Imagine that!

Rowena introduced her into a sensual world full of lavish shows of attention. Cecilia listened for hours on end as Rowena talked about herself, her family and her life. What if it was nothing and everything at once?

Too fascinated to complain, Cecilia hung from every word. The way Rowena said them was a treat in itself, with a husky voice that sent shivers running down her back.

Hard to believe this was happening to her. *That for the very first time, she did not feel left out or rejected. Best of all, her mind was not interfering with the physical tempest wracking every fiber of her being.*

Then again, she had no time to think.

Rowena's frantic life dragged Cecilia out of her shell and threw her into the world shining under Stella's bright light. A world made of endless parties and downright fun, chatting for hours on the musical notes of Rowena's throaty tone.

To Cecilia, it was like opening a window on a brand-new universe and absorbing it all at once.

Readjusting to reality was more like it.

She had been losing perspective and without even being aware of it until the most passionate of phases had changed everything forever.

Exactly how did it begin?

Oh, yeah, it was on one of those days, one similar to many others. Rowena was sitting on the bed in her room and talking about something or other.

Cecilia simply reached over and kissed her full on the mouth.

Just like that!

It had been as easy as taking a breath, except she was holding her breath.

"I like it." Rowena licked her lips as though to savor her kiss. "Let's do it again."

Mouth pressing more decisively, Cecilia's tongue plunged into her wet cavity.

Into another dimension, it seemed.

Next thing she knew, she was tossing away Rowena's clothes and sinking into her essence. Having her naked was like a dream come true. Flesh quivering under her touch, she tasted her all over with hungry intakes that tried to gulp down the full breasts. Firm and very round, they were too big for any effective swallowing. Still, they were intoxicating her senses, which was just the beginning of a dull throb between her legs.

Teasing the hard nipples that peaked excitedly at every stroke did nothing to assuage her craving. Worsened everything, to be honest, swamping her cunt into a veritable pool.

When Cecilia had the bad idea to press a couple of fingers on the center of her pounding, she jolted.

Literally!

Out of sheer pleasure alone!

Still, it was nothing compared to the exquisite sweetness Rowena hid between her legs, and that exploded in Cecilia's mouth at her first tentative lick.

No, nothing had prepared her to this wet universe.

Oh, how to forget the silky feel of that drenched pussy? Or the way the tender folds opened up to her inspection? Begging her to lick each one with luscious laps? What about that very greedy knot throbbing like a heart from the need to burst?

Cecilia loved it all.

So did Rowena, considering how far up she arched her back to get more.

Cecilia did not dare budge. Between the widespread legs, her face, nose and chin drowned in the heavy honeydew dripping to Rowena's thighs. The mere smell filled Cecilia's nostrils and senses to intoxication. So pungent and spicy, it drove her tongue to brush more forcefully the entire surface. From clit to ass, she made the rounds, never getting tired of the tight circles until she hit the bull's-eye.

The throbbing bud.

Too good to ignore, she lapped it all then sucked it to her stomach. Or such was her intent, had not the slippery surface prevented her from holding it inside her mouth.

It did not matter anyway. Not seeing how Rowena swelled in repeated throes that had her continue the delightful exploration. She was getting high from merely sticking her tongue tip down the voracious slit wanting to devour it all. Clench it frantically was more like it, what with those hips swaying in a steady and most erotic rhythm that increased the thrashing and moaning.

Which pushed Rowena beyond any feasible edge.

It was no small measure of satisfaction, and Cecilia could not believe she was so good at this new game that had nothing of the mind's twists she usually preferred.

It was all physical. Nothing mental about Rowena's muscles tightening and releasing whenever Cecilia hit a particular spot in the eager cunt.

With fingers and tongue now digging in Rowena's moist softness while drinking down her bittersweet juice, there was no way to stop the thrill from going straight down to her own dripping center. Which triggered the need for some serious touching.

Obeying this primal urge, she rubbed the aching knot until she nailed it.

And everything sort of burst.

Scorching waves coiled from her pussy up, firing her every fiber to a spasm. Now, she knew what the blonde goddess was experiencing herself and did not want to stop those incredible sensations from melting her.

Stroking herself and Rowena at the same time required a few adjustments. Particularly that bit about shoving her fingers in and out of her lover's velvety slit while covering everything with her tongue. Somehow, she managed it, and the reward was immense. Not just because of the raw flesh wrapping around her fingers. Between the taste, smell and other sensations, Cecilia was going crazy with the new need to explode.

She heightened the pressure on what had started hammering the second after she had come and climaxed again, right alongside Rowena.

If that was the beginning, the hot sex kept coming.

Long hours spent adoring her goddess, passion and excitement clouding her senses until the burst of pleasure made everything start over again.

Cecilia learned all about her phase mate's splendid body. Not just the physical side of it. The unexpected reactions were tantalizing new games that she relived again and again once the sex was over. She was utterly under Rowena's spell, unable to deny her slightest whim, allowing her to take it all.

To receive more than she gave for sure, but what could one expect from a goddess?

Cecilia played along, quite happy to spend hours merely imagining one torrid sex scene after another. Lying in bed with closed eyes, she lost herself in the details, fantasizing about positions and touches, precisely what pressure to use to provoke the maximum pleasure. Yet, even if she repeated the imaginary sequence once Rowena was finally in her arms, she did not always get it right.

It was the one true lesson of her phase. Reality was not always as satisfying as her imagination. There was no way she could overcome such a limit, abstraction inevitably closer to perfection despite all her attempts.

Still, it did not matter to her.

This was an exciting new game, after all. One she could play with one person alone. That was the reason she preferred to overlook the more negative side effects, like having to put up with Rowena's unpredictable moods and occasional absences. Her phase mate grew easily bored with people, after all. So what?

Anything! Cecilia would have done anything *for her blonde goddess, no matter how controlling and desperate her anxiety ate up her heart. She would have succeeded, too, had reality not turned on her and bit back with all the force that she lacked.*

Weeks had passed without a word from Rowena. When at last Cecilia managed to corner her, Rowena appeared different from the start.

"Oh, stop that, Ceci!" Nervously, she loosened Cecilia's grip on her supple breast. "We have more serious things to talk about."
More serious than us?

"I finally did it!" The deep blue eyes sparkled with a new light. "I had sex with a man! It was incredible!"

By then, Cecilia was barely listening.

Barely holding on to be precise.

Her hand fell on the bed, frozen along with her heart.

"They're plain magnificent, with that huge piece between their

legs that promises delights." A naughty smirk curved Rowena's lips.

Nonsense! *That was what it sounded like to Cecilia's ears. Nonsense as hard as a rock! That was what it felt like to her stomach.*

"Delivers them, too." *This time, Rowena smacked her lips.* "You wouldn't believe how good it was with Jake." *She shifted on the bed.* "Uh, he satisfied my every whim."

The more Rowena talked about that insignificant man. The more Cecilia realized she was at the end.

Not of her love, for she could never stop loving Rowena even if she lived forever.

Of her game.

Like all the ones with the Blue Oasis's children, this one had also come to an abrupt close.

Yet, once again, she could not salvage any part of it.

"Oh, Ceci, you should go out there and try one yourself." *Clutching her arm, Rowena squeezed it.*

"Not interested," *Cecilia scoffed.*

Not an excuse.

All she craved was the blonde goddess. No puny man could ever do. No one else, either. Not then. Not in any foreseeable future. Not ever!

How could she go on living with that overpowering love crushing her heart to bits?

"Come on." *As though having caught up on her feelings, Rowena's intriguing eyes scanned her face.* "I swear they aren't bad, and you should be with one of them instead of wasting your time with me."

"But I love you." *Shocked, Cecilia could not believe her ears.*

"I love you, too, darling." *Rowena seemed positive.* "We'll always have each other, even if the phase is over. We had a wonderful time. But now, we have to grow up and get on with our lives. To experience new things like men and get to know their bodies as much as we know ours." *A delightfully malicious smirk twisted her lips.* "Don't you think so?"

No, I don't! *Cecilia wanted to scream.*

If she did not dare, it was because Rowena's mouth curved in that peculiar way that tolerated nothing less than an agreement.

Why can't we just keep being lovers while you screw as many men as possible? Why do you have to cut me off?

This kind of escaped her.

But since there was no use saying any of it out loud, despair sank her in the bottomless pit of her mind and drowned her in Blue Oasis's uncommunicative maze.

CHAPTER SEVENTEEN

"Hem . . ." *Clearing his throat, Duncan refocused her attention to the here and now.* "If you need someone to talk to, feel free to use me." *His penetrating black gaze studied her face intently.*

Cecilia *had the feeling he had caught all her distress from the bat of her eyes.*

"No, really." *How could she trust a stranger with her most intimate secrets?* "There's no need to – "

"Love gone wrong hurts so damn much." *His tone deep and grave told her that he knew exactly what she had gone through.* "But it's nothing compared to the pain of repressing its memory."

"I . . ." *Pushing out a heavy breath, she forced her voice not to crack.* "I love my phase mate." *There, she had managed to say it, though it hardly conveyed the depth of what she had felt.*

Truth was – she had embraced this love wholeheartedly, surrendering with total and complete abandonment. In short, she had lost her sanity to it. It had been like shutting her eyes and falling off a high cliff headfirst, rewarded tenfold by an incredible passion that had the taste of the flesh's revenge over a domineering mind.

"But now, it's over." *Alas!*

Had it been up to her, she and Rowena would have lived happily ever after and never come to the same abrupt end as her childhood games.

"Now, she considers me only as a friend." *It fucking hurt merely acknowledging it.* "Nothing more." *Or maybe what got to her this time was the fact she had let go of something no one else knew, not even Rowena.*

"There are many other women in the world." *There was a note of real concern in Duncan's throaty voice.*

"But I love her!" Like a stubborn child, she would have stomped her feet had she been standing. "I want her, not just any other woman."

"If her phase is over while yours isn't, you don't have much choice besides accepting it." He sounded so downright reasonable that her heart sank way below her stomach. "Believe me, friendship is a most generous offer on her part."

"You don't think I can try to make her change her mind?" Without even realizing it, she gripped his hand as though asking for reassurance.

He understood her heartache perfectly, had probably experienced it himself. Yes, but on which side of the fence? Did he leave his phase mate, or was it the other way around?

Not that she could believe for one moment someone, anyone could ever leave such an incredibly handsome and intelligent man. Not if he was in his right mind.

Whatever the case, one thing seemed abundantly clear by now. Phases had no rational ending. No rational beginning, either, which explained her frustration and inability to set it inside her logical grid.

"If your phase mate ends it, there's nothing you can do about it." Gently untangling his hand free, Prince Caldwell had rolled on top of her, pressing her down to stare into her eyes. "I bet she told you that she wanted to try out men for a change."

"That's exactly what she told me." Now, she was getting an accurate picture of which side of the fence had been Duncan's. "You seem to know the drill too well not to have gone through it yourself with your phase mate."

"Yes, I've had a similar experience." An indefinable flash crossed Duncan's beautiful eyes.

Had he loved him as much as she had loved Rowena? Did he miss him as much as she missed Rowena?

All questions she did not dare ask.

"I know it's no consolation, but life goes on." Fixing an invisible point in midair, he seemed to be talking to himself. "And your feelings change with each passing day." Shaking his head free of *whatever memory had focused it, he returned his gaze squarely on her. "We're amazingly adaptable creatures if only given half the chance."*

Sure, tell that to Rowena!

And to the irrational phase that had shattered her in so many pieces that she was still trying to retrieve them all.

CHAPTER EIGHTEEN

"Excuse me, Leader." *After knocking on Arthur Fairchild's office door, Cecilia hovered above the two steps separating the small landing from the rest of the room.*

If she hesitated, it was because she had never received any sort of invitation to see the place despite being one of the twelve High Council permanent members. A duty she had inherited along with the rest of the Hurst's legacy when she had been old enough to read her father's will. A task that required her to be part of the highest ruling body of all the lands.

"Yes?" Lifting his gaze from the papers he had been reading, Arthur regarded her coldly. "What is it?"

"I'd like permission to study the structure in the Nephis Valley." Tentatively, she descended the two steps and approached his desk.

Going to him had taken more guts than she would have thought. Maybe because he never encouraged anyone to address him outside council meetings except for the two Templetons who ran the Hall behind the scenes. If one did it in the daytime because he was the vice-leader, the other had such a free hand in the nighttime entertainment that no one doubted he was as high up in the ladder as his father was.

Then again, Arthur was so obsessed with the striking and very seductive man that he never let him out of his sight and out of his bed, a treatment he reserved to none of his other boys.

Or so the gossip assured.

"Why?" Leaning back on his chair, Arthur glared at her, a flash of annoyance clouding his expression.

"'Cause I think it has something to do with our way of life." To give herself courage, she ignored his reaction and threw back her

shoulders on reaching his desk.

"Of course, it does," he scoffed, getting irritated. "Or we wouldn't use it to pledge."

No lie that it was the whole purpose of the place and of the structure it contained. Cecilia knew it well enough, having witnessed Rowena's pledge to Oliver Sentry. Remembered it despite her crushed heart to be precise. Probably as crushed as Steve Templeton's, Oliver's phase mate and the second witness to this particular pledge.

Not her fault, it had come too soon after Rowena had decided their phase was over.

At least, for her taste during the approximately three years that had intervened.

Nor did it seem fair that it should require two witnesses, one for each mate, and that she had been Rowena's choice. Alongside Steve, she had struggled every step of the way, weighed down by the pulse of her broken heart while following the couple down the narrow canyon that gave access to the breathtaking Nephis Valley.

Too bad, she had not been able to appreciate it fully, for the place had seemed hazed by a blinding light that had hurt her eyes and dulled her perception. To the point, she had to squint simply to catch sight of Arthur standing in front of something that looked like a bizarre tower.

A geometric structure of sorts closely resembling a pyramid had been her safest guess, though a weird one, if considering all those other smaller pyramids making it up from the broad base to the pointy tip. The fact Arthur had seemed to have no problems with the intense light behind him had made her wonder whether he was unaware of it or merely unaffected.

"But it's just a symbol." The leader made it sound as though it had no real value of its own. "A reminder of who we are, where we come from, and where we're going."

Which she was sure was not the case.

Not by a long shot.

"I believe it's much more." Standing now in front of him, she took a deep breath before spitting out, "'Cause we can't have

children without it."

"Nonsense!" Of course, he would think her crazy.

She had kind of expected it. Only she had applied her mind to it too often to have him deflect her rationalizations that easily.

"What's important is the vow exchanged during the ceremony." That he wanted to set her straight was evident from his condescending tone. "Not the structure behind them." He talked to her like she was dumb or something equally offensive.

Too bad for him. She was nothing like his tone implied, and it was too critical to let it go like Arthur seemed to be demanding.

No, she had to find a plausible explanation to the doubts crowding her mind of late. "I think it's so much more."

Once her sight had adjusted, and she had been able to see more of the intriguing tower, she would have liked to take a closer look, if not touch it outright. Which was not her call alas, for only the couple had such privilege.

She had just watched the show.

While asking the ritual question and receiving a simple, "Yes," as a reply, Arthur's white robe with gold leaf embroidery had been in sharp contrast with Rowena's fine blue silk that displayed all her tantalizing curves. Right after, he had joined their hands, and it had been over.

Clearing her throat, Cecilia returned to the leader's office. "If I could study it up close —"

"You'd get as much information from it as from any other rock," he sneered contemptuously.

Undeterred, she insisted, "But —"

"Permission denied." Raising his hand, he ended the argument, seemingly fed up with her stubbornness. "Now, leave." Having dismissed her, he glanced down at his documents. "'Cause I'm somewhat busy."

If he thought he could get rid of her that easily, he was dead wrong.

"Oh, I didn't mean to take up your precious time, Leader." She worked hard to suppress the irony that would have laced her words, had she only allowed. "It's just that haven't you ever wondered why

our life seems so . . ." Lazy? Indolent? Meaningless?

Just because all of the above applied did not mean she could blurt them out. A suitable synonym was in order, one that would not offend the leader.

"Idle?" *Happy with her choice, she took a step forward.*

"What's idle about it?" *Arthur retorted icily.* "We have a wonderful life that fulfills all our needs." *His piercing gaze looked her up and down as though she just could not get it through her thick head.* "There's no suffering, no hunger nor poverty. Best of all, there's no violence." *He shifted on his chair to stare her in the eyes.* "What more could we possibly want?"

"How about scientific progress or technological advancement?" *Leaning on his desk, she made sure to lock her gaze on his.* "Since we lack nothing, we don't grow, nor do we need to, so nothing ever changes." *Just saying it made her angrier than when she had first analyzed it.* "The only thing progressing is our extreme absorption with sex and everything related to it."

"Correct me if I'm wrong, but isn't sex a great thing, neither harmful nor deadly?" *His eyes twinkled in amusement.* "Isn't everyone quite happy to be so sexually active?"

"They're just fools out to have a good time," *she snorted.* "Without even caring about what's going on."

"While you do, Lady Hurst," *he taunted openly.* "Maybe, you think this Game of yours has made you a real expert in the matter." *A dry, brittle laugh, then he continued,* "Now, you can't wait to share your observations about what sex is — "

"Whatever it is, it can't be our only interest or reason for living!" *Her face went hot from the biting edge in his voice.* "There must be something else." *There just had to be because it made no sense otherwise.* "Something more productive — "

"We are very productive as it is," *he cut her off brusquely.* "In case you haven't noticed, we have highly organized artisans and traders, an advanced farming system, and a hierarchy that makes sure everyone receives what they need. Our villages flourish by sharing their resources in peace and harmony, in full respect of nature's laws and of its balance." *He pursed his lips.* "Which, *everything considered, makes for a damn good bargain."*

"If for hierarchy you mean the High Council, I just see a bunch of complacent people who do nothing from morning to night except have sex with anything that moves." If that contributed to her Game's success, it did not make her feel any pride for the group she represented.

It was the goddamn truth, and it was time someone said it to the leader's face. To let him have a piece of her mind was her goal, for she had nothing except loathing for most of her so-called peers. Arthur, with all his boys, was not helping matters, either, turning the Hall into a sex-only zone that had nothing to do with the responsibilities the place should have promoted.

"Morning, evening and night, all they care about is their sexual fulfillment." On the offensive, she had to pause lest she choked on her own bile. *"Not just the council members, everybody at the Hall can't think of nothing else."* And your Lord Christopher Templeton is the worse of them all. *"Or do anything besides sex as often as they can."* Having it out in the open made her feel better at once. *"So, forgive me, Leader, but I don't think it's natural."*

"No, I won't forgive you or your intolerable rant." Eyes ablaze, Arthur spoke through clenched teeth, *"What do you know about* normality *anyway? Or about nature for that matter?"* He hissed, *"Your overactive mind keeps you so detached from it. You're the least qualified to discuss it."*

"My overactive mind *is precisely the reason I question this way of life,"* she bit back. *"'Cause things aren't adding up as they should if we lived by nature's laws as you claim."*

"What do you mean?" Suddenly standing down, he changed register as though curious to know what was on her mind.

"That animals don't need a pledge to reproduce." Helped by his switch, she relaxed a bit. *"They have sex and get an offspring out of it. Totally unlike us, who have to wait for a pledge before having a child, no matter how much sex we have in the meantime."* This still baffled her. *"Don't you find that odd?"*

"Not at all." He waved a dismissive hand in the air. *"Pledges*

serve the express purpose of making people aware of their responsibilities. Without them, our world would have to pay the consequences of too many mouths to feed."

"That's not nature's way of doing things." Stubborn, she held her point. "I mean, animals don't need any special ritual to have an offspring." More than that, she seemed driven to the extreme measure of defying her own, usually brilliant logic, in spite of the leader's sensible statements. "They have their heat — "

"So do we," he was quick to block her.

"Yes, I know." It was the madness of the senses similar to the phase, yet different because it happened between opposite genders. "We get a sort of heat after the pledge. Only difference, animals have it all the times regardless of — "

"If we were to follow their example, we wouldn't have survived." Now, Arthur seemed exasperated with her continuous objections. "Our world could not possibly sustain millions of people. We just don't have enough resources. If something didn't regulate our reproduction, we'd have all died." His eyebrows rose. "Do you understand now why the pledge works better for us?"

"Perhaps." Now that he mentioned it, she had to admit she had not given too much thought about the consequences of what she was prospecting with so much emphasis. "Still, it all comes back to that structure in the Nephis Valley. I mean, words alone can't have the power to stop what is a natural process. Something else must influence it." The more she thought about it, the more it made sense. "If you only gave me permission to study it, I'd put my doubts to rest and — "

"Permission denied." This second refusal sounded final. "Now, run along." Ignoring her, he shifted his gaze back to his papers. "You've wasted enough of my time already, and I have better things to do than argue with an unreasonable child."

CHAPTER NINETEEN

"All right, Ceci, I get it." David glanced at the shades, drawn to keep out Stella's fierce desert light. "You think things aren't adding up." Lying in her bed on a lazy Blue Oasis afternoon, he shifted to stare at her unique face that resembled a man's, with its hard chin, high-pronounced cheekbones and thin lips.

Too long apart, he had missed her and that exceedingly masculine body of hers. Yeah, his reservations notwithstanding, it seemed like an eternity since he had last been with her. With that amazing mind of hers mostly, which managed to surprise him every time.

Now, why did everything in Cecilia Hurst seemed designed for a man's body, including that impressively impeccable logic of hers?

Damn if he knew.

And damn it twice because he was far from displeased.

Quite the contrary.

Those straight lines of hers, the practically non-existent breasts and the flat stomach, where no curvy hip led to her cunt, had always turned him on no matter what.

If sometimes he wished her body's reactions were half as intriguing as her insights, it meant nothing because he liked her just as she was.

"But why is it so important to you?" He examined her face hoping to read the answer straight from her dark, mesmerizing eyes.

"'Cause it's not natural," she huffed, annoyed.

Probably because she had gone over it already.

"Why would Rowena have Ronnie right after her pledge?" Her eyes widened. "Considering all the sex she had, why should a pledge make any difference? How could just a few words in the Nephis Valley accomplish what loads of sex could not and make her pregnant?"

"I don't see what's odd about it." Just for the fun of arguing with her, he repeated his earlier objection. "It's what happens all the time. Couples pledge. Then, women get pregnant." He narrowed his gaze on her. "It's as simple as that, so what's all the fuss?"

"Sex makes babies, not pledges." She sounded adamant. "Haven't you ever watched your precious horses breed?"

"Yeah, they get the heat, have sex and conceive." Inevitable for his mind to return to Black Rose and John Meyer, the Caldwell's stable keeper since forever.

Now that he had fallen ill, Duncan was going crazy trying to find a replacement worth its name, which David knew was a material impossibility.

So did the prince.

"It's nothing different from what happens to us." Snapping to the present, he shook his head clear. "We also get the heat, have sex and conceive."

"Sure." Cecilia smiled sweetly. "Only horses don't pledge beforehand." Her voice became pleading, "Can't you see that there's something wrong with this system?"

Well, he had to hand it to her. Her reasoning was always dead on track. Focused and sharp like nothing else, she deserved a small prize.

"In the Caldwell family, it might've happened." He was sure this bit of information would catch her immediate attention.

"What do you mean?" Without fail, it lit her dark and masculine features like nothing had so far.

"That Prince Charles, Duncan's father, was very much in love with a servant in Black Rose . . ." Mary Jane Elspeth.

His memory retrieved the sketchy images he had of the beautiful woman, and he got lost in a time that did not exist anymore. His nine-year-old self did not exist anymore, either, and that had been when the poor woman had died suddenly and mysteriously.

"They had a child together?" Cecilia was quick to jump to the conclusion.

"No, they didn't." He did not doubt it, however many insinuated the contrary, blaming it on all sorts of witchcraft or sorcery. "She *pledged to Black Rose's stable keeper, but her daughter came out looking like a Caldwell." How that could have been possible was still beyond him. "So similar to both Prince Charles and Duncan that people could not resist running their mouths off and spreading all sorts of lies and gossip, as though Prince Charles had fathered her." He had not approved of it back then. He certainly did not now. "Which is ridiculous." He pursed his lips. "We all know that no pledge, no babies, and both had pledged to someone else."*

"What happened to this girl?" Curious, Cecilia edged closer.

"She lives with her father, the stable keeper, over at the village." After Lady Sophia Caldwell in person had kicked her out of Black Rose, her native home.

Not the sort of detail he wished to share, so avoided it all together. Mostly he had to suppress that clenching of his stomach at the thought he had done nothing to stop the harsh woman from playing out her jealous revenge on someone too little to defend herself.

If that had not been bad enough, he had also allowed Ylianor's memory to fade from Black Rose. Which was unforgivable, however hard he tried convincing himself he had no choice in the matter.

"Lately, he has fallen ill, and I think she looks after him." To be precise, he had not bothered enquiring, too guilt-stricken even for such a simple task. "Anyway, this is beside the point." With an effort, he pulled himself together. "And it's got nothing to do with your latest obsession about breeding and reproduction." About the significant correlation between sex and pledges. "Or with your need to understand this apparent disregard of natural laws."

No, make that driven to understand, as though she would not rest until she found a logical explanation for it.

Then again, Cecilia Hurst had a history with obsessions, her primary one being with sex and with her mind preventing her body's full enjoyment of it.

"It's not an obsession." She beamed at him. "It's a scientific quest."

"Don't give me that!" David provoked on purpose. "I know you too well, Ceci, so you can't fool me." His gaze bore deep into hers. "This isn't just about intellectual curiosity, is it?"

Of course, he had better sense than to take her words at face value. Not that she ever lied intentionally. It was more of a defense mechanism. A way her fertile intelligence had devised to force her to admit what she would rather not.

"Well . . ." She blinked twice in palpable unease. "I've been thinking . . ." Like a little girl, she would have hidden her face in his chest had it stopped his probing.

When this happened, he almost loved her. Gone her hard edge, he glimpsed her real essence. The lonely little girl buried way down the confident façade of the permanent council member and the heir of the Blandry District.

Not that Cecilia ever showed it. Just his luck, he had caught sight of it upon first meeting her and had grown attached to it in spite of his better judgment.

"I've been thinking about having a child of my own someday," she breathed hoarsely.

"Nothing is easier." Even if he acted as though this would not affect him any, his heart plunging to his stomach told a different story. "Just pledge."

"To you?" Fixing her gaze on him, she spelled out the words, "'Cause I'd like your child."

David winced. He had hoped it would never come down to this.

"Why the maternal impulse?" He sidetracked her focus. And who knows?

He might just get lucky, and she would forget she had ever asked him to pledge.

"I'm not sure." Uncertain, she bit her bottom lip. "The last Game got me thinking about what would happen to it if I wasn't around anymore." Her expression brightened as if she had already seen it. "About who would continue it since I'm the last of my family."

"The Game begins and ends with you, Ceci." Affectionately, he tapped her nose. "You should know that."

"Maybe." Unconvinced, she shrugged. "Just means my son or daughter will have to find a better occupation," she teased. "With you as a father, I doubt there'll ever be a lack of things to do." She glanced at him shyly. "If you want to pledge to me, that is."

"I don't know . . ." Now, it was his turn to be evasive. "I mean, I'm honored, but . . ." It did not feel right.

Not since the world was broken up in classes. Not since masters belonged with masters and servants with servants. And the sad reality was that she was in the former while he was in the latter.

"Ceci, you should have children with someone of your own standing," he argued, appealing to her sense of rationality.

"Nonsense." He would have to do better. "With very few exceptions, those in my position aren't worth half as much as you are. I just have to think of Christopher Templeton to know I'm right."

She had no great liking for the odious Lord Templeton. What else was new?

No one in his right mind could like someone as jealous, possessive and exclusive, which made it all the stranger that Prince Duncan Caldwell did.

No, more than liked, the prince loved the gorgeous creature like he loved no one else in the entire world. That was something David for one found hard to grapple.

"Could be." Still, and despite her logic, it did not prompt him to jump into pledging her. "If we figure out why our world seems to defy the natural order of things."

"You mean, why no pledge, no babies?" Rolling aside, she settled in a more comfortable position. "To me, it must have something to do with the pledge itself."

"Or maybe with the Nephis Valley," he offered, glad for the chance to be off the hook at least for now.

"Yeah, the Nephis Valley." She frowned, deep in concentration. "It gave me a creepy sensation when I was there." Her gaze clouded as though she were reliving the moment.

Or rather, the pain of her shattered heart at having to witness her phase mate's pledge.

He knew all about it. She had told him about Rowena, just like about everything else concerning the woman she considered a goddess, still hankering after her big time like when her phase first started.

"What's the structure really like? What's the purpose of it?" She *said it like she was talking to herself. "Arthur said it's a reminder of who we are, where we come from and where we're going. But he wasn't all that open with me, and his ambiguous answers explained nothing."*

Though a bit extreme, David let it slide. He had not confronted the leader, after all. Nor had he ever seen him more than once in his life. Just thought that a rational man like Arthur Fairchild would not have beaten around the bush the way Cecilia implied.

"There must be more to it than what Arthur said, and that I already told you." She furrowed her brow as though going over the conversation she had already recounted. "'Cause either the structure or the ritual does something to people that ensures reproduction from the pledge on." She heaved. "That's why I asked him permission to study the structure in the Nephis Valley, and he refused."

"On what grounds?" Not at all surprised, he leaned his weight on an elbow to stare her in the face.

"He said I was talking nonsense, and that there was no point in studying a symbol of our origins." Kind of evident, the leader had grated more than one of Cecilia's nerves. "But I want to go there and see for myself." She turned huge eyes on him. "Will you come with me?"

CHAPTER TWENTY

Sure, Cecilia had asked.
But why had he spoiled it all by accepting?
Damn if he knew!
David simply followed her to the Nephis Valley, a place he had only heard about, without the slightest inkling of what would come.
Thank the stars for that!
Or he would have never agreed to go in a secluded valley surrounded by high mountains. Blazing from such intense lights, he had to shield his eyes just to see what was in front of him. Only thing, it was the dead of night.
All right, something was not quite adding up from the beginning. Still, it prevented neither him nor Cecilia from sitting on the damp grass to examine the situation further.
As if there could be an end to the strangeness of it all!
Which there was not.
Once his eyes adjusted, he could not believe what he saw. Or thought he saw. A jumble of pyramids all thrown together to form a bigger one. A peculiar one, if he was any judge of pyramids, tall enough to reach the sky, with so many different colors and materials that he had to stop staring. Better to concentrate on figuring out how it worked.
Something told him this thing had a life of its own, plus a heart hidden in between the confusion of opaque stones and transparent glass making up its odd surface.
When Cecilia spotted it, he was not surprised that it was the centerpiece at the very top.
To him, the real question was, "How did she find it?"
Not something you would see that easily, not unless someone or

162

something had called her attention to it.

To her, the real question was, "How can I bring it down?"

She need not have worried. At least on this, he had it all figured out, and it hinged on the power he had been experimenting with of late.

Discovered quite by chance, it allowed him to move objects from a distance, without touching them. Why and how he managed it was a matter of speculation, but there could be no better time than the present to test it.

Focusing on the structure, he called it. When nothing happened, he was severely disappointed.

Somehow, the prospect of trying out what so far had worked only in his room had been the driving force behind his decision to help Cecilia. Moving small objects around had excited him into believing he could replicate it anywhere.

Yet, he had been a fool!

He was about to turn to Cecilia and admit his failure when the million lights became red. Loud sounds of rocks or pyramids clashing against one another hit his ears and plunged him into utter chaos. In the middle of a battlefield was more like it since he had the nagging sensation that a fierce struggle had erupted inside the tower.

Taking Cecilia by the arm, he scrambled to get away. Not an option, though, not since he caught sight of a new shining light carrying a small object down to the ground. Down to Cecilia's feet to be precise.

Speechless, he gawked at a blue pyramid on the grass, apparently made of solid stone. Or maybe, it was just another illusion.

Because what he observed whirling inside had nothing of the stone's consistency. It was a glass-like material that revealed a shimmering sphere composed of many tiny particles.

The more he looked at it. The more the fight raged. The more he feared he had done something terribly wrong.

Hence his resolve to leave it right there and get the fuck out fast!

Which was not Cecilia's intention.

She had come too far to leave empty-handed. Regardless of his reasonable objections, she was interested only in bringing the damn thing home and study it at leisure.

To no avail, did he try to dissuade her. As stubborn as only she could be, she did not listen to a word he said. Simply bent down, picked up the solitary pyramid and headed back to Blue Oasis, with a dejected David tagging along.

CHAPTER TWENTY-ONE

"They're here." Cecilia approached her bed, where David lay curled on a side.

"I know." He did not even blink, stretching as he was half rising to sit up straight. "I saw their horses." A scowl crossed his handsome face.

Her heart sank to her feet.

Not because he had warned they would.

If he had been right about this, he had been right about everything else, too.

"You think they came after the pyramid?" In spite of knowing it already, she provoked him on purpose.

"Of course, I do," he scoffed as though annoyed with her playing dumb. "I told you they would."

Oh, yes, he had, and more than once since his return to Blue Oasis. Which had been a couple of days before.

"I told you that Prince Caldwell would come looking for it," he insisted in repeating a point he had abundantly stressed already.

"How could you have known?" Until that evening, she had only half-believed him.

"As soon as I heard that Lord Fairchild had summoned him and Lord Templeton, I knew it had to do with the missing pyramid." He sounded so confident that Cecilia wondered why she ever doubted him.

"Why them of all people?" Still, this escaped her. "Why should the leader call them?" Suddenly feeling tired, she landed on the chair next to her dressing table, still facing

David. "Neither one is a council member."

"Could be the reason he chose them," he argued sensibly.

"Or maybe, being a council member has nothing to do with it." Her gaze switched to the pyramid she kept wrapped up in a silk scarf on her dresser. "Maybe, it has to do with this . . ." *How to call it?*

Needless to say, she had been more than impressed with his little trick of moving the small pyramid and convincing it to come to her. Precisely how he had managed it, she still had no idea. Nor did he, if given his lack of scientific explanation. It could not be enough simply to want an object to move for it to do so. Or could it?

"Power you have." She could not suppress a sense of pride from lacing her words. "Even if I returned the pyramid, how could they possibly put it back?"

"Not your problem, Ceci." His hazel eyes sparkled in impatience. "If that's what they'll need to do, I'll be more than happy to help them put that thing where it belongs."

"But I still need to learn its secrets." Damn! Between her council duties, the district's affairs and organizing her Game, she had had no time to do any serious studying. "Its connection to sex and babies."

"If you want babies, pledge." His tone was kind of exasperated since he had already said as much before she had taken the pyramid. "Afterward, you'll have as many as you wish."

"Then, let's pledge." Leaning forward, she locked her gaze on his. "'Cause I want your children."

She knew she sounded like a spoiled brat rather than a woman choosing her future. But she could not help it, not since David had turned her down before.

This was unfair and unfounded because, and despite all his reservations, she wanted him in a way she did not want any other man, not even the very striking and very perfect Prince

Duncan Caldwell.

"I can't pledge to you, Cecilia." The harshness of his tone was probably due to her stubbornness. "We're two different classes, so it's out of the question."

Sure, he was a stickler about hierarchy.

But she was not buying it this time.

If she had accepted his reasons before, now she questioned them.

Or rather him, for he had changed. Though she had no basis for this conclusion, she suspected that it had to do with the new woman in his life. Same woman who had held Prince Caldwell spellbound during the whole nighttime of playing her Game.

As though realizing he had been too abrupt, his tone softened, "If you and I ever want to pledge, we should do it with someone at our same level."

"I suppose you already found someone at your *same level*." Hard as she tried, she could not keep the icy edge out of her voice. "Right?"

David's face flushed.

Which was all she needed to know she was on the right track and that she had added up all her facts correctly.

"That stable keeper's daughter you told me about, right?" Angrier than she had ever felt in her whole life, she kept attacking.

Because she had not expected how beautiful and uncannily alike to Duncan, the woman would be.

"I presume her father died." Reasoning helped to quell part of her rage, just like recounting Lord Templeton's explanation. "That's why Duncan offered her the position."

"I didn't ask." On the defensive, David refused to be intimidated. "And he didn't tell."

"But she's the one people say was Prince Charles's daughter, isn't she?" No, not even David's words had prepared her adequately for the shock.

Or the insane jealousy.

"Only you failed to tell me they had all the reasons to believe it." Staring intently at him was a way to control the painful pulse of her heart. "'Cause she doesn't just look like Duncan. She's like his twin!"

This had grated most on her nerves, not to mention the trifle about the amazing way they had played, which had not helped matters.

Not one bit!

"You saw her then?" He gazed at her with a falsely innocent look stamped all over his face.

"How could I not?" She nearly lost it. "He used her as his slave," she practically shouted. "Didn't you tell me he wasn't keen on servants?" Just one more inconsistency she could not fit anywhere.

"He isn't," David confirmed testily. "It was probably the only way he had to enter your Game."

"Ha! That's a laugh." Even more, if considering everything Master Duncan had done with his slave. "It looked like he couldn't wait to get his hands on her and show her off to the rest of the world. And my Game had nothing to do with it."

"It was probably a ruse," David did not let it go. "To distract you and hide the fact he's here for a definite purpose."

"If that was the case, he did a magnificent job of it." She felt sure of it, having watched the two play until the end. "'Cause he looked like he had not a care in the world."

David was quick to point out, "He's good at concealing his real emotions —"

"Sorry, darling, but Rowena and I had sex with him," she rushed to contradict him. "I can say for certain he didn't seem focused on anything except his own pleasure."

As soon as she had blurted it out, she was sorry she had. This bit about the stable keeper's daughter was messing with her perceptions, something that had started from the moment she had laid eyes on the strange creature.

"I see." His pursed lips told her he did not appreciate her sharing.

How to blame him?

She would not have, either had she only been in his shoes.

"That was before he started playing for real." She tried to make it up to him by leaving the chair and sitting next to him on the bed. "And shattered everybody's illusions." *Not just mine.* She attempted a smile that came out crooked.

"What do you mean?" Mollified, he made room for her.

"He was so taken by her that he practically ignored everybody else." She lifted a shoulder, acting like it meant nothing to her.

Which was a lie pure and simple because, like everyone else, she had not been able to tear off her gaze from him.

"Their game was . . ." *Exciting? Arousing? Heart pounding? Cunt wetting?* "Extreme." Or so it had seemed from the outside. "He pushed her to the hardest possible edge, yet she never got enough. Kept raising the stakes — "

"How could she?" His eyebrows flew upward. "I mean, if slaves can't talk, how could she — "

"Well, the funny thing is that it seemed like she could." She knew she was not making much sense. "It was like they talked among them somehow . . ." If her voice trailed off, it was because she had no rational explanation to offer. "Or something to that effect." She stared hard into space, replaying some of the hottest scenes between Prince Caldwell and his slave. "I know you must think me crazy." Her focus spun back on David. "But I wasn't the only one who noticed this." *Or who was envious of it.* "He did everything he could to attract notice."

"Like what?" Exceedingly curious, David bent in her direction.

"For starters, he had her service half the men in there." She licked her lips. "Good thing, his guest took care of the other half, or they'd still be at it." She laughed out loud.

"I presume his guest was Lord Templeton." David had to set the record straight.

"The one and only," she snickered. "He went through every able male body he could find and consumed it like he didn't want to leave anything for anybody else," she sneered. "Between the three of them, they kept all my players quite busy. Those they didn't screw were too busy watching or talking about it to do anything else." She shifted and settled in a more comfortable position. "And they're still at it." She had caught more than one group of people gossiping among themselves in spite of the hour having grown very late.

Or very early, depending on who was keeping track.

"It's kind of inevitable since he proved to be the best master of all, to the point he could command her with a single glance." It had been all the proof she had needed to know she had been right all along in choosing him as her paragon. "Also, the most highly irregular master, who had eyes for her alone like she had bewitched him or something." Which perhaps she had if any of those rumors David had told her about had any truth in them. "He used her like he actually cared for her. No one ever dared during any of my previous Games. Nor had anyone ever kissed his slave the way he did her." Like he was starving, thirsty or both. "Not just once, twice." She was still reeling from the enormity of his gesture. "The first time when he picked her up from Jeff Macy's place, he kissed her right there in the middle of the chamber." Boy, how that particular kiss had scorched her all over! "As if it wasn't bad enough, he was carrying her to his place, rather than having her walk behind him."

"So, he broke more than a few of your rules." David chuckled.

"Actually, it's not exactly a rule, more of a custom." No,

there had been no real breach of etiquette on Duncan's part, however much she played it like there had been. "Though his second kiss could well qualify like being against the rules." For sure, it had been against any measure of decency. "This second one was at the end of his game when he was leaving the chamber. He just had to do it while he carried and devoured her like he ran the risk of losing her any time soon. And of course, people stopped whatever they were doing to stare at them." She eyed David's face. "Can you believe it?"

"You said it wasn't against the rules." He pulled Cecilia closer.

"It isn't." Though now, she would have to amend them for sure. "Masters have the right to do whatever they want with their slaves." *Except to kiss them in such a public way from now on.*

"Where was Lord Templeton during all this?" A blaze lit his hazel eyes.

"Oh, he had split long before any of it started." She remembered the flash of his blond hair as he had headed down to the pool area. "But I think he saw at least one of the two kisses." Frowning, she seemed to recall catching sight of him on a side, though she could not tell whether it had been during the first or the second kiss. "If I'm wrong, by now, he must've heard about it."

"Wasn't he there in the chamber?" Only natural for David to wonder since he always kept well away from the actual play.

"He was downstairs, in the pools, getting his ass thoroughly ravaged by two new masters who were playing for the first time." She giggled. "It was a nice variation despite some of my reservations, and it worked great for them and for your prince, who could dominate his slave like she belonged to him." Like she was his property for real.

"With everyone gawking." He definitely got it.

"The women were the worst," she sustained his

assumptions. "Most of them would have given their right arm to be in your girl's place."

"She's not my girl," he huffed. "And her name is Ylianor."

"Ylianor, eh?" Oh fuck, the damn woman also had an arresting name.

As if things were not bad enough!

"Yeah, Ylianor." The way he said it, it was like he was savoring each letter. "Now, come on." Drawing back, he raised the cover to invite her inside. "It's late, and it's high time you got some sleep." He patted the place by his side. "'Cause you look very tired."

Now that he mentioned it, she felt exhausted.

"Whatever her name, she still feels like your girl." She quickly undressed and slipped inside, pressing against him.

"After everything you told me about tonight, I'd say she's more *Prince Caldwell's girl*." A bitter snarl curved his lips devoid of any trace of humor.

"Doubt he'll ever take her seriously." Or so she ardently hoped. "Given everything I've seen of him, she's probably just a passing fancy, like Rowena says." She prayed that her phase mate was right. "While with you, she stands a much better chance. You two are of the same level, and I get the feeling that you —"

"All right, so I had sex with her." That it cost him to admit it was evident from a certain clenching of his teeth. "But it's not like you think. She's in love with the prince."

"Does he return her love?" She felt stupid asking it, for every bone in her body screamed that he did.

"He certainly cares for her." If David fidgeted nervously, it was probably because he knew it, too. "Though I wouldn't know how to call his feelings."

"After what I saw of those kisses, I have a definite name in mind." Which started with an *L* and ended with *Ove*.

David shrugged as though it made no difference to him.

"From what I can tell, the only one he's in love with is Lord Christopher Templeton, his phase mate." Even if she knew he could not stand the man, his tone had all the respect people always associated to phase relationships.

"They're still lovers, aren't they?" Not that she needed David's confirmation. It was kind of obvious just by watching them together.

"Yes, they are." His voice was sweet and full of understanding, as though he feared this truth would hurt her.

Which, for the record, it did in the worst way possible.

Bringing up all sorts of nagging questions, she had no desire to ponder.

Things like why were they still at it when Rowena had made it clear that sex between them was over? Why did some people have all the luck in the world while she, Cecilia, could only pine after the woman she loved beyond her very life?

Just thinking it killed her inside like the first time she had realized her phase had really ended.

"She must feel very jealous." She tried hard to keep her glee at bay.

"Hem . . ." He hesitated as though he had the answer, only did not wish to share it. "I don't know. We haven't talked a lot."

"Just screwed a lot," she was quick to connect his dots.

David's face became bright red.

"Hey, darling, I understand." Snuggling closer, she caressed his face gently. "At least both of you love the same person. That ought to mean something." Lightly tracing his cheekbone, she tried to reassure him. "You know I'm not jealous," she lied smoothly. "We each love someone else, after all. If there's a new person in your life, I'm happy for you."

"Are you really?" Somehow, her show did not impress him.

No, make that it did not fool him.

"I am." Her vigorous nod was another attempt at convincing him of the contrary.

"Well, I'm grateful for your *open-mindedness*." Was it her impression, or did she detect a hint of sarcasm? "But I suppose it's beside the point now that they're here and will ask for the pyramid." His eyes flashed at her. "So, what are you going to do about it?"

CHAPTER TWENTY-TWO

"Wakey-wakey, sleeping beauties." Tossing open the door of Prince Caldwell's room, the black cloud that had engulfed Chris since leaving Patrick threatened to swallow him whole.

Not because of everything that had happened at the blasted Game! Not because of the gossip, either, even if both were reason enough to strangle Ylianor with his bare hands!

Because his striking lover clung to her like he was holding on for dear life! Curled around her on that big bed like she was about to slip from his grasp any time soon. So tight, her ass seemed glued to his crotch. Her every curve fitted against his as though she had been built for his exact measures.

Which sent Chris flying off his horses worse than he had been during the entire conversation with those idiots of the Arthur boys. His cock yelping for a taste of that same magnificent ass did not improve matters any.

Had he only been free to do it, he would have obliterated her from the face of every known land. Like he had done in his earlier days when he had gotten rid of her to avoid the very same thing she was attempting now. To steal his lover from under his very nose. Who gave her the fucking right anyway?

Prince Duncan Caldwell had always belonged to him, marked and sealed from the first moment he had laid eyes on the stunning dark-haired boy. He had the hottest, most torrid phase ever to prove that the spectacular prince was his in a way he would never be with anybody else. So, why did that very same prince have to claim her so publicly? Why did he have to tell the whole world that he owned her, body mind and soul his for the taking?

To no avail did his memory remind Chris that such had been the case before he had reached Black Rose on that fateful summer day. The one thing he could not forget was how attached Duncan had been to the intolerable witch, back in the days when she had been just a brat following him around like a hopeless lovesick puppy. Now, she had taken everything that one-step further, challenging him openly and in front of everybody.

The mere thought made his blood boil. If he did not calm down, he might just snap her neck right there and then, and be done with her once and for all.

He slammed the door and went to the bathroom. Neither had stirred, anyway, nor budged an inch from their tight entanglement.

Relieving the full bladder that had been pressing from the moment he had woken up, he switched his attention to an even bigger problem, his growling stomach. Now that he thought of it, he had not eaten since leaving the shelter next to Blue Oasis, and that seemed like an eternity ago. Since Cecilia's maddening rules permitted only masters the privilege to be fed, he had to wake up his lover and, with some urgency, if he did not want to starve.

Shaking the last drops off the tip of his penis, he closed it back inside the pants and returned to the bedroom, where her ass still dug in what did not belong to her. And would you believe it?

His goddamn shaft jerked, as though it would not rest until he had her. As though he craved her or something.

Which was pure ludicrous.

Ignoring his body, he sauntered away from her and knelt next to his phase mate.

He smelled of sex and of the musky grave odor that was Duncan's alone that had his senses swimming.

Not his fault if he loved the man so fucking bad. So much, he would have done anything for him, even died had he just asked.

With an effort, he pulled himself together, trying to focus on something besides his raw need of the gorgeous dark-haired prince.

Upon straying his focus, his gaze fell on that odd blemish on the left shoulder. More similar to a bump or a mark, it looked like the result of a faraway wound that somehow had never healed properly, given the jagged edges he felt under his fingertips.

"It's the seventeenth hour." His hand traveling upward from the scar, he brushed the black-raven hair. "Way past lunchtime." Bending, he pressed his lips to Duncan's ear. "I also skipped breakfast."

His earnest appeal failed to move Prince Caldwell in the least.

"Oh, come on, lover." Burying his head in the nape of his neck, Chris inhaled his scent to his lungs. Then, bit him before trying his luck again. "Wake up," he whispered seductively. "I'm starving and not just for food."

A groan escaped the full lips. "You're insatiable, Angel."

His voice groggy with sleep sounded even throatier than usual.

"You know I am." Chris chuckled amused, wishing he could reach his cock for some serious fondling. "If you only get a move, I'll show you just how much."

"You'd just love it, wouldn't you?" Slipping his arms from under Ylianor, Duncan stretched and yawned before opening his eyes.

"What if I did?" Oh, yeah, Chris would love nothing better than to stifle the black cloud with some proper ramming of his ass. "What would you do about it?"

"For starters, I'd be impressed." Shifting to a side, Duncan finally unglued his crotch from her despicable backside. "Since your ass worked overtime last night."

"You heard?" Of course, he would have.

This Game that Cecilia supposedly invented was nothing different from what everyone did at the Hall, having loads of sex and gossiping about it for hours on end.

"You should've seen how good I was at taking two cocks at once." He could not help bragging. "And milking them dry at the same time."

Duncan chortled as he rolled to face him. "You're a real slut."

"That's what they thought, too." Chris beamed in an enthusiastic response. "That's why they couldn't get enough of it." Taking advantage of the new position, he clutched the limp piece.

A few strokes and it was on its way to the impressive size that he adored.

"And that's why they had to pump it all night long." He smacked his lips, proud of his achievement.

"Without any success." Raising the stakes, Prince Caldwell grasped his buttocks. "Or you wouldn't be here, begging for more."

"I'm not begging." Haughtily, he threw back his shoulders. "Just reminding you of all that you missed yesterday." His rhythm became more decisive. "Speaking of which, was it necessary to make such a scene with your slave?"

If it had not been his intention to blurt it out like this, it slipped through before he even realized it.

"What was the idea of kissing the insufferable witch like she actually meant something to you?" But now that it was out, he could not stop. "Like you didn't care less about breaking all of Cecilia's rules?"

"Kissing a slave isn't against the rules," Duncan rectified immediately.

"Maybe not now," Chris scoffed irritated with himself mostly and with pursuing a track that was sure to lead nowhere besides his fuming anger.

"But, for sure, she'll amend them before the next edition." It was too damn intimate for her to tolerate it in any way. "'Cause what you did last night went well beyond every damn restriction Cecilia has ever thought of."

"She never thought of someone as scorching as the princess." There was a malicious intent in the prince's voice that he did not like.

Not at all.

"For I got so hot for her, I couldn't stand my own skin, even if I had vowed not to touch her." Bending, Duncan almost touched his forehead to Chris's. "I just had to have her." The emphasis was similar to a blow to the stomach. "It got unbearable when I saw her with Jeff Macy. Remember him?"

"The jerk?" How could he forget?

Even if he had, those fools of the Arthur boys had made it their business to remind him and blab their mouths off about all the sordid details of his screwing the nosy witch in the chamber while her master gawked and probably gave her silent orders.

"Sure, I do." He left it vague on purpose.

"He kept her for something like a couple of hours." A wicked gleam sparked the black eyes. "And he couldn't get enough of her. Fucked her everywhere, in her ass especially. I watched a good part of the action, at least the one I didn't live myself when I linked to her sensations." Was Duncan goading him or what? "So, you can understand why kissing her was the only thing that gave me a measure of relief without spoiling the rest of the night." Undoubtedly, the pause was a strategic one. "Or would you have preferred that I fucked her in front of everyone?"

"Nobody would have given a damn if you had." Stubborn, he pushed back. "In case you haven't noticed, masters fuck their slaves all the time—"

"Not one like her," Duncan cut him off abruptly.

"Gee, lover, the way you're telling this, you couldn't get enough of her, either." No, he really could not understand this.

"Jealous, Angel?" Duncan taunted.

"Of a nobody like her?" *Never!*

Scornful, he made a show of refusing even to glance at the despised creature as he tried to pull himself together.

"That day has yet to dawn!" He tossed back his head to stare into the amazing black eyes. "But since it never will, let me make it clear that this isn't about her!" Taking a much-needed breath steadied his voice. "This is about you and the fucking hot game you played with her."

"It was just a game." Duncan shrugged as though it had meant nothing to him. "Nothing more."

"Didn't seem like you were play-acting much." Somehow, he could not let it rest. "Not according to all the details I heard and to how fast news traveled."

"You could've stayed and played with us." The biting tone cut deeper than Chris would have admitted. "Or need I re-mind you that I wasn't the one who disappeared the entire night long?"

"Just screw you, lover!" *'Cause you're all I wanted last night.* "And that goddamn princess of yours!"

"Why didn't you say it sooner?" With a sudden move, Duncan flattened him to the ground, trapping him under his more massive build. "Instead of depriving me of this fabulous ass of yours?" Despite the pants standing in his way, he man-aged to stuff three fingers through the narrow ring at the cen-ter of the cleft. "Same ass, I'll claim when I'll feel like it."

Pressing more weight on him, Duncan leaned to whisper in his ear, "'Cause whatever game I decide to play, I'll always be the master." Releasing him, he got to his feet. "You better never forget it." He was naked and oh so mouthwatering that Chris's tongue almost fell to the floor.

His stomach, too, considering how caved in it had become merely watching him heading to the bathroom. While his every instinct screamed to surrender everything to the only man worth a damn to him.

Why was it that no one else could ever compare to him? Why was he more beautiful and cock-wrenching than any of the many men who had fucked him the previous night?

No, make that all the days and nights since his phase had ended.

"How could I ever?" Jumping up, Chris was ready to take things that one step further. "In this damn place, no one can do anything except a master." Which was all bullshit as far as he was concerned. "Not even ask for food." His stomach's loud grumble reminded him how urgent the matter was becoming. "So, why don't you order something to eat before I starve to death?"

"It seems you won't take no for an answer." Returning, Duncan landed on the bed.

"Hey, I gave you an alternative." Quick to take fire, Chris was on him, clamping the equipment now at half-mast.

"Let's stick to food for now." Smiling broadly, his lover removed the greedy paw from the delightful piece. "The princess needs to eat."

And who fucking cares?

No, he did not say it. But he wished he could, for the mere reminder of the tenderness oozing from every word was about to choke him.

For real!

Whirling around, he reached the servant's bell with two strides, pulling it as though he wanted to tear it off from the

181

wall.

"Princess, are you awake?" Duncan's fingertips tracing the contours of her face were the last straw.

For his heart plunged to his stomach.

No, further down, for the awareness he read in those few touches was enough for cold sweat to break on his forehead.

Suddenly, everything made sense as the dots connected. The caring, the treating her like a precious charge, the request to give him more time, what it all came down to was a feeling so strong it would be next to impossible for the prince to deny it for much longer.

Thus, the damn witch had done it. Somehow and against his lover's better judgment, she had managed to crumble his reservations. Or perhaps it was the Game's fault for accelerating what had started the few months since the three of them had left Black Rose. It was like Duncan had just realized his time was up and that he had to reckon with her in a forever type of deal.

Which infuriated Chris.

Not because he had feared it would come down to this, to the prince falling for her. Because he had been unable to stop it. What about the long-term consequences? What if his lover would want her as a permanent addition to their ménage?

The gods forbid!

He despised her enough as it was, without having to wonder how he would react were his lover to admit it outright.

"It seems I've no choice in the matter," Ylianor mumbled sleepily.

Nor will you ever, dearie. "Slaves don't have choices." *Not if I can help it.* "Once a slave, always a slave."

As he ducked to avoid a pillow that Duncan threw at him, someone knocked.

"I'll get it." Since he was the closest, he flung open the door.

A handsome dark-haired young man entered. "I'm Colin."

He bowed to Duncan. "At your service, Master."

"We'd like something to eat." Detaching himself from her, the prince sat up straight.

"Yes, Master." Colin eyed Ylianor skeptically. "For how many?"

"For three." Reaching over, Duncan found it indispensable to drag her next to him.

Chris's rage mounted again.

"Wouldn't want the princess to go hungry." A heartbreaking smile split his face.

"I'm touched, Master." Unmistakable, the irony in her tone. "You're most gracious."

"Aren't I always?" That his phase mate was getting a kick out of it was equally obvious.

"Very well, it's breakfast for three," the servant summed it up for everyone's sake. From his expression, it was kind of clear he had not expected Prince Caldwell to be so generous. More used for sure to masters starving their slaves.

"I'll be right back." He retreated until he exited.

"That . . ." *What's his fucking name?* "Servant wasn't bad at all. Very cute, don't you agree?" His gaze swung from the door to his lover.

"I prefer blonds." Duncan grinned. "And just for the record, his name is Colin."

"Whatever." It made no difference to him. "He just happens to be a handsome dark-haired type," he teased playfully. "Which is my favorite kind, as you already know."

"No, Angel," Duncan retorted. "You like any cock that moves."

"That, too," Chris sniggered. "But at least I have more class than this here slave of yours," he just had to add. "Who from all accounts was so voracious she went through all the able men on the floor."

"Only the ones who didn't go hiding in the pools," she was

quick to snap back.

"We weren't hiding, dearie." *Fuck!*

That was all he needed to fire up good and proper.

"We were having the time of our lives." Staring at her splendid ass as it swung off the bed was making everything more difficult. "Without annoying women around."

"You were just scared they'd steal your spotlight," she attacked venomously before disappearing in the bathroom.

"Ha! As if they could ever!" He followed, determined to give battle if it were the last thing he did. "They're good for nothing, not even for any serious competition."

"Is that why no one could talk about nothing else beside me, your lover, and those fiery kisses he gave me?" Ylianor snarled in triumph.

Ouch! That fucking hurt!

Though he would be damned if he let her know.

"Don't overrate yourself, dearie." He played it cool. "Those kisses meant nothing. Just one more show among the dozens more interesting ones that people played all night long." He huffed, "Or so they told me 'cause I certainly didn't stick around to see them —"

"Liar!" Rising from the toilet seat, she fixed her arresting green eyes on him. "I felt you watching us the second time." She took a step closer. "Like everybody else, you couldn't take your eyes off," she spat. "Not even if it was killing you inside."

That did it!

He completely lost it.

So did his shaft, gone slab of marble from the moment she had confronted him.

"The only one dying today is you, honey." Gripping her by the arm, he would have slammed her to the nearest wall, had Duncan not intervened just then.

"Not today." Wrenching her away, the prince dragged her back in the bedroom. "Or who's going to take care of this very hungry cock of yours?" He flung her on the bed, belly down, pressing her with his weight so that she could not budge.

"Not this worthless piece of hide you should've gotten rid of long ago." Incensed, he could only stare at that delectable ass wriggling to get free. "She's no good even for this simple task."

Whom was he kidding?

His lust had grown so out of any boundaries that it was clogging all his senses.

"Then, why the standing ovation?" The black gaze dropping to his exaggerated crotch needed no elaboration.

'Cause I fucking want her like I've wanted nothing else in my life before! "Just a coincidence."

No way would he give her the satisfaction of admitting it outright.

"Coincidence, my ass!" But of course, there was no way he could fool the man who knew him better than he did himself.

Tugging him closer, Prince Caldwell managed to keep his tight hold on Ylianor while whispering in his ear, "You're about to explode simply watching her goddamn ass."

At the words, Chris's equipment became even stiffer than before, if at all possible, and he could not stand his pants' extreme constriction.

"So, why don't you do us all a favor and take it now?" Duncan stroking the swollen bulge from above the fabric was making him dizzy. "Before I forget, I'm in a sharing mood and that she's my slave?"

"If that's the case . . ." Tossing his clothes aside and impaling that narrow asshole of hers was one and the same. "No use wasting more time!"

Better yet, he went for it as though it was ready for him.

Which it was not, considering how cramped it felt.

Her problem, not his, though he did like how she tightened everything from the pain of his possession.

Given his tautness, it had taken just one minor adjustment

to crack her open like a nutshell.

To reach her guts, mostly.

Duncan crashing in his behind spun things so far out of proportions that Chris was sure none of it would last for any meaningful length of time.

Still, he put up the semblance of a fight, pumping her viciously. Glad that his lover's powerful slams provided double the impact force. Already his ass had become as large as when those two fools of Brome and Shydan had taken it together, which left him to wonder how one man alone could pull it off so effortlessly.

It was simply uncanny. The way Prince Caldwell fucked him was something so otherworldly that there was no comparison possible. Not even two cocks taking him at once gave him quite the same sensations or the fulfillment he got from just one cock. One very particular and skilled cock if he had to say it all.

The way Duncan moved in his ass had no equals. Nowhere else had anybody ever fucked him like the dark-haired prince. Not even Arthur.

Everything was only getting more scorching with his own beast embedded to the balls in the most confined space ever. As much as he hated to admit it, he had missed her almost as much as he had Duncan.

Had missed everything about her, especially that way she had of heightening his pleasure whenever he was stuck in her ass. Maybe because she reacted to the pain he inflicted on purpose. Just too bad, she always managed to turn it into pure bliss.

This time was no exception, however much he had stepped up the tempo blowing her butt to bits.

"You weren't kidding when you said you wanted to kill her," the prince's raspy breath snapped his attention back to something that wasn't his body's extreme pleasure.

"I wish." Of course, his lover would have no problem determining she had overcome any sort of pain. "But your damn princess isn't any good for that, either."

"You can't win them all." His breath short, Duncan seemed about to reach the finishing line.

"I could still punish her like she deserves." On spotting her wrist sliding down her belly, he tried to grab it.

But the infuriating witch was quicker. Her hand disappeared between her legs before he had the chance to prevent it.

He was about to wrench it out when he felt her burst. "Fuck you, slave!"

At her first swell, she shuddered like there would be no tomorrow.

"Too late, Angel." The ragged breath sounded too smug for Chris's taste. "She got you."

On and on in perfect synch with her scream, her ass clenched him on every side. So fiercely, she might as well have severed his stick from its root, had he not spilled his very essence at that moment.

Just like Duncan was doing all over his guts.

CHAPTER TWENTY-THREE

"That was . . ." *Fucking awesome!*

Still reeling from the shattering force of his orgasm, Chris was thinking of the most appropriate word that would not give the smug witch any satisfaction, when the new knock had Prince Caldwell vacating his ass and opening the door.

Full tray in hand, the servant arranged everything on the table before turning to leave again.

"Thanks, Colin." Approaching, Duncan scrutinized his handiwork. "By the way, I need to speak to Lady Hurst after I'm done."

"I'll ask her if she wants to receive you." This sounded like another of those goddamn rules Cecilia was so fond of, to the point of obsession. "If she consents, I'll take you to her."

"All right," the prince agreed. "You ask her, then wait for my call."

"Sure will." After an exaggerated bow, the man left.

"So, the next item on the agenda is to confront dear Ceci." Chris drew the obvious conclusion as he unscrewed his cock from her ass.

Which was a real shame, for he was still as hard as before and would have gone for a second round, had his empty stomach not growled in protest, forcing him to grab a seat.

"We might as well." Following his example, Duncan settled on the chair next to his, at the head of the table. Ylianor chose the side opposite Chris. "Since she must already know what we're here for." Pulling the teapot to him, he poured the scalding brew in three cups. "Maybe, we'll also discover why she took it in the first place."

"Yeah, why did she go to all the trouble of stealing it?" It did not make any sense to him. "What does she plan to do with it?"

"Why is the damn thing so important anyway?" Duncan divided the cups between the three of them.

"We'll find out soon enough." Grabbing a plate, Chris began piling it up with whatever came under his hand. "Though it would help knowing where she keeps the damn thing."

"It's probably in her room." Dish in hand, his lover was also filling it. "Right, Princess?" He handed it to her.

"Hem . . ." On taking the full plate, an adorable blush spread on her lovely face, as though she had not expected him to be so mindful of her needs.

Which goddamn him, he was.

"I'm not sure if it was her room." After setting the plate in front of her, she did not dive into it. "When I came up from the pools, I passed a room where I thought I felt something calling me." Instead, she went through every single piece as if looking for something specific. "I also felt David's presence, so I figured it must be the place where they keep the pyramid." Having evidently spotted it, she uncovered a piece of a particular cheese and took her first bite. "I couldn't tell you exactly where that room is." To think that both he and Duncan were halfway through with their food. "It's such a maze in here. It'll be difficult to find."

"Not at all." The prince's firm tone held no doubt he would succeed in his intent. "What color was the door?"

"It was gray." There was no hesitation in her tone.

"Then, we know exactly where the pyramid is." Duncan spooned up the last of his beans before wolfing down a boiled egg. "If memory holds, only Cecilia's room has a gray door."

"I hadn't noticed there was a color code in here." Chris, instead, was hard at work on the delicious eggplants and peppers with a generous piece of freshly baked bread.

"That's because there are too many of them." Duncan frowned as though trying to remember them all. "Blue is for significant rooms. Green is for average rooms. Red is reserved for slaves and servants. Black is for service rooms like a kitchen or mess hall. The only gray door I remember is for her room."

"So, what's the plan?" Figured that the impossible woman would keep her home as organized as her mind was. "We barge in and ask her to give us back the pyramid?"

"Even if she did, we could never put it back in its place," she argued. "We don't have that kind of Virt."

"While she does?" Chris simply refused to believe it. "Is she more powerful than the three of us combined?" This was even more preposterous.

"It's not a question of how much, rather of what kind," Duncan was quick to set the record straight. "Since they took something from the structure, I'm assuming we're talking about a Virt that moves objects."

"Not Cecilia's for sure." Chris was adamant. "I'm betting on David." However minimal his consideration for the man, he might just have what it took to pull it off somehow.

"That would certainly explain why I've had trouble read-ing him." Her plate practically as full as when Duncan had handed it to her, all she had touched was the cheese.

The same kind she had worked so hard to uncover from under the stack of food the prince had piled on it.

"But I doubt he did it all by himself." She nibbled that piece of cheese as though it were the most mouthwatering thing she ever ate in her entire life. "Whatever her Virt, it must have joined with David's, or that heart would still be in place."

"This just means we'll need to work together to put it back." His phase mate took a second serving of green beans and mushrooms.

"Can't wait," Chris growled. "Couldn't imagine anything less exciting than taking a trip with the two of them to the Nephis Valley." His stomach revolted at the mere thought. "With someone who would love nothing better than to kill your princess."

"I know she would." Her eyes became huge. "What I can't understand is why."

"She's jealous." Devouring more hotcakes, Chris looked at her. "She and David must've been lovers for who knows how long."

"Yeah, and I wonder why he never breathed a word about it." Duncan stared at Chris as if he could supply a viable clue. "Like he never did about his Virt."

"'Cause he was ashamed." For him, the answer was obvious. "You know what a stickler for class distinctions he is." The mere notion was ridiculous, of course. "Screwing a noblewoman isn't exactly something he'd be proud of, or that he'd tell his adored master." An icy snarl twisted his lips. "On top of it, he must've told her about your new stable keeper." He paused to gulp down a generous sip of hot brew. "Or maybe Cecilia found out by herself. Either way, you're much more to his taste." He cocked his head to her. "Not to mention his level—"

"Not that again," she flared, getting angry all of a sudden.

He would have, too, were someone to remind his lover's aristocratic sense that she was still a servant, despite everything that had happened.

"Not my fault, he'd never consider Cecilia pledge material." This clarified the whole thing of the masculine woman's jealousy. "She must know it herself by now, or why else would she have given her right arm just to know your slave's name?"

"I thought I had been clear about that." Prince Caldwell seemed surprised that Cecilia would have kept insisting.

"Not by a long shot, lover." Chris set his records straight. "She asked just about everyone in that goddamn chamber if they knew who Ylianor was and what was her relation to you." He gulped down the last of the hot brew. "The fact that no one could answer made her only more persistent and downright mad," he was happy to report. "Which, to me, is a sure sign that she considers your princess a rival."

"Nothing new, then," the contemptible witch quipped. "I already survived one deluded fool who considers me a rival—"

"Fuck you, bitch!" The nerve of the woman was sheer incredible!

And someone still had to tell him where she found the spunk to get back at him every fucking time!

"I never considered you anything but a pastime that my lover will soon grow tired of." Or so he ardently wished. "Not his fault if his unfortunate taste for your despicable gender has made him overlook your many shortcomings." He glared at her. "Were it up to me, I'd have set you straight from the start, punishing you the way you deserve—"

"That's exactly what I did the whole Game long!" Grabbing her neck and dragging her to the ground took Duncan only one second.

Even less to feed her Chris's piece.

"Sure, and I suppose that kissing her was another punishment, right?" Getting angry, he disregarded how good she had become at sucking him.

"It absolutely was." Increasing the pressure, Duncan forced her mouth to slide to his balls.

And gag on them.

"Or did I forget to mention that I forbade her from coming the whole time we were there?" Now, her head bobbing in synch with her hands over the whole of his engorged rod was a welcome addition.

"You what?" His cock went slab of marble in a second flat. She choked.

Not before she tried pulling back, something that such an iron hold did not allow her to do. He clamped her neck over what had become an absolute monster, stiffened out of proportion from her loud gurgles and inability to breathe.

Served her right, anyway. Her and that fucking nerve of hers of having conquered a foothold in his lover's heart.

"You heard right." Setting a steady rhythm, Duncan snapped her head up and down. "It's called orgasm deprivation." She had no choice besides swallowing the whole of his long thick length. "It's the reason why she was so irresistible." Best of all, he controlled her intakes in a way that would end up smothering her in the end.

Which was totally fine.

"Why everybody on that damn floor wanted to fuck her like crazy and couldn't get enough of her." He pushed so hard that she jumped back despite his clamping clutch. "It's what made her special and different, had not her bare cunt already singled her out."

Right!

How to forget that exceedingly naked pussy of hers?

Even those dimwits of the Arthur boys had taken due notice and commented on it! And the stars only knew how little they cared for cunts.

"But what made her deliciously tense was that she couldn't come." As his phase mate slammed her down again, she sputtered from lack of air. "Ever."

"Did she obey?" However, swimming his senses, Chris knew things were not quite adding up. "She's such a slut that I doubt she managed to restrain herself—"

"Let's say it wasn't easy." Duncan licked his lips as though thinking back at what he had her endure. "But she managed it except for one time when she came despite my orders."

"What did you do?" Gripping Duncan's hand, Chris increased the pressure and decreased her margins for breathing.

"What do you think I did?" A snarl twisted the full lips.

"Punish her." Realizing all control was in his hands, Chris obliged her to take the whole of his engorged erection, though it stuck beyond her throat.

None of her choking moved him to pity or convinced him to release her if not the second before she would have suffocated on his piece.

"I did more than that." Pressing full lips against his ear, the prince whispered, "I had her punished by the masters fucking her. Even if she disobeyed me just once, I played it like she came more times, just to have them discipline her over and over." His hot breath tickled. "And they were real vicious, blowing that magnificent ass to bits to teach her a lesson in manners."

"They must've been real hurtful." The mere thought sent his juice speeding to the exit.

"Let's say she couldn't sit for hours after they were done with that tantalizing ass of hers." Duncan shoved her head so far down that Chris's piece almost made it to her stomach.

This spelled the end of the second round for him.

Unstoppable, his load shot down her throat.

"Uh, I just got to crack it again." Still as rigid as though he had not come twice already, he lifted her and brought her to the couch. "While you can have mine." Pure provocation on his part, he wriggled it as he fell on the plush cushions. "'Cause I'm sure you got fed up with hers."

If his lover did not rush to confirm, he still made no objections. Just went to him and grabbed the witch from under her armpits.

"I suppose you won't make her come this time." The prince chuckled as he flipped her around to face him.

"No way will she be able to do it," he snarled malevolently.

Feet firmly on the ground, he straightened his beefy piece to center the target in between her buttocks. After Duncan plunged her down, her backside stretched all together, all at once.

"Not like this." Instead of savoring the cramped feel of her delicious ass ring, Chris gripped her arms and twisted them behind her back.

"If you think that works . . ." Duncan's dubious tone did not sound too confident.

"It will, provided you aren't too good to her," he retorted.

Now, drilling her guts, he slid downward to invite the prince to take him.

"And that you ignore her like she deserves." Cruel and indifferent, he just wanted her to pay for all the gossip he had to sit through, unable to turn it off in any way.

Unable to stop thinking and desiring her, either. As though he had fallen under a spell, like his lover before him.

"Don't worry, Angel." Acting as though he could care less about her, Duncan knelt and went straight for his ass. "Like you said, I've had enough of her to last me a while." One merciless blow and his gigantic equipment sank to the root, enlarging the space to its convenience.

Chris would have drooled from the sheer pleasure of having him reclaim what belonged to him by default, had his perceptions not been the prey of her maddening intoxication.

"Enough of her worthless hide to last me a good long while." That Duncan was challenging her was apparent.

"It was about time you found out." He doubled the dose.

To make things worse for her, he tightened his hold in the most hurtful manner possible.

"That there's nothing special about her." *Except for her Virt.* Which was indeed out of the ordinary, but had no place as far as sex was concerned. "That she's nothing but an insignificant slave." He enjoyed so much this picking on her that his tempo accelerated.

She did not protest.

Not even in her master's head.

He was pretty sure about that because he was getting better at perceiving their silent way of communicating.

"No, she isn't any good for that, either." Duncan rammed the whole of his inches inside the butt that swallowed them completely. "'Cause I've seen far better slaves."

"Yeah." No use denying a self-evident truth. "With a much better ass than what I'm forced to fuck." Up and down, his hips moved in perfect synch with Duncan's shoves. Best of all, her ass was now so large his balls slapped her buttocks every time he impaled her to the hilt.

But, in spite of his treating her like a mere object, she was not crumbling. Not begging for impossible mercy. Not asking him to slow down any.

In fact, he had the sneaky suspicion she was liking it way more than what he had intended for her.

Glancing down on her puffed-up slit, the heavy honeydew coating it was a sure sign she was losing it regardless of his efforts to the contrary.

"We could always have her just watch," Duncan offered.

It was so out of context for the prince that Chris wondered why he had not noticed it sooner. That he was daring her to come, pushing her to that extreme edge he must have played with her all night long.

He would have agreed to the prince's suggestion, had not the sperm risen without control. The way his cock had penetrated to her guts was more than enough to convince him of the need to spill it all. Pressing on the tip of his erection, it exploded without any warning. Or maybe, denying her the very pleasure coursing through his every fiber had driven his load to the exit.

With his phase mate shoving twice, then pulling out and spraying her buttocks, things could not be more perfect.

Too bad, it lacked the completion he had grown used to ever since he had to accommodate her in his sex with his lover. That way, their energy had of joining and becoming one was the most incredible thing of all, and he missed it. Had missed it all through the past night. It was something so unique that belonged to the three of them alone. Something he could not replicate with anybody else.

Which was nothing like what she was going through, her body screaming for the release he had just deprived her.

"Ready for round four?" Without giving him time to re-cover, Duncan unscrewed her butt and carried her to the bed. "I get the feeling you haven't had enough."

"What if I did?" Chris challenged, unwilling to give him the satisfaction.

"Suit yourself." Shrugging as though it made no difference to him, the prince arranged her flat on the mattress. Raising her legs, he was about to plunge into her. "I need something more—"

"Me, too." So, what if this was just another trap?

Truth was—he needed to hear her scream to quench the deep burning for her that scorched his insides.

"But her ass is mine now." Taunting black eyes, Duncan lifted her legs some more. Centering the puckered edges, he flung her rear channel wide open.

"I'll retake her mouth." Reluctantly, he straddled her, and his massive piece fell in her gaping cavity.

Just a few sucks and his senses began spinning again.

She was good, no question about it. Not just because now she could hold his entire length for a good number of seconds before choking on it. She had mastered his only lesson, deliv-ered on the shores of that faraway lake, and perfected a style all her own, which he was coming to love despite his demeaning it.

Plus, having Prince Caldwell on the opposite side, blowing her ass to bits, was tipping him overboard. Without hiding anything, his lover had escalated everything to incendiary, for them as well as for her.

Good thing, he could intervene this time.

Reaching over, he pinched her clit. So ruthlessly, she jolted from the pain.

"The deal is that you don't get to come," he hissed threateningly. "Remember?"

Her crushed expression made his juice rise fast.

"Put your arms behind your back," he ordered thickly.

This would take care of her once and for all.

When she complied, her discomfort was evident. But he concentrated on his pleasure alone and came in her mouth when one of Duncan's fiercest shoves split her in two.

No sooner had he started unloading that also his phase mate climaxed, jerking an uncontrollable piece that splashed his come all over her belly and breasts.

For the fifth round, he sprawled on the mattress and impaled her not-so-narrow rear sheath. Duncan had flattened her back down on him and had gone for his enlarged back ring.

But the absence of her orgasm was driving him crazy.

This time, he knew that he would not succeed in coming was she not right along with him.

"What's the matter, Angel?" How the man had managed to pick up his sensations was a matter of speculation. "Getting tired of the slave?" Banging his considerable stiff size inside him, he pressed his weight on both him and her at once. "Want me to get rid of her?"

"No, I . . ." His mouth dry, the only thing he wanted her to do was to come.

Already, he felt her quiver under the pressure building

with the force of something wild blocked by his cruel way of treating her. Yet, this attitude was also the reason it was mounting to an explosive climax that would soon be unstoppable.

"Or is this treating her like an object that you can't handle?" Biting, Duncan bent on his ear. "'Cause she's so fucking open and defenseless that you could do just about anything to her." He puffed hot air on Chris's neck. "Except make her come." The long black raven hair fluttered at the same rhythm of his drills to the guts. "Or maybe that's all you want." The liquid black eyes flashed. "Am I wrong?"

"The gods help me." A groan escaped his lips. "It's all I want!"

"Your wish is my command." Faster than lightning, Prince Caldwell pulled out of his snug backside and stuffed her pussy to her ears.

So, she shattered.

Literally.

With his cock firmly embedded in her ass, Chris felt the convulsions shaking her to pieces. The frenzied coils clenched her every fiber and did not abate until they came out of her mouth. But, once her scream started, her climax intensified and sucked his monster beyond her guts. Same thing she was doing with Duncan's beast. Only, with him, it was to the throat.

Not that either of them had any time to complain. Both of them were flooding her front and back with surprisingly abundant jets.

Next thing he knew, she grabbed their essences and blended them. Gone the barriers, he felt her as close as only his lover had ever been.

Unlike all the previous times, he did not fight her.

Not at all.

Welcomed it as a matter of fact, if not downright craved it.

Because for once, this seemed so right that he did not want it to end.

When unfortunately it did, the angry black cloud was gone. Disintegrated. So effectively, he felt spent and sated as he had not once during his whole night's worth of wild sex.

Which would have been sheer incredible, had it not been so absolutely frightening. For who would have ever guessed she was the key to his true fulfillment?

CHAPTER TWENTY-FOUR

"Welcome, Prince, it's quite an honor." Standing in a spacious blue living room with two couches facing one another and divided by a low table, Cecilia bowed.

On stepping inside her room, the first thing that caught Duncan's attention was how rigid she looked, to the point of being uncomfortable.

She's agitated all right, Ylianor confirmed. *So much that her lights are trying to flutter.* She giggled in his head. *Only she won't let them.*

Shut up, Princess. He tried to sound stern so that he would not crack up as her pun deserved.

"I must admit I didn't expect your visit." Cecilia's dark red robe emphasized her black hair and pale complexion, making her look more imposing. "Not with the entire delegation, including the one who has no voice."

As always, she was too formal for her own good.

"We're not here to play games." Annoyed, Duncan went to Ylianor and covered her with a robe he had brought from his room. "As of now, we're officially out of the Game."

This is undoubtedly a first, my love. Wrapping herself inside the warm fabric, Ylianor gave him the sense she was cold.

Yeah, but don't get used to it. Now, why did his every instinct scream at him to take her in his arms? And hold her until time stood still? *You know how I prefer you.* He suppressed a grin. *And dressed, isn't it.*

"Don't fret, lover." Chris's hot whisper in his ear caught him off guard. "The sooner we're out of here, the sooner you can have her naked again."

Sure, his angel was plain incredible when it came to reading his mind, but this was bordering the ridiculous.

Not that he could say anything about it right now, so he just ignored the comment and returned his focus on Cecilia.

"Please ask David to join us," he ordered.

If she hesitated, it was just for a fraction of a second. Or for the time it took her to knock on a closed-door behind her.

After a moment, his valet and friend opened it and came forward.

"Good afternoon, Prince." An apologetic expression crossed his face.

"Hello, David." Squeezing his arms, a million questions that were neither the time nor the place to discuss crowded his mind.

"Lord Templeton, good evening." David went all ceremonial before relaxing his stance the moment he swung his head in his princess's direction. "Good to see you, Ylianor." His hazel eyes lit up in pleasure.

Duncan could not help the jealous twitch of his heart.

Which he quickly silenced, for it had nothing to do with his task. Or with his business, since she was not his property, however much he felt she belonged to him.

"Hello, David," Ylianor's soft voice could not hide her gladness at seeing him.

"Now, Ceci, I'm sure you know why we're here." Taking a hold on himself, he blocked out the unimportant details. "Where is it?"

"In my room," Cecilia's tone sounded strained.

"I'll get it," David offered as he disappeared inside the same room he had just exited.

He returned with a small triangular pyramid made of some sort of bluestone that he set on the table.

"Please sit." Cecilia gestured to the couches. "To observe it better."

Duncan accommodated at the center of the large sofa, his gaze already at work in scrutinizing the object.

"Is this it?" Upon sinking on his left-hand side, Chris's blue-gray eyes brimmed with curiosity. "Why is it so special?"

"You tell me." Sitting on the couch opposite his, Cecilia pointed at it.

That the woman would never stop playing games was something he was just beginning to discover.

"I suppose it has something to do with the pyramid itself." To humor her, he peered more closely at it. "Not with the entire structure from which you stole it."

David wincing visibly as he sat next to Cecilia was a true sign that he regretted his action.

He sure does. Picking up his sensations without any effort, Ylianor sat on his right-hand side. *And he'd take it back in a heartbeat if he could.*

Not a possibility. He pursed his lips. *Unfortunately for him.*

Catching a strange shift in the pyramid with a corner of an eye, he concentrated back on it, hardly able to fathom what he saw.

The bluestone exterior was melting away to leave the place to glass-like walls.

No, it did not change shape. Still a triangular-based pyramid, only its outside coating turned from stone to glass in the bat of an eyed. It was like a window opening upon a world Duncan had no idea existed at all.

Or so it felt on glimpsing at what was beyond the permeable boundaries.

For the pyramid hid a core made of a small twirling sphere suspended in its center.

This was one unique piece. Composed of tiny shiny plaques that moved up and down, each ticked and hummed at various speeds and sounds.

Same humming, he remembered hearing in the Nephis Valley.

More disturbingly yet, the whole thing looked like some kind of mechanism directing everything.

This was fascinating and impressive, also considering that the candlelight filtering through the glass shell remained trapped inside. Bouncing on every side, it created colors where none had existed before it beamed out in the form of a rainbow ray.

Impossible as it sounded, this thing felt like it had a life and a mind of its own!

"What the fuck? It's alive!" Of course, his angel summed it up for everyone's sake with his usual gift of synthesis and brilliant intuition. "I've never seen anything even remotely similar to . . ." He obviously tried finding a proper name for it. "This." And failed.

Like Duncan would have.

"What exactly do you see?" Smug smile stamped all over her face, Cecilia glared at Chris.

"A glass pyramid with a ticking sphere inside," the angel supplied.

"That hums, too," Duncan added.

"Don't hear any humming," Chris objected. "But the pieces seem to move fast as if they're dancing to some kind of tune."

"I don't hear any sounds." Cecilia exchanged glances with David. "Do you, darling?"

David shook his head without averting his gaze from the object.

I don't hear any humming, either, the princess breathed in his head. *But those plaques whirling around seem to be dancing like the demon says.*

"What's important is that we're all seeing the same thing." Cecilia looked around the table before stopping her focus on him. "A sphere made of tiny pieces that move inside this pyramid. They go up and down, apparently without any cause or pattern."

"What's its purpose?" Shifting position, Chris leaned closer to the pyramid.

"I still don't know." Cecilia shrugged in frustration. "The only thing I'm sure of is that not everyone sees the inner core."

"What do you mean?" If he knew anything of Cecilia Hurst, he would have bet that this had something to do with the reason she had taken the pyramid in the first place.

"That the others I've shown it see it only as a blue pyramid." Cecilia sounded sure of it. "Nobody mentioned anything about a sphere, and Rowena even went as far as saying this shade of blue clashes with the furniture."

"Maybe, they just didn't notice it," Chris retorted.

"No, I think people simply don't see it," Cecilia insisted. "And I'll prove it." Reaching over, she pulled a bell. "With Colin's help."

At the man's knock, she raised her voice, "Come in."

"Milady." Entering the room, the servant bowed low. "Command."

"Please, you should do me a favor." Going all cool and sophisticated, she reclined on her seat. "We disagree on the composition of this pyramid." She gestured at the table. "How would you describe it?"

Taking a step forward, Colin looked closer. "Can I touch it?"

"Yes," Cecilia encouraged him. "You may."

Picking it up, he weighed it, turned it around and stroked each side until he put it back on the table.

"It's a three-sided pyramid made of some sort of bluestone . . ." His eyebrows furrowed from his intense concentration. "I've never seen the likes of it before." He frowned as though to get his facts straight. "It's also surprisingly light, considering its material."

"Nothing more?" Cecilia provoked deliberately.

"No." The man's brow creased in concentration. "I don't see anything else."

"Thank you, Colin." A spark of satisfaction lit her dark eyes. "You've been most helpful." She beamed at him. "Now, you may go."

After the servant left, she turned to him and the angel. "What did I tell you?"

"He could've been lying," Chris argued.

"No, he wasn't," Ylianor's soft voice was barely audible. "He clearly saw only a piece of bluestone."

"Well, well, we have an empathic slave." Cecilia snarled spitefully. "Don't we?"

Which irked every one of his nerves.

"Her name is Ylianor," he rectified coldly.

"Whatever." Cecilia's wave of dismissal did not fool him one bit.

Since he had just provided the information, she had yearned for the entire nightlong.

"So, that was what your game was all about last night." Evidently connecting all her dots, Cecilia glanced at him maliciously. "Why you seemed to have more fun than anyone there."

Impossible to miss the load of envy and jealousy clogging her voice. All directed at his princess, even if she was taking pains to avoid looking at her. The angel gripping his thigh was all the confirmation he needed.

"Have to admit it was more than I expected." Just to spite her, he circled Ylianor's waist and pulled her closer. "And I haven't thanked her enough for it."

It was my pleasure. Snuggling closer and melting all over, she raised her gaze to his face.

He intercepted it, getting lost in her green depths. Drowning in her essence was more like it.

A mistake for sure, for he could not tear himself away from

her and the burning images flashing in his mind.

"Hem . . ." Cecilia clearing her throat was an attempt at recapturing his attention. "Whatever happened during your private game has nothing to do with this pyramid." Kind of obvious, she was sorry to have brought up the matter. "Or with the reason we can see what others can't."

"That's because we've got powers," the angel snorted disdainfully. *Though for the life of me, I'd have never guessed you had one.*

If he did not say it, Duncan had no problems reading it in the scornful blue-gray gaze while rushing to prevent him from blurting it out, "You know about power?"

"Not really." Hesitant, Cecilia latched on to David's gaze. "But I'm beginning to."

"You think you have power?" Of course, Chris would not stand for it.

Not that Duncan blamed him any. Who could ever qualify as having any Virt when in the presence of a towering pyre of pure fire that could destroy or heal just about anything?

Unable to hold his tongue, Chris sneered sarcastically, "What kind of power exactly?"

"I . . ." As though feeling the flames licking her very spirit, Cecilia had enough sense to lower her gaze. "I don't think I have any special powers except perhaps that of a logical mind." To him, it qualified as some sort of Virt, however different from his angel's.

All of a sudden, he understood why he had been attracted to it from the first time he had set eyes on her.

"That can solve or create complicated puzzles." Happy with her rendering, Cecilia looked to him for support.

"Isn't that what your game is all about?" Now that he thought of it, her Virt could come in handy for so much more than just sex.

"I guess so." Instantaneously bolder, Cecilia leaned in his direction. "I trap people in a logical illusion, which for some becomes more real than reality itself." She smiled sadly. "Which is nothing like what David can do—"

"Move objects with his mind," Ylianor provided in a soft tone.

"Your slave is very acute." Surprised, Cecilia cocked an eyebrow.

"I told you her name's Ylianor," Duncan reiterated.

Her persistence in demeaning his princess was just further proof of her jealousy.

"Yeah, whatever." Turning an icy hard stare on him, she twisted her lips in a snarl. "But I doubt you need her to reach a conclusion you have probably figured out on your own." Her focus strayed to the arm still clamped around Ylianor's waist.

Which told him in no uncertain terms how little Cecilia could stand the princess for being the perfect slave that she would never be. Like his angel had so rightly guessed from the start.

"You're wrong, Ceci." Determined to prove just how much the princess meant to him, he tightened his grip on her pliant body already flattened against him. "Her perceptions aren't just invaluable in defining my own. She's also the one teaching me about power." *Another thing I haven't thanked you enough for, Princess.*

He just had to catch her stunning green eyes before he could continue.

"I had no idea it could be such a complicated issue." *Nor such agonizing closeness.*

Clutching Ylianor's hand, he squeezed it hard and felt her heart liquefied worse than before.

Then, his voice became stern as he addressed David, "Which doesn't excuse you from having kept silent about it."

"I'm sorry, sir." David's face reddened all over. "I would've said something. Only I didn't know where to begin." He hung his head. "Plus, it's something I discovered so recently that I had no idea—"

"None of us did, darling, thanks to Arthur." Cecilia was quick to jump to his defense.

"What's that supposed to mean?" Chris's growl had a threatening undertone that warned Duncan his angel would not take any slander about the leader.

"That he keeps secrets and hinders people's pursuit of knowledge," Cecilia spat.

"He's entitled to." Barely holding it together, Chris seemed ready to strike at her. "He's the leader, remember?"

"Hard to forget when he keeps the council in the dark about the crucial matters," Cecilia rebuffed.

"He does the best he can," Chris retorted. "Considering the idiots he has to put up with."

That Cecilia was among the *idiots* Chris referred to was evident from the sheer loathing and contempt oozing from his words.

"How dare you?" Of course, Cecilia had done the math, too. "You're not even in the council, yet you dare judge us—"

"I'm not the one judging you, Lady Hurst." Full of scorn, Chris snapped on the aggressive, "Arthur is."

"You'll never get over your bad habit of defending him." Piqued beyond words, Cecilia was fast losing that cool exterior of hers. "You're just like your father, Lord Templeton." With a visible effort, she calmed down enough to breathe normally. "Always defending Arthur, even when he's wrong." She shook her head. "Like when he denied me permission to study the structure in the Nephis Valley."

"Is that why you felt authorized to steal this particular piece?" Chris bit back.

Which got Cecilia more enraged than before. "I didn't—"

"All right, enough!" Raising his voice, he glared at both his angel and her. "This sort of attitude isn't going to get us anywhere, while I have every intention of understanding what has happened." He shifted his attention to Cecilia alone. "I'll play fair with you, Ceci, and I expect you to do the same." Not waiting for her consent, he pressed his point. "As you probably guessed, Arthur sent us to retrieve this pyramid and put it back where it belongs." He glanced briefly at the rainbow rays spreading a soft glow in the room's half-darkness and at the sphere still twirling inside the glass. "And we're going to carry out his order." He made it sound like there was no margin for appeals. "But before we do, I'd like to know why you took it in the first place."

"'Cause I think it's related to our way of life." Throwing back her shoulders, Cecilia seemed ready to get into a fight to uphold her beliefs.

"How?" Very interested, he locked his gaze on her.

"I have a theory." She returned his look. "It starts with a comparison between animals and humans."

"I believe they're different." Chris chuckled. "With a few exceptions."

"Not as different as you'd think, Lord Templeton." She frowned in concentration. "True, we don't fight or kill one another like they do. But we eat, drink, have sex —"

"No, we have more." Chris smacked his lips. "'Cause we have lots more sex than they ever will."

"We do." Cecilia's lips curved downward. "We push it to such extreme limits that I can't help wondering why we need so much sex in our lives."

However ridiculous the question considering where it came from, Duncan did not feel like laughing.

Nor did anybody else.

"'Cause it's fun." Chris had no doubt. "And I don't see anything wrong with it."

"Or why you think this pyramid has something to do with it." This still escaped him.

"Before I answer, Prince, let me return to the differences between animals and humans." Evidently relishing her spotlight, Cecilia shifted on her seat. "As you know, we both use sex to ensure reproduction. Just like them, we have the heat. But unlike them, we have children only if we —"

"Pledge." Again, Chris completed the information.

"Which also means that humans can't reproduce without a ritual formula." Cecilia trained her gaze on him and Chris alone. "Don't you find it odd?"

"If my father were alive, he'd argue your point." The pain crushing his heart reminded him that it was still a touchy subject. "Since he believed the princess was his child." He pressed Ylianor to him, so Cecilia would not doubt who the princess was. "Though born of a woman he hadn't pledged."

"Really?" Cecilia's head swung in David's direction, enough to suggest they had talked about it. *That's why she was so curious about you, Princess.*

No, only because she's still very interested in you, Ylianor contradicted.

Nonsense! He refused to believe the woman would harbor any kind of feeling for him. *She has David now.*

Do you think that could ever be an adequate replacement? Ylianor's ironic tone reverberated in his head.

"Is that a fact?" Cecilia requested. "Or simply his belief?"

"I'd say the latter, Ceci." *And thank the stars for it.*

For he could never consider the princess like a sister.

Not now.

Not ever.

"As you said, no pledge, no babies." He summed up the fundamental cornerstone of their way of living.

"Exactly, Prince." Cecilia nodded. "Humans need the pledge to have the heat and then conceive." She pursed her lips. "Too bad, none of it is natural."

"You think this thing . . ." Chris gestured at the pyramid. "Is to blame?"

"I think this can explain," Cecilia huffed as though the angel was too thickheaded to understand. "'Cause it comes from where pledges take place —"

"The Nephis Valley," the princess mumbled.

"Precisely." Cecilia did not even glance Ylianor's way, never wavering her gaze from either him or Chris. "But how can a few words have as much power as to unleash life's creative force?" It was clear she had given this considerable thought. "The only way it makes sense to me is that it must have to do with the structure itself. After I overheard Arthur talk about some sort of Elected Group controlling it, I became convinced that more than mere words are at work when we pledge."

I wonder if it also explains the demon's madness of the senses and the uncontrollable urges in the Nephis Valley. Ylianor suppressed a giggle.

Shut up, Princess. Duncan laughed. *I doubt he'd appreciate your humor.*

"Need I remind you that it was just damn witchcraft?" Not giving him time to recover from his angel's low whisper, Chris straightened and confronted Cecilia once more, "But why this particular pyramid out of the many making up the structure?"

"'Cause only this one contains a sphere inside." Cecilia checked the object in front of her. "All the others are empty."

"'Cause only this is the heart," the princess repeated what she had already told him and Chris.

Something she had picked up from the structure itself during the night they had spent examining it.

"Or technological birth control." Chris's sarcasm did not escape Duncan's ears.

"Which is impossible, since we have no technological or scientific advancement in our world." Cecilia's earnest tone was trying to drive her point across. "Sure, no one gets hungry. No one knows any sort of violence."

Duncan glancing at his angel would have had grounds for disagreeing.

Which was so beside the point he did not even linger on it. Simply switched his focus back on Cecilia and her so very logical arguments.

"Everything is set at birth, our position as much as the tasks we'll be asked to do. And we're fine with it," she spurned. "Satisfied with peaceful and uneventful lives as though they were the best deal we could ever get."

"What's wrong with that?" Duncan defied.

"Nothing, except I don't think it's natural." She lifted a shoulder. "Even if I can't say exactly how this thing works, I believe it influences our sex." She took a deep breath. "If it explains the heat, why couldn't it also be the reason we have a phase? Or any of our feelings—"

"Love, too?" That Chris did not like the idea was kind of a given.

"Why not?" Cecilia rationalized. "That's why I took it, to study it and verify my theory."

"But you haven't done much of either, right?" Duncan was sure that, if she had, there would be fewer conjectures in her reasoning.

"Haven't had too much time for it," Cecilia admitted reluctantly. "I'm also not sure how to go about it, what to do or—"

"Have you tried stopping the sphere from spinning?" Chris suggested, looking specifically at David.

"No, Lord Templeton, I haven't touched the thing since we took it." Shifting uncomfortably, David heaved. "Technically, I think I could try to move a few of the pieces around, but . . ." He glanced at Duncan, unable to hide the emotions he felt. "Prince, I've never wanted to do anything against you, and I regret my foolish act to steal something that didn't belong to us and now—"

"That's all right," Duncan was quick to set his mind at ease. "If I was surprised when the princess read your presence in the Nephis Valley, now I know you were only helping a friend." He clamped David's hand. "Like you've done with me countless times. So, I can't blame you." He let go of David. "I wish you had told me sooner, but I understand it wouldn't have been easy."

"Believe me, I tried." Deeply touched, David lowered his gaze. "Only didn't know where to begin." Feeling more confident, he raised his gaze again. "Thing is I was wrong, so now I'll do whatever you command to set things right again."

'Cause whatever he feels for her, Cecilia will never prevail against you, Ylianor's husky breath floated in his mind. *You're the only thing essential in his life.*

Can't say the experience was all bad. He suppressed a smile. *I think he learned a lesson about trust.*

So did you. Her conclusion was inevitable.

Oh, I've always known I could trust him. No matter what had happened, David remained the precious reference point he had grown used to over the long years spent with him. *But he needed to know he could trust himself.*

"Ahem . . ." Cecilia cleared her throat. "David could move a few plaques for a second, simply to see what happens."

I'm sure it was a calculated risk on Cecilia's part. She looked adorable when hard at work on a new thought. *Even if she must've known, David would never betray you.*

"After a second, he'll put them back, right, darling?" Cecilia sounded pleading and seductive at the same time.

How can you be sure? This he could not figure out on his own.

She knows David loves you. Ylianor chortled as though the notion amused her. *If it were Rowena sitting where you are now, she'd have switched sides in a matter of seconds.*

"Only if the prince agrees." David's steady gaze on his face snapped his priority to the possibilities at his disposal.

"Well . . ." Only natural, he would be intrigued. "I . . ."

"It's too risky, my prince." Something in Ylianor's tone sent a shiver down his spine.

"It would be just for a second, Princess." Against his better judgment, he tried to reassure her that everything would be fine.

"Yes, only for a second." Cecilia pressed her point. "To see what happens. Then, David will put everything back as it is. After all, if I'm right and we are mere puppets, wouldn't you like to know what pulls our strings?"

"I wouldn't if I were you." Ignoring Cecilia, Ylianor's arresting green eyes begged him openly.

"How about that?" Which, of course, got Cecilia furious. "Who'd have thought your slave was just a scared little girl frightened of her own shadow?"

"Stop it, Ceci," David burst. "Her name is Ylianor."

The tender note of caring and the need to protect the princess was so similar to Duncan's own that it went straight to his heart. And quelled that jealous itch that had tormented him ever since catching the two of them in their intimate pose at Black Rose's stables.

"She may have a point." This time, the flash of concern lighting David's hazel eyes was all for him.

"Or she may be wrong." He could not tell why, but something was pushing him to take his chances.

Maybe, the necessity to know more about a world he had taken at face value until Chris and Ylianor had opened so many doors he was still having trouble grappling with them all. Or Arthur's words confirming them, including the many layers he perceived beyond this new surface and that he still had to explore.

Either way, it was time to learn more, like Cecilia advocated.

Mind made up, he nodded in David's direction.

Right after, what looked like a couple of metallic pieces detached from the central body and floated upward.

No, stop him! Ylianor's shout in his head was too late.

For one second, nothing happened.

Then, the pyramid shot a violent burst of light in the princess's direction.

Nooo! Upon hitting her fully, the beam cut off her painful scream.

And things were never the same again.

CHAPTER TWENTY-FIVE

When everything went dark, Ylianor precipitated in a bottomless void.

Down and down she went. Entirely in the blind, she kept falling until she hit the hard ground.

Or what she thought was hard ground.

Point of fact, she could feel nothing.

Not even her body.

If that was most puzzling, it was just the beginning of the strangeness. For wherever she was, she was not in Blue Oasis anymore.

"No," a metallic male voice startled her. "Now, you're here with me, little girl."

"Me who?" She regretted the question the moment she uttered it. "Who are you?" What are you would have been more in order.

For what she sensed in the cold, vast emptiness was dreadful. To the point, it crushed her to the same hard ground that was just a figment of her imagination.

"I am Virtus." Big, dark and oppressive, a tall shape confronted her.

Cloaked in a long black mantel, she could not quite define it human. Not since it had hard metallic stumps where hands should have been. No face, either, save for an oval disc covered by a black hood and sparked by a series of intermittent lights. But what most disturbed her was the lack of eyes. If the ominous red flash crossing the oval disc was their replacement, she was in even bigger trouble than she had initially assessed.

"I am chaos." The loud boom seemed to emphasize his claim. "'Cause I intend to finish the mission I've sworn to carry out." The red light running from one end of what she could not bring herself to call face flashed menacingly.

"No, wait." With an effort, she suppressed the shiver of fear evoked by his mere words. "First, tell me. Where am I?"

Not that she cared a fig about it, just hoped to stall him before the irreparable occurred.

Because it was only a matter of time before it would regardless of her attempts to the contrary.

"Guess," Virtus goaded her on purpose.

If this monster wanted to play games, she was ready for him.

Well, almost.

Truth was — she had no idea where she was. In the darkness was her only certainty, since also the stars had gone dead. The ground, if such it was, gave her the impression of being rocky, warm and . . .

Her heart skipped a beat.

Whatever lay below her was alive.

Abruptly, a flame burst and pierced the darkness just as a swell snaked through the ground and ripped it wide open. Right after, a gigantic mass of fire and stone exploded in the air. On falling back down, red streaks of incandescent liquid appeared out of nowhere and advanced toward her.

Rooted to the spot, she dared not move.

Not breathe, for that matter.

She had no physical body, after all, so nothing could harm her.

A second passed, a new blast lit up the sky. The fallback increased the streaks of molten lava accumulating on the ground. Another blaze, another fallout, and her heart filled with dread. Since the explosions kept following one another, she was afraid for her world.

"Yes, you're on a volcano." Virtus glanced around him as though it was all his doing.

As though he was directing it somehow.

"Now, look into the crater," he ordered. "Only then you'll know what your world is really like."

Startled, she lowered her gaze.

Oh, boy!

She was so close to the edge she would have fallen into it, had she been corporeal at all. As it was, she simply bent over and peered inside the deep cone.

At first, she could see nothing except a whirling red mass.

Then, the surface broke, like a lake ruffled by the wind. From the bottom, an image began forming, taking a more definite shape as it blew upward. What she saw iced her blood.

Entire villages gone to pieces, buildings shattered everywhere as though an earthquake had shaken them down to their essential components.

Only the earth had not budged.

The few people going through the ruins seemed to look for something specific. From where she stood, she could not make out what it was until someone uncovered a still body and dug it out from the wreckage. Not just one. The first of a long line of corpses that people were excavating from under piles of stones and rocks.

All at once, she was sick to her stomach.

"Like the show?" Virtus sneered contemptuously. "These petty humans look even more miserable when they're dead —
"

"Stop it!" If it came out as a shriek was because she could not stand the sadness and pain flashing in the survivors' auras. "Can't you see they're suffering?"

"Not enough." The ominous figure shrugged as though it did not matter to him. "But perhaps, you're just as fainthearted as all the rest of this insignificant species called human." He roared with sinister laughter that sent chills down her spine. "Or perhaps you just need a different show." The nipper he had in place of a hand waved over the crater. "Take a look now."

"No," she spelled it out, so there would be no margins for misunderstanding. "I'm not going to humor you—"

"I said, *look!*" A cold pincer clamped her neck and snapped her head down to face the crater.

For being without a body, her neck was aching like crazy.

"When your master orders," his voice turned threatening. "You obey."

Since when are you my master? Between Prince Caldwell and the odious Lord Templeton, she had enough of those to last her a lifetime.

Too bad, she could not even come close to sharing the thought, given how inflexible this particular master seemed to be. She would have loved nothing better than to defy him. But the familiar face in the image rising upward caught her complete attention.

It was none other than Elizabeth, Duncan's sister.

She was in Black Rose. Of that, Ylianor was quite sure, since she recognized the familiar place. But something was off with her. Or why else would she be yelling?

That the young woman was distraught was an understatement. When she slapped Missus Merryweather, the housekeeper, Ylianor could not believe her eyes. Mousey, submissive Elizabeth could not be doing what she was seeing her do!

She just could not!

Things got worse the moment she grabbed a knife and chased her mother on the hills, driven by the hate and rage of a lifetime's frustration. Poor Elizabeth, an unappealing child, in love with a brother too beautiful for words and with his unreachable phase mate. With a father too taken by his son and his little princess to give Elizabeth the attention and love she deserved.

Yes, life had just been so very unfair to poor Elizabeth, and now she was taking her revenge on the one who had wronged her most of all.

Sophia Caldwell screaming in pure terror was not a pretty sight, though a very satisfying one. However irrational, a part of Ylianor rooted for Elizabeth's success in putting an end to the terrible woman. Same woman who had made her last ten years the most miserable ever. Who had kicked out of Black Rose her deeply hurt and very defenseless nine-year-old self, out of the place she had been born in, and that was the only home she had ever known.

She deserved whatever Elizabeth would do to her.

Just Ylianor's bad luck she would not witness it, for the image grew out of proportion and blew over like steam.

Another rose from the depths of the crater to stare her in the face.

This scene was not in Black Rose. The place was quite different, sprawled in a sort of valley surrounded by high peaks. She would have had no clue where it was set had she not caught sight of a blond-haired older man. He resembled Chris too much to be a coincidence. Were that not enough, lights did not lie. They were telling her this was indeed the demon's father, James Templeton.

He was not alone.

Next to him, two dark-haired young men holding menacing knives were about to jump at each other's throats and slash them to bits.

Literally!

In the middle, James seemed paralyzed by the sheer horror of it all. Something clicked, and he sprang into action.

Shielding his younger son, James pushed back the eldest of the two, yelling in fear and bafflement.

As before, the uncontrollable hate and rage rose to the top, distorting reality into a grotesque fight for dominance, until it burst into a million pieces of lava and molten rocks.

No time to think, somebody pushed her to the hard ground. This time for real, she could feel pebbles and dirt scrunching her delicate skin. Maybe, the man pressing on top of her had something to do with it, though she could not be sure of anything.

Not since the screams for mercy of terrified women filled the air, drowning out any other sound. To the point, she could not even hear herself think.

Something was horribly wrong. Something that began with the groping hands on her breasts and got worse with the swollen male equipment slamming deep inside without her consent. Hurting and tearing soft tissues. It did not pump for her pleasure. Rather, for her humiliation and shame.

Feeling violated, Ylianor opened what should have been her mouth to scream. Only nothing came out.

It was too late anyway.

The scene burst, just like all the previous ones.

Which did not end her torture.

Not in the least.

More violence followed. More hatred, anger and vengeance enflamed everyone's cores and pushed aside all the inhibitions that had kept them trapped into a semblance of civilized human beings. The barriers crumbling, all that remained were savages — cruel monsters more frightful than the demon himself during his bloody knife play.

She could do nothing to stop the tide overwhelming her. Nothing except shudder at the sheer enormity of the evil Virtus had brought to the fore.

Or maybe it had always been there, restrained by something that was not there anymore.

Something like the heart of the blasted pyramid-like tower.

Just as the dots connected, she latched on to Arthur's hard stare trained on her.

Standing near his office window, the one that opened on the great valley below Rockyhorn, an odd relief sparked his eyes, as though he were glad she was there. She, who meant nothing to him!

It seemed so ludicrous that she would have laughed, had not the sneaky suspicion that he had somehow planned all this stopped her cold. As though it were all a ruse to have her right there, to become his unwilling witness. Somehow, this was the scariest bit of all.

The woman in front of the leader was mad at him.

No, make that raging mad.

That she might be Arthur's pledge was a possibility that crossed her mind, though nothing in either of their auras indicated they had any sex. It was more of a stance on her part that had Ylianor wondering whether this was indeed Claudette Fairchild.

Yelling in frenzied agitation, she blurted everything out without taking any pause. It was all Arthur's fault. Or so it seemed, as she vented the disappointments of a lifetime, the hurt of a woman too long neglected, denied any contact while betrayed at every turn with young and beautiful men. Like an avenging fury, she reached Arthur with two strides and pushed him out the window.

Calming down, she took a step back to watch his inevitable fall.

Arthur's body hovered for a second on the windowsill. Half in and half out, he did not seem concerned.

Not at all.

Not since his focus was all on Ylianor alone. That he could see her seemed evident, however puzzling the notion. She was sure that none of the others whose scenes she had observed had noticed her. Not Elizabeth, not James and his sons, not even that brute plundering her yielding flesh as though it was the spoils of an undeclared war.

Only Arthur seemed to be aware that she was there for real. Not an imaginary figment of somebody's fertile mind, he had no trouble perceiving her from whatever dimension she was watching.

"He's the one, child." His words came out raspy and short of breath. "Never forget it." The lurch backward destabilized his balance. "And never forget *me*." Out he went.

As the image dissolved, the awareness that Arthur had just died hit her like a blow to the stomach. Had she possessed one, she would have doubled over from the sheer pain and utter bewilderment.

Not because Lord Arthur Fairchild had just plummeted to his death.

The position of High Council Leader suddenly vacant, the apex of the pyramid-like hierarchy collapsed in the blink of an eye!

The organization Arthur had controlled and regulated was now sagging on itself!

The very foundation of her world was shaking and about to crumble along with everything else. The void so palpable, she had no doubt everybody felt it, whether council members or not, and the despair sank in worse than before.

Just when she thought that she could not take it one second longer, an abrupt shift filled the void. Someone had stepped in and taken over Arthur's place, his powerful Virt coalescing the vital energy of every single living being and equilibrating once more Virtus's attempts to unbalance everything her people had accomplished.

That someone was Prince Duncan Caldwell, the new Leader of the High Council!

The news so overwhelming, she wished she had more time to analyze it. Instead, the full load of every emotion she had picked up since Virtus had flung her way out there was draining her very spirit.

No more!

"Stop!" Ylianor shouted. "I've had enough!"

"Welcome to my world, little girl," Virtus spat. "This is what you are." His voice turned dark and creepy, "Always have been and always will be," he sneered contemptuously. "While I am the reason for your worthless lives," he snickered scornfully. "Without me, you'd have all long extinguished your miserable existences." From an odd twist in the grating tone, she guessed this would have pleased him a whole lot. "Wiped out by your violence, like it has already happened to countless other foolish and dastardly races similar to yours," he scoffed disgustedly. "'Cause you are nothing but a pitiful kind bent on destroying everything, yourselves included." The red light crossing his oval disk increased its speed. "Exactly what you'd have done, were it not for me." Proud of his handwork, a low beep escaped from what she could only guess was his mouth. "You forced me to keep your horror at bay, but I've had enough of your sickly peaceful world." His metallic voice resembled a sinister crackle. "No, better, I'm finally free to do what I damn well please. And I owe it all to you!" Upon bowing in mock pretense, the metallic edge became derisive.

That was his real intent, to trap her inside his sick world. To force her to stay there with him, for whatever his reasons, he needed her.

Not just as a member of the progeny he claimed to despise, but as herself, Ylianor Meyer.

Which gave her the creeps.

"Now, I want it all!" He was determined to succeed. "From pain to pleasure without any limits."

This was simply too close to home for her. Had she not said those same words to her prince just last night when bragging about her plotting to conquer the demon?

"Yeah, I want your worthless species to live in the same chaos I've had the pleasure of controlling since the beginning of time." Simple and effective, it sounded like a definite agenda to her.

It also gave her the strength to react, taking advantage of his fascination with the eerie scenario he was painting.

The flaming red-hot streams of liquid lava brightening the darkness seemed enough of a backdrop to hasten her intervention before things became unmanageable.

Prince! Ylianor screamed at the top of her mind. *Tell David to put the pieces back.* She just hoped her message was getting through to him. *Now!*

And mercifully, the world went dark again.

CHAPTER TWENTY-SIX

"Princess!" The trace of worry in Duncan's tone was unmistakable, no matter how out of it Ylianor felt.

Out of this world for sure. Still atop that volcano witnessing those terrifying scenes if she had to take a wild guess.

"Wake up!" Cradling her head to his chest, his dark energy wrapped around her like a blanket.

"Come on." The refreshing balm of a healer's touch made her realize she was back in Blue Oasis.

Back in her body, lying on the cold hard ground.

"Time to get a move, Princess." At the renewed shake, but more at the gentle slap on her face, her eyes flew open.

"What happened?" Mumbling, she raised her gaze.

And met the blue-gray eyes trained on her. Full of so many contrasting emotions, they cut off her breath. Next to him, David also peered down at her with an equally anxious expression clouding his face. All three hovering over her as though she was about to die or something.

Which maybe she was, for the world was falling to pieces.

While she was doing nothing to prevent it.

"You tell us." The demon laughed half-amused, the extreme apprehension she had read in his aura fading in the background.

"You fainted." Nearing her on the opposite side, David pushed away a few loose strands covering her face. "And slid to the floor."

"Just when the show was getting interesting," Chris retorted with a dry laugh. "David just moved a few pieces around — "

"We've got to put them back." She tried scrambling to her feet and failed miserably.

"Easy there." Duncan's hold tightened. "The pieces are already back in place." *But it's the least of our worries.*

In a flash, he flooded her with the same horrible visions Virtus had just shown her.

You were there, my prince? Strange, she had not felt him linked to her.

Yet, there was no doubt he had lived the same exact things she had.

Aye, I was. He searched her face for signs that she was all right.

So, you know you're our new leader. The awareness made her want to sit up and salute him properly. *That Arthur appointed you to take his place.*

He knew.

Of course, he knew.

There was a new edge about him, but also a heaviness like darkness trying to smother him. *Yeah, I know about that, too.*

His voice sounded so weary and tired that she had to study him one second longer just to make sure he was all right. *Good, 'cause you must also know chaos has broken loose.* She replayed the images of the devastation that Virtus had forced her to witness. *That it needs healing . . .*

This particular awareness stung like crazy. Given the amount of pain, bewilderment and sheer fear, there was no way around it. For only one man, and one alone, had the necessary Virt to stop it all.

Same man whom Prince Duncan Caldwell loved more than life itself.

I know. Of course, he did.

The heaviness of his words was all the proof she needed. *Your angel will have to . . .*

If her voice faltered, it was because she could hardly

fathom the enormity of what the prince would have to ask of his beloved. Yet ask he must or condemn his world to extinction like Virtus demanded.

"David didn't just move a few pieces around, did he?" That Chris was getting better at reading her mind was a reality she would have to reckon with sooner rather than later. "Right?"

"Unfortunately not." Duncan's face turned to Chris. "Angel . . ."

She had to avert her gaze, for she could not stand the terrible ache in the black eyes.

"Yes, lover." But the blue-gray gaze melting in the black one seemed ready to take the world, had Duncan only asked.

"I need you." Untangling from her, Duncan got to his feet, bringing Chris with him.

"I'll do whatever you command." No trace of fear or hesitation, the demon stood up and faced the prince as though he knew this was a matter of life and death.

Which was not what caught her eye.

No, what struck her was Chris's solemn tone, as though he was not speaking to his lover but his leader.

"People are suffering out there," Duncan lowered his voice as his arms wrapped around the lither body. "They need healing," he whispered.

Loud enough to hear.

"And oblivion." Pulling back, he gripped Chris's arms tight. "'Cause they have to forget what happened."

"How many people are we talking about?" Practical and to the point, Chris looked like he was already analyzing the situation.

"A lot." The prince heaved. "Too many to count for sure."

"No problem." She had the sensation Chris was downplaying it on purpose for his lover's sake. "Only I'll need an enormous amount of energy."

"We'll supply you." Duncan's focus snatched on her.

"Right, Princess?"

"We will." Finding the strength she lacked before, she bolted to her feet. "So will everyone else." With a hard stare, she made eye contact with Cecilia.

"Yes, of course," Lady Hurst was quick to agree.

"Oh, all right . . ." That it pained the prince to give the final order was not hard to guess.

It would have her, too, had she to send off her lover on a suicidal mission. With no choice in the matter, either, and just a handful of seconds to stop Virtus and the harm he had caused.

My prince, we can't afford to waste time. She tried to keep the harshness at bay. *You must send him immediately.*

Yes, I know. Unbearable, the weight crushing his heart. *But will he survive?*

The searing pain slicing her in two was just the tip of his dismay.

He will. She made it sound more confident than she felt. *'Cause you'll be the one feeding his fire.*

Flattening Chris against him, the prince's cool power surrounded the flaming essence. Ready to jump into the sky itself, his body disappeared as if devoured by the increasingly powerful flames. His heat and brightness increased as the prince fused more into him. Like he did every time they were on a bed, she could not tear her eyes away from how beautiful they were. How deep could they be into one another?

So deep that not even a world's crisis could come between them.

At least, for the space of the eternity they spent entwined around one another. Which was closer to the few seconds before Duncan gave him a vigorous shove.

The tower of pure incendiary Virt rose and was gone from Cecilia's room.

Just like that, one moment he was there, the next he had soared away.

Not in the flesh, of course.

His material body discarded, it stood apparently lifeless within Duncan's embrace that conveyed his inexhaustible reservoir to his adored angel, fueling his drive to save the world.

This flow of energy between them resembled a bridge, a very shiny one. No one better than Ylianor could appreciate it. Hooked as she was to the prince's sensations, she perceived that Chris was doing a fantastic job of it, soothing and healing those still alive with small fire-like darts, while his healer's heart bled at the sight of the many dead lying under the ruins of what had once been flourishing villages.

Not that she could linger.

Her task was to keep track of the energy flow she perceived from the shifts in his aura. To sustain him, she had already surrendered her meager allowance, letting him borrow as much as he wanted, without holding anything back. He dipped liberally, reaching out and grabbing more and more with each consecutive minute.

But when his requests became more pressing, she knew she could not sustain them.

He needed more, and the only way to satisfy him was by adding Cecilia and David's energy.

Which could prove to be a problem, especially given Cecilia's little propensity for sharing. Make that no propensity at all, considering the high walls cutting her off from the rest of the world.

Not just her.

Her energy, mostly, trapped as it was behind those impenetrable barriers of her creation that kept everyone out except for David.

He alone seemed to have a privileged channel, a way to reach her despite her defenses, and Ylianor took immediate advantage of it.

Drawing out his energy, she connected it to Cecilia and

showered the roaring fire with the full force of their collective power.

Chris's lights gained new strength as he erased everyone's memory of the brutality unleashed by a heartless monster. On and on without fail, the demon lent his entire Virt to restore the world to a semblance of normality until the worst of it faded from people's minds and bodies.

Nothing left to do except return to his physical shell. Not the Christopher Templeton she knew, the man repossessing of his body was a pale and oh so feeble imitation of the splendid blond man who had flared into action just minutes before. His lights were dimming so fast that her heart clenched in fear.

"I think I did it, lover." White-faced and exhausted, Chris twisted his lips in a smile that came out crooked. "Got rid of everything like you ordered." His stance uneasy, he faltered and grasped Duncan's arm for support.

"I know, Angel." Quick to catch him, the prince laid him on the couch. "I can't even begin to tell you how grateful I am."

Too bad, Chris could not hear. Half-fainted, his eyes closed, his breathing shallow, his aura dimmer than ever was like a blow to the stomach, and she could not help remembering how intense and vivid it was.

More similar to leaping flames, his lights had been the first she had ever seen. Back in the days, she had lost count of how many nights she had spent awake just picturing them.

"Quick," she barked at Cecilia. "He needs food and sugar now."

Cecilia rushed to the bell and repeated the order to the first servant who knocked at the door.

Within seconds, Duncan took the sweetest drink available from the full trays just delivered and poured a few drops on Chris's lips.

Please, tell me he'll be all right. The anguished black gaze was all for her.

The problem is that he's lost a lot of energy. Bending, she checked that he was still breathing. *But he's strong and very much in love.* She beamed her most confident smile to convince him.

Unsuccessfully, alas, for it failed to impress him in the least. *If only that were enough to save him —*

It will be, she cut him off abruptly. *'Cause he loves you too much to leave you.* Duncan himself could not deny this truth.

I'll never forgive myself if he does. The agony in his voice was so raw it had her cringing.

He isn't going to die! Ylianor snapped back to stop the useless self-pity. *He just needs plenty of rest, and you'll see how fast he'll recover.* Approaching, she gripped his hand. *Now, let's get out of here. We need food ourselves, and you'll need your energy —*

"Fuck!" Chris coughed convulsively. "Where am I?" Opening his eyes, he spat the last drop of the liquid that had obviously choked him.

"Angel!" Duncan's relief was palpable. "You're back in Blue Oasis."

"I'm so tired." A yawn escaped from his lips.

Next, he curled to a side, ready to faint again.

"No, you have to eat something first." Grabbing a spoon of sweet jam, he neared it to the thin lips. "'Cause I taxed you a little harder than I intended."

Obediently, the demon opened his mouth and swallowed every bite of what the prince fed him.

Not just a matter of food.

The energy play between them was just as vital.

"May I help?" Fetching a plate of cheeses, David neared the prince.

"No, thanks." Duncan swung his gaze to David. "There's not much else we can do."

"We're sorry." Moving to his side, Cecilia communicated

more with her contrite expression than any words she uttered. "We never wanted to hurt anyone . . ." She looked to David as though wanting confirmation. "Much less for this to happen." Her dark eyes clouded. "Or for Lord Templeton to end up like this."

Kind of clear that she had no clue about what had happened.

"But it was all my fault." Nervous, she scanned Duncan's face. "Wasn't it?" Since the prince did not give her any satisfaction, she became frantic. "Please forgive me. I wish I'd never taken the damn thing." Cecilia glared at the pyramid sitting peacefully on the table.

"At least you realize how foolish you've been." Duncan's tone was as cold as the look he sent her. "Now, I need to take Chris to a bed and let him rest."

Cecilia immediately called for help, and the servants came back.

"Yes, Milady?" Colin asked.

"Help our guests to their quarters." Cecilia gestured at Duncan, hovering on the couch. "And bring them food, juices and plenty of water."

A few servants scuttled away.

Reaching Prince Caldwell, Colin bent on the couch. "I can carry him to your room—"

"Don't you dare touch him." If it came out as a sinister growl, Ylianor supposed it was due to her prince's extreme agitation. "He's *mine!*"

Brushing Colin away, he picked up the unconscious form and cuddled it tenderly, as if afraid to break it. Headed for the door, he stopped on the threshold and addressed her, "Princess, please bring the pyramid with you."

Complying took just a few seconds. The time necessary to clamp it and follow Duncan to their room, leaving behind a very bewildered Cecilia and David.

CHAPTER TWENTY-SEVEN

Don't despair, my love. She could not help the trembling in her voice. *We may be able to help your angel yet.*

How? Even though he had reached their room, he stopped to gaze at her, his velvety eyes full of hope.

Chris's unconscious body held between them by his powerful arms only increased the unbearable tension knotting her stomach.

I'll tell you as soon as we've settled down and eaten something. Through the open door, she noticed the table loaded with food and beverages, the bright fire crackling in the background and a handful of servants arranging the last details. The prince's curt thank you dismissed them all.

Going straight to the bed, he placed the demon on it and pulled up the covers. "Tell me how we can help him."

That it sounded like a command, she put it down to his extreme anxiety. "I will." Unruffled, she proceeded to close the door before spinning around to face him. "But first, we need to regain our strength." Nearing the bed, she sat in front of him.

"He could die because of my order." Miserable and dejected, he gripped Chris's hand tighter. "I can't bear to lose him." The intensity of his sadness sliced her heart in two. *I love him so damn much.* He wrapped it possessively between both his palms. *What am I to do if I lost him for real?* One of the palms went to caress the pale face, then moved up and got lost in the thick blond hair.

"He's not going to die." If she kept talking rather than let her words flow in his mind, it was solely for Chris and his need to feel his lover's presence as much as possible. "I told you." Cupping Duncan's face between her palms, she compelled him to look into her eyes. "He has you to live for." She spelled the words slowly so that they would leave no doubt.

"I swear I'll never ask him anything like this, ever again." Pulling the demon closer, he squeezed his shoulders fiercely.

"Don't make promises you might not be able to keep," she reproached. "Not since you've become the new Leader of the High Council."

"It's true then." He heaved as though he would have gladly left this duty to someone else.

"Yes, my prince, it is," she confirmed, even if there was no need for it.

He had known it from the moment Arthur had died, and she just had to remember the new awareness she had read in his liquid black eyes upon escaping Virtus's clutches to be sure. As if that had not been enough, Chris's response had been the final proof.

"I thought so." Defeated, he averted his gaze on the unconscious form by his side. "But I can't believe it." He frowned in puzzlement. "I mean, how can that be?" From his pained expression, it was evident he was trying to work things out in his usual analytic fashion. "I haven't even claimed my father's seat yet." The empty permanent Caldwell Seat in the High Council was something Arthur himself had brought up during their visit at the Hall, before all this mess of the missing heart in the Nephis Valley had started. "Why choose me?"

Yeah, why him?

True, leaders had no set rules or conditions when they chose their successors. He could be anyone from any social class, though she had the feeling Lord Fairchild had chosen Prince Duncan Caldwell because he had been born for it.

"I don't know." Since she had no evidence to support her

belief, she shrugged in lack of a better answer. "Your great power probably has much to do with it, but I'm sure that's just skimming the surface. All I can say is that you've always been our leader, for me and the demon, and now you are everyone's new leader. Which is what I felt from the moment Arthur died." Her certainty had only grown since her return from Virtus's wretched place.

"That's also true? Arthur is dead?" Snapping up his head, he looked at her. "But Claudette couldn't . . ." His voice faltered. "Wouldn't . . ." He just could not get over it. "We didn't see him actually fall—"

"He died. Trust me." She knew it beyond the shadow of a doubt, the scene too eerily similar to the one of Prince Charles's death that she had witnessed as a mere child. "Right after, you became the leader and had to stop the madness breaking loose everywhere. That's why you had to send your angel," her tone was very gentle, almost apologetic. "He was the only one who could set things right again. He alone has that kind of Virt, so you had no choice." She kissed his lips softly.

"I don't want this leadership if it means sacrificing the ones I love," he spat vehemently. "Like my angel or . . ." Reaching out, he pulled her close. *You, Princess?*

"Nonsense." Resisting the urge to melt in his embrace, she dismissed his objection with a wave of the hand. "You might have no choice in the future, either." However strained he seemed to be at the moment, she knew no better or more suited man could assume such a responsibility in her world than Prince Duncan Caldwell. "Leaders often have to give unpleasant orders, even risking the lives of those closest to them." She raised her gaze to fix him steadily. "Do you understand now why Arthur was so worried you only had two channels?" Straightening, she leveled their gazes. "We limit your potential."

"As if love could ever be a limit," he snorted contemptuously.

"That's not the point," she scolded lightly. "And you know it." Stretching, she felt every tired bone of her body, not to mention the hole that had taken her stomachs place. When her gaze fell on all the untouched food, she could not stop the hunger devouring her from the inside. "Come on." Getting up, she pulled on his arm. "Let's eat something." Mustering all the force she had, she managed to detach him from Chris's side and pull him to his feet. "You have to build your strength for your angel's sake, while I need it if we're going to try to revive him and if you want me to keep talking—"

"Damn right, I do!" A little push and shove finally convinced him to reach the table and sit on the first available chair. "Let's continue with, *What in the gods' name was that thing that kidnapped you?*" After taking an empty plate, he began piling it with cheese, vegetables, beans and oatmeal. "Is it the pyramid itself or something that lives in it?"

"Something that haunts it, you mean." And would keep haunting them all if they did not put it down fast. "I wish I knew." Perplexed, she shook her head in frustration. "But it had too much life to be just a pyramid."

"For sure, it's as evil as nothing I've ever felt." With a concerned expression crossing his beautiful eyes, he set the full plate in front of her.

She tried hiding the look of dismay at the sight of the sheer quantity he thought she could eat. He was just like Anne in this respect—another incurable optimist when it came to her eating habits.

"That's an understatement." Tentatively, she reached first for a glass of juice. "I've never seen anything so black in my life." No, not even the demon's unspeakable tortures were quite as comparable. "Not even your angel when he came to Black Rose the first time." And he had been pretty pissed off with the whole world that he would have blown it up, had Duncan not intervened.

The prince suppressed a smirk while glancing at Chris from behind his shoulder. "Did Arthur know this was coming?" Returning his gaze on her, he picked up another plate and filled it without bothering to pay any attention to what he was selecting.

"I think he did, or I'd have never picked up that stuff about his death." In a flash, she shared the sensation Arthur had given off the first time she had seen him at the Hall, and that had so upset Chris when she had talked about it. "This creature seems too cunning and dangerous to let Arthur stop it." Gingerly, she scouted for her favorite cheese, half-hidden under a stack of eggplants. "I get the feeling that our old leader knew it was coming after him, but he didn't have the strength to contain it anymore." She swallowed a generous forkful of green beans before attacking the cheese. "He must've expected Virtus would kill him eventually."

"Then, the question is why." His forehead creased in concentration as he polished off his eggs. "Why did Virtus wanted Arthur dead?"

"I believe Virtus wants everyone dead, not just Arthur." Philosophical to the point of sounding cynical, she took another bite of cheese. "That's why he sent us after it." Delighted, she munched slowly to savor it to the fullest. "As if we could ever stop it," she huffed sarcastically.

"Maybe not, but we should at least try to understand it." His black eyes brightened as though he had the first inkling of a solution. "It's our only hope to defeat it." With new vigor strengthening his voice, he took a second serving of beans. "You know it, too, or you wouldn't have reacted the same way you did when my angel played his *scary game*, as you call it, with you. Goading it at every turn so that it kept talking and feeding you valuable information you might later use against him."

Well, she was damn impressed!

Not many would have been able to draw the comparison, much less to use it to their advantage. She had hardly been aware of it until now. But thinking back on the experience, she could just applaud him for his keen intuition. For when the demon had brutally stabbed her, she had not only been terrified out of her mind. She had also been gathering information to use against him the first chance she got. And if payback with the demon was still some time in the future, with Virtus she might get it sooner than she anticipated.

"Let's go over everything together to see what we've missed so far." His confident grin was a sign he had latched on to her thoughts despite her shields.

"All right," she grumbled. "For one thing, this Virtus freak is a real piece of work." Cheese finished, she nibbled on a piece of bread. "While it was trying its best to plunge our world into chaos and mayhem, it was telling me that it was born to guard us against violence — "

"How could it possibly stop every human being from committing violence?" He slowed down on his eating to stare at her. "Our world has never known anything of what it showed you on the volcano."

"Maybe, we should just assume everyone has those kinds of impulses all the time." It seemed the most logical explanation after what she had seen. "That it must be thanks to Virtus and its intervention if we haven't all killed one another yet."

"You might be right." Deep in concentration, he chewed on a slice of cheese. "Things happened so fast. It was like people couldn't wait to be free to do something they've wanted to do for a long time."

"It isn't just powerful, which would explain its name and why the ancients referred to power as Virt." She grabbed a honey wheat cake and munched it. "This Virtus can also affect people at an individual level—"

"Controlling our emotions—"

"And replacing them with others." She stopped eating and looked at him dismayed.

"Or maybe not." His lighter tone was just a ruse to mask the concern she read on his face and spotted in his lights.

"Well, maybe we're just making too many assumptions," she teased without the slightest trace of humor.

"Maybe not." He pushed out a heavy breath as if the new twist had left him without air. "If everything was true, what went wrong? Why did this creature first make the world a safer place, then turn around and try to destroy us all?"

Reflecting on the question, she uncovered a solitary flat cake beneath several cheese layers. "Maybe, all the violence it had to curb from the beginning of our history made it evil somehow."

"Turned it into that . . ." He searched for a word. "Human-like monster?"

"Such an evil mind can only live in an evil body." Shivering at the memory, she rushed to add, "I wonder though if that's what it really looks like." She bit her lower lip as the image of the pyramid-like tower flashed in her mind. "Or if it's just another illusion it created while it was locked up in the Nephis Valley structure."

"Yeah, that structure was its cage." Obvious how this made sense to him. "But it wasn't strong enough if David and Cecilia alone managed to break Virtus free." He reached for a honey scone. "How can we stop it?"

"It's not going to be easy." At the moment, it seemed her only certainty. "If that freak convinced Cecilia to take it away, we can safely say that it's one scary monster." She sighed at the enormity of the task at hand. "It's so determined that it might just do anything to get what it wants . . ." If she paused, it was to cool her parched throat with a refreshing glass of water. "Whatever that is."

"Nothing good for sure." He frowned. "Not since it didn't give a damn about control, bent only on total havoc regardless of the consequences." Now, his gaze narrowed on her. "But one thing seems clear." Clutching her hand, he pulled her closer. "He wants you, Princess, and badly."

"I don't think . . ." She felt her face grow hot. "It was probably just my imagination playing tricks —"

"No tricks." He seemed to have no doubts about it. "I felt its raw need. Not to hurt you. To possess you somehow." There was no mistaking his erotic undertone. "Like he was obsessed with you or something."

Which made her think of the demon and the perverse attraction he had revealed during his scary knife game.

"So, if we ever manage to defeat it, it'll be only thanks to you, sweet princess." He leaned on the table. "Our key to unlocking its secrets."

"Nah." She lifted a shoulder, hoping against hope that he was wrong. "I'm not all that important."

"Oh, but you are," his voice grew husky. "Bringing you on top of that volcano, into his dimension, is all the proof I need." Pulling away from the table, he came to her side and embraced her, holding on tight. "I have the feeling that it showed its true face to a human being for the first time ever." His fingers raked through her long hair. "Since it happened with you, I have to assume that you're special."

"Then, I'm doomed." It seemed like the only logical conclusion, one she refused to consider as she snuggled closer inside his arms and allowed his scent to seep to her very core.

"Not necessarily." As though reading her craving, he intensified his strokes on her head and back. "Another thing I'm convinced of is that it's losing it somehow. All that uncontrollable rage and this opening up to you are signs it's escalating to the point of no return."

"But why now?" This still escaped her. "What happened now that caused things to go so horribly wrong after they've worked fine for our entire history?"

"I have no idea, nor do I care right now." Gripping her shoulders more firmly, he intensified his hold on her. "Not while my angel is still unconscious." His touch sent goosebumps of pleasure rippling down to her cunt. "So, why don't we try that plan of yours to revive him?"

CHAPTER TWENTY-EIGHT

"Prince, are you there?" A knock followed the female's voice.

Sorry, Princess. Letting her go with a twinge of regret, Duncan stood up and retreated from the table. *I gotta get this.*

She would have rather he did not, much preferring he kept cuddling her.

But it couldn't be helped, not since he opened the door to a deathly white Cecilia.

"May I come in?" Anxious beyond description, she looked like she might faint at any second.

He stepped aside, and she advanced, her gaze fixing on the demon.

"Will he be all right?" Cecilia's voice sounded hoarse.

"He'll be fine." Kind of evident, from his lights and cold tone, he was not pleased with her interruption, either. "What do you want?"

This also explained his brusque manner and rigid stance.

"I . . ." Cecilia's voice broke, and she threw herself in his arms, leaving him no choice except to catch her. "Arthur is dead!" Violent sobs shook her body.

"I know." He stroked her hair to give her some measure of comfort.

"You do?" Her head snapped to stare him in the face. "How could you possibly?" A confused expression spread on her hard features. "The messenger from Lord Templeton, the vice-leader, just reached me."

"Let's say I have my sources." Deliberately cryptic, he

glanced at Ylianor, who had not moved since Cecilia had entered their room. *The best one to date,* he mused softly in her head.

Which had her liquefying all over the place like she had been right before Cecilia's unwanted intrusion.

"Oh, I see." However taken aback by his reply, Cecilia did not waste time dwelling on it. Instead, she lowered her head once more, pressing it against his broad chest. "Do you also happen to know who the new leader will be?" Not just her head. Judging from her frantic aura, she craved nothing more than melting against him. "Lord Templeton was kind of vague in his message."

Meaning that Chris's father had provided no clues as to the identity of Arthur's successor.

"Hem, no." Only natural, Duncan would not jump in to fill in her blanks. "But I hardly think we should be worrying about this right now, not after all the chaos and destruction we've suffered —"

"Which is all my fault." Suddenly reminded of her responsibilities, she started crying again. "I didn't mean to hurt anyone." Fresh tears hung on her eyelashes before rolling down her cheeks." I never thought it would lead to this," she bawled uncontrollably. "People and animals are dead or dying as we speak. Entire villages have been destroyed. Roads are useless. Crops and fields are ruined. Buildings are crumbling or lie in heaps of rubbles and debris. Our precious water is at risk." The grim list appeared to be never-ending. "In short, it's a mess everywhere."

"I know this, too, Ceci." Yeah, unfortunately, he did.

Ylianor wished she could turn off once more the images rushing back to the fore, conjured by Cecilia's grief-stricken words. To think she had worked so hard to chase them away since escaping Virtus's kidnapping, succeeding only when the prince had held her tightly in his arms.

"Really? Your sources are well informed." There was a slight trace of irony in her voice. "The worst thing is that no one knows what to do," she relapsed in her earlier hysteria. "Or where to start doing something—"

"We'll figure something out." He continued to caress her head, as it to soothe her guilty conscience.

"Not by ourselves." She looked uncertain, her dark eyes huge with fear and puzzlement. "The High Council has called for a special meeting," she informed curtly. "Which requires your immediate presence, Prince, even if you're not a member."

At the news, he swung his gaze to lock it on Ylianor's, as though he still harbored doubts about everything that had just happened and everything he had felt since Virtus had crashed into their lives.

I told you, my love. She suppressed a smirk. *You are the new leader.*

I wish you weren't so damn right every time, he grumbled with a hint of amazement at the accuracy of her perceptions.

As if feeling she had lost his attention, Cecilia snuggled closer. "Have your sources told you this, too?"

"Not in so many words," he admitted. "But this call comes as no surprise."

"What are we going to tell the council?" Her gaze did not waver from his handsome features. "About what happened, I mean."

There's not much to tell. He exchanged glances with Ylianor. *Is there, Princess?*

Not if you want people to keep their wits. She grimaced, knowing as well as he did that this would have to be their secret— the demon's, his and hers.

"That something went out of control. Only we don't know what." Reluctantly, he returned his focus on the dark eyes filled with tears and dread. "Which is the truth, by the way."

However much more they knew than Cecilia did, it was

barely enough to make sense, much less draw reasonable con-
clusions.

"What are we going to do?" Worried, Cecilia frowned as
though her logical mind was having trouble processing too
much information in too short a time.

"Pick up the pieces." He seemed to have everything figured out already.

Ylianor could not be more impressed with his rational approach to the calamity that had hit them and risked drowning
her entire world from the weight of the next tasks.

No, she could not be more in love with the man.

Same man Cecilia appeared to be childishly jealous of, going as far as ignoring her and trying to grab all his attention
with every trick in the book.

"Most importantly, we'll handle one thing at a time," he
continued. "First, we'll deal with the emergencies, then with
all the consequences." The way he talked, Ylianor was willing
to bet he had a definite plan in mind. "Using everybody's
help, we'll organize teams and groups to clean up and repair
the damage." This plan of his was shaping up as he spoke.
"I'm afraid it's going to take time and hard work . . ." He
snickered, "Lots of it before things can go back to normal."
His full lips curved in a tentative smile. "But when it's all
over, we'll have a Festival." Now, the smile became a heart-
stopping grin.

"A Festival?" Curious, Cecilia fixed him with raw expectation stamped all over her face. "What sort of Festival?"

"The best sort." He beamed evidently proud of his idea.

And Ylianor realized he was already thinking as a leader.

"It's going to be a grand event dedicated to food, drink and
sex." He scrutinized Cecilia's face. "That's how things work
here according to your intuition, so we might as well take advantage of it. This, if nothing else, will help people forget."

Which was another considerable preoccupation on his

mind, however lightly he had mentioned it.

"Actually, no one around here remembers a thing," Cecilia was quick to point out. "No one knows what happened."

"That's better for everyone," he assured nonchalantly.

"You know, though, don't you?" She looked up at him, trembling and shaking until her focus cut to the pyramid, lying sweet and innocent on a table. "What are we going to do with it?"

"One thing at a time." He pulled away, his lights signaling he had enough of their forced closeness. "Let's set things right again. Then, the five of us will reconvene to discuss our options regarding the pyramid and decide on some sort of action."

The only option was to put the damn thing back in its place like Arthur had ordered a lifetime ago. Still, it made sense that the prince might want to reflect on other, better alternatives.

Right, Princess, he confirmed, latching on to her thought without any trouble. *These other alternatives will present themselves only after we gain a deeper understanding of who or what this Virtus really is.*

Something you plan to do while cleaning up Virtus's mess, she sniggered. *Right, Leader?*

His scowl was not an optimistic one, even if she detected the quiet acceptance of his title and of the new role that would be his prerogative from now onward.

It was about time!

"Shouldn't we get going?" Taking a step forward, Cecilia clung to him as though she had no intention of ever allowing him to get rid of her.

"Yes, absolutely, go." Once again, he broke free from her hold and moved closer to Ylianor, obviously attempting to set enough distance between them. "The High Council is waiting for you."

"What about you?" Suspicious, Cecilia followed him. "Remember, you've been summoned along with every other member of the High Council."

"First, I must make sure the angel is all right." As a way of a strategic move, he approached the bed. "Then, I'll leave for the Hall." Inevitable for his hand to stray on the ashen—yet still incredibly gorgeous—face of Chris's unconscious form.

"The sooner, the better," Cecilia countered. "James Templeton's instructions are quite clear, and no one is to do anything until your arrival."

"I'll be there. Don't worry." Refusing to let her rush him, he continued stroking the demon's delicate features. "You have my word." Straightening, he left his beloved's side and walked toward her to see her out of the door.

"I prefer your kiss." Taking advantage of their renewed closeness, she reached for his lips with a naughty twinkle.

He did not push her away but brushed his lips on hers.

That Cecilia wanted way more was kind of a given. Exploiting the situation, she deepened the kiss, her tongue darting in his mouth and begging for more substantial, not to mention proper, ravishment.

Since he had pulled her into his awareness, Ylianor felt it all, along with his sense of impatience at Cecilia's unscrupulous attack. It was the reason he hurried to end it, succeeding in drawing away only after considerable effort.

"I think you should leave now." Unceremoniously, he shoved her gently toward the door.

"All right." Resigned, she nodded. "I'm going." One foot still inside, the other stepped into the hallway.

"Oh . . ." He detained her as if struck by a sudden thought. "Ceci?"

"Yes, Prince?" Eyes ablaze, she spun quickly around full of hope and anticipation.

"Please leave David behind." Four simple words were enough to crush all her expectations. "I need him with me on the road."

Cecilia remained perfectly still for a long moment. "As you wish," she managed to breathe out eventually. "I'll send him to you, Prince Caldwell."

"Thanks." His smile had something vaguely apologetic about it. "Have a safe journey, and I'll see you at the Hall."

At these words, she crossed the threshold and closed the door behind her.

CHAPTER TWENTY-NINE

"Now, Princess." As soon as Cecilia left, Duncan jumped on Ylianor. "Let's revive my angel."

"I can't promise anything." She stopped his enthusiastic turn to the bed. "But since his Virt has the healing power, if we can make it work on him, he should be all right." She approached Chris hesitantly. "I'll just have to reach his core and get it to heal him." She hoped she sounded more confident than she felt. "You can monitor the situation and pull me out in case he wakes up." Of course, she need not add more since the prince knew precisely the risk involved should the demon's fire collide against her. Still, it was better to be safe than sorry. "Before he inadvertently burns me, without even realizing it."

Not that it would be a significant loss for His Haughtiness Lord Christopher Templeton. Aware or not, nothing would give him more pleasure than to reduce her to cinders and be rid of her once and for all. It stood to reason, after all. She could have never contemplated much less dared something so outrageous, had he been feeling himself. Just his bad luck, she had no obstacles now that he was unconscious, hence less harmful.

"Got it." He beamed his best smile as though to show he had the utmost confidence in the success of her plan and her capability to get out of it alive.

"My life's in your hands," she provoked him on purpose.

"Hasn't it always?" Duncan retorted playfully.

Suppressing a giggle, she neared the bed and focused on

the pale demon. He was so breathtakingly beautiful that her heart skipped several beats. Not just a question of looks. His silent tongue was too good a novelty, and she tried imagining what he would be like without his biting remarks and bitter sarcasm. Since it was as unfathomable as the absence of his snappy comebacks, she pulled herself together. She had a task to perform, after all.

Staring at the gorgeous man like a silly love-struck school-girl would not help her, not at all.

Concentrating, she slipped inside him, past his skin, past his blood, deeper yet to his fiery core. Or rather, to what had once been a burning core.

Now, after saving the world, it was just a heap of smoldering cinders sparked by a feeble light suffocating under the cloak of darkness attempting to snuff him out for good.

But he refused to go down without a fight, his flames leaping to pierce the blackness despite their evident lack of strength.

As she went to examine the dying embers, she noticed his Virt comprised two separate rays, a red and a blue one.

All at once, she understood how his power worked.

"That fiery core of yours is capable of the most opposite things. From healing to destroying, you can go either way faster than the bat of an eye," Arthur had commented.

It could not be otherwise. Not since that red ray held all the destructive fire in the world, while the blue counterpart took care of the soothing healing she had felt after his vicious knife game. Come to think of it, Arthur had also added, "That's why you crave pain and pleasure in equal measures." This made perfect sense as well. She could just imagine how the contrast between the two separate forces would drive the demon to lust after such irreconcilable sensations, apparently as different as night and day yet, in fact, two faces of the same medal. Like when he had flooded her with pieces of himself, a combination of shiny particles fused with black ones, of light and darkness that had hit her on all sides.

Now, it was up to her and her Virt. To ensure that this precious and most singular being did not perish.

Shrugging off the unwanted responsibility, she surrounded his essence with her energy and squeezed tightly. Stroking it forcefully, she used the same pressure she had learned he liked on his cock. Almost lovingly, she continued with her seductive handjob, a steady up and down rhythm that had the blue ray glowing in no time at all, stronger, harder and more powerful.

Not all her doing.

Duncan's potent mix overflowing his angel with an extra surge spun things out of control. The aura mostly, now shining so bright until it flared up unexpectedly. One more second and the demon would have incinerated her on the spot had the prince not intervened. His energy falling like a heavy curtain between them, he infused his beloved with all the strength and love he could muster.

With a gasp, Chris opened his eyes.

"Angel, you're back among the living." Duncan's arms wrapped around the slender frame in a tight bear hug. Leaning over, he planted a soft kiss on his neck.

"Did we win?" Chris's lips curved in a grin that came out crooked.

"Of course, we did." Duncan beamed in response. "Thanks to you."

"Glad to be of help, lover." Despite his apparent exhaustion, Chris reached for the prince's lips for a quick kiss.

A chaste affair, this kiss, completely unlike the ardent exchanges she had witnessed more than once between the two stunning men. Still, it was heartbreaking to feel the depth of their connection that nothing, not even a near-death experience could lessen.

"Now, I feel tired." Dropping back down on the bed, Chris opened his mouth in an exaggerated yawn.

"You should eat something first." Worried lines furrowed Duncan's brow. "Then, you can go to sleep."

Since he was evidently too busy smothering his angel, she took it upon herself to fetch a glass of juice and hand it to Chris.

He drained it in one gulp.

Next, she arranged a selection of cheeses on a tray along with dried grain cakes, flat scones, honey muffins and fragrant seedy bread that she offered him.

"You'll see." Duncan nodded in pleasure the moment Chris began munching on a wheat cake. "Tomorrow, you'll feel like a new man."

"I guess I have you to thank." Raising himself, Chris rested on one elbow while devouring two flat scones in rapid succession. "For getting me out of the woods."

Glancing at her, Duncan cleared his throat. "Actually, Angel—"

"I know." The demon sighed heavily, turning to her with a resigned look. "It's you I have to thank, Milady."

"It's not necessary," she snapped with a tone that sounded colder than she intended. "You don't owe me anything." However much she reprimanded herself, she could not help feeling hurt by his reaction. "I've done nothing special." She buried it under her ironic words. "The little I did actually do was only for the prince's sake, not out of any concern for your life." Since this was a lie, she worked hard to make it ring as credible and as venomous as she could.

"Princess." Duncan's pained expression told her she had overplayed it a bit. "That's not true." Or maybe she was just a terrible liar.

"No, you're right. I deserved it." Chris, however, got her point loud and clear. "I apologize, Ylianor." Swallowing down a slice of bread and cheese, he looked at her earnestly. "I didn't mean to sound caustic." He shook his head in frustration. "I felt your touch inside, and it made me all the sorrier we're not compatible . . ." His blue-gray gaze roamed her body, undressing it at leisure and leaving her naked at his mercy.

Only natural, her face should grow unbearably hot until it blazed.

"Energy-wise, I mean." He managed to grin correctly this time. "You have the sweetest and most erotic touch I've ever felt. The way you stroked my energy back to life . . ." His pause was clearly a tactical one. "Well, if I hadn't been between life and death right now, I'd have come." Reaching for the tray at his side, he downed more cheese and a few honey muffins.

"It was a unique experience for me, too." It took no effort to admit this, mollified as she was now. To be honest, mellow had nothing to do with it.

She was downright excited. To hide it, she brought the pitcher of fruit juice and refilled his glass.

"Wherever I touched, you released electric sparks that sent shivers through my every fiber." She still could not get over the sensation, the mix of pleasure and annoyance always driving her insane. "I'm also sorry we can't do this under normal circumstances."

"Like on a bed?" He raised his glass with a naughty twinkle brightening his expression as if he wanted to toast her.

"Exactly on a bed," she confirmed readily, watching him empty his second glass.

"I'm glad you're feeling better already." Duncan tousled the blond hair affectionately. "At least judging from your topics."

"You know me." A sheepish smirk twisted his thin lips. "There's nothing like sex to make me feel better."

Eating and drinking had also its advantage, for his appearance had improved with every bite down his stomach.

"How could I ever forget?" She could swear she saw glimpses of their hottest male scenes flickering in his velvety gaze. "I guess I can—"

A hard knock made the prince stop and turn around to yell in the door's direction, "Come in."

"Forgive me, sir." Popping his head round the threshold, Colin fixed him. "I just wanted to inform you that David will be here shortly."

"He doesn't need to come here," Duncan objected. "Just tell him we'll leave in a little while." His gaze was about to connect back on the demon when it settled on Colin again, as though a new thought struck him. "Has Cecilia left?"

"Yes, sir," Colin confirmed. "She had to go straight away, what with all the chaos and Lord Fairchild's death—"

"What?" Chris's dismayed cry cut him off. "Arthur is dead?"

Damn! Duncan scoffed. *Why couldn't he keep his mouth shut?*

The demon was bound to find out soon enough, she argued sensibly, hoping to quell his agitation regarding Chris's despair.

Sure, but like this? "Yes, Angel, Arthur is dead." Clasping the demon's hands, he locked their gazes. "I'm so sorry."

"Dead?" Chris paled beyond his extreme pallor. "Why . . . when . . ." He had to catch his breath lest he choked on the emotions strangling him. "How did he die?"

"You need not worry about this now." Duncan caressed the beloved face full of so much misery that his own heart was near breaking. "You have to recover your strength." However sensible his suggestions, she knew Chris's grief was too overwhelming for anything as fundamental as mere comprehension, much less coherent thought. "We'll talk about it when I get back." Spinning to Colin, he waved him away. "Please go. I'll be right down."

"I'm sorry, sir." As if realizing he had made a mistake, Colin's contrite face stared back at him. "I didn't know —"

"Of course, you didn't," Duncan's tone softened. "It just seems that today everything is going the wrong way." A wry snarl curved his full lips. "Please, tell David to get the horses ready and pack food and blankets. I'll be down in a few minutes."

"Yes, sir, I will." After bowing, Colin closed the door.

"Where are you going, lover?" Chris grasped his arm.

"I have to get to the Hall." After patting his hand in reassurance, Duncan grabbed a bowl of dried fruits. Choosing a big fat fig, he fed it to Chris. "It seems Arthur intended me to succeed him as the new leader." It was the turn of a few shelled nuts and almonds to find their way to the demon's mouth.

"Wow, really?" Hastily gulping down, his blue-gray gaze glimmered in anticipation. "When did that happen? You haven't even claimed your permanent seat at the High Council yet."

"I know." Setting the bowl aside, Duncan shrugged as though such details meant nothing. "But I got confirmation of this destiny of mine from the greatest authority of all." He reclined on the demon in a conspiratorial fashion. "The princess," he whispered in his ear, loud enough so she could hear him, too.

"If she said it, then it must be true." The demon glanced at her from over Duncan's shoulders. "You know she's always right," he snickered. "That's why we've never won an argument against her."

"How true." The prince made a show of sighing loudly.

She stuck her tongue out at both of them. It was the only answer they deserved, but she felt it her duty to add, "Why do I keep wasting my breath on the likes of you?"

"Because you love us," was Duncan's amused reply.

Which made all three of them burst out laughing.

"No, I think she just likes to show off," Chris continued with the playful banter. "It's great news anyway about your leadership." Serious again, his attention was all back on the prince. "Though I'm sorry to see you go." The way he clung to his arm gave her the impression he would have loved nothing better than to detain him.

"Not as sorry as I am. Believe me." Bending, Duncan kissed him lightly, clearly afraid of causing any harm. "I thought I had lost you, and I would've never forgiven myself if I had." To be on the safe side, he fed him more succulent figs in between nuzzles and cuddles. "I should've never asked you to go out there, knowing your life could be at stake—"

"You were right to order it." Fixing a distant point midair, the blue-gray gaze filled with such despair, the likes of which she had never seen before. "There was so much misery, hatred, and . . ." His forehead creased as though he had trouble naming the sensations he had experienced. "Pain and hurt in the world. It almost killed me to get rid of it." His gaze cut back to Duncan. "I know I've caused my share of damage." He lowered his head in shame, probably prey to a vivid memory of his scary knife game. "But nothing can ever be comparable to what I saw." Anger coursed through him and reddened his aura's hue. He snapped his head upward. "That deadly force unleashed on the innocent people by . . ." His gaze wandered to the blue-stone pyramid on the table.

"Virtus," she supplied.

"The pyramid has a name?" Surprised, Chris stared at her wide-eyed. "It talked to you?"

"Yes." She nodded. "But not the pyramid itself, more like some entity that lives in it."

"Well, whatever it is, this Virtus freak is one fucked up monster when it comes to humans." In the intervening pause, Chris pushed out a heavy breath. "He practically wanted half the population to wipe out the other half."

I told you. Virtus is dangerous. She searched for the prince's liquid black eyes. *And evil.*

I never doubted you, Princess. His gaze swung to the pyramid, standing all blue and innocuous atop the table.

"Yeah, lover, that's a real menace over there." The demon had clearly followed Duncan's gaze.

"After everything that's happened, I can certainly concur with your assessment." His full lips split in a half-smile that broke some of the tension. "I just wonder if it will try escaping as soon as I leave?"

"I don't think so." Stepping closer, she studied the pyramid for a moment. "All this chaos and mayhem must've depleted its energy like it has ours."

"Mine has certainly never been scarcer," Chris joked, helping himself to more dried grain cakes.

"I wonder what will recharge it." The prince seemed captivated by the blue-stone object given how intently he observed it. "Now that it's outside the Nephis Valley's structure."

In reality, she knew he was analyzing every possible angle to come up with a logical solution to what had now become a great big mess.

"It's probably resourceful enough to survive no matter what," the demon sniggered.

"Not if we can help it." Kind of obvious, the next item on Duncan's agenda was how to shut down this damn threat. "We'll talk about it when I get back." He squeezed Chris in a sweeping, passionate embrace. "Now, you have to promise you'll rest and build up your strength." With a finger under his chin, he lifted the blond head. "I need you by my side as soon as possible, or I'll keep getting lost every time I turn a corner in that damn maze that's the Hall." The grin spread from his full lips to his eyes. "Think you'll be up to it?"

"I won't let you down, lover," Chris agreed immediately

before a scowl darkened his face. "If you're the new leader, you'll have to work with my father."

Right, James Templeton was the High Council Vice-Leader, the one who had summoned the council members and read Arthur's last instructions.

"Of course, I will." Duncan seemed to look forward to the prospect. "I'll have to see him as soon as I reach the Hall."

"Life is strange, isn't it?" Chris heaved.

"That's an understatement." The ironic black gaze was all on her. "But now, you have to rest, Angel." He placed a loving kiss on the demon's forehead.

"Yes, sir." But instead of obeying, Chris watched as Duncan moved about the room to get ready.

First, he went to a cabinet and changed into his traveling clothes. Picking up a satchel, he began stuffing it with whatever came under his hand.

"Here." Having spotted a wool sweater, she handed it to him. "For the cold nights."

"Promise you'll look after him, Princess." He took it and put it in the satchel he was filling with other items. "I'll hold you personally responsible should anything happen to him."

"Don't worry." She pressed a hand on his chest. "I'll nurse him back to complete health."

"Don't believe her, lover," Chris teased. "She'll be the death of me."

"Hush, you, unfaithful puppy." Prince Caldwell did not just smile broadly.

He showered his angel with a veritable deluge of unrestrained emotions, among which she glimpsed scorching love and palpable relief.

"If no one were to look after you, you'd rush into the first available bed." His black gaze unwavering, he could not look at anyone except Lord Christopher Templeton. "And drain the little energy you have left."

"At least it would be for a worthy cause," the demon was quick to raise the stakes.

"More worthy than saving the world?" Breaching their distance, Duncan returned to the bed and sat next to Chris. "You have a twisted sense of priorities." His arms snaked around the lithe frame as if they had a mind of their own, pulling him so close their chests glued to one another. "Never forget I love you, Angel." Given their closeness, it was no surprise that their lips pressed together in a most possessive and fiery kiss. "So fucking much, it hurts if only I think about it." Kind of amazing how he had managed to break the sensual exchange.

The way both men had been carrying out, she would have never thought they would ever untangle.

"I'd give up any responsibility right now simply to stay by your side." Shifting Chris's head, he burrowed his nose on the crook of his neck.

"You mustn't even think about it for a moment." Cupping his face, Chris raised it until their gaze leveled. "I'm not that important—"

"Hush, Angel." Another cunt-pounding kiss had them melting into each other once more. "You're the most important thing in my life!" There was no disguising the depth and fierceness of Duncan's declaration. "I'm just relieved I can still tell you in person." Kissing him again, he ran a hand down the demon's back. "Now, do try to be a good boy while I'm away, for your own sake."

"You know I'm incapable of being good, lover." Snug and conceited as only Christopher Templeton could be, she was sure he would start misbehaving as soon as the prince turned his back.

"Don't I?" Raking his fingers through the short thick hair, Duncan buried the blond head in his chest. "Now, please go to sleep." Lifting Chris's head again, he scrutinized the tired face attentively. "You look worn out and ready to drop at any moment." He traced the lines of fatigue crossing his lovely face. "If I don't see you resting, I won't be able to get anywhere."

"All right, if you insist." A huge yawn split Chris's face. "I'm kind of tired anyway." What he meant was that he was so beat he would sleep through an entire week.

And his pretenses be damned!

Turning on a side, he snuggled down, and the slowing of his breathing indicated he had indeed fallen fast asleep.

Duncan tucked him in tenderly, lingering a few minutes to deposit one last kiss on the blond head.

She thanked the stars she was not the jealous type, or she would have ensured that Chris never woke up from his sleep.

When the soft breathing became shallower and the face distended, Duncan got to his feet and went to pick up the satchel he had discarded earlier.

One quick check, a few more things thrown in, and he closed it. Balancing it on his shoulder, he advanced toward the door.

She expected him to step out and vanish without looking back. It would have hurt, but what had just occurred with the hateful demon was a tough act to follow. It had reminded her — as if there was any need — that his heart and senses belonged to one man alone. The force of their attraction was so overwhelming that no one could ever stand in the way. She was just a fool if she still harbored illusions about the striking prince despite the cock-wrenching game they had played together and the even more cunt-wetting one-on-one that had followed. It would serve her right if he left without glancing at her or uttering a single word —

Hey. Too wrapped up in her self-pity, she had failed to notice that he had spun around and opened his arms, watching her from the threshold with a strange glimmer lighting his dark pools as though he had intercepted all those negative thoughts she was now ashamed of acknowledging. *No good-bye kiss for your master?*

It was a provocation pure and simple.

I thought you had enough kissing for one day, she quipped, wanting to make him sweat for her but falling into his embrace, nonetheless.

He took immediate advantage, tilting up her face to claim her lips with a hungry growl of satisfaction.

He still craved her, his beautiful lover notwithstanding, and this awareness was enough to topple all her restraints.

Her body liquefying the second he tightened his hold, she drowned in his smell, touch and warmth. She breathed down his scent to her lungs in deep gulps of air that further sank her into his essence. With his lips and hands all over her, she surrendered. Everything belonged to him, anyway. Body, heart and mind, his for the taking, had he not already claimed it all.

His tongue ravaged her mouth all the way to her throat. His hard kiss bruised her lips. His triumphant sweeps started a dull throbbing in her cunt and wetness pooled between her legs.

I'm sorry I can't stay to finish this. His apologetic grin was heart-stopping, however maddening his statement.

I'm sure I'll find someone to take care of it, she taunted thinking that it would serve him right. Her tone turned serious, *Be careful, my love.*

I will. He squeezed her tighter than ever. *Don't worry.* His gaze caught hers. *Just watch out for Virtus.*

I will. Suppressing the urge to switch her focus on the pyramid, she snuggled closer. *Have a safe journey.*

Another ardent kiss, another luscious tongue slide to her stomach, another titillating touch, then Prince Caldwell was gone.

While she was alone, body burning in desire, mind confused and unsettled by a very frail demon who still hovered between life and death in spite of his earlier passionate show.

CHAPTER THIRTY

"How is Lord Templeton?" David asked the second Prince Caldwell stepped out of Blue Oasis's front entrance.

Not that he needed to bother about it.

The relief was so palpable he had no trouble reading it all over his master's handsome face.

"Much better." Duncan pushed out a heavy breath. "For a moment there, I feared I might lose him . . ." He averted his gaze as though trying to hide the swirl of emotions rising to the surface faster than he could conceal them.

Which was useless for David knew all about it. Had known way back when the phase had begun, seeing how easily that blond tantalizing creature had sucked the prince into a sensual vortex that still held him prisoner years after it would have been supposedly over. Too deep their bond and inevitable, given how young they had been when they had first met. Which had not improved matters for him, David Smith, who had loved Prince Duncan Caldwell ever since he had become a privileged part of his life as his personal valet and trusted advisor.

"It seemed like touch and go for a while." Upon regaining his composure, Duncan's voice steadied, "But then the princess intervened and saved his life." Impossible to miss the sense of profound gratitude oozing from his every pore. "Literally." He fixed a point in midair, a concerned expression veiling his beautiful black eyes as if contemplating how horrible things could have turned out had she not succeeded.

"I'm real glad to hear it." It was the truth, no matter how

little he could stand the smug Lord Christopher Templeton.

And having spotted the same in Ylianor, he did not comment on the role she played in saving what she must consider a competitor.

"Me, too." Duncan shook his head free of that worst-case scenario and glanced at Fuzeon. "Shall we go?"

"Absolutely." David handed the bridles he had been holding after fetching the horse from Cecilia's stables. "I hear congratulations are in order."

"Is that what Cecilia told you?" Swinging a long leg across Fuzeon's back, he mounted gracefully.

"Well, she has no certainty." He followed his master's example, settling on Oscar. "But from Lord James Templeton's summon and Lord Fairchild's death . . ." The pause was in order.

Even if he had hardly seen the deceased leader, just once for the record, everyone concurred he had been a great man. He had absolved his duties and responsibilities with efficiency and efficacy.

"Anyway . . ." Clearing his throat, he led Oscar toward Blandry's northeastern boundary. "She's convinced that these two events together can mean only one thing." He turned to level their gazes. "That the High Council will proclaim you as our new leader." He could not restrain the beam of pure, unadulterated pride, the same he had felt when Lady Hurst had first prospected this news.

"Cecilia and her sound logic will be the death of me," the prince joked, obviously referring to her decision to steal the pyramid from the Nephis Valley.

"Not in this case if she's right," he joined in the amusement.

"She must be since the princess has been telling me the same thing." Stifling a grimace, Duncan gripped his left shoulder as though it hurt. "But we'll know for sure as soon as we reach the Hall." After rubbing the sore spot, which seemed to be where he had always had that odd-looking scar, he grasped the reins firmly once more.

"About that . . ." Being on the lead, David slowed down. "There are two routes to get there. The first and fastest takes you through the mountains. It's a bit taxing for the horses, but I'm sure both Fuzeon and Oscar are up to it." Both beasts were well-rested, after all. "That's where Cecilia went," he added as a way to persuade his master, remembering how much she had stressed the need for expediency.

"What's the second road?" Unconvinced, Duncan stared forward at the desert's vast emptiness.

"It goes through many villages," he provided. "We won't have to cross the mountains, so it's less dangerous but infinitely slower." Cecilia would be anything except pleased should he go for this one.

"Let's take for the villages." Mind made up, Duncan kicked Fuzeon's flanks to get moving. "I want to see what we caused and help people deal with it," he offered as a way of an explanation.

"All right." Nodding, he matched Oscar's pace to Fuzeon's, wondering at the same time how he could ever make it up to his prince.

The brief remark had made his guilt resurface all at once, the same he had struggled with ever since moving those blasted pieces around. Once more, he wished he had never laid eyes on the damn pyramid or Cecilia for that matter, the weight of having betrayed his adored master twice pressing heavily on his chest.

"I'm sorry," he blurted eventually, unable to stand his heavy conscience and the unbearable distance from the man he loved and had vowed to serve for the rest of his life. "I didn't mean to . . ." *Be such a traitor? Set the pyramid free? Make it beat to a different tune? Plunge the world in chaos? All of the above?*

A strained breath escaped from his lips. "About

everything," he mumbled at last, talking more to himself than to anyone in particular. "Ceci told me about the wreckage we caused to people and things." He hung his head. "I didn't mean for any of it to happen —"

"I know," his voice soft, Duncan understood somehow.

For which he could not thank him enough.

"None of us wanted any of this," the prince continued. "I suppose we all misused our powers in one way or another." From his intense expression, he guessed Duncan alluded to something more far-reaching than what had just occurred. "Speaking of which, why didn't you tell me about yours?"

Yeah, why hadn't he? "I wasn't sure of it at first," he began apologetically. "For a long time, I thought my imagination was playing tricks on me. After I realized it wasn't, I didn't know what to do." He recalled his uncertainty and bewilderment at the strangeness of it all, not to mention the sheer intoxication. "With Ceci, it only came out because of the pyramid."

"It's a great power you have." Gone the earlier scolding, Duncan now sounded admired.

"One I obviously misused," he was quick to make the connection. "Like you so rightly observed."

Funny how this amazing man always seemed to be one step ahead of everyone else.

"No, David." The black eyes flashed in disagreement. "I was speaking for all of us, so don't blame yourself." He settled himself more comfortably on the saddle. "If anyone is responsible, it's me since I ordered you to do it."

"No, you don't understand, Prince." Driven to prove his point, he raised his voice, "It was my doing that brought that damn pyramid to Blue Oasis." Which was not the worst part of it. "Still my doing, I didn't tell you anything, not just about my power but also about Cecilia." He would make a clean slate of it even if it killed him, even if his master might never want to see him again. "I'm to blame 'cause I betrayed you not once but twice in such a short time." Real sorrow crept in his voice at the enormity of his misbehavior. "I don't deserve to serve you, Prince—"

"Nonsense!" Duncan cut him off abruptly. "Just because you were seeing Cecilia doesn't mean you betrayed me." He dismissed that claim with a mere wave of the hand. "There was never anything between us, only sex and my fascination with her brilliant mind." This came as no surprise, for they had talked about it often enough in the past. "There's still nothing between us, even if I'm sure you heard I had sex with both her and Rowena during the Game."

"Yeah, I heard." He pursed his lips the same way he had when Ceci had recounted the experience.

"I just thought that, given our closeness, you'd have dropped a hint or two." A vaguely reproachful glimmer lit the dark pools confronting him. "Not that I want to know about your private affairs." He shrugged as though to emphasize he was not pushy or anything. "For they are none of my business."

"You're not angry with me then?" *You're not going to cast me off for being disloyal?*

"No, David," Prince Caldwell reassured. "I'm just sad you didn't find it in your heart to tell me about the new things in your life, pyramid included." The velvety gaze swung to catch his. "Didn't we use to share everything, old friend?"

The affection in the term made his stomach cave in, and his heart stopped dead. "You're right, Prince." Swallowing, he was glad to notice that his heartbeat had resumed. "I would have, had Ylianor not returned and complicated things good and proper." Unbidden, her lovely face and dazzling green eyes filled his mind. "She . . ." She was just too beautiful for words, and her striking resemblance to Duncan had mixed up matters beyond any safe level. "What happened with her was . . ." Frantically, he searched for words. "Embarrassing and incredible at the same time."

"I'd say uneasy most of the time," Duncan summed it up brilliantly. "At least if I remember how fidgety you were at Black Rose right after she arrived." His intelligent eyes sparked as if prey of a new awareness. "But I'm guessing I was the source of your nervousness, not her."

"Hem . . ." As usual, his master's intuition was unbeatable. "I dare say it was." Just admitting it was like a load had suddenly been lifted.

"Look, David." He spun his head gracefully, his long black hair fluttering around his shoulders. "I already told you. Like Cecilia, the princess is *not my property*." Piercing black gaze bore into him, evidently wanting no misunderstanding to stand in their way. "*I don't own her*," he spelled each word slowly and distinctly. "She's free to do as she wishes, and that includes being with you."

"Yes, I know she's her own person." She had more than proven it, first at Black Rose and now at Cecilia's Game. "But she isn't the only reason I didn't breathe a word of what was going on with me." He threw back his shoulders to give himself the courage to speak his mind. "Truth is—I felt you distant." Surreptitiously, he glanced at the prince from under his eyelashes to determine his reactions. Since he perceived nothing but interested attention, he charged on, "You seemed so distracted and preoccupied with other things that my stuff didn't seem all that important, just like everything else. Whatever the subject, I got the feeling you were so far away I couldn't reach you, no matter how hard I tried."

"You're right." Duncan's words seemed to tumble out like pebbles falling from a waterfall. "I was," he acknowledged wearily. "Distracted, as you said, by my angel first and foremost." His gaze shifted to the road they were traveling. "I love him so fucking much. Always had and always will." Such was the unmistakable fierceness in the possessive undertone that it hit like a blow to the stomach. "Yet, I worked hard to deny it in the two years that followed the end of our phase, pretending it didn't exist." His focus did not waver. "Imagine, I was so foolish I thought it would be enough never to see him again to erase my feelings for him."

"But now, it's different." He had no doubt it was, considering the newfound closeness he had seen of late. "Right, Prince?"

"Today, I'm a new man," Duncan confirmed. "I love my angel, and the phase has nothing to do with it." The angles of his full lips curved upward. "More than that, I quit fighting this captivating pull he has over me. He holds my heart in the palm of his hand, and I wouldn't want it any other way." His satisfaction was tangible. "Accepting this love has made me free, and my life is all the better for it." His forehead creased as though he had just thought of something new. "At least until the princess came along." He smirked naughtily. "Like you said, she complicates things good and proper," he sniggered. "No, make that she has a rare talent for it." Somehow, he did not seem to be thinking of himself alone.

Which got him wondering how Lord Templeton was putting up with the nuisance of having a rival so close to the man he considered his personal property.

"I thought that, after the angel, nothing would ever challenge my choices again." A wry grin curved his full lips. "Boy, was I wrong," he admitted flatly. "She had me question my entire set of beliefs, and I'm not done yet." He paused as though struck by new consideration. "Nor do I know where it might take me." He squared his shoulders as though getting ready for a fight. "The only thing I'm sure of is that we share something unique, something I can't replicate with anyone else, not even my angel."

Was it his impression, or did he detect a trace of regret in the prince's voice?

"Which means she'll have to become a permanent fixture in our lives." Oddly enough, he seemed weighed down by this awareness.

David could not help wondering what was really going on, and the reasons for his ambivalence regarding Ylianor.

But then, something in the prince appeared to shift, taking the heaviness with it. "Which also means that her purpose is to mess up my life," he joked, his tone implying he was far from displeased at how she was going about her task. "Not only is she the most irresistible woman I've ever had the misfortune of knowing, so damn attractive I'd keep her chained to my bed as you probably heard during the Game." He practically smacked his lips as though remembering the hottest scenes. "She's also . . ." He hesitated, evidently debating an issue with himself. Having made up his mind, he plunged ahead, "When the lawyer came to Black Rose, he told me that my father wanted to include her in the will. He felt so strongly about her that he wants to adopt her and give her the Caldwell name."

"Really?" David could not wrap his head around this news. "She will become a Caldwell?"

"She might." The prince nodded. "Let's say the choice to honor this clause is mine, and I wasn't too favorable at the idea when I first heard it." In other words, he must have been dead set against it. "Now, I see it a bit differently." The twist in the full lips gave the sensation that it had been anything but easy to come to terms with this unusual provision. "I still have some issues to work out, but I have to decide by the end of the summer, before the official reading of the will."

"So, what will it be, sir?" Curious in spite of himself, he raised his gaze to peer at the gorgeous man by his side.

"I don't know yet, David," he breathed after a long spell. "I must confess that my father's request rattled my certainties. I found that I took for granted our rigid class distinction, despite my protests to the contrary. Truth is—things get twisted if you start considering people as individuals, not labels."

"I see." He beamed understanding where his master was going with this. "I'm sure Ceci will be pleased," he quipped sarcastically.

"She'll be anything but, given how she feels about the princess." Unavoidable for his master to notice.

Then again, how could he not given Ceci's antagonism.

"Must've been tough for you when she found out about her." Duncan grinned.

"Well . . ." He coughed dryly, unwilling to reveal just how awful it had been. "I've had better days."

"I bet." Somehow, his brief remark appeared to have reinforced the prince's convictions. "That's why she was so interested in her during the Game," Duncan mused with an ironic glint lighting his dark eyes.

"Let's say her competitive side got the better of her," he interjected as an apology. "But then, as you said, Ylianor is so unique. I guess Ceci felt . . ." *Downright jealous and envious!* "Threatened," he opted for a softer approach. "And overreacted—"

"She was downright jealous and envious." The prince set the record straight once and for all. "And afraid to lose you."

"Me?" This was news to him. "I think her jealousy was directed at you, sir."

"Nah." Prince Caldwell rejected his suggestion with a shrug. "In case you haven't noticed, she seems genuinely attached to you."

"We get along well, Prince." His face flushed hotly. "But I know where I stand, and it's not the same place she's at."

"While the princess is?" Duncan frowned.

"Right now, she is." That was an undeniable fact. "If she becomes a Caldwell, though." *I won't stand a chance.*

The abyss that would inevitably separate them would be insurmountable.

"David, you're wrong to let the class issues limit your choices," Duncan objected. "People can pledge whomever they like regardless of their classes. Whether you want Cecilia or Ylianor, just reach out, and everything else be damned."

"That wouldn't do, Prince." No, no way it could. "As I said, I know where I stand."

"Have it your way." The prince raked nervous fingers through his long hair as if fed up with his stubbornness. "But if I do become the leader, I'll ask you to manage everything at the Hall, like you do at Black Rose." Catching his gaze, he held it. "This will certainly raise your level to a new height. More than that, it'll make you a very powerful man in your own right."

"Sir, it'll be an honor and a privilege to serve you in your new role." He bowed stiffly, elated yet confused at the same time. "I didn't expect to —"

"You should," the prince retorted. "You're a competent man and a trusted friend." He patted his shoulder, given their proximity. "Who better than you could I charge with the responsibility of managing an important place like the Hall?"

"I understand." He bowed as a sign of acceptance. "I'll be happy to look after things for you just like I do now in Black Rose." He pursed his lips, knowing the prince would not like his next remark yet unable to let it slide. "But it won't change my status."

"Suit yourself." Duncan's lighthearted tone did not fool him one bit.

Prince Caldwell was the most unconventional man he knew. No one tried as hard as he did to crumble the social barriers dividing the world into privileges and classes determined by birth. The only line he drew was in bed. His aristocratic taste and rigid selection allowed no servants anywhere near it. So, why had he thrown all reservations to the wind and gone after Ylianor?

"I'm sure Cecilia feels differently." Spurring Fuzeon, Duncan picked up his pace.

"She certainly does," he had to agree. "She even went as far as asking me to pledge."

Leaping forward, Oscar caught up with Fuzeon, and both horses set on a brisk throttle.

"Which you refused." There was no trace of a question in his master's confident analysis.

"Of course, I did." No other alternative would have been possible! "How could I ever accept?"

"Still, it didn't prevent you from helping her steal the pyramid." Luckily, the prince did not sound harsh, just matter of fact.

"I know, and I'm sorry." He hung his head, for he would never be through apologizing. "But there's something about Ceci that gets to me in a way that . . ." He had to take a breath to clear his head. "I mean, I don't feel like this about anyone else." His heart throbbing loudly protested to the contrary, conjuring up one enticing picture after another of Ylianor.

Not something he could dwell on, so he silenced it in haste to cover his partial truth.

"She's so very lonely that I just can't stand it." He sighed for it tore him inside. "Most of the time, she reminds me of a lost little girl, trying to play grown-up," his voice breaking for a second, he struggled to steady it. "When she talked about her plan, I was afraid she'd do something she'd regret later. That's why I thought it best to go with her." He bent his head in shame. "Believe me. I had no other purpose."

"I believe you, David." To prove his point, the prince showered him with a most dazzling smile that crushed his stomach to a pulp. "Let's hope this serves us both as a lesson to trust our friends in the future."

"I always trusted you, Prince." Overcome by emotions, there was no hope of recovering his self-control if not by averting his gaze.

"Good." Incredible yet true, Duncan's smile deepened, and there was no describing the man's allure. "It's important, especially now that I'll need you more than ever." Raising his gaze, he fixed the vast emptiness in the general direction of the Jeruashi Mountains.

"I won't fail you, Prince." He would not, even if it killed him.

"You better not," Duncan teased. "'Cause you're an integral part of how we're going to solve this pyramid business."

"We ought to put it back." It was the most logical course of action.

"We'll decide together, the five of us like I promised Ceci," his master's tone was cautious as though he had not yet made up his mind. "And you're an essential part of this group."

"We're a group now?" David joked, not sure he liked this twist.

Not since the group comprised the very obnoxious Lord Christopher Templeton.

"Yes, whether we like it or not." Duncan seemed to pluck his concern straight from his mind. "We're the only ones who know what happened, and I want it to stay this way."

"To be honest, I still don't know exactly what happened." To say that he and Cecilia had been baffled would be an understatement.

The moment the pieces had stopped spinning, he had been conscious only of Ylianor's black-out. Next, she had returned with an urgency he had not yet comprehended. Right after, he had seen the prince's anguish as he had clutched Lord Templeton with a vehemence that had spoken volumes about the depth of his feelings. To the point, he had clung to his lover like he would never set eyes on him ever again.

275

Like he was about to die or something.

Which maybe he was, given how he had collapsed.

And maybe, it had been the same thing that had yanked out his insides and left him weak and uncertain.

And why had Ylianor seemed to be orchestrating everything? Like she was in control or something?

Someone had a lot of explaining to do, and he could not wait.

"We'll discuss it after things have settled down," Duncan guaranteed. "For now, the fewer people know, the better." Lines of worry creased his ample forehead. "Our priority is to stop it from happening again. As for the others, we'll say that an unknown force has attacked us."

"Will they believe it?" In other words, could people be so gullible. "If the reports that were coming through are any indication, people won't be satisfied with simple explanations."

"Oh, they will." His master sounded quite certain. "The angel made sure everyone forgot everything about this ordeal."

"He did?" He opened his eyes wide from the amazement. "He has that kind of power?"

"Yes, absolutely." Duncan nodded with ill-concealed pride. "Virt is how our ancestors called it, and his own is to heal and erase memory." The sheer power of it made his head spin. "He can cure people's wounds and make them forget they were ever injured."

"He also managed to do a spell on all the lands?" He still could not believe the potency of it all. "That's why he was so weak afterward."

"Yes, despite all the energy we supplied him," the prince clarified.

"We?" *When? How?*

"Didn't you feel like your inside was pulled out?" At his nod, Duncan resumed, "That was the princess's doing. She transferred all of our energy to the angel. His mission was extremely dangerous, and he could've died." With a wounded look, the prince grimaced as if he were still living the threat of losing his lover.

"But he came through in one piece," he recalled.

"Yes, my angel is a tough one." Prince Caldwell could not suppress the note of unconditional love lacing his tone. "May the gods always keep him so," he continued softly. "Now, enough of the past." Kicking Fuzeon's flanks, he accelerated. "It's time to meet our future and start reconstructing our world."

Time for discussion over, David prodded Oscar to keep up, bracing himself for the death and desolation that was sure to be awaiting just beyond the horizon.

CHAPTER THIRTY-ONE

"Leader, we must go." Catching Prince Caldwell during a break from his latest task, David approached him. "They're waiting for you at the Hall and . . ."

He did not have the heart to continue, the sheer havoc of this last territory shutting his mouth however right he knew he was.

"Yeah." Duncan rubbed his eyes as though they were tired. "You're right." He looked at the wall he was helping to build. "We should get back on the road."

Not just on the road. Onto the High Council like Cecilia had stressed.

If only the degradation had not reached the remotest corners of the land, causing a general shortage of food and water, David would have managed to set a brisk pace. As it was, the sheer abnormity of what he had unwittingly unleashed had numbed him ever since their first mile on the road.

Merely a stone's throw away from Blue Oasis, people had looked so totally out of it that it had been the most natural of impulses on Duncan's part to jump off Fuzeon and get down to work. What other choice did he have?

They had needed a leader and badly, considering how utterly lost they had been in that big field of crumbling ruins that had once been their village, their home. Everything had lain in heaps of smoldering stones, some pressing on human forms that seemed too still to be alive. Without a leader worthy of his name, those people would have never managed to survive the days to come.

Just their luck that Duncan Caldwell was the right man for the job.

No other would have been as quick as he was to respond and take immediate action. He had assigned them to collect and burn all the corpses as fast as possible, lest they infected the little water and food the community had managed to salvage. He had personally helped erect the funeral pyre, a stack of bodies so high that it had probably taken more than one day and night to burn them all.

But by then, he and Prince Caldwell had been on the road again, shortening the long-distance that separated Cecilia's Blandry District from Rockyhorn, the seat of the Hall and the High Council.

Not that they would reach it any time soon!

Given the desolation of it all, people detained them at every turn to ask for advice and help. Being the incredible person he was, Leader Duncan Caldwell found the time for everyone. Stopping at every bewildered village they crossed, he gave support, alleviated the suffering, cleaned up the terrible waste of lands that once thrived, and detailed plans for a fast recovery. In short, he was simply one-step ahead of anybody David knew, which infused people with the belief that things would return to normal.

Not mere words alone.

Duncan set the example for all, working despite the little time at his disposal that was running twice as fast.

This was the reason he and Duncan were still on the road, traveling with such unusual slowness that a journey of a weeklong had already lengthened to more than ten days.

"Will you be leaving soon?" One of the men working alongside the prince to repair the half-crumbled wall raised his gaze.

"Have to." Duncan looked sorry he would. "They're waiting for me at the Hall, so . . ." He shrugged apologetically.

"I understand." Getting up from his crouched position, the man stretched his legs. "But we'll miss you." He glanced around at what remained of his hamlet.

Not much to be sincere.

Having seen his fair share of disintegrated sites, this was in a particularly bad state, given the few buildings left standing. The majority of what had once been a flourishing townlet lay in ruins that would require a lot more effort than what the few residents still alive could afford.

"'Cause the situation seems kind of desperate . . ." And for the record, it looked pretty desperate to David.

"We just have to be more efficient and organized if we want to pull through this," the leader stated philosophically. "For the time being, join forces with the neighboring communities and organize teams that work on reconstructing one village at a time while sharing the little food you have." Confident in his analysis, he tapped the man's back. "'Cause you have few resources, human or otherwise. Only if you share everything will you survive."

"Yeah, you're right." The man nodded gravely. "It's just that everyone is still under shock from what happened." Taking a step back, he lowered his gaze. "No one expected such calamity to fall on us." He pushed out a heavy breath. "My pledge mate . . ." He winced. "She remained trapped two days under the rubbles of our house, and I still can't believe my luck that I found her alive."

"I know." Impulsively, the prince squeezed the man's shoulder. "I almost lost my phase mate, so I know exactly how you feel."

He was telling no lie.

His pain was still so raw that David could not help feeling it himself. To think he had never stood Christopher Templeton, not since the time they had all been kids. Too exclusive for his taste, the gorgeous boy had set his mind on having the prince all to himself, to the point he had driven away anyone and anything he perceived as competition. Little Ylianor had been the first one to pay for his misguided belief that Duncan Caldwell could be his and his alone.

Yet, seeing how he had jumped to do what would have killed a lesser man, then witnessing Duncan's unfathomable black pit at the thought he could ever lose him, David wondered whether he had missed something about the stunning blond. Maybe, just maybe, he was not just an egotistical narcissistic who thought only about himself. Maybe, there was something more to him, something the prince had evidently seen from the start, but that had escaped most everybody else's notice.

David had only to remember Anne Peacock's reactions, to know he was speaking the truth. For the cook in Black Rose had never had any great love for the vain boy, and time had not improved her opinion any.

"I'm sorry, Prince." The man clasped his hand. "I hope he's better now."

"He's . . ." David figured Duncan's hesitation was to silence his heart from beating too loudly. "Recovering. I've left a competent person to look after him, so I'm sure he'll be fine."

Briefly and not for the first time, David wondered how that particular relationship was evolving. Given how little Lord Christopher Templeton and Ylianor could tolerate one another, it seemed ironic Duncan would have left her in charge of his precious angel's wellbeing. Or perhaps, he had counted on the fact Lord Christopher Templeton was in no shape to hurt anyone at the moment, not even by mistake.

Right, but what had made her agree to it?

David put it down to her blind love for the incredible prince she had adored since forever. She had fallen for him without even fighting it, unable to hide those feelings that made her huge green eyes shine like stars. Then, Ceci's Game must have escalated everything to an unbearable level, given all the accounts that had circulated.

No one could stop talking about the two of them, about how differently they played from everyone else and how little they resembled a master with his slave. Passionate lovers was more the sensation they gave off in that chamber, to the point everyone on that floor had wished to be in Ylianor's shoes, including Ceci and Rowena. Or to be more precise, every woman had been jealous of Ylianor, of the sparks she gave off every time the prince simply looked at her.

It had not surprised David in the least.

Little Ylianor had adored the prince from way back then. Ever since she had been old enough to walk, she had followed him around like a lovesick puppy begging for the slightest bit of his attention. The difference now was that he did not simply pay her attention. He seemed bewitched by her like his mother had claimed from the start. Then again, what could you expect from a witch's daughter?

Actually, David had never believed the wild tales about witchcraft and sorcery that had plagued Mary Jane and her Caldwell-like offspring. Since she had not pledged to Prince Charles Caldwell, Ylianor could not be his daughter, however attached Prince Charles had become to the child after her mother's death. Duncan himself had not been immune from her allure, either, protecting her from his mother's vicious attacks despite his young age. Chasing after her on Black Rose's every hill while growing up, he had been her privileged playmate until the stuck-up lord had the bad taste to show up at Black Rose's front gate, and things had changed forever.

Shaking his head free from the unbidden memories, David returned his focus on the here and now.

"I'm glad to hear." A luminous smile split the man's face. "You already have so much weight on your shoulders."

Since the load was going to grow if they did not get a move, David tried to bring the leader back to his duties.

"Which is why we should be going," he cut in softly as he advanced.

"Yes, we can't delay it any longer," Duncan heaved in evident weariness.

"Is it true you'll be our new leader?" Eyes ablaze in interest, the man did not allow him to budge.

"I wouldn't know." Of course, the prince downplayed it. "I haven't talked with anyone from the High Council, not even with Lord Templeton, our vice-leader."

"I'm sure they'll offer you the position." The man patting his back appeared to have no doubts. "They must," his voice rose a notch. "For there's no better man for the job!"

"Thanks for the vote of confidence." Duncan beamed enchantingly. "That's why I must leave immediately." He extended a hand, and the man squashed it forcefully. "I know you'll be looking after things here. But as soon as I get to the Hall, I'll send you extra manpower." He tightened his grip.

"I'll be sure to finish up here." The man let go of Duncan's hand. "So, we can help anyone here or in any of the other districts."

"Thank you." The prince grinned.

"No, thank you for being here with us. For *us*." Abruptly, the man grabbed back Duncan's hand, as though he wanted to press his point. "For taking the time to stop and oversee our work."

There was so much gratitude and admiration in the man's tone that it was kind of inevitable for David's heart to melt on the spot. This man, repeating what countless others had already said, proved that people could not help loving their new leader.

No questions about it.

David saw it all too clearly from the light shining in their eyes, the interest and respect with which they followed Duncan's every word.

Which was nothing new as far as David was concerned.

He had always believed his master to be so far above ordinary mortals that such reactions did not surprise him. Like everyone else at Black Rose, he had the certainty Duncan's destiny would be a great one. His words and his every deed testified to it, to the point David had no doubt he was witnessing the beginning of a legend.

Prince Duncan Caldwell would turn out to be the most exceptional leader of all times, fast eclipsing any other before him, Arthur Fairchild included.

And David, his servant since the time he was a mere boy, could not have been prouder to serve a man so far superior and with such a shiny path in front of him.

"It was my pleasure," Duncan assured. "Should you require it, feel free to come to the Hall to discuss whatever problem you may encounter." He hesitated slightly. "Though I'd much prefer it if you came to share your solutions." A wide smile broke his handsome features.

"I will most certainly take you up on your offer, Leader." The man returned the infectious smile. "If I have something noteworthy to bring to your attention."

"Not mine." Duncan spun to David and to the others who had gathered in the meantime. "To everyone's attention, 'cause we're all in this together." After a quick bow as a way of saluting them all, he moved off finally.

David was at his heels. "By the way, I have news from Blue Oasis."

"Yes?" The quickening of the step and the somber expression clouding his beautiful face was the most telling evidence that the thought of Christopher Templeton was always on his mind.

Not a second went by that the prince did not worry about

his blond lover in a way that tightened David's heart every time, and he would have given an arm or a leg just to make sure he pulled through safely, for nothing and no one would be able to withstand Duncan's bottomless despair.

"Lord Templeton is recovering," David was quick to set his mind at ease. "He's still weak, of course, and spends his time in bed, sleeping most of the time." Unconscious actually, if he had to be honest. The man had also eaten next to nothing since all chaos had broken loose.

Something David accurately avoided mentioning.

Once he had realized their journey would take forever, he had set up a system of relaying information back and forth from Blue Oasis, designed to give Duncan the freshest news possible.

"Ylianor is constantly at his side." He cleared his throat, unwilling to let his feelings for her strangle him in any way. "Though they tell me he isn't aware of anything much right now." Fearing that his words were not precisely cheering up the prince, he gripped his shoulder hard. "But he's getting better, sir. Believe me."

"Thanks, David." Duncan clutched his hand. "I have the utmost confidence in my angel and his ability to pull through." His face split in the most handsome of smiles.

David hoped he meant it for real. That it was not something he told himself because the situation was not as good as he was making it out to be.

"Now, come on." Picking up his pace, Duncan walked away. "We've got work to do, so time to get moving."

"Yes, sir." Eagerly following, David fell in step next to him.

Fuzeon and Oscar were grazing nearby. With a few brisk strides, he reached the horses, mounted and rode off in the Hall's direction alongside his prince.

CHAPTER THIRTY-TWO

"Fellow members . . ." Raising his gaze, James Templeton glanced at the tired and drawn faces of the few men and women who had made it to the Hall in one piece.

The others, the majority unfortunately, seemed lost to the chaos that had broken loose from out of nowhere.

Same chaos that had taken Arthur.

His dear friend, Arthur.

He had to suppress the wave of sadness, threatening to overcome him. For unlike everybody else, he had not just lost the Leader of the High Council. He had lost the one tie to his past.

To Charles.

His focus shifted to the Caldwell Seat, which had been empty for far too long. And it would continue to be so since Charles's son was to become the new leader.

Imagine that!

Duncan Caldwell, the new leader!

He still could not believe it. Not even now that more than ten days had passed since Arthur's death and Duncan's nomination. He knew it better than anyone since he had been the first to be called in upon Arthur's demise.

As Vice-Leader of the High Council, it had been his duty to see his friend's lifeless body lying in a heap at the bottom of the valley. It had been a long plunge downward from that window in his office from where he had supposedly fallen. Which was as hard to swallow as the notion that he had been sitting there in the first place.

Arthur had never been one to linger next to the windows. He always sat at his desk or on the comfortable couches next to the fireplace. Knowing that his pledge mate, Claudette, had been there with him in one of her extremely infrequent visits to the Hall made it even less likely that Arthur might have been dallying near a window.

Or had he?

When he had questioned her, another of his duties, she had seemed to be coming out of a trance. The poor woman seemed to have no recollection of having ever reached the Hall, asked the servants for a word with Arthur or talked to him in the privacy of his office.

The two of them alone.

Yet, she had not even realized he was dead, and it had been up to him, James Templeton, to break the sad news. She had been stunned, to say the least.

No, there was no end to the strangeness or the bafflement of it all. Like reading Arthur's will and discovering that Duncan Caldwell, his son's phase mate, was to become his friend's successor, the new Leader of the High Council.

"Hem . . ." Someone clearing her throat snagged his attention back to the here and now. "Forgive me, Lord Templeton." Lady Cecilia Hurst rose from her seat as a permanent representative of the Blandry District. "Have you any news?"

"Reports keep pouring in." Regaining his composure, he squared his shoulders and faced the assembly gathered in the semi-circular chamber that was the High Council official meeting place. "They're anything but good." He grimaced, feeling weighed down by the enormity of the downfall.

The worst thing was that no one knew anything. No, make that no one *remembered* anything, which was the oddest thing of all.

"Too many people have died and more still because of the injuries they suffered." Worriedly, he noticed the expressions around him were void of any hope for the future. "There's no telling how many villages have been destroyed in total or in part. Every day, I think I have the final count, yet every day I have to increase the numbers."

He groaned inwardly. *Will this nightmare ever end?*

"What about your son?" Still standing, Lady Hurst fixed him with her dark, intelligent eyes. "Do you know if he is better?"

She had sketched out the events that had taken place at her home, Blue Oasis, while her Game of Masters and Slaves had been in full progress no less!

He had not needed to ask what his son had been doing there. All the Arthur boys could talk about at the end of last season had been this renown Game and how to weasel an invitation, if not from Cecilia, from any suitable body going. Since he knew Chris could not stand the woman, he wondered whether he had convinced Prince Caldwell to take him as a guest. Yet, Duncan was the last person he would have imagined attending such a sex-filled event, much less receiving a master's invitation from the woman. This bit of news ran contrary to everything he knew and had heard about the serious-minded young man who was Prince Charles's beloved son and heir.

"No, I'm afraid I have no news." Noticing the anguish softening her hard features, the same that had tormented him ever since learning of this incident, he added in a gentler tone, "But I'm sure he's being taken care of at Blue Oasis."

"I left strict orders that his wellbeing was a priority," Lady Hurst assured firmly. "That it had to come before any other concern, including the personal ones."

"I have no doubt he's recovering as we speak." Or so he ardently hoped, for he loved this stubborn yet dazzling son of his, however problematic he could be at times.

Which was the reason he had been less than forthcoming

about his feelings to his son's face.

"He must!" The fierceness in her tone took him aback. "From everything Prince Caldwell said, your son acted most bravely to stop the chaos."

"He did?" If a part of him was proud of it, another was struggling to fit his impetuous blond boy into this new role.

Not at all an easy task.

Christopher Templeton was simply too damn beautiful and sensual to do anything as selfless as Lady Hurst implied. *Too gorgeous for words. Nah, too gorgeous for his own good.* That had always been the problem, the one thing that had amazed yet frightened him. To the extent that he still found it difficult to accept this incredible son of his, especially if compared to his elder brothers.

Steve and Bran were smart boys, intelligent and reliable fellows, dependable to a fault. But they had none of the allure Chris had in such abundance. Their handsome looks did not come anywhere near the explosion of the senses that was his youngest son, and there was no way around this fundamental truth.

For whatever his shortcomings, there was just something so unique about him, something that set him apart from anyone else. It was enough to look at his elder sons to see the abyss separating them. Same abyss that would have inevitably spoiled the boy in the end, had he not intervened at the right time.

When Chris had been a mere eight-year-old, he had shipped him off to Charles's place, Black Rose, and his son, the young Prince Caldwell. It had been the perfect solution. Just a few years older than Chris, Duncan promised to be a good influence, would have surely set him straight. And he had, at least in the beginning.

When their friendship had turned into the phase, James had not been so sure anymore. Or rather, he had not known whether to be happy or worried over his son's passionate response to a temporary parenthesis in life.

For such were phases, as he had learned only too well from his own. An apparently eternal storm of the senses that dried out after a couple of years of torrid sex with the chosen friend of the same age and gender. If this was true for most men, some clung above and beyond any safety level.

Like it had happened with him and Charles Caldwell.

Like it had with his son and Duncan Caldwell.

There was no doubt in his mind that Chris had come to the Hall to hide after Duncan had broken up with him. Same way, he had hidden behind his mother's skirt every time he had done something wrong or wanted to avoid his responsibilities. Chris's steadfast refusal to have anything to do with him had only confirmed this impression.

Arthur pumping his ass so publicly had not helped, either. Nor had the Arthur boys, a harmless group of young men that had turned nights into endless orgies since Chris had joined them. Most distressing of all had been discovering how taken the dead leader had been with his son.

Downright in love, if James was any judge of it.

To the point, Arthur had ceased to be objective or supportive of a real change, almost protecting him against himself.

Now, Cecilia's words had opened a door he had not even known was there. *Have I been wrong all this time?*

"How?" He searched for an answer in Lady Hurst's masculine face.

"I don't know." She bit her lower lip nervously. "I can't remember anything."

No surprise there.

This had been everybody's standard answer these days.

"But I promised Prince Caldwell I'd do all in my powers to look after him." Her sense of agitation increased as though she felt guilty and responsible for what had occurred to Chris.

"Speaking of him, do you know when he'll be here?" She looked around the chamber as if expecting Duncan to pop out from behind a seat.

"No, I have no news about him." He pursed his lips, for he did not approve of this delay any more than she did. "Didn't you say he left Blue Oasis at the same time you did?"

"Not exactly." She shook her head. "I left before he did." As the pressure got to her, she seemed unable to maintain her usual detachment. "He must've taken the longer route to get here." She fidgeted anxiously. "The one that goes through the villages and takes forever."

"What are we going to do in the meantime?" Richard Ellis frowned. "People and lands are still suffering." The permanent council member for the Ridgely District was evidently concerned about the deteriorating situation. "Yet, we're doing nothing about it."

"'Cause we can't." It was not his call. "We must wait for our new leader—"

"Prince Duncan Caldwell." Stephen Penbroke interjected. "Right?"

He turned to the permanent member from the Coreley District, wondering how far gossip had reached despite the crisis. "Yes."

Not that it should have been kept secret. It was just that he was pretty sure he had told no one about it.

Then again, nowhere did gossip thrive better than the Hall. Stopping it would have been a more significant task than recovering from whatever had thrown their peaceful lands into such havoc.

"Arthur chose him as his successor," he continued as his attention spun to Lady Hurst. "That's why I asked you to bring him along."

"How did you know he'd be there?" Suspicion clouded her dark eyes.

"I didn't." He pursed his lips in annoyance. "Arthur did." This was just the umpteenth time his old friend had not shared information until the very end. Sometimes until it was too late, like on such occasion. "He left instructions on how to contact him."

"I see." Something must have clicked because her expression was one of understanding.

"So, you are the last one to have seen him." Richard sent her an accusing look as though she were concealing the man or something.

No, worse, as though it were her fault Duncan was not yet there.

"Why didn't you ride together to the Hall?" Lord Ellis fumed impatiently.

"He wanted to be sure that Lord Templeton recovered." Not rising to the bait, she kept her tone cold and detached like she always did. "And he preferred to ride here with his valet."

From her disappointed frown, he guessed Duncan's decision had not pleased her. Could it be that she harbored some kind of feeling for the handsome prince?

"As I said, I don't know when they left exactly." Her gaze met his hard stare. "Or what route they traveled. Hence, I have no idea where he is or when he'll reach us," she concluded haughtily.

"There's no way out of it then." Stephen grinned in forced amusement. "We're stuck waiting for his arrival. Right, James?"

"Right, Stephen." Without a trace of Duncan, there was nothing to do, not even for the vice-leader himself. "But I'm hoping he'll turn up soon 'cause the situation is dire enough, and it's not going to get any better if we don't—"

"That's right, Lord Templeton." The deep male voice so similar to Charles's made his gaze snap up toward the door of the chamber where Duncan Caldwell had just entered and was striding confidently down the aisles. "I've personally seen how dramatic it is out there, so we should set immediately to work."

"Absolutely." At the sight of the determined man advancing his way, a surge of relief coursed through his every fiber. "But first, let me say how glad I am to see you, Prince Caldwell."

As the assembly rose, he walked to Duncan and clasped his arms and squeezed them affectionately. Then, he peered into the amazing black eyes, and he almost came undone.

By the gods, how much he resembles Charles. Up close as he was, he could not deny the jumble of memories raging in his heart. *Too damn much!*

To hide the flush he felt spreading on his face, he swung his head behind a shoulder to fix the council members. "We'll take a break and reconvene in one hour."

"Prince, please follow me." Taking charge, he led the way out of the chamber. "I need to talk to you urgently."

CHAPTER THIRTY-THREE

"Before we begin, how's my son?" Following Duncan Caldwell inside what had been Arthur's office, James closed the door.

Wherever he looked, Arthur stared back as if he had never left.

As if he were still sitting and working at his desk.

Too much to handle, he glanced over his shoulder, yet the glimpse he caught of the black-haired Prince Caldwell did not assuage his anxiety.

"Chris is recovering." Duncan's deep, throaty voice gave him a start. "He was too weak to travel, so I had to leave him at Blue Oasis." The note of sorrow and regret was hard to miss. "Otherwise, I'd have brought him along."

"Well, that's comforting." Brushing off his useless despair, he locked gazes with Duncan. "Was the excitement of Lady Hurst's Game too much to handle?" He hoped the joke would lighten the mood.

"Hardly." Prince Caldwell's smile split his handsome face. "Your son is the most indefatigable man I know when it comes to sex."

How true!

He had only to think of the Arthur boys, all the excesses and vices he had heard about firsthand to have no problem believing it.

"Also, when it comes to trouble." Sobering up, he shook his head sadly.

"I beg to differ, Lord Templeton." Evidently wanting to

make a point, Duncan's voice became stern, "Chris almost died to save our lands."

"Yes, Lady Hurst said as much." He pursed his lips. "So, my Chris is a hero?" Recalling some of the extremes Chris had reached, he had to suppress a smile. "Who would've guessed?"

"I never had any doubts about him." The black eyes flashed at him in a challenge. "In fact, he has the most determined character I know, and I respect him for it." The profound emotions playing on the handsome face spoke of a love so deep that James had to avert his gaze to give the prince the privacy to get a grip on himself. "Perhaps, you misjudged him all this time."

"Have I?" Again, the unsettling feeling that he was missing a vital clue about his beautiful boy punched him in the stomach.

Yet, this young man, no more than a boy himself, the son of his phase mate, had that unwavering faith that should have been a father's prerogative.

To think he had always admired Duncan's brilliant mind, quick intelligence and analytical reasoning, not to mention his striking good looks, so similar to his father's. *By the gods, I wish he didn't remind me of Charles so damn much!*

Not possible, of course.

Somewhat inevitable, given how distracting the man was.

"I think you have," Duncan asserted. "Please forgive my bluntness." Clearly annoyed, the prince took a step forward. "But you haven't always been fair to your youngest son, often believing the worst of him, even when untrue."

At the accusation, something broke inside him, something he had kept tightly locked for who knows how long. "Hem . . ." His brain scrambled to come up with something to say before his old heart gave out in front of the prince. "He's always been such a stubborn and difficult child." It sounded like a lame defense, even to his ears. Still, he continued,

"Never prone to listen much less follow good advice." He had to chuckle upon recalling many of Chris's most rebellious stances. "He's just . . ." Words failed him in the rush of emotions assailing him. "A hothead and a bit superficial at times, like when he does things simply to spite me." Wearily, he faced Duncan. "Which I admit has restrained much of my affection."

"I believe the opposite is true." A naughty twinkle lit up the black eyes. "I think you have always loved him too much and have been afraid to show your real feelings."

Could it be? James's heart stopped cold, and he felt the color drain from his face. *Have I been wrong all this time?*

"Listen," Duncan's voice softened. "I'm not criticizing. Whatever happened between you and your son, it's a private matter, and I should've never brought it up." He bowed slightly. "I had no right to question you as a father, so please accept my sincerest apology."

"No, Prince." Ashamed, James bent his head. "It is I who should apologize for doubting my son when you have such an obvious trust in his capabilities."

"I'm sure you will, too, given time." Prince Caldwell sounded way too confident for James to object. "But now, we've got more pressing issues at stake."

"You're right, of course." Straightening his shoulders, he moved toward Arthur's desk. "As you know, Arthur Fairchild, my friend and a close friend of your father, died after falling out of the window, here in his office." Turning, he caught Duncan's glance going to the one window out of the three from which Arthur must have fallen. "You know what happened, don't you?" He breached their distance. "Did you see him die?"

Duncan squirmed uncomfortably, without answering.

"Please, tell me what happened," he insisted.

"I'm not at liberty to discuss it, sir." Kind of evident, the prince felt weighed down by this impossibility. "Please, don't ask." He took a deep breath. "But one thing I can guarantee is that I'll face up to the emergency and help in the rebuilding of our lands and villages."

"So you must," James confirmed. "'Cause Arthur nominated you as his successor."

"Even if I'm not a council member yet?" Duncan's eyebrow rose in puzzlement. "Is this nomination legal?"

"It absolutely is." He nodded emphatically. "A leader can choose whomever he wishes as his successor." Tired of standing, he drifted toward one of the couches and sat down. "Besides, you're already part of the council in name if not in fact. Your father's permanent seat is waiting for you, and it would've been yours already had you read his will sooner, instead of waiting until this summer as Arthur informed me." He scanned the prince's face. "You should make it your priority once our situation is better."

"Yes, my father's will . . ." Duncan's voice trailed off evasively as he perched in front of him.

"You know it's important, don't you?" James was quick to elaborate. "It's a symbolic passage into manhood by which the eldest son or daughter inherits the High Council seat, among other things."

"Only if he or she deserves it, sir," Duncan demurred calmly.

"What do you mean?" Frowning, he settled more comfortably on the sofa.

"I'm just saying, perhaps this rule is not always appropriate." Duncan did not budge. "I'm beginning to look at the High Council as a place of power that should include only those who have Virt."

"Power? Virt?" Confused, he scrutinized Duncan's face. "That's a word I haven't heard for a long time." He sighed as his mind traveled back to the first time Arthur had spoken it, remembering his utter bewilderment at what it implied. "I suppose Arthur must've filled you in on its meaning—"

"Not just that," Duncan interrupted. "Mostly, on the importance of people becoming aware of it and using it for the greater good."

"You don't believe that the High Council just oversees our lands and the people's welfare?" Needless to mention how intrigued he was by this revelation.

"Not at all, Milord." Duncan's confidence seemed to have no bounds. "I think the High Council is a place of power, so its tasks go well beyond simple administrative duties. From now on, I'll make sure everyone is aware of it."

"How do you plan to do that?" Intrigued despite himself, he leaned forward.

"I have several ideas in mind," which he was not prepared to share judging from his significant pause. "Let's say I'll start by accepting only people with Virt as our new members." He eyed James without blinking once. "And with all the havoc we've suffered, I suppose I'll need to swear in lots of new members."

Definitely, the man was intelligent!

Sneaky, too!

James could not but applaud him and the way he would succeed in his intentions, given how right he was on all counts. Leaders, after all, chose without any restriction the person best suited to fill empty seats, sometimes even disregarding traditions or nominations suggested by other council members, including those who had previously held the position. He shook his head disconcerted, already guessing where Duncan was going with this. "Are you implying I shouldn't leave my seat to Steve?"

"I'm just saying that firstborns don't always inherit the family's Virt." His tone became soft and sincere, "In your case, I believe that person is Chris, your youngest." He pushed out a heavy puff of air. "And so did Arthur."

"Yeah, he nagged me about it often enough." Something James had put down to the old leader's infatuation with his son rather than to a heartfelt conviction. "Truth is I had my reservations—"

"Arthur Fairchild sent your son and me on a delicate mission that has required all our strength and powers combined." Duncan did not mince words. "Now, Chris lies in Blue Oasis spent after using all that power to save our world." The black gaze turned fierce. "What more reservations could you have now?"

"None, I suppose." Defeated, he had to admit that Duncan was right. "But then, you don't need my consent. As the leader, you have the final say on who sits on the High Council, and who doesn't."

"I don't want blind obedience, Lord Templeton." The black eyes glittered despite the encroaching darkness of late afternoon. "I want cooperation and collaboration from everyone, particularly from my vice-leader."

"All right." Impressed by the man's clear-headed thinking, James nodded. "I promise I'll think it over and come up with a better recommendation that will please both you and Arthur." He grinned in a mockingly conspiratorial fashion. "I wonder if this is why he chose you as his successor." He chuckled at the absurdity of it. "Just kidding, of course."

Duncan smiled ironically. "However much he may have loved Chris, I doubt Arthur would've gone to the trouble of dying just to see him replace you."

"You knew about it?" That he was surprised was an understatement.

"It was kind of hard to miss," Duncan admitted. "Even if I wasn't around the Hall."

"I only wish Chris could've taken better advantage of Arthur's advice." He sighed wearily. "Instead of just . . ." *Fucking him.*

Frustrated, he waved a hand aimlessly in the air, while the black eyes twinkling told him Prince Caldwell understood perfectly what he meant.

"As you said yourself. Chris is not inclined to listen to advice." Once more, a strong emotion curved the prince's lips. "Not even for his own good."

"I guess you know him well enough." Reacting to the infectious feeling, he could not help smiling, too. "When I last saw Arthur—"

"You saw him before he died?" Duncan stretched forward. "Did he tell you anything that could explain his death?"

"I'm not sure." He went back over that fateful last meeting, trying to remain clinically detached from it all. "He called me shortly after you and Chris had left for your mission, which he naturally told me nothing about." Why bother to sound so aggravated?

Arthur had never been one for sharing, not even with his vice-leader, and there had been not a damn thing he could have done about it. Not one in the more than forty years of service.

"Actually, now that I think about it, he seemed somewhat scared." He frowned at Arthur's image playing in his head. "I thought it was because of your mission, but maybe he feared for his life." He searched his memories to confirm his impressions. "He must've known he was going to die, or why else would he write his will the day before it happened?"

"Could be." Duncan shifted position. "Had he received threats?"

"I wish I knew," James huffed. "Arthur was very secretive, and I was often the last one to know about important matters." Not true, of course.

Everyone at the Hall had a spy network worth its name to keep abreast of the relevant facts, usually a mix of reliable gossip and servants' accounts. No one topped his information system, with the possible exception of the one his son had so brilliantly and effortlessly set up in the short time since his arrival.

"I'll change that, Lord Templeton," Duncan was quick to interject. "I promise."

"I'm not sure I believe you, son." His lips curved downward. "You already told me you're not at liberty to discuss the recent dramatic events."

"Only because I still need to understand them myself." A worried expression furrowed Duncan's brow.

"I guess I'll just have to trust you as I did Arthur," was James's logical conclusion.

"Right," the prince agreed. "I think we should return to the meeting." He rose to his feet. "And plan a course of action."

"Of course, rules require leaders to be sworn in before they can start on any official duty." Slowly, James started to get up as well. "There's a formal ceremony for it called—"

"The Fitting," Duncan cut him off. "Even if I've never seen one, I know what it is . . ." A winning smile split his handsome face. "At least in theory."

"It's a ritual to make you fit to handle the responsibilities of a leader." He was happy to provide more details. "But we don't have time for it now, not while everything else is falling apart."

Duncan placed a hand on his shoulder. "I'm sure people will understand if we postpone it until . . ." He creased his forehead, obviously trying to determine a date. "Let's say next spring."

"Yes," he concurred. "It may be a wise choice."

"For the time being, I'll say a few words to the assembly," Duncan proposed. "Then, we have to get to work, serious work if we want our people to survive the winter."

"I agree, Leader." James bowed, full of deference for a man he was sure would turn out to be one of the greatest ever to hold this position. "I think Arthur understood much more about you than he led me to believe."

"About your son, too." Duncan chortled.

"Well . . ." He cleared his throat. "Maybe." Unwilling to dwell on it, he hurried toward the exit. "What are we waiting for?" Having reached the door, he opened it and gestured for Duncan to go through before following him out of the room. "Let's go."

CHAPTER THIRTY-FOUR

"My fellow members," Lord Templeton addressed the assembly. "Before dying, Arthur nominated his successor as Prince Duncan Caldwell." James gestured at him. "The respected son of Charles Caldwell, a dear friend of mine . . ."

However contained and fleeting, the strangled choke of emotions was not lost on Duncan. Standing center stage beside the vice-leader, he was at the large table at the auditorium's lower flat area. Looking up, he glanced at the rows of seats arranged in concentric half-circles rising above him, accommodating the twelve permanent members and the additional twelve temporary ones. That more than one-third of the chamber was empty was something he had noted upon his arrival.

"The valued council member who was in charge of our Shelter System," James continued having recovered his wits.

All eyes ran to him, Duncan Caldwell, the new Leader of the High Council, their only hope against the Virtus Monster he had somehow awaken.

The eager faces peering down at him were mostly unfamiliar, apart from Cecilia sitting on one side and beaming her full support. The rest, those who had made it he would get to know in time.

"Although Duncan isn't a council member yet, he would've filled his father's seat sooner, had events not prevented him," Lord Templeton's loud voice pulled him out of his musings and reminded him of their earlier discussion.

Whatever their social standing, whether permanent or

temporary, council members with Virt would be the new norm. This simple clause would secure Chris's succession to the Templeton Seat. It was his call, after all. He would use it to his best advantage and the council's, given the number of replacements he would have to take care of, including the Caldwell Seat. He needed someone to fill it, doubly so since he had moved up the ladder, yet remained Charles's rightful heir. The good news was that he might just have the perfect candidate in mind.

Yeah, sure, if only this were not the tricky part.

Not because he still had to read his father's will, which both Arthur and now James had urged him to do.

Because he would have to consent to that unbelievable request and adopt Ylianor Meyer in the Caldwell family!

Problem was—did he want it?

No, make that—did he want *her*?

"As you all know, Arthur was free to choose whomever he wished as his successor." James eyed him significantly. "But this wasn't a spur-of-the-moment nor a last-minute decision." His gaze broadened to the assembly once more. "Arthur himself told me he trusted this young man to carry out the highest duties of the land." He nodded as though he were still debating the issue with the deceased leader. "More than that, he motivated his selection to my complete satisfaction." Raising his gaze, he took his time to make eye-contact with every council member. "After talking just a few minutes with him, I'm delighted Arthur chose so wisely." Turning to face him, James bowed.

Duncan had to wonder why all he could think about was that James was the father of the man he loved above and beyond life itself, the man who had almost died to obey his command, the man at whose side he would have preferred to be right at the moment. Since that was not an option, he would have taken James in his arms, like he would have his father, and made him believe in that fantastic creature that was his son, Christopher Templeton.

"As second in command, I feel honored to welcome Prince Charles Caldwell's son, Duncan, as the new High Council Leader." Extending out a hand, James presented him to the entire assembly.

Everyone rose and applauded.

"Thank you," Duncan acknowledged them. "Please, be seated." He gestured for them to do so.

"Yes, please be seated," James chimed in, waiting until everyone had settled back down. "Since we're facing a crisis, I'm afraid we cannot hold the Fitting, the proper succession ritual." He looked at the people confronting him as though testing their reactions to this news. "Once the upheaval is over, we'll hold the grandest Fitting ever." He made it sound like it would be the most exciting event in everybody's life. "For the time being, I declare him our chosen leader." He invited Duncan to the fore. "He will say a few words before we get down to work." Then, he retreated to a seat that was next to an empty one.

"Council members, I'm Duncan Caldwell, son of Charles Caldwell, at your service." Looking up at the people assembled, he briefly wondered whether he had what it took to lead them. It was one thing to guide his lovers, quite another to command the ruling body of their lands.

Or maybe, he was born for it, like his father had implied in his letter.

The searing pain at his left shoulder brought him back in focus, back to the weight that had crashed down on him the moment he had seen Arthur falling out the window.

The moment he had become the leader.

Right after, a charge had coursed through him, sparking every bit of flesh, and he had heard the strange humming that had drowned his senses in the Nephis Valley. The multi-pyramid structure had filled his mind with its fierce glow, and the sharp sting of an innocuous childhood scar on his left shoulder had him almost doubled over from the scorching pain.

Since then, there had been no time to tell anyone much less understand what had happened.

No respite, either.

The persistent melody was still there, however muffled it had grown. The intense lights were another torment, blinding him at times and eerily similar to the princess's perception.

These alone would have been enough to drive him crazy, had not the damn scar beaten them to it.

What had been an unremarkable skin blemish had erupted and become pronounced, embossed as if something had yanked it out from under the surface. Now, its angry red borders flared up whenever he thought of the leadership, burning and throbbing like it were on fire all the time.

Resisting the impulse to rub it, he resumed his speech, "Like all of you, I'm devastated by the death of our long-standing leader, Lord Arthur Fairchild." Bending his head as a sign of respect, he recalled the last time he had seen Arthur alive. "I didn't know him well, but he was a great friend of my father. More importantly, a true and esteemed leader whom we'll all miss deeply." The sadness reflected in everybody's gaze told him that indeed the feeling was shared. "Yet, we must go on. Despite the pain in my heart as in all of yours, we are in a calamity that requires immediate action. Arthur realized that something was angry with us, but he never found the strength to face up to it." Probably because he was alone in his leadership.

A mistake he had no wish to repeat.

"That's why he summoned me and my phase mate, Lord Christopher Templeton, the vice-leader's son." He inclined his head in James's direction. "To stop the impending threat."

A pang of guilt sliced his stomach in two at the blatant omission of *her*. She had been just as essential as Chris in dealing with the darkness they had conjured up out of nowhere.

More so, if he had to be honest.

She might even be the key to it all. Or why else had things precipitated since he had reconnected with her?

However intriguing the notion, he had neither the time nor the effort to explore it. Her voice inside his head had simply been another distraction he had not known how to afford, not while the dastardly pyramid blared its incessant notes and flashed its disturbing lights night and day.

That had been the reason he had closed their channel while on the road to the Hall.

It had cost him.

No use denying it.

But he had been unable to take it anymore.

Something had to give, and shutting her out had been the obvious choice.

No, the only choice, the only one over which he had a measure of control.

Worst of all, had he even wanted to acknowledge her, how could he have introduced her? *My soon-to-be adopted sister? Lover? Friend? Stable keeper? Slave?*

With an annoyed shake of the head, he dismissed the thought entirely.

"Well . . ." He cleared his throat to dispel the last lingering doubts. "We tried until it came to the point that I had to order Christopher Templeton, my phase mate." *My beautiful angel.* "To limit the damage by using his incredible power." His voice grew husky and pained, "And he . . ." His voice nearly broke, "He almost died in the process." His heartthrob was so intense that he had to take several breaths of air. "To his honor and our eternal gratitude, he didn't hesitate once, not even with his life at stake." *Never again, Angel, never again!* "And he succeeded in what looked like an impossible task." However much he tried, he could not hide the immense pride and love oozing from his words.

Intercepting James's stare, he noticed the same emotions shining from the old man's eyes, glad that he had taken Duncan's suggestions at heart.

A clap interrupted the silence. First one, then another rose to show appreciation until the whole assembly was on its feet and bringing the house down.

"It's terrible that we couldn't save Arthur," he resumed after order had been restored. "Or the many good people that have died in this catastrophe." He saw the concern etched in everyone's face. "But now's not the time to grieve our dead. It's the time to act, to prevent further havoc and repair what has been devastated." His words seemed to return people's optimism. "I have a plan." Pausing, he realized that he had captured everyone's attention. "Our priority is to collect the bodies and burn them fast, to avoid contamination. We need to clear the debris and replenish our food and water supply. The only way for quick and efficient results is for everyone to collaborate. From the highest noble to the lowest servant, everyone will be assigned to specific teams with different tasks that will run in each district. The High Council will organize and steer operations for all the lands, but each district will have its own steering committee to regulate things on a more practical level. This way, we will share the workload, until every corner of our lands is as healthy as it was before." He hoped he had been comprehensible. "The Hall will be our headquarters. Here is where all information and provisions must transit before being spread out to every district. This will be the cornerstone of the network connecting us all, from the nearest to the farthest. We'll draw up a map to indicate the places in urgent need of help and the storage facilities for supplies and materials, which will give us a fair assessment of what's available and where." He raised his gaze to make sure people were following him.

And they were, their intent focus never wavering away from him.

"Keeping in mind that our priorities are food, water and improving our production output, there's no obligation for council members to remain here. You can just as well help your people on-site like I've done every step of my journey from Blue Oasis. Those of us who stay here will oversee the districts' needs, manage the teamwork and provide regular updates to keep the situation under control. All of you will report to me directly and to my personal assistant, David Smith." He smiled confidently as he wound down for the close. "Together, we'll monitor the progress, send people and materials where needed."

With a sigh of relief, he detected agreement with his heavy schedule on the brave faces surrounding him. "But enough about work. Once the worst is over, to reward our collective efforts, we'll have a grand celebration, a three-day Festival with plenty to eat and drink. *Fun for all* will be the theme. Each district will host at least one Festival. Our estates will be opened to all and will provide the basics, including the beds." Winking mischievously, he was not surprised to see this idea had even more consensus. "Are there any questions?"

"Thank you for your inspired words, Prince Caldwell." A dark-haired man stood up to address him. "I'm Stephen Penbroke, permanent council member for the Coreley District, and I would like to know what happened exactly? What hit us so horribly that we don't even know where to start picking up the pieces?"

Beats me! All I know is that it's big, black and mean. Scary, too. And it's called Virtus.

"I'm not sure, Lord Penbroke." Evasiveness was his best strategy. Plus, no one remembered a damn thing thanks to Chris's intervention, which allowed him to play with the truth as much as he wanted. "Arthur believed something threatened our peaceful way of life, so he sent Christopher Templeton and me to investigate. Unfortunately, we were late. We could just stop some of the more negative effects." He pushed out a deep breath to emphasize his point. "I think Arthur was right. Judging from the amount of destruction it wreaked in just a short time, it's something very powerful and extremely dangerous, but that's as far as I go. I can only hope we'll be able to shed more light on this matter while working to repair things."

"I'm Richard Ellis, permanent council member for the Ridgely District." Another man got to his feet, younger and more distinguished than Stephen, though with lesser hair. "Are we still at risk?"

"Not immediately, Lord Ellis," Duncan reassured with a confidence he was far from feeling.

For it appeared pretty obvious that the monster had no intention of returning to the darkness that had generated it.

Not of its own accord anyway.

"If something should change, we'll face it together." The softening of Richard's worried expression was a sure sign that he had provided the right answer.

At the silence that followed, council members eyeballed one another before returning their gazes squarely on him.

"If there are no more questions . . ." When no one else spoke, Duncan wrapped up things. "Do you all understand what I need you to do?"

Heads nodded.

"Great!" His lips curved up in praise. "Let's get to work."

CHAPTER THIRTY-FIVE

"Wait, little lady." The man coming toward Ylianor raised his hand. "Let me help you with that bucket."

"It's not that heavy," she lied, halting on her tracks. "Really." She switched hands so that the clay and straw she had just finished mixing did not weigh on one arm alone.

"Let me be the judge of that." Snatching it from her hold, the man took possession of it. "'Cause I don't like to overtax the members of my team." The effortless way he held on to it made her wonder whether it had become suddenly weightless. "Speaking of which, I'm Terence Blaise, in charge of this team." He extended his free hand. "We come directly from the Southern District."

Given his offer, she had to shake it.

"And who might you be, little lady?" Instead of releasing her, he tightened his grip.

"I'm Ylianor." Trying to get her hand back was a useless endeavor, considering how forceful the man's clutch had become.

"You're from around here?" Eventually, he freed her, his inquisitive gaze scanning her up and down in blatant interest.

"No, not really." She shook her head, strangely disinclined to tell him or anyone else for that matter her business.

Not that there would have been much to tell, except perhaps of how lonely, lost and abandoned she had felt ever since Prince Duncan Caldwell had decided to close their channel. Gone his voice from her head in the blink of an eye, he had condemned her to the same dreary isolation as after Prince

Charles's death. She was not sure she could take it for the second time in her life. If she could withstand that awful load of misery and loss that had cost her a good ten years simply to survive. The sheer load of it had almost crushed her, and at times, she still wondered how she had managed to pull through it.

Which was the last thing she wanted to think, much less talk about, lest the pain of the eerie silence drowned her completely.

"You were here for Lady Hurst's Game, uh?" Not being stupid, Terence had drawn the most logical conclusion.

"I suppose I was." A heavy puff of air remained stuck at the lump pressing to the back of her throat.

"Didn't think you were old enough for it." He scrutinized her as though he could read her age from the curves of her body.

"I'm old enough." To prove her point, she threw back her shoulders and tried to look more mature.

Given how tired she looked — thanks to Virtus's nightmares keeping her company the whole night long — she was sure she could fool him.

"Are you, really?" Then again, maybe not. "Come on." Taking her by the arm, Terence led her toward the stables that had been her intended destination. "The men over there need this concrete."

Located in this small village near Blue Oasis, it was one of the many buildings in bad need of repairs. This specific site was in a better shape if compared to most. A lot of them had not withstood the lethal sweep of Virtus's intervention and had crumbled to the ground.

She had seen it for herself while toiling around the district with one team or another, heaps of rubbles the only lingering proof that once life had flourished there. And it just added to the desolation of her heart.

"What role did you play?" Although he kept his face fixed on the men working around the stable, she could tell from his lights that his attention was all on her.

Not just his attention.

His cock had almost given her a standing ovation the moment he had caught sight of her.

"Mister Blaise, I'd have never imagined that someone from a faraway place like the Southern District would know about the Game," she teased, hoping to get off the hook.

"The Game's fame has reached even our distant corner of the world, Milady," he replied with an equally mocking tone. "We all learned its rules, even if few of us ever played it." Halting in mid-step, he leaned on her more intimately than before. "Tell me," he lowered his voice. "What did you play?"

"I thought you'd have already guessed," she provoked him on purpose.

"Let's say I want to hear it from your lips," he insisted.

Keeping this up was sure to get him over-excited. Already, his aura was blazing out of control, which only worsened when she had to admit that she had been a slave.

"Aha, I knew it!" Grinning broadly as though he had won a victory of sorts, he dragged her until their bodies practically touched. "Who was your master?"

"Hem . . ." Swallowing the lump that had grown bigger was an impossible task. "I doubt you know him." She kept it deliberately vague.

"Try me." He did not seem to stand for it.

"He's . . ." *The best. Yet, also the worst. The new leader himself.* "From the Silcamore District."

"Isn't that the same district as our new leader's?" It was apparent this new twist had captivated Terence good and proper.

"I think so . . ." She kept it vague on purpose.

How was she ever going to quit thinking about him if

everyone kept bringing him up?

From the second the gorgeous dark-haired prince had stepped out of Blue Oasis, no one had managed to stop blabbing about him. About the great things he had done in the short time that it had taken him to get to the Hall. Of his grandiose speech when he had seized power. Of all his selfless exertions in setting up and coordinating teams to deal with the calamity that had left death and destruction in its wake, from one side of the lands to the other.

At Blue Oasis, in particular, servants had no other topic besides the striking prince turned leader. When they were not talking about His Haughtiness Lord Christopher Templeton, that is.

"But I don't keep up with politics." This other lie slipped out more easily than the first one. "Sorry."

"I'm sure you know about the new leader." Disbelief made his light shimmer uncertain. "People can't talk about anything else."

Don't I know it!

"Besides this catastrophe, of course." Thankfully, his gaze shifted to take in the village's dire conditions. "So, you must've heard." His focus snapped back on her.

"Yes, of course, I did." *How could I not?*

This conversation was stirring up so many unwanted emotions that all she wished for was to crawl away from everyone and cry her eyes out forever.

Damn it all!

She missed him like crazy!

His absence in her head was unbearable, and nowhere had it hurt more than during the long days and nights spent at Chris's side, worn out from worry and fear should he not make it. That he might not, had been a reality she had discovered right after her ministrations to his core had not proved to be as effective as she had believed.

No, her near burning had not been enough to pull him through the worst of it.

Still, she had given her word to nurse him back to complete health, and she would keep it, even at the cost of her own life.

Truth was—she could not bear the thought of what Prince Caldwell would have to go through, should he ever lose his beloved angel for real.

So, she had cared unceasingly for the feverish body lying still in bed, fighting against the darkness that wanted to devour him.

Him!

Who was all fire!

The brightest light she had ever known, outshining any star in the night sky and blinding her with that oh, so brilliant aura.

Thinking had been her sole distraction back then. Since the stunning demon had been half unconscious most of the time, hardly aware of her presence, of her hand holding his and trying to give him what little strength she had at her disposal, her mind had gone round and round in frantic circles.

What has happened to Prince Duncan Caldwell? Why has he shut me out? Why does he leave me so cold and miserable? At the mercy of the awful silence choking me?

Lacking answers, she had fabricated a ton of them to make sure it was not his fault. He had become the leader, after all. He could not possibly have time for the likes of her and even if he did, no way could he spare a single fraction of it on her. His undivided attention must all be devoted to the far more significant issues facing him, to the point their connection had become a burden.

Yes, indeed, she had used up every justification in the book and more, just like she had when the hateful Sophia Caldwell had thrown her out of Black Rose, her native home, and her handsome prince had failed to come to her rescue.

Anything!

She would have clung to anything rather than admit he cared nothing for her. Had he not said he needed time? Or had that been just another lie?

Was it any wonder she wanted to curl up and die on the spot?

"But not in any detail since I've been kind of cooped up inside Blue Oasis all this time." Trying to pull herself together, she averted her gaze and took a tentative step in the direction of the stable.

"You didn't get the chance to go back home once the Game ended?" Full of concern, he rushed to detain her.

"I . . ." How could she tell this stranger what had plagued her after the world had fallen to pieces? "I couldn't." A deep breath steadied her voice, "I had to look after someone —"

"Lord Christopher Templeton, I bet!" His lights flaring like it was the most awesome thing he had heard all day, he nearly shouted, "It's him, isn't it?" So aroused by this bit of information, Ylianor feared he would start jumping on the spot. "The leader's phase mate, right?"

"The one and only," she confirmed wryly.

"Wow!" Eyes ablaze, he regarded her as though she could provide a privileged insight about Christopher Templeton. "That speech the leader delivered at the Hall had everyone wishing they were his phase mate." He, too, hearing how enthusiastic he sounded. "Especially after the leader thanked him in such a public way, for all his heroism in destroying the darkness."

Yet, not one word about her, like she had not even been there alongside him, kidnapped by an evil black monster forcing her to watch how he went about punishing her world.

"When I discovered Lord Christopher Templeton was here, I just had to come in the hope of catching a glimpse of him," Terence confessed candidly. "I just had to take advantage of Blue Oasis's accommodations to see him for myself."

Right, how to forget that Terence here would be sleeping under her same roof?

"I've pestered David to give me all the news he could." He raised a quizzical eyebrow. "You know who David is, don't you?"

"More or less," she mumbled.

She had heard it say from Lady Hurst's servants that he was the coordinator in charge of all teams, the one who traveled to the farthest territories to ensure that everything received proper care. Had he only shown his face round Blue Oasis, she would have welcomed him with open arms instead of wondering how his newfound responsibilities were affecting him.

"He's the leader's right hand, his personal assistant." Without hesitation, he plunged into a new explanation.

Which was fine.

The more he talked, the less he would require a meaningful contribution from her.

"He keeps communication flowing from the Hall to the most faraway land of all." Sincere admiration laced the man's tone. "He has overseen the setup of the various teams and has assigned them to several locations. He's really the best. That's why I thought he'd know about Lord Templeton."

"And did he?" Remembering David's discretion, she was quite sure he had not divulged a single scrap of information about Chris's condition to Terence or to anybody else for that matter.

"No, he didn't." The man shook his head regretfully. "But you will." His mood picked up considerably at this unexpected opportunity. "So, tell me, how is Lord Templeton doing? Has he recovered and all?"

"He has." This came out so low it was doubtful he had caught it.

But at this point, she could care less.

She could not hold it together any longer.

"Would you mind excusing me for a moment?" Spotting the makeshift bathroom, she commanded her feet to move to it. "I have to pee."

"Sure." He let her go reluctantly. "I'll wait for you here."

Barely holding herself upright, she took her first hesitant stride toward the shack that would give her a measure of cover. One foot in front of the other, she concentrated on the simple task of getting there without breaking down. The lump was about to burst, and she could do nothing except hurry.

Once she made it inside, the bitterness of it all strangled her, and no amount of tears could melt it. But Leader Duncan Caldwell's cold indifference was only half the problem. Lord Christopher Templeton's icy distance was the other half.

The day she had spotted something different in Chris's aura, she had known he would wake up soon. The dim hue of the past weeks gone, his lights had been getting ready to soar again, to become the roaring fire she had grown familiar with from her childhood onward. That extreme heat of his had oozed from every pore for the first time since he had cleansed and erased the evil unleashed by Virtus.

She could not have been happier or more relieved. She had missed the tantalizing licks of his aura.

That his own had been the first she had ever seen still baffled her at times. Same time she had realized she was not yet over the awe of seeing lights around people's heads.

In Blue Oasis, she had never been gladder to see them sparking in impatience around the demon's blond hair.

Her duty absolved, she had stood up, caressed his beautiful face and left his room. He would have soon been alert and demanded something more substantial than what she had provided so far. Something like food, drink and sex, of course.

Oh, yes, if she knew him any, it would be the first item on his list, no matter how feeble he still was. Not surprising, either, given how Christopher Templeton could not function without it.

Knowing how little he could stand her, she had left him to the capable hands of the many servants employed at Blue Oasis. Too weak to stand much less leave his room, Chris had relied on them for food, sex and gossip. She had arranged it so that it was only the cutest of them, all young, dark-haired men who would have no qualms in servicing him whatever way he requested. Blowjobs mostly, or so the young men had assured when they had bragged to the rest of the staff about what Lord Christopher Templeton had asked of them.

She had been right there in the kitchen when they had not been able to stop talking about His Haughtiness as though he were a god come down from above. Which maybe he was because the leader himself was as smitten with him as those cute young men who could not shut up about the gorgeous lord.

Yet, not a word about her.

In the weeks that had followed, she had kept out of his way, never intruding nor going to his room except sometimes late, very late at night to check on him as he slept peacefully for a change.

Well, guess what?

Ever since he had rejoined the living, there had been no signs from him. In spite of all he had solicited, never had he asked to see her. Never called for her, not even once, not even by mistake.

She, who had gone beyond herself to save his worthless hide. Who had sat at his side night and day to help him recover. Who had skipped food and sleep lest her guard dropped. Who had quietly retreated once he had been conscious again.

His callous unconcern had wounded her worse than when

he had slashed her with his knife.

If she had believed it to be the most despicable thing he could do to her, now she knew he was capable of far worse.

Foolish woman that she was, she had hoped against hope that he would inquire after her if for no other reason to see if she was still alive.

Of course, he never bothered.

Closing her eyes, she tried stopping her hysterical sobs.

Virtus playing horrible nightmares had not helped, either.

They had begun as soon as she had returned to her quarters. Scenes of torture and inhuman monstrosities terrified her every sleeping moment. People assaulted, brutalized, maimed, then killed after atrocious sufferings — such was the essence of the sequences plaguing her night after unending night.

No, not people.

Just her.

She always ended up as the victim of Virtus's violence until she woke up with a frightening jolt.

Maybe, the pyramid she kept on her dresser had something to do with it.

Hard to forget how it glowed in a snarl-like way when she bolted upright, trembling and sweaty from the latest night terrors. No question about it! The ghoul took a sinister satisfaction in harassing her.

She should have tossed it away, should have locked it up somewhere and thrown away the key.

She dared not.

She had vowed to look after it, and like with the other promise, she did not intend to default on her vow.

She dried her eyes with the back of her hand. Crying would not stop the pain. Nor lessen it in any way. How could it?

She was hooked on them big time!

It was the undeniable truth that was fast unraveling due to

their despicable behavior.

Making it a point to become unreachable, Duncan had disintegrated her illusions about any sort of lasting relationship. Chris's total disregard had smashed her ultimate fantasy about turning it into a successful trio.

So hard the blow, she had not even attempted to make up excuses. She had just accepted the fact they both refused to have anything to do with her.

Well, she had news for them!

She would not let them bring her down. She would not fall prey to defeat. Screw them and their pretense that she deserved everything they were piling on her!

Determined to prove she was not as worthless as both their attitudes implied, she had joined the teams that came to work on the Blandry District. So, what if most days she had trouble standing on two feet?

She simply pushed herself. Now, she had something to do all day besides sitting around mooning over Prince Duncan Caldwell and his phase mate, Lord Christopher Templeton.

Yep, killing herself was the better of the alternatives, and at least her sacrifice would help someone.

A fresh pair of hands was always welcomed. The things to do were so many that no single team, however capable, could ever hope to do all the work. Plus, the leader insisted they shifted around to guarantee adequate rest-time for all, meaning there was a continuous shortage of manpower.

Lucky her!

The different groups rotating in the Blandry District had given her the chance to escape. Whatever the crew, she had gone out in the nearby fields to lend her little energy to the reconstruction effort. It had also turned out to have more advantages than she had thought at first, given the number of men wanting to have sex with her.

Like Terence here, who would be just one of the long line

she had gone through already. A sturdy body and cute features, she would forget him as soon as he left the district for his next assignment.

Her outburst quieting down, she washed up and was presentable again. Nothing left to do than exit the shack and let her body tell him she would love to spend the night in his bed.

Would he mind?

From the way his lights colored red with lust, she was pretty sure he would not.

Not at all!

CHAPTER THIRTY-SIX

"Hem . . ." The clearing of a man's throat broke Duncan's concentration. "Excuse me, Leader."

Sitting in what had been Arthur's office, he raised his gaze from the latest document he had been skimming. "Yes, Kevin."

"Sorry, I didn't mean to disturb you." The young man hovering on the threshold seemed to be asking permission to enter.

"You're not disturbing at all." He smiled brightly. "I just wasn't paying attention to the time." Stretching, he got up from his chair. "I suppose you're here for our meeting."

"Yes, sir." The man brightened and took a decisive step inside.

"By all means, then." He gestured at the large oval table on a side, surrounded by many chairs. "Come in, everyone." He caught sight of the group of men and women now crowding his entrance.

From Clay Myrtle to Shelby Landin, from Frannie Golan to Ashton Brighton, to Sander Krystek and Betsyan Yaren, all the teams' coordinators filled his room and began moving the chairs around the table. All young, a few even younger than himself, all handpicked with David's assistance, they were the Hall's reference points for the reconstruction effort, above council members themselves. If not everyone had taken this breach in the chain of command too kindly, no one had been in a position to complain, given the extra load weighing down on each district.

Then again, ranks in the High Council had never been thinner. Virtus had wiped out a whole generation, but the sons and daughters who were to fill those empty council seats did not have enough experience.

Which reminded him that he still had to read his father's will. Just one more duty in the long list he had set aside for when things would be back to a semblance of normality. He owed it to his family and his name as Charles Caldwell's son and heir, even if it had lost much of its symbolic meaning as a rite of passage into adulthood.

"Good evening, Leader," Frannie's melodious voice covered the noise of everyone settling down.

"Good evening, Frannie." As the last one to reach the table, he sat closer to his desk. "I hope you all have good news for me."

"Not just good." A naughty twinkle lit Sander's brown eyes. "Excellent." He beamed confidently, his gaze fixing on Duncan. "I know that in our last meeting, every district except for my very own, the Southern District, had completed the clearing-up stage." He glanced at a note. "I've just heard now that we aren't lagging behind anymore. All villages are good to go. No more dead bodies lying in the streets, no more crumbling ruins, no more devastated fields. All hamlets are back to the normal farming activities, and there are no traces of ruins anywhere around." There was no describing the excitement in the man's tone. "Nothing is out of place *anywhere*, not just in the Southern District but nowhere else, either."

It was really over!

Incredible yet true, his world had defeated Virtus's brutal attempt at wiping it out.

He still could not believe it!

Sander's infectious smile split his handsome face. "The worst of it is over, and they survived all thanks to you, Leader."

The note of respect mixed with a sort of awe clenched Duncan's heart, but what did it for him was the sense of profound relief coursing through his every fiber.

"Yes, you did it!" Betsyan pitched with the same admiration veining her voice. "'Cause things in the Dartmouth District are looking better than ever, now that all boroughs are running as before."

"No, better than before," Clay was quick to add. "Everything in Fountaintops is as good as new, and people are now focusing on getting their lands up to the agricultural standards they had before this thing hit them."

"That's exactly what people in the Sephora District are worried about," Shelby confirmed in her sweet voice.

"Thanks again, Leader." Sitting opposite him, Ashton leaned on the table. "'Cause none of us would've made it without you."

"No, thanks to all of you." Suppressing his emotional response, he made sure to make eye contact with everyone around the table. "I could've never pulled it off without your precious support, your great work or your unwavering effort."

A simple, matter-of-fact statement. The mass demolition unleashed by Virtus on a global scale had required all the organizational skills he had at his disposal. Under his supervision, all districts had joined forces. Every able pair of hands assigned to one team or another, they had worked on specific tasks across the land. Starting from those sites that had been hit the worst to the remotest places of all, men and women had picked up his challenge and got down in the reconstruction effort.

"Or without David," he added, regretting that his faithful friend had not yet returned to the Hall.

"Oh, he's been invaluable," Kevin Roan was quick to jump in. "If it hadn't been for his skillful coordination of all the accounts we got day in and day out, we'd have never figured out our priorities."

"Yes, I totally agree." Reports of all kinds had flooded the Hall, some with urgencies that would have gone unattended, had it not been for David's efficient handling of every piece of information. "After we had set up the patrols going to and from the Hall, all the messages they brought back would've meant chaos for sure." Problems and progress sometimes mixed up in a way that would have caused quite a confusion if only Duncan had stopped to think about it. "Instead, it has ended up being the most efficient way to speed up communications and bring fast aid wherever required."

Most important of all, David had selected all the scouts making up the network that was responsible for everyone's survival. A resourceful group of people, they had traveled everywhere to bring advice, food and supplies, getting back to Rockyhorn with news and fresh petitions.

"Yep, and he chose every one of us for this task." As though reading his mind, Kevin fixed a clear gaze on him.

"For which I could never thank him enough." Duncan charged the words with all the appreciation he felt for them and for everyone who had enabled the delicate task of setting their world back on its feet.

All of a sudden, his vision blurred while an explosion of lights and sounds blinded his every sense.

Damn them and their annoying presence in his head!

Never a moment's relief, the excruciating nuisance had endured with its jumbled mass of deafening hums and flashing sparks. It was like living inside the Nephis Valley's pyramid all the time, except that Ylianor's voice and Chris's fire overshadowed everything. If added to the constant throbbing on his left shoulder, there seemed to be no end to the torment that he managed to keep at bay with much effort and willpower.

Which, of course, was nothing he should be worrying

about right at present, much less allow it to distract him.

Reason why he overcame the unwanted background noise after an imperceptible struggle and resumed the briefing.

"Now that the situation is under control, our next concern is to have enough food and water to survive the winter." This was the real purpose of the meeting. "From now on, agriculture will be our priority. I've already asked Oliver Sentry to lend his expertise to the cause."

"He's the best man for the job." Sander's expression brightened all together. "His work on Lady Hurst's desert land is short of prodigious, so I'm sure he can help everyone grow things faster and more efficiently everywhere."

"That's precisely what I'm counting on," Duncan confirmed. "Through Lady Hurst and David, we'll get not just Oliver but also his assistants to work on raising our production standards so that no one will have to suffer."

"I suppose we'll get to work with Lord Steve Templeton, too, our vice-leader's first son and your phase mate's brother," Sander observed with an awed tone that testified to how impacted everyone still was by Chris's heroism. "He's one of Lord Sentry's most gifted assistants, and I've heard he's worked more than one miracle on those drylands of the Blandry District."

"Good thing 'cause we need all the help we can get," Clay interjected. "Some places are still in critical condition."

"I know." Duncan peered at the man before his gaze widened to the rest of them. "That's why I called you all here today." Shifting, he settled in a more comfortable position. "To be sure, our present situation isn't so awful. Thanks to Arthur's careful planning, we have enough supplies to last us through the wintertime, provided that you start on delivering them where they're most needed."

"What exactly do you want us to do, Leader?" Practical and down-to-earth, Shelby sat up straighter as though she did not want to miss any of his instructions.

"Quite simply to continue what you've done until now. Only, instead of sorting through appeals of aid, you'll have to coordinate your scouts to bring food supplies." Turning to his desk, he grabbed a map and laid it on the table. "These are the locations of the major silos." He pointed at five areas he had marked with red ink. "I've increased the manpower dislocated here and assigned horses and wagons that your runners can use to carry food to the remotest corners of the lands." He studied the map along with the rest of the group. "Your job will be to coordinate the requests you'll be getting and to send your teams from the depots to the final destination."

"We have to direct traffic to and from the silos." Frannie's finger trailed on the map.

"To and from the communities that have the most pressing demands." Intercepting Frannie's finger, Ashton steered it aside.

"Exactly." He nodded, satisfied.

Of course, doubts were far from over, so he spent the rest of the evening sorting out problems and finding solutions until no one had any questions left to discuss.

"Thanks, Leader." Rising from the chair, Kevin was the first to approach him, hand extended, eyes flashing. "It's always a pleasure to work with you."

"And with you." He shook the man's hand vigorously. "Like I said before, you all have been a great aid, and everyone is in your debt." Letting go of Kevin, he grabbed Frannie's outstretched hand.

"Did I hear that you'll be proclaiming a Festival soon?" Frannie squeezed it, her warmth seeping to his bones.

"Yes. It'll start in ten days from now, and it'll last three full days." Detaching from Frannie was not as easy as he had imagined. "It'll be everyone's feast, to celebrate the end of the hardest times anyone has known and bless the better ones to come."

"Wow!" It was Ashton's turn to shake his hand. "Sounds awesome!"

"It'll be even better." He grinned, already envisioning it. "The home of every council member will be open for the occasion." He could not wait to see how beautiful Black Rose would be for the event. "There'll be plenty of food, drinks and sex for everyone."

"Now, that's an invitation I can't refuse." Giggling happily, Betsyan approached him to shake his hand before moving to the door.

"Where will you be spending your Festival?" Shelby's inquisitive gaze trained on him.

"Home," he breathed the word with all the force of his desire to see the beloved place again.

He missed it like crazy, and this forced stay at the Hall only reminded him of how long he had been away from it.

"Where you'll hold your own Festival, right, Leader?" Clasping his hand tightly, Clay held it in a firm and steady grip.

"Yes, and you're all invited in case you're looking for places to go to," he offered.

"Thanks, but I'll get back to the Southern District." Sander was the last one to clamp his hand as a way of a goodbye. "Speaking of which, one of my teams stayed in Blue Oasis and told me that your phase mate is feeling much better."

He did not expect Sander to know that his adored angel had made it safe and sound. David had kept tabs on him, and that had provided him with all the relevant updates. He could not have used the most reliable source, after all. Not since he had closed her out while on the road from Blue Oasis to the Hall.

"But that's not all," Sander continued. "Terence Blaise, the head of the team that has spent more time at Blue Oasis, told me that there was a dark-haired young woman that the servants say looks a lot like you, who helped his team the most. It seems she worked real hard with every group passing through Blue Oasis, and Terence, in particular, was very taken with her."

The undertone was not lost on him.

All at once, he was back in the Game, back to being her master while she provoked him to push her boundaries out of any context. Unavoidable then for his insides to be liquefying from the craving to have her, same way it had happened during Cecilia's blasted Game!

"Not just 'cause he told me she's beautiful." Sander sounded sorry that he had not been able to see her for himself. "'Cause she did selfless work in the fields, even if her strength wasn't always up to it."

Kind of evident, the strain must have gotten to her, as well. So, what else was new?

He could see her, driving herself harder than anybody he knew, beyond her energy for sure, just to prove her worth. Which started a wave of tenderness he had to block lest it strangled him.

"Anyway, Terence thought you ought to know." Sander's lips pursed. "Which is why I'm telling you."

"I appreciate it." After patting the man's back, Duncan watched him leave together with the others.

CHAPTER THIRTY-SEVEN

Goddamn it! Upon sitting behind his desk, Duncan's fist hit the wooden surface. *Why did Sander have to bring* her *up?*

It had all been going so well. He had cast Ylianor out of his head after a fierce inner struggle that had lasted three days from the moment he had set foot out of Blue Oasis.

It had been too much, the stress coupled with the new commitments. She had been just one more complication over which he had neither time nor energy to spare. So, he had severed their link, silenced her voice and pretended she had never existed.

Too bad, everything seemed to begin and end with the damnable witch, including that compelling voice of hers that would have drowned every other sound, had he only allowed it.

It grated on his nerves. To the point, it blurred all his perceptions when it came to her and her relationship to him.

Not a slave, yet after Cecilia's Game, he could not deny that his mastery over her was complete and total. For she belonged to him like no other person he knew, not even his angel.

Not a lover, yet his body lusted after her with an intensity he had felt for no one except his angel. For the craving to have her, again and again, had become unbearable. Uncontrollable, too, to the point of justifying his shutting her out completely.

Not an asset, yet he could not fathom his life without her. For she meant so much more to him in ways he was just beginning to discover.

Not a troublemaker as Chris had claimed from the start, yet

she seemed strangely connected to the same catastrophic events that had nearly wiped out their world. For he could not shake the sinking feeling that, whatever he had unleashed, was after her and that their world just happened to be in the way.

Not a twin, yet she had awakened his Virt and seemed to control it. For she was the primary note that blared in his head and covered all other sounds.

Not a relative, either, yet he would have to make her a part of his family. For he would have to assign her the Caldwell Seat in the High Council. This was a necessity he had been grappling with for reasons that were not just political.

On one level, Cecilia and Chris's support alone could prove insufficient, however renovated the assembly might be after Virtus's mayhem. He required all the allies he could get, and she was the most readily available one.

On a second level, if James Templeton agreed to have the angel replace him, Duncan was sure he would ask for something in return. He would ask his son to pledge.

It was only customary, after all. Traditional, too, given the increased obligations and responsibilities to one's family that such a position entailed. It was only a matter of time before James brought it up. What would happen then? What woman would Chris be willing to pledge if not *her*?

What a mess!

He was back to square one, with her taking it all and his inability to stop her in any way. Like he never had a choice when it came to the blasted witch.

Which pissed him off like when he had learned of his father's will and its insane adoption clause. Downright furious with the likes of her, no wonder he had cut her off without the slightest possibility of appeal.

No, he really wanted nothing to do with her.

Least of all as a sister, even if it meant one more supporter in the council. The mere thought of having to shield her from his mother's inflexibility and wrath would have been enough to dissuade him from fulfilling his father's request. Even less did he relish the idea of pledging her to his lover. As if she were not trouble enough, the irony of it all was that, as the leader, he would have to perform the ritual himself. Something he already knew he was not inclined to do.

On the bright side, the world could end tomorrow, which did not seem like such a bad alternative, everything considered.

Ha! Whom was he kidding?

His insane rant was nothing short of *bullshit*!

Convenient lies from start to finish, he had been telling himself nothing but, incapable of facing what was really eating him.

Like the fact he had failed her.

Wholly and utterly.

Worse, he had dismissed the attraction, the power and the intimacy they had shared like they had meant nothing.

Like *she* had meant nothing.

Which was as far from the truth as night was from day.

He fucking missed her, and there was no way around this awareness!

She and that seductive voice of hers exploding in his head and stiffening his cock into hard rock solidity in the space of instants. He could not bear her deafening absence, not even now that a thousand other voices hummed continuously in his head.

She was simply too close to him, however much he tried to forget or confuse her among the million lights and sounds clogging his perception ever since becoming the leader.

Now, he could not take it anymore, the emptiness that devoured his heart and made him regret his decision.

Which was why he reopened the channel he had shut an

eternity ago. *Princess . . .*

No answer for the longest time.

He tried again, determined to reach her, was it the last thing he did. *Princess, are you there?*

If she did not scramble to reply, he felt her just a breath away, hesitating on the threshold. How to blame her?

After how he had treated her, he could not expect her to welcome him with open arms.

Princess, I know you can hear me. His tone deliberately huskier, he knew she would not resist his call.

Thought I'd never hear from you again. Not her usual pitch, this had a wearied strain that went straight to his heart and filled it with dread.

The sense of abandonment so overwhelming, it choked him, as did the pain and suffering that came with it. But before he could analyze it further, she attacked him.

Who would've guessed? Now, it was her again, the heavy sarcasm dripping from this biting remark made him think he might have mistaken his sensations. *Already tired of visiting your angel?*

No lie, he had lost count of the nights he had lain awake in bed while trying to reach out for his beloved Chris. His absence was another devastating hole in his heart that throbbed night and day painfully. He so fucking missed him that it physically hurt, like having lost an arm, a leg or both. To the point, he had refused to believe Virtus could ever have the better of him.

Once his angel had pulled through, he had attempted to touch, albeit at a distance, the fiery essence lying weak and feeble in Blue Oasis. Which had been his only measure of relief and comfort during the months of hard work and strict organization.

No, I'll never grow tired of him. Not just because he loved the man so damn much!

Because, if Chris had been there with him, he would have

never flung her out in the cold.

Just thought I'd check up on you for a change, he provoked.

Your consideration is appreciated, Revered Leader, she taunted mercilessly. *But highly unnecessary.* There was a strange note of barely suppressed pride and harshness he had never suspected in her. *As you can see, I have no problems surviving on my own, without anybody giving a damn whether I live or die.*

I'm sorry, Princess. She was totally justified, of course, and he totally deserved her scorn. *I've been so busy lately that —*

You had to close our channel. Hardly fooled, her cold and distant tone testified to how clearly she saw through his deceptions.

It was just a way to handle things over here. He groaned inwardly at the lie. *You have no idea of the amount of work I've had to —*

You don't give me the chance to know, she cut him off brusque, clearly fed up with his attitude. *You just delude yourself that the weight of being a leader is incompatible with the sharing you believe I forced on you!*

Fuck it!

No, fuck her!

And that impressive logic that had cut to the chase! Nailed him to his responsibilities!

Why did things always have to get complicated so fast, so soon?

He had not figured them out himself. How could he possibly do it while talking to her from so far away, without even having the benefit of sinking into those arresting green eyes of hers?

You're right, he snapped back. *I've been making up my mind about us.*

There! He had done it!

Had blurted it out without the least consideration for her feelings.

There's something between us that I need to understand before I can handle everything else. The rush of thoughts seemed unstoppable now. *You upset all my efforts at finding some sort of balance in all this chaos. I . . .*

Awareness punched him like a blow to the stomach.

He was obsessed with her!

Same way, he had been only with his angel.

He could just kick himself for the foolishness of thinking he would never fall under her spell.

Listen, I know I should explain. First, the sex had hooked him good and proper with its blend of hot scorching passion that quenched his senses in a way it never had with any other woman.

Then, the realization she just might be what he had been looking for had blown his mind. Now, he would have given just about anything to have her one more time, instead of relying on inconsequential replacements that could only warm his bed, not fill the void in his head and his body.

But this is neither the time nor the place. It would take him too long to admit he had been dead wrong in closing their connection. That it had not made him feel better, merely worse. *You'll have to wait until we see each other again.*

Sure, I get it. Her faint whisper carried her anger, her hurt and something else he could not quite identify. *As you wish.*

Ha! That was a laugh!

He could not even begin to describe what he wished!

All I wish is to know how you feel.

Why do you bother asking if you don't give a damn about me? Not mollified in the least, she called his bluff.

Because I know something is wrong, he dared her back. *Terribly wrong.*

No, really. Such insistence proved how stubborn and reserved she could be. *I just miss you.* It was the first truthful bit of information she provided, and the intensity of her need got to him.

I miss you, too. He charged the words with all the ache

piercing his heart.

Doubtful she caught it.

All he felt were her barriers going up, and he lost her again. There was no way he would get her back now.

His fault, for sure.

He and his shutting her out gave him no rights to pretend what he was not willing to give himself.

We've been apart too long. She could not deny it, not even if hiding behind her wall of reticence. *That's why I'd like for us to be together in Black Rose for the Festival if the angel is up to it.*

Oh, he's already in top shape, she sniggered.

Which to him sounded more like relief at being off the hook.

Itching to get back to you, she concluded.

I'm sure he found more than one way to cure his itches. Duncan chuckled, imagining how insatiable Chris would have become after his forced inactivity.

Let's say he knows his way around Blue Oasis a lot better now. She giggled. *Servants here are very accommodating, without mentioning the various work teams.*

Speaking of them, it seems I have to thank you. He chortled amused.

Me? Kind of evident, she had not expected this turn in the conversation. *Why? I haven't done anything worthwhile –*

Oh, yes, you have, at least according to your friend Terence. From her embarrassed silence, Duncan guessed his initial assessment had been right all along and that the man had been more than just a teammate. *He made it a point to inform me of how selflessly you dedicated your time and energy to the reconstruction effort, which is why you have my sincerest thanks.*

It was nothing. Breathless, her voice faltered most deliciously, *Really.*

If you say so. He knew it!

Knew she had overtaxed herself simply to stifle the pain of his abandonment.

Just be sure to save your strength for the journey, he urged her.

I will, she promised. *I'm sure the demon will make me leave straight away for Black Rose.* Of course, she missed the place as much as he did, given how homesick she sounded.

I can't wait to see you, Princess, both of you. His stomach clenched in anticipation. *Just remember to bring the pyramid along.*

Exactly what he would do with it, he still had no idea. Put it back, then hope life continued as usual?

Not his best option, though the only one at the moment, however dissatisfied he was with it.

What if Cecilia was right, and it controlled sex? Maybe not just sex, but everything else, too?

With Virtus looking over everyone's shoulder, it was logical to consider emotions less than real, as though everyone had lived a lie all along.

Which was unacceptable on so many levels he could not even begin listing them all. Starting from the simplest one that a damn mechanism could never be responsible for what he felt for his blond angel. For the hot, passionate love tying him to the incredible man who was his lover, his friend, his brother and phase mate. Beyond the sex and the sensual potency that connected them, Chris belonged to him. No Virtus monster would have him believe that his raw hunger for his amazing angel was anything less than what his heart yearned for every day, all thirty-six hours of it.

Right now, though, it was beside the point since the sole link to the evil monster remained *her*.

Ylianor Meyer.

The only one capable of talking to it was the same woman he had to make amends to before the situation got out of hand for real.

Will do, she assured. *Goodbye.* What followed was the slamming shut of their channel, a forceful impact that reverberated in his mind with the potency of a thunderbolt on a fine summer day.

Stunned, it took him a few minutes to recover before the emptiness began swallowing him. Was that how she had felt until now?

She had gone before he could assuage his guilty conscience or ask if she had something to wear to the Festival.

Which she probably had not.

No question about it, her skimpy wardrobe would not have grown since he had last seen her. If it had been the perfect excuse for keeping her naked and at his disposal, it would not do for this occasion. He would get her something special to celebrate more than just the Festival.

A new beginning was in order. Enough fighting himself for what he mistook as an intrusion. Enough of seeing her as the enemy. Of blaming this Virt that required such a close connection between two people, whether they wanted it or not. No more fierce resistance to the intoxication of having her locked up inside of him. So deep inside, she had become a piece of him.

Whether he liked it or not, she was part of him and he of her. There was no way he could keep denying it.

Not to himself.

Certainly not to her.

To the woman who had exalted his senses like no one before her.

What he had to do was accept her, like she had been urging from the start. It was his most logical course of action. Or rather, what his heart longed for, now more than ever. Just being away from her had made him sick to his stomach.

Literally.

It was high time he acknowledged her and her power over him.

Thank the stars, he had not blown his chances.

The way forward was to have a good long face-to-face talk,

decide how to leave communication open in the future and let the Festival seal their deal.

And he could hardly wait!

CHAPTER THIRTY-EIGHT

"Come in." The loud knock at the door interrupted Duncan's stream of thoughts.

"Hello, darling." Cecilia popped her head around the threshold. "Busy."

"Not at all." Gesturing her forward, he sat straighter. "What's up?"

"Just checking in before I leave for Blue Oasis." Tentatively, she took a few steps inside his office, closing the door behind her. "Gotta get ready for the best Festival ever." She winked in a sexy, conspiratorial way.

"You've more than deserved it." He invited her to take the chair in front of his desk, and she was quick to land on the leather cushion. "You've done a heck of a job these past weeks!" The note of praise was sincere and heartfelt. "You amazed me the way you coordinated your teams. You managed to get not just Blandry up and running again, but also the entire area around it before anyone else. Your boroughs have the fastest recovery rate of any other, with everyone helping on a vast scale." He gave her an appreciative glance. "You've set an example for all, and I'm really impressed with your efforts."

"Thank you, Leader." She smoothed down her long skirt in an attempt to hide the deep blush spreading on her cheeks. "Let's say I felt . . ." A bitter scowl twisted her lips. "Responsible."

"You shouldn't be." He peered at her intently. "I gave David the order to move the pieces around—"

"Yeah, but you wouldn't have, had I not stolen the damn thing from the Nephis Valley," she moaned.

True enough, but things were more complicated than that. Plus, his damn shoulder flaring up was an unnecessary reminder of just how tangled things really were.

"I'm not so sure." Still, he was not about to lay all his cards on the table. "I've been working on some new theories . . ."

Rubbing the sore spot on his left shoulder, he pondered how easily Virtus could have instilled doubts in Cecilia about what was real and what not, clouding her judgment and muddling her priorities and options.

"Should they prove correct, what you've done would pale in comparison of what we have to face." Leaning forward, he bore his gaze into hers. "To be honest, I need an expert game player to unravel this whole mess."

"You need me?" Evidently taken aback, she was still processing the first part of his speech.

"Of course, I need you," he confirmed readily. "As I said at Blue Oasis, the five of us will have to figure out what to do with the wretched pyramid—"

"It's like you're setting up a special team for this task." She giggled at her pun.

"Hadn't thought of it like that." Liking her sharpness, he rewarded her with a huge smile. "But I suppose I am."

The Goodbye-Virtus team!

"With its members being David, Lord Christopher Templeton and your slave." A twitch of her nose told him how little her attitude had changed toward his princess, in spite of everything that had happened!

"She's Ylianor Meyer." Refusing to dwell on all the personal issues that would divide rather than unite this particular group, he groaned. "And she's not my slave."

"Whatever." She waved a dismissive hand in the air. "What's the first order of business? When and where should we all meet to discuss it?" Her dark eyes flashed as if she had just thought of something new. "Hey, why don't you spend the Festival at Blue Oasis? This way, we'd all be together—"

"Thanks, Ceci, but I'd like to go home, too." No way would he pass up the chance to return to Black Rose. "A place I'm starting to forget." He smirked apologetically. "That's how long I haven't seen it."

"What about Lord Templeton?" Cecilia's inquisitive gaze inspected his face. "My staff tells me he has made a remarkable recovery."

"Yes, I know." He beamed at her from the sheer pleasure he anticipated from his imminent reunion with the blond angel. "He and Ylianor will be on their way to Black Rose shortly." He could not wait to see them, *both of them.* "And to the Festival I'm hosting for my district, Silcamore." Which would be worth celebrating only if they were at his side. "After the Festival, I'll read my father's will." He frowned, remembering that he still had not told the lawyer whether or not to include the adoption clause. "Which reminds me." He looked up at her. "If you don't mind, I'd like to ask David to deliver a message for me to Black Rose if he has returned."

"He has," she informed. "I saw him coming in from Ridgely, Lord Ellis's district."

"Good." He was glad to have David back. "You can send him over as soon as we're done."

She inclined her head in agreement. "What about the pyramid?" She tensed up at the mere mention of the blasted thing. "I presume Lord Templeton is bringing the pyramid along."

"Technically, Ylianor has charge of the damn thing." His lips curved in an ironic snarl. "Otherwise, you presume correctly."

"Oh, all right." Once again, his reproachful tone did not affect her in the least. "We should meet after the Festival."

"After I've read my father's will," he retorted. "As to

where—"

"I'd like to see Black Rose," she blurted out with excitement stamped all over her angular face. "With all I've heard about it, I'm dying of curiosity."

"All right." This worked perfectly, and it would leave him ample time to do everything. "Ten days after the Festival, the five of us will meet at Black Rose and decide what to do with the pyramid."

Cecilia nodded in agreement. "Thank you, Leader, for everything." She stood up awkwardly. "If you hadn't been here, I . . ." As her voice broke, she seemed about to give in to the emotions she had been repressing since entering his office.

Going around his desk, he reached her. "Come now." He took her in his arms. "Everything is going to be all right."

"Only because you are our leader now." Obviously grateful, she snuggled closer. "Arthur would've made me pay dearly for my mistakes."

"Hush, Ceci." He bent on her ear. "I promised we'd work things out together, and that's precisely what we're doing."

Raising her head, she kissed him. Sweetly at first, it soon turned into a passionate affair, his tongue sliding down her throat and making her sway against his groin, awakening a desire that had been dormant for way too long.

"Why don't we continue this tonight in my room?" So, what if Cecilia Hurst was not quite his first choice? "I still have a few things to finish up here. Then, I'm free."

"Can you make it for dinnertime?" Her eyes shone from sheer lust.

"Yes," he confirmed. "Come to my room, and we'll take it from there."

"Great!" Giggling ecstatically, she reached the door, looking as happy as a child. But then her step faltered, and she turned around with an anxious expression crossing her features. "Are you sure you want to spend the night with me?"

Nervously, she chewed on her lower lip while waiting for his answer.

"Ceci, you'll never learn, will you?" Amused, he shook his head. "I didn't say I love you." He grinned wickedly. "Just asked to spend a night with you."

"I thought you didn't like me much." Clearly ashamed, she lowered her gaze and stared at her feet in rapt attention.

"I don't like the unbalance between your body and mind." Nearing her, he tilted up her head. "But there are attractive sides to you that I can't wait to explore." His hand trailed down to her breasts, pinching each aroused nipple in turn, begging as they were for his touch.

"Will you give me more lessons tonight?" She pressed her body against his.

The hot afternoons he had spent in her bed at Blue Oasis flashed in his mind. "When I did, they didn't seem to help you much." His lips curved downward. "At least judging from our time at your last Game."

"Oh, come on!" Affronted, she took a step back. "That wasn't so bad," she protested. "It would've been better if Rowena hadn't been there," she pointed out as though it explained everything. "You know what I feel for her . . ." She trailed off, embarrassed.

"Yeah, I know damn well what you feel for her." *Obsessed!*

That was the only way to describe it.

Cecilia was as obsessed about Rowena as Chris had been about him, which had been the reason he had to kick him out of Black Rose and end their phase in such a cruel way.

"Tonight, we'll see how it goes one on one." Bending, he kissed her hard.

She did not put up any sort of defense. She surrendered everything and went limp in his embrace.

"See you tonight." Pulling away, he went to his desk.

Breathless and unsteady on her feet, she was about to leave

when something stopped her mid-step. "Do you want me to send David to you now?"

"Yes, please." Sitting down, he leaned back in his chair.

"Fine." Spinning around, she opened the door. "See you later." And she was gone.

CHAPTER THIRTY-NINE

As soon as Cecilia was out of sight, Duncan wrote, "Yes," and a date on a piece of paper. Folding it, he addressed it to Mark Hamill, Harbor Town. He was just adding the finishing touches when another knock shattered the silence.

"Come in." Expecting David to walk through, he did not bother to look up at the door.

"My dear prince."

Since the strong male voice sounded more like James Templeton, he quickly raised his gaze. "I'll be leaving tomorrow for Fair Haven and wanted to say goodbye." Advancing, James closed the door behind him. "I need to celebrate the Festival with my family."

"Don't we all?" Getting up, Duncan gestured at him to get comfortable on the couch nearest the fireplace. "I'm also leaving for Black Rose in a few days." He settled on the opposite couch.

"Do you think I'll have the pleasure of having Chris with me?" There was such a tender, hopeful note in James's voice that crushed Duncan's heart.

"Sorry, Lord Templeton." He tried to be as gentle as possible, feeling oddly protective of the older man.

Like he was his father, not just Chris's.

"I've invited Chris to Black Rose," he continued softly. "Not just for the Festival, but mostly to sort things out and get them back to normal." *As much as possible.*

"I understand." James leaned back against the soft cushions. "Don't worry about it." However light the tone, it was clear he would miss Chris. "I'll do with the rest of my family."

"Again, I'm sorry." A pang of guilt sliced his stomach. "Once our business is over, I'll tell him to visit you," he promised. "I believe you have much to discuss, especially if you've made up your mind about stepping down."

"I have, Leader." James sighed. "I'm an old man, and I've seen too many of my friends die." Deep lines of sorrow furrowed his face. "It'll be good to get some rest finally, even if there's still that nagging dilemma about who will take my place."

"Please, let's not talk about this anymore." Stretching over the low table that divided the two sofas, he caught the other man's gaze and held it. "Instead, why don't you keep an open mind and spend some quality time with Chris when he'll be home?" The advice had James's full attention. "You might feel differently about him, discover how gifted he is, and why I won't accept any other candidate from your family."

"After what you said during your first speech, I can understand why you'd insist on it." James nodded slowly. "By the way, did I thank you?"

"For what?" Puzzled, Duncan stared at him.

"The wonderful words you said about my son . . ." James's voice broke for a second before he managed to get a grip on himself. "In front of the entire High Council."

"I only spoke the truth." He could not suppress the heated wave surging through him, only thinking of how close he had come to losing his precious angel.

"No, you did much more than that." James's watery blue eyes flashed. "Not only did you make me very proud of him. You also turned him into a hero, even if no one is quite clear on what he did exactly."

"Not much." Duncan smiled mischievously. "Besides saving the world."

"I'm sure it's all thanks to you." Something like an

emotional wave coursing through James reddened his cheeks. "I always thought you'd be a good influence on him. That's why I sent him to you when he was just a boy." He paused, and Duncan remembered what Chris had shared while on their way to Blue Oasis. "Today, you've become a man who cares about him."

"Oh, no, it's much more than that," he blurted out, not wanting any misunderstanding to stand in the way of his feelings for the fantastic creature that was Christopher Templeton. "I love your son." He gave the words all the depth and passion he could muster. "I did from the first time I laid eyes on him." He pushed out a heavy breath. "And will keep loving him until the end of time."

There, he had poured his heart out, and he was not sorry about it.

Not one bit.

If anything, he should have done it sooner.

"I was afraid of it." James locked gazes with him. "At least until Arthur told me it was the best thing that could happen to Chris." His harsh glare softened. "And to you, son."

Grateful for the consideration that mirrored his own, Duncan bent his head.

"Thank you for your honesty, though this love of yours has been in plain sight from the start." He laughed. "It lights your eyes whenever you talk about Chris, so there's no hiding it. Of course, my son is so in love with you that both Arthur and I feared he'd never get over his phase." He threw back his shoulders. "My son is indeed a lucky man, for such strong feelings are rare once the phase is over." He sighed as if he had something weighing on his mind. "While we're at it, I have something to confess . . ." His voice trailed off, uncertain and hurt at the same time. "Something I've lacked the courage to do so far."

Reading his anguish, Duncan tried to block him. "Milord,

you shouldn't—"

"No, please," James implored, almost pleading. "Let me say it, or I'll never face up to my responsibilities." He shifted position. "When I sent Chris to you, it wasn't just to get him away from certain bad influences around Fair Haven." Evidently embarrassed, he lowered his gaze. "No, I'm ashamed to say I disowned him in a way," he admitted. "It was like I thought he didn't need me anymore. Like there was someone better qualified to take charge of him." He shook his head in dismay. "I know it doesn't excuse me, but it might explain how difficult I considered Chris to be then . . ." He raised his gaze. "And still do at times, which is probably why he didn't want to have anything to do with me when he stayed here at the Hall." Eyes moist from the emotions threatening to overwhelm him, James had never looked frailer. "It was like we were living in separate districts when, in fact, we were under the same roof."

"I could never replace you, sir." Leaving his couch, he sat next to James.

"No matter how much I love him, your son needs his father." He squeezed the older man's shoulder to give him strength. "And these words, which you should tell him, not me."

"I will," James assured. "This tragedy we barely survived has given me a different perspective on things and made me understand what's really important in life."

"Then, it wasn't all in vain." He beamed, relieved to see James riling up to the occasion. "Once you have your heart-to-heart talk, you'll see that Chris is the best choice for your replacement."

"Now that you mention it." James pressed his hands together. "Steve doesn't even care about the council, much less getting my seat." He examined Duncan's face. "My oldest boy is much happier spending his life outdoors, taking care of all sorts of vegetation—"

"For which I hear he has a special talent," Duncan was quick to pick up the thread. "He and his phase mate, Lord Oliver Sentry, are behind Lady Hurst's success in getting production levels of her district back on track."

"Yes, Steve and Oliver are very dedicated to improving agricultural methods," James confirmed. "And so is Bran, my second boy. Steve has converted wholeheartedly to his love for farming and experimentation. All together, they've been studying and applying revolutionary techniques for years, which is how I know that neither one cares for the responsibilities here at the Hall."

"Whereas Chris has been preparing for it all his life." He had just to think of the two and a half years his angel had spent with Arthur to feel certain of it. "He's been so good at it that he had practically ruled the nightlife."

Which was a coded way of saying that his angel was in charge of the Hall's sex life, particularly the one that went on in the attic between the Arthur boys.

"Not just that," James retorted. "He rose so fast in the Hall's hierarchy that I'm still wondering how he achieved it." He frowned in concentration. "In all my years as vice-leader, I've never seen anyone go so fast to the top, and not because he was my son." He lowered his voice, "And now that his phase mate has become leader, there'll be no stopping him."

"Oh, I'm aware of it." Phases, after all, were privileged relationships, often valued above pledges. No wonder that a leader's phase mate would have as much power as the leader himself.

No, in Chris's case, it would be way above any leader's!

"He's already ahead of me." He chuckled in amusement. "Especially when it comes to gossip and networking."

"He's way ahead of everyone in those skills." James grinned widely. "I think you may be right, after all." He patted Duncan's back. "With all he's got going for him, Chris might be the best replacement I could ask for." His tone grew somber, "What about your father's seat?" He pursed his lips. "With your becoming the leader, the Caldwell Seat will remain vacant, and you need to fill it."

"I will." He had the perfect woman for the job if only he could work out the details.

"You already have someone in mind?" Very interested, James raised an eyebrow.

"Let's say, I do." The scalding sting on his left shoulder agreed with his assessment. "Though it might be a bit tricky."

"I'm sure you can work it out." James's vote of confidence was unmistakable. "Like I've seen you work through the worst of our crisis." He gripped Duncan's arm. "I must say I've been really impressed with your dedication and effort. You've worked twice as much as anyone else in organizing, giving advice, setting down guidelines and helping whatever way you could. I know for a fact you are a source of inspiration for everyone, both in and out of the council. You have great assistants." His brow creased as though reviewing a list of names. "That David fellow, for example, has been an excellent reference point for everyone here. He's quick, efficient, thorough, capable and very discreet."

"He's more than an assistant," Duncan pointed out. "David is a close friend, and I have to thank my father for having chosen him to be my companion when I was just six years old."

"Charles was always an excellent judge of people." For a moment, James seemed lost in memory. "A skill I'm glad to see his son inherited." Coming out of whatever reverie had imprisoned him, he smiled sympathetically. "Well . . ." He got to his feet with some effort. "Now, I must go and finish up my packing."

Duncan stood up, too. "Have a safe journey to Fair Haven."

He pulled James into a tight embrace.

"Thank you, Leader." Disentangling, Lord Templeton went for the door but soon stopped. "Just one more thing." Spinning around, he confronted Duncan once more. "If you want him on that permanent seat, Chris will have to pledge."

The man did have a point, one that, fortunately for him, Duncan had already anticipated.

"Are you haggling over Chris's future?" Still, he would not tolerate blackmail.

"Actually, you are." James licked his lips smugly like he had succeeded in cornering him. "By insisting he'd be the Templeton sitting on the High Council. That's a responsibility to his district and to his family that he can't ignore," he declared. "Especially since it becomes necessary for Chris to pass on this prodigious power you talk about."

There, the older man had just sealed his angel's fate! After all, no pledge meant no babies, so Chris was trapped in a no-win situation.

"I suppose fair is fair," he conceded cautiously. "But not if you have to extort his compliance."

"Let's say it's a non-negotiable condition," James offered.

"Everything's negotiable," he mused, recalling how he had persuaded his princess to play the slave.

"Not in this case," James demurred. "So, my question is — how will we convince him if he still hates women?"

Not all, fortunately. "You can start by talking to him when he comes to Fair Haven."

"I sure will," James concurred heartily. "But we both know you'll have to do much of the convincing."

Hey, I'm already working on it, would have been Duncan's reply had not a knock prevented him. "Come in," he hollered.

"Forgive me, Leader." Opening the door, David stepped inside his office. "Lord Templeton." Noticing James, he bowed deeply. "I'm sorry. I didn't mean to disturb you."

From the way he hovered on the threshold, it was clear he was about to bolt. "I'll wait outside—"

"No, David." James moved toward him. "I was just leaving." Turning to Duncan, he extended a hand. "Goodbye, Leader, and have a good Festival."

"You, too, Milord." He clasped James's hand tightly. "Safe journey to Fair Haven."

"Thanks." Going up to David, James tapped his back. "It's been a real pleasure working alongside you."

At the unexpected compliment, David's handsome features became bright red.

"You've done excellent work, as I just told the leader." Seemingly unaware of the tumult he was causing, James continued on the same note, "I hope you get the chance to rest and enjoy yourself in the coming Festival." He held out his hand to David.

"Thank you, sir," David stammered, shaking it. "It was an honor working with you, and I wish you a safe trip."

"Thank you and take care." Letting go of David, James strode into the hallway and closed the door behind him.

CHAPTER FORTY

"Thank you for coming, David." Slapping his back, Duncan brought him forward.

Still shaking from Lord Templeton's earlier compliment, he simply nodded.

He had not been expecting it, much less from the vice-leader, a man who, after all, was Christopher Templeton's father. The man who also ruled the daytime activities almost behind Lord Fairchild's back, while his son had free rein in the nightlife. From the little he had gathered, father and son had divided the responsibilities between them quite nicely and effectively.

Now, looking at his leader and adored prince, he could just wonder how this would affect things once that menace of Christopher Templeton would be well enough to return to the Hall.

Which would happen sooner than he had anticipated, judging from his latest information.

"What's the news from Ridgely?" Having gestured for him to sit, Duncan went around his desk and settled in his chair.

"Things are up and running again," he was happy to report. "They've finished rebuilding, and they're talking with Lord Bran Templeton as we speak about Lord Sentry's innovative farming techniques—"

"James was just telling me of how dedicated Bran is," Duncan observed. "Yet, people only talk about Steve, but not a word about him."

"Probably because Lord Steve Templeton is Lord Sentry's

phase mate," he pointed out with all the respect that such a relationship deserved. "But Lord Sentry has many assistants and assistants, and one of the most gifted is Lord Bran Templeton."

"It seems that we owe the Templeton family a bigger debt of gratitude than I originally assessed." The prince chuckled.

"Yes, they've all exerted themselves pretty hard," he confirmed. "Traveling to faraway districts to spread Lord Sentry's knowledge and raise productivity levels."

"Speaking of which, I've heard that the princess has been doing her bit." There was an undeniable note of admiration in his master's tone. "Helping several teams in their reconstruction efforts."

"Yes, sir, she has." He went over in his head what he had learned about her lately, trying not to picture her dark, slender form. "Mostly clearing the debris in the villages around Blue Oasis."

"I hope she doesn't work herself out," Duncan worried out loud.

"I hope so, too," he concurred softly. "But then, we've all worked pretty hard lately." His tentative smile was a way to move the conversation away from dangerous topics.

"No one worked as hard as you did." Duncan beamed in response. "Like Lord Templeton pointed out, your efforts in getting things back to normal deserve all the praise you can get." The black gaze flashed in satisfaction. "I'm proud of you, David, and as you heard, I'm not the only one!" The applauding note was so infectious that David's heart had a meltdown. "We could've never done it without you."

"I . . ." He felt himself turning purple. "I just did my duty," he managed to blurt eventually.

"No, you did much more." It was kind of obvious that his humility would not deter the man from commending him all the more. "You were selfless, quick, efficient and effective.

You went beyond it all and gave a heck of a lot more than what was required." He had to pause for a breath. "Not only did you train the scouts, but you also directed their work and traveled yourself to the most dangerous spots, bringing supplies to those in need and creating the most solid network I could've ever hoped for." Duncan regarded him with something close to amazement. "You've earned my everlasting thanks and respect," he assured. "Now, it's time to rest."

Since he did not feel all that tired, he ventured to say as much, "I don't need to—"

"Nonsense!" Duncan raised a hand to stop his objections. "I know for a fact that you hardly slept these past days," he contradicted. "Being as you were on the road all the time, supervising everything and everyone." It was kind of evident that the leader not only had noticed how strenuously he had applied himself to the rebuilding effort but remembered everything he had done, too. "You must now recover your strength, and that's an order." Despite the cackle, he knew this was a serious command. "I need you at your best for the tasks ahead, all right?"

"Yes, sir." He almost jumped up to prove his acquiescence. "Thank you."

"No, thank you." Duncan grinned widely. "Forgive me if there are a couple of more things I need to ask you before I free you for the Festival," he added apologetically.

"Sure, no problem." Shifting position, he got ready to memorize the leader's new instructions.

"I would like you to deliver a message over in Harbor Town to our lawyer, Mister Hamill." The prince leaned forward. "Remember him?"

"Of course, sir." He had no trouble recalling the young man, who had ridden under a veritable deluge just for the chance to speak to Prince Caldwell in Black Rose.

"I'd go myself," Duncan continued. "But I'm tied up here

until tomorrow." He handed David a slip of pleated paper.

"All right, sir." Taking the sheet, he pocketed it. "I can leave tomorrow if that's all right with you."

"Good," Duncan smirked. "Once you've delivered the message, I'd be much obliged if you went to Black Rose."

"Shall I tell Reginald to expect you in a few days?" He searched for confirmation in the handsome face.

"Yes, but there's more." Reclining, Duncan shifted his focus to the window at his left, and he got lost for a moment in a fixed stare of the encroaching darkness.

Which reminded David that night was about to fall, and that he would have to check on the leader's dinner in the kitchen.

A hand rubbing his left shoulder as though it hurt him, the man turned his attention back on him. "The angel and the princess are on their way there, and I don't want any problems."

"That may be difficult to accomplish." He shrugged, thinking of all the complications waiting for Ylianor at the Caldwell estate.

"I dare say you might be right." Duncan groaned audibly, imagining for sure the same complications. "They're bound to arrive before I do, so tell Reginald to accommodate them in the western tower, in the rooms next to mine." That took care of the organization. "As for my mother, inform her that they are my guests, whether she likes it or not, and she has no say in it."

"Shall I tell her these exact words?" David offered mischievously.

"Yes." Duncan grated his teeth. "No." He waved a dismissive hand in the air. "Oh, fuck!"

The interjection was so heartfelt that David found it his duty to try and calm him. "I know your mother can be difficult at times —"

"That's an understatement," the prince admitted readily. "'Cause she'll be upset no matter what."

Upset was putting it mildly. Raging mad would be a fairer assessment.

"You mean about Ylianor?" If he asked, it was only because he did not want to misunderstand the root of his master's distress.

"Yeah, it's all about the princess." From the loud sigh, David surmised that the issue might be bigger than an oversensitive Lady Caldwell. "And the fact that my mother will never accept her." Duncan's shoulders sagged as though the weight of it all was unbearable.

"She'll never accept the sleeping arrangements either." His lips distorted in a wry snarl. "When she finds out, your mother won't be pleased."

"Not to worry," Duncan growled. "She'll be furious when she learns about the will." Frowning, he shook his head, the long, dark strands of hair fluttering around his shoulders.

"You're going through with the adoption, then?" Sitting up straighter, he regarded Duncan intently.

"Yes." The heavy breath the prince pushed out told him that it had been far from an easy decision. "I need her on the council."

If he does, he sounds none too happy about it.

Now, why should that be was a matter of conjecture. Something was off for sure — something that spoke volumes about the leader's less than enthusiastic response to this new twist.

Still, he supposed it was a necessity if the rumors he had heard proved right. "People say the vice-leader is going to retire and leave his seat to his son, Lord Christopher Templeton."

"Word really travels fast here." Evidently taken aback, Duncan stared at him in wonderment. "James only discussed it a few times . . ."

"It's more than enough to get tongues wagging," he

assured. "So, both of them will sit in the council?"

"Yes, and not because of our involvement," Duncan stressed the point. "It's because the High Council is a place of power, and you've seen for yourself what they're capable of."

"I understand." He bowed in acknowledgment, trying to ignore the ache in his heart at the thought of how above him Ylianor Meyer would become.

"Speaking of power." Luckily, the deep, throaty voice snagged his attention back to the matters at hand. "The five of us need to sort out what we started in Blue Oasis."

"I'm ready." *Ready for action! Ready to set things back to normal! Ready to forget that Ylianor will soon be out of my reach!*

"Good," the prince approved. "The plan is for us to reconvene in Black Rose ten days after the Festival, all right?"

"I'll bring Ceci and see you then." Feeling his emotional control slipping the longer he looked at the man who so closely resembled Ylianor, he unfolded from the chair and stood up awkwardly. "If that's all, I think I better leave and start packing."

"Sure." Coming round his desk, Duncan pulled him in a tight embrace. "Goodbye, David, and have a safe journey."

"You, too, sir." For good measure, he squeezed his master's hand before going to the door and exiting.

CHAPTER FORTY-ONE

The tip of Duncan's erection swallowed by Cecilia's pliant mouth was an excellent start to his night.

Sucking then lapping every side meticulously, she gave a better performance than her usual. Still, it could stand some improvement, reason why he held her head and fucked her face without constrictions.

But ramming his cock to the back of her throat was only the preliminary to get the show on the road.

Cecilia gagged but did not miss a beat, rubbing the hard stem as if afraid to miss even a tiny spot. Appreciative of her efforts, he watched her head bobbing more frantically. If she kept it up, he would have a good chance of reaching her stomach.

Which was not his aim.

Her ass was.

Although not as tempting as his angel or his princess's, it was still his best bet for oblivion.

Then again, Ceci did not have much going for her besides her brilliant mind. She had none of Ylianor's allure or seductive curves, none of her smoky green eyes bewitchment nor her keen reaction to pain and pleasure.

Goddamn it!

He better stop thinking about the blasted dark-haired witch if he did not want to turn this into the worst pity fuck of his life.

Obliterating the picture of the princess taunting him, he pinned down Cecilia and tested her narrow back passage with wet fingers.

She moaned and pushed back, her swamped slit proving beyond a doubt how ready she was for him.

He propped her up on all fours and thrust. Inch by inch, his monstrous equipment slid into her until fully wrapped by the narrow channel. Her butt swung back, and he set a beat that was sure to crack it sooner rather than later.

Boy, it felt so tight she was about to explode from the effort of containing it whole.

Something that would have sent him straight to the finish line had she not leaned down to dig her elbows on the mattress and spread her knees, forcing him to slow his acceleration.

She was in obvious need of a little incentive, so he gladly obliged. Bending, he brushed her drenched cunt, not neglecting to dip into the moist folds, stroke the throbbing clit and penetrate the enlarged slit. The position allowed it, after all, as well as the thorough ass fuck that soon beckoned him more than her pussy's satisfied drippings.

"Now, it's your turn, Ceci." Grabbing her hand, he placed it between her legs.

She took the hint naturally, and her fingers burrowed in her sleek cunt.

Free to focus on his release, he straightened and impaled his long shaft all the way to her guts. Embedded to the hilt, he pulled back and slammed forward, beginning a frantic rhythm that would not last long.

Could not, to be precise, because the fleshy walls of her behind had all but imprisoned his colossal beast.

The faster he shoved, the hotter he became with each consecutive slide.

Not to mention bigger.

Every sensation concentrated on the fathead. He was ready to blow out of control.

Cecilia's orgasm unraveled him. Her contractions sucked him deeper and drained his every last drop in repeatedly convulsive jets.

The end of round one signaled the beginning of round two.

Flipped on her back, he took her slit, pumping hard and nailing her clit with a prolonged rub that made her come in a matter of minutes.

Resistance futile, he let go of his second load, already planning round three.

Four and five came and went. By the fifth, exhaustion overtook him, and he concluded with a tremendous come all over her breasts and belly.

Chapter Forty-two

"My darling." Stroking Duncan's bare chest before snaking her hand through the mass of his long hair, Cecilia placed a soft kiss on his nipple. "Have I ever told you I'm in debt with you?"

"What for?" Sprawled in bed, senses satisfied, he relaxed all his muscles after the whole night's worth of passionate exertions.

"For teaching me about sex." As spent as she was, she still found enough strength to be all over him. "During those glorious afternoon lessons."

Her body curled so tightly around his own that he could barely move.

"Yeah, those were the days," he mused fondly.

Had he been pressed into describing what Cecilia meant to him, he would have had to admit that she occupied a special place. She had been the first person—more like the first woman—he had sex with after his angel. Two more opposite people in bed, he could not fathom, and the irony was not lost on him. Not when considering how long and far he had to travel from Black Rose just to find her. Or that, without such an enormous distance from his angel, he would have never been able to have sex with someone new. Not to mention that other trifle—how hurt and damaged both he and Cecilia had been from the end of their phases. Unforeseeably, it had created a connection where none existed. Not that they had been on the same side of the fence.

Far from it!

He had kicked Chris out of Black Rose, thoroughly fed up with his aggressive sexual tactics, while Rowena had unceremoniously dumped her. Still, the pain of the breakup had been an undeniable reality for both of them. Nor had it helped that half the time, he had wished he were in bed with his angel instead of her.

Worst of all, he had drawn unnecessary comparisons that had threatened to spoil his enjoyment in more than one occasion.

"But you didn't even seem to listen." Pulling free of memory lane, he caressed her dark hair.

"Not true," she flared in protest. "I listened closely and treasured every bit of information," she assured vehemently. "So much that they inspired my Game."

"Really?" It was damn impressive! "How?"

His interest went beyond mere accomplishment.

Everything about her mind fascinated him. At times, he could almost see the wheels clicking and turning, working hard to make sense of the world around her. Or as the princess had so aptly described, "It's like she lives in a reality of her creation, where everything has to fit inside her complex grid. Like everything must have a rational purpose to it or, at least, a plausible explanation."

Cecilia snuggled closer in his embrace. "After you ran off with Rowena—"

"I most certainly did not," he corrected. "She was someone new, who just happened to take my fancy."

"All right." She sighed in defeat. "After you paired off with Rowena, I realized you are a—"

"Master!" Something finally made sense. "That's why you kept inviting me to your Game."

"Yes," she confirmed with a smug smile that curved up her lips. "You're the only one I've invited to every edition." She sounded proud of herself as her fingertips strayed over his chest and arms. "Because you're the perfect master."

"Out of your head, too?" Grinning widely, he shifted position to lie on a side, leaning on his right elbow. "Now that you saw me in action, how did I perform?"

"Do you need to ask?" Cecilia cooed coyly.

"Humor me." Just then, his left shoulder heated up, and he resisted the urge to massage it.

"I wanted to be your slave." Given the veracity of her assertion, which mirrored what he and the princess had picked up during the Game, it was no surprise that her face was becoming bright red. "Actually, half the women there wanted to be your slave, and everything else be damned."

"Even if I bent the rules?" He could not help the shiver of excitement at the way he had used her Game to test his newly found Virt.

Which had turned out to be one of the best training he could have ever devised!

"Who noticed?" Cecilia joked, although the amusement did not reach her dark eyes.

"You did," he was quick to catch her inconsistency.

"I'm the Game Master," she declared, clearly relishing her own self-importance. "It's my job to know."

Which was not what galled her, at least judging from her expression.

"But I'm still wondering about the others." A baffled scowl crossed her harsh features. "They had no idea you and your slave could head talk, yet they couldn't take their eyes off either of you." There was a note of awed amazement that was hard to miss. "In all my games, I've never seen an act more followed, more watched than yours." She bit her lower lip. "All anybody could talk about was you and your slave, and what a lucky woman she was."

"Was that what you thought, too?" He scrutinized her face.

"I may have been as envious as everyone else," she

admitted reluctantly.

"When I first heard about your Game, I knew it was just a matter of finding the right slave." He chuckled, recalling the first red-carton invitation landing on his desk at Black Rose.

"Most people think the slave plays the least important role." She pursed her lips in disapproval. "What fools!" Cecilia spat. "The entire Game revolves around the relationship between master and slave," she explained unnecessarily. "In all those years, you're one of the very few who has understood this, yet you played master just once!"

Did I win some sort of prize for my insight?

From the way she beamed at him, he just might have.

"This proves I was right in choosing you as a model for that role," she concluded, complacent to the extreme.

"Glad to be of service, Madam." He followed his words with a mockery of a bow. "Now that I've found my perfect slave, you'll see me more often in the future." Since he did not want to sound pushy, he added, "If you'll still want me."

"Of course, I will!" Her eyes flashed as if to dispel any doubt. "Not because you're the leader," she expanded on hurriedly. "Because of your gorgeous looks and great skills." She giggled.

"You want me even more under the spotlight." He had no trouble perceiving where she was going with this.

"It'll be inevitable." She waved a dismissive hand in the air, before slanting her gaze to meet his. "The way you moved, the way you treated your slave, the way you simply were in that sex-filled chamber commanded everybody's attention, and that was before you became the leader. Just imagine how much more attention you'd get now." As usual, her logic was impeccable.

"I'm ready for it." He chortled, enjoying this new twist in the conversation.

"Also, for the women who'll be all over you?" She raised a quizzical eyebrow. "I mean, you're young, beautiful, powerful and un-pledged." Sitting up, she had ticked off each quality on her fingers. "Need I say more?"

No, you've said enough. Though he had to applaud her impudence. "Is this an offer?"

"What if it is?" Going all business-like, she threw back her shoulders. "Your most important duty to yourself and your family is to pass on your great power."

Why did she sound just like his mother all of a sudden?

Like James Templeton, too, come to think of it.

"I'm not pledged. Like you, I come from one of the oldest and noblest families of our land. We both oversee large and important districts. We're both in the High Council, albeit my position is just that of a permanent member." There she went with the counting again, her slender fingers flying all over the place.

"All right, we've got all the qualifications we need to get pledged." He straightened to mark the seriousness of their discussion. "Now, let's talk pros and cons."

"Only pros, darling." She patted him on the back in a way he found a bit condescending. "There are no cons."

He was not so sure. Still, he gave her the benefit of the doubt and did not interrupt her.

"The first is I know you don't love me, which is an advantage since pledges are only about having babies." Funny how she glided over how infatuated she still was with him despite her assurances to the contrary. "Which brings me to the second asset," she continued smoothly. "Can you imagine how exceptional an offspring of ours would be?"

"I thought you wanted David's child," he challenged.

"Yes, I did." She did not even blink. "Until he told me it wouldn't be . . ." Her brow furrowed in concentration. "Proper to pledge to me."

"Proper?" David could be such a pain in the ass when it came to class and social distinctions that Duncan had half a mind to call him right now and get it out of his system one way or another.

"Yeah, proper." She nodded before taking a deep breath. "Don't get me wrong. I like David . . . a lot." More than was good for her, if the slight trembling in her voice was any indication. "But he's made it abundantly clear he's not looking for any permanent relationship." From the bitterness lacing her words, it was clear this awareness still stung as much as when David had said it. "At least with me," she scoffed wearily.

So, she knew it, too.

She knew that David would go for Ylianor without thinking it over twice.

"Then, there's Rowena, the love of my life, but she's no pledge-material either." Her lips twisted in a wry snarl. "You, on the other hand, have Chris, who is the most important person in your life, but he's got as much chance in the pledge department where you're concerned as Rowena and me. Hence, the third advantage—I'd let you live your passions just as you'd let me live mine." She eyed him triumphantly, as though she had him right where she wanted him. "To summarize our mutual benefits, we know one another well enough to accept that we both have significant others, whom we truly love and won't ever give up." She licked her lips, probably savoring her victory. "We're also smart enough to know that those we love are in no position to tie the knot, not even that slave of yours."

"Her name is always Ylianor," he chastised her for the nth time. "Other than that, you've thought of everything . . ." He racked his brain for something to sink her enthusiasm.

And get him out of a sure fix!

"Except for the heat." How he came up with it, he was not sure, nor did it matter that it was a last resort. "Won't it change things between us?" True, he had no idea what he was talking about, which did not mean he would not pursue it.

The heat was a myth his mother brought up whenever she tried bullying him into a pledge. Too bad, she had never gone into any detail about what it was.

"Won't it alter the balance somehow?" Still, it made for a good argument.

"Did you find Rowena any different?" Folding her legs to her bosom, she wrapped her arms around her knees. "Yet, she's pledged, has the heat and a child."

Feeling trapped, he shifted uncomfortably, inching away from her and crossing his arms on his chest.

"I see you don't like what I'm suggesting," she blurted after a moment or two of silence on his part. "Is my logic faulty?"

"Your logic is faultless as usual, Ceci." He heaved, pondering how to let her down gently.

Because the very last thing on his mind was a pledge like he had tried to tell his mother countless times already.

"That's not the problem." Unfastening and lowering his arms, he cocked his head toward her. "It's pledges themselves. What if it's all a big lie like you guessed? What if pledges and phases aren't what they appear to be? What if they serve another purpose entirely?"

"Anything is possible if the pyramid has enslaved us all," she concurred. "For sure, it's been playing some kind of game with us." Her chin rested on her knees, even if her gaze never wavered from his face. "A game more elaborate than any that my mind could ever conjure up."

"I wouldn't be so sure." He smirked persuasively. "Tell me honestly that pledging to me wouldn't be just another of your games."

"I . . . I . . ." The purple blush covering her face was a sign that he had hit the bulls-eye. "I like you, Prince Caldwell." Affronted, she tilted up her head. "Maybe because I seem unable to deceive you. Or maybe because we think alike on many subjects." Her arms dropped to her side, and she lowered her legs. "Whatever it is, we'd make a great team together."

"Well . . ." He cleared his throat to come up with a good excuse. "I feel honored that you asked me, and it's a very tempting proposal." He pretended to consider it for a second. "But right now, I will have to decline." Since she had jolted to full attention, ready to shout her objections, he held up a hand to block her. "No, it has nothing to do with you or with your flawless analysis." *Just with my impossible lovers and me.*

That was it in a nutshell!

A pledge, any pledge, might come between him and the two people who continually occupied his every waking and sleeping moment. He could not, would not abide it, and all his rationalizations crumbled miserably.

"Naturally, I could never pledge to the angel, however much I'd want to. As for the princess . . ." He shrugged helplessly, unwilling to thread on such a tricky path.

If he adopted her, could he then turn around and pledge her, too? Would it be legal? What about Chris? Whom would he pledge? After his assurances to James, there was just one woman his angel might consider. It was the same one he would have chosen for himself, alas.

"It's complicated," was his most honest assessment.

"Do you love her?" Cecilia leaned so far forward that she was about to fall in his lap.

"Getting jealous already?" Duncan taunted.

"Simply curious." Her piqued tone did not fool him.

"To be honest, I don't know what I feel for anyone anymore," he confessed wearily. "What has happened with that damn pyramid has taken away the few certainties I used to have." It was best if he did not speak of Virtus, of what it had told the princess or of their conjectures.

"Bottom line is that you don't want to pledge?" She stared

at him, wide-eyed as if she could not believe him.

"Oh, I will." *One day perhaps.* "I'm just not ready for it now." He worked to make it convincing. "Not with every-thing else going on." He assuaged her disappointment with a winning smile. "Like learning to become a leader." *Like living in a Virtus-free world before I make any major decisions about my future or my feelings. I have enough doubts as it is.*

"So, it's no." She looked so crestfallen that his heart went out to her.

Clasping her hands, he squeezed them tight to lessen the impact of the blow. "For now," he murmured softly.

"It doesn't have to be now." She immediately clutched at the door left open on purpose. "Just promise that you'll think about it," she implored.

"All right, I will." But deep down, he knew he would not.

CHAPTER FORTY-THREE

"Welcome back, sir." At Black Rose's front entrance, Reginald bent his head. "We missed you."

The butler stepped aside to let him through, and Duncan crossed the threshold.

"I missed you, too." But mostly her, Black Rose, his native home.

It was the reason he had flown from the Hall, forcing Fuzeon to devour the miles separating the two places.

Not the only reason, though.

The other one waited for him upstairs—something he did not want to dwell on, lest his cock tightened more than it already had.

For the time being, he was content with breathing deep of the salty sea air, taking in the graceful hills and the rugged countryside. It was part of him, after all, along with those waves crashing on the cliffs, the green valleys and extensive forest surrounding it. Now that he had returned, he could not believe he had managed to be away from it for so long.

"The great news we heard only makes us gladder you're back," Reginald's voice cracked under the intense emotions veining it. "Please accept my sincerest congratulations on your appointment as our new leader." To hide some of his turmoil, he shifted to close the door. "It's an honor and a privilege to serve a High Council Leader." Again, he had to bow.

So low, his forehead almost touched his knees.

"Thank you, Reginald." Moved beyond words, Duncan gripped both his arms forcefully and helped him upright.

"I'm deeply touched." Another squeeze, then he let the older man go. "But nothing has changed. I'm still the same man who left only a short while ago." Not exactly the truth, but Reginald need not know all the details. "How have things been around here?" Of course, he already knew.

David had kept him informed about everything concerning Black Rose.

"We have the situation under control." Reginald's words confirmed David's. "Your mother and sister are fine if a bit shaken by the past events."

How to blame them?

The image of Lizzy chasing Sophia with a knife in hand popped to the fore.

"As you requested, much of our staff have left to help reconstruct the nearby villages." Reginald's calm tone was a clear indication he was oblivious of what had indeed happened.

Like everyone else, he had no memory of the incident. Something Duncan still had to thank his beautiful angel for, and that he would do as soon as he freed himself from his duties as a host.

"Work will take longer than expected, but they'll all be back in time for the Festival," Reginald concluded.

"Great. Tomorrow, we'll talk about all the arrangements we need to do." One less thing to worry about for now. "Any other news?"

"Your guests arrived today, as David anticipated." If Reginald's expression brightened, Duncan did not have the heart to tell him he knew this, too, having spotted both Black and Starlet in the stables. "Lady Caldwell was not happy about the accommodations." The butler pursed his lips, evidently unwilling to reveal the whole of it.

Duncan had no trouble figuring out that she was pissed off for real.

"Have they eaten?" Setting aside the image of his mother making one of her scenes, he focused on practical concerns.

"Hem . . ." Reginald hesitated. "Not really," he blurted eventually. "Your mother invited Lord Templeton to join her for dinner, but it seems he refused to go without Ylianor." His watery gaze widened as though he could not comprehend how anyone would ever dare deny Her Ladyship. "Your mother ate with Elizabeth while your guests stayed in their rooms."

Perfect! Just what I need! More problems!

As if he did not have enough already. Yet, somehow, all of Virtus's cruel violence seemed a trifle compared to his mother's stubbornness.

"Please, ask Anne to fix dinner for three." Taking a profound breath became a way to steady himself. "Just give me a couple of hours to rest." *Or rather, to crack my angel's ass, and I hope it's enough!* "Then, we'll eat in the small dining room." Summing it up, he looked at Reginald.

"Very well, sir." A limpid gaze met his own. "I'll tell her."

Heart thumping in his throat, he flew up the stairs, expectation twisting his stomach like a knot. Accelerating, he threw open the door of the room next to his, and there he was.

The most beautiful and cock-wrenching creature of all was in front of the fireplace. Just one glance and Duncan went so stone-hard he could not wait to reaffirm his claim on what belonged to him by definition.

"Angel!" Advancing, he latched onto the blue-gray eyes that had swung his way.

"Lover!" Jumping up, Chris was on him with two strides. "Missed me?"

"So much that I don't even know where to begin." Crushing the lithe body to him, he attacked the thin lips.

Tongue sweeping the wide-open cavity, he drank the familiar taste and smell down to his balls. His piece flared up worse than before.

Which was nothing compared to the marble-like consistency digging in his belly. Or to the incredible rush of excitement that melted all rationality as soon as the angel freed his shaft and jerked it forcefully.

"Let's start from here." Pulling away, Chris bent and swallowed him whole.

Balls included.

Literally.

"Shall we?" A quick breath, then Chris had him down to his throat again.

It was so goddamn good that he would spill it with just the first suck if he did not do something about it.

And fast!

Chris set such a delicious rhythm it was near impossible to play out things for any decent amount of time. Sliding down to the root with each consecutive head bob, he wrapped an amazingly adept tongue around the fat crown to brush it lavishly.

"We most certainly shall." Yanking the thick hair, he tossed back the blond head. "But not like this." Pushing him back, Duncan threw him on the bed. "'Cause I want my share of you." Straddling Chris, his beefy monster plunged into the fiery mouth it had just vacated. So fiercely, it practically reached the ass.

Nailed to the mattress, Chris did not have any choice except to suffocate.

Which did not move Duncan to pity. Quite the contrary, it increased his drive and his determination to reach what it obviously could not. The flames scorching the engorged stem also hastened the juice to the exit.

He would have come right there and then, had he not been taking out Chris's cock and gulping it down to his stomach.

No, further down, given the considerable impact from the upward hip swing.

Nothing he had trouble handling. Too long, he had been fucking the angel not to have learned how to tame that unruly piece. Tricks like curling his tongue around the fathead and blocking its more dangerous lurches while squeezing it with the cheeks' pressure. Allowing it to slide to his throat, whetted its appetite. It also catered to its illusion that it could actually reach beyond the natural limits of a mouth's constricted space.

That Chris loved it was kind of obvious. Not just because he had stiffened to the point every lap risked to sever his beast from the crotch. Visibly pulsating, it was doubtful it would resist the urge to discharge for much longer.

He was not faring any better. Not while so deeply embedded in the angel's velvety hotness that sped up everything. In and out, his stick hammered Chris's mouth like it was his ass, making him sputter despite his tight control over every intake.

Not always successful, it took more to master it when it had been so long apart from his very reason for living. Since he could not take it anymore, it was time to end it for both of them.

With one well-adjusted blow, he smothered Chris's rod, and it exploded in his mouth. Same thing he was doing in his angel's cavity, shooting unstoppable jets of sperm down to his stomach.

With a cock still as hard as though he had not come at all, Duncan scrambled to his feet.

"Now, for the serious fun." Shedding both their pants, he spread Chris's legs wide. "'Cause I've missed this ass way too much for my taste." The tight ring seemed to agree, enlarging as it did under the pressure of several fingers.

"I would have, too, if all I had to fuck was Cecilia Hurst." Twisting his hips, Chris impaled the fingers to the hilt.

Duncan added one more to widen it some more. "How the

fuck do you know that?"

True, his angel always did have a phenomenal intuition. But this bordered the incredible!

"Easy." A smug smile curving his lips, Chris rotated to ease Duncan's task. "With all the chaos that happened, the Hall must have been pretty empty." From his slight wince, Duncan understood he was prey to a world of pain still as raw and as fiery as when he had erased it. "Given your aristocratic taste and how busy you must've been, I'm sure you didn't waste any time looking for suitable bedmates. Just went for the most convenient one."

"I'm impressed." Deeming the back ring ready, he slammed his very hungry equipment in the yielding butt.

Well, not so yielding, if truth be told.

"But I'm guessing you didn't have such a great time, either." The tight fit was something of a novelty. "Couldn't find anybody good enough to stuff this voracious ass of yours while I was away?"

"Thought you'd like it nice and tight for a change," Chris joked, smashing down to drill the whole length to his guts.

Only natural for his breath to falter, given how suddenly his balls slapped the pliant buttocks. Or perhaps, what got him was how quickly the scalding sheath enveloped him to the root.

"Liar." Adjusting his position, he tried overcoming the cramped boundary. "None of those cute servants at Blue Oasis had what it took." Impossible as it was, he banged more inches in that capacious rear, regardless of the friction standing in his way. "Nor were any from all the work teams going in and out of that place."

The fleshy walls squeezed him like crazy. So ferociously, he would soon have to stop talking if he wanted to last longer than he had with the blowjob.

"While I was working my ass off, someone had way too

much fun," he concluded his fake scold in a teasing tone.

"While someone else should've kept her trap shut," Chris snorted in mock annoyance. "Especially since she took shameless advantage of them, as well." Following the rapid beat, he screwed the balls along with the rest.

If not quite, it certainly felt so to his enormous shaft, ramming at full speed.

Which flung him to a new edge.

"Yeah, someone should have." It came out before he even realized it had. "But you can relax," he was quick to add, to silence the twitch of his guilty conscience. "She didn't reveal any damaging secrets." *Why the fuck did I have to bring her up, instead of keeping my big mouth shut?*

"That's comforting." Something in Chris's tone alerted Duncan that he had picked up how awfully he had treated his princess and how badly he regretted it.

Which was so impossible, he refused to believe it.

"At least, she didn't blurt out how compliant and eager to please me all those cute boys were." At Chris's licking his lips, he wondered whether it was from his latest shove or from remembering how serviceable everyone had been. "Including at the tip of my knife."

This was a provocation if he ever heard one. Oddly, though, his only reaction was to miss her worse than before. She and that longing she had to continue where his angel had left off, even if she did not dare confess it.

Not even to herself.

"Must be the reason your ass is such a poor lay today." If Chris wanted to play, he was ready for him.

"I think all that screwing with Cecilia has made you forget what a good lay is." Piqued, his phase mate arched so far back that his behind became ten times its size, and Duncan had no problems perforating his guts. "I almost miss the times you could think of nothing besides blowing your princess's magnificent ass to bits." Now, why did he sound angry all of a sudden? "At least, you had better taste then."

If the angel wanted to make him mad, he was succeeding brilliantly.

He needed a change of position to suppress all thoughts about her since they had no place in his furious pounding of this fabulous backside.

"My only taste now is to crack you open like you deserve." Unscrewing from the narrow confinement, he flipped the angel on his stomach. "Since you've obviously forgotten what it feels like."

Impaling the guts from above took no effort at all. Just a forceful thrust and he sank to the hilt. Ravaging the restricted channel with consecutive blows, he drove his rod so deep he wondered whether he would ever retrieve it.

Chris was clenching it so hard that it was doubtful he would get it back in one piece.

Not that it mattered either way.

The scorching waves coiling from the tip of his erection were making him lose all perspective. Rough and ruthless pumping, it would be impossible to keep up his frenzied rhythm for much longer. Not since everything burned so hot that bursting was his only option to bring down the temperature.

Chris spilling his guts on the bed was the last straw.

Reclining on the prone body, he banged twice and flooded the ass convulsing on his cock.

For round three, he pulled the slender frame to his feet and flattened it to the nearest wall. Legs far apart, back bent, butt flung out, he made the most scrumptious sight of all.

Since his demanding shaft had never gone limp, he penetrated way beyond the guts with the first shove alone.

Chris moaning and flinging back his buttocks was all the indication needed to know he was loving it. Drooling over it, as a matter of fact, given how swollen his unparalleled beast had become. Not to mention his backside, now as wide and easy to stuff as it had been during their phase.

"I'm finally starting to recognize your ass." Blowing it mercilessly, Duncan widened it to the maximum. "You just needed some practice." Weighing on his back, he pinned the slimmer body to the wall.

"You know what they say." Barely holding on, the angel matched his rhythm without missing a beat. "Practice makes perfect."

"Then, you'll have the *perfect* Festival." He nodded. "With plenty of cocks."

"They'll never beat yours, lover." There was a definite note of regret in Chris's voice.

"Tell that to the two monsters that made mincemeat of your ass when they fucked you together during the Game." Just remembering that particular incident had him stiffening in anticipation of the most tremendous come.

"I will." Panting, Chris signaled he was about to reach the finishing line. "First chance I get." His hand went to grab his erection.

"Oh, no, you don't." Intercepting it, he wrapped his palm around the humongous gland. "This belongs to me." He jerked it at the pace the angel loved best. "You're not allowed to use it until I say so."

"Fuck, no!" The groan escaping the thin lips sent a jolt of pleasure coursing down his spine. "I can't—"

"You better 'cause I'm nowhere done with you." That is if he managed to hold it together.

Something he had doubts about, for his senses were about to take flight whether he let them or not.

To distract himself from climaxing too soon, he flopped out of the snug hole and sprawled his phase mate on the table. Back to the wooden surface, Duncan lifted his legs until the puckered opening gleamed in front of his large crown.

Claiming it and increasing the butt drill was one and the same.

Now that his angel was at his complete mercy, he could concentrate on ramming that sweet behind until it would explode from the feat of containing something too big for it.

Not his problem, of course.

Then again, his slutty lover would gladly erupt just to have the satisfaction of having gobbled up the biggest stick of all.

Pressing down to sweep the mouth with decisive tongue strokes pushed everything overboard. As he took his unhurried time in brushing the wide-open cavity, he felt Chris surrendering body, mind and spirit.

His chest rubbing on the erection stuck between them accelerated things to the explosive point he had tried to delay.

Which literally blew his mind.

His cock, too, spilling every last drop inside Chris's overly stretched rear.

CHAPTER FORTY-FOUR

"Let me look at you." Barely sated, Duncan straightened to check over Chris.

The hard shaft still embedded up the rear hole kind of dampened his perceptions, though not enough to miss the pronounced rib cage and the narrow hips. Not to mention, a penis that was now more humongous than ever, given the exceeding flatness of the stomach.

"You've lost weight." It tightened his heart to know he was the cause of it.

"Not much." Of course, the angel downplayed it on purpose. "I still have my great looks and huge cock." Clamping the rigid stem, he flicked it vigorously. "And a quite aching butt." He wriggled it in impatience, stiffening both their equipment to their previous solid consistency.

"I know a way to cure that itch." His amused chortle became lost in his latest shove to what had once been tiny.

There it went again! The madness of the senses that always devoured his spirit whenever he was with his adored angel. It was just uncanny and defied any logical explanation. The more he had of Chris, the more he wanted.

Astounding in a way, considering they had been fucking together for almost ten years. Very right on another, since no one was ever quite like his angel, whose bright flame eclipsed all the lights and sounds that were messing with his awareness.

Which was the best side effect he could ask for of late.

He did not fight it anymore. What was the use when

everything in him screamed for a new release? For a fulfillment that he could find in Christopher Templeton alone?

Feet still planted on the ground, cock stuck to the hilt in the
most delightful place of all, he hammered the yielding ass like
there would be no tomorrow. Tonight, he just could not get
enough, which justified his extra blows aiming at splitting
open his lover.

Not that he ever ran the risk.

The backside he was trying to crack was simply too experienced to crumble under that sort of pressure. Instead, it accelerated the throwbacks, stepping up the rhythm for both of
them until things spun out of any sequence.

Grabbing Chris's twitching monster, he jerked it at the
same tempo pushing his own beast overboard. In and out, he
moved without slowing down the beat ravaging that splendid behind.

Which spelled the end of this new round.

With a loud gasp, Chris's load sprayed all over his belly.
Just to raise the level of excitement, he pulled out and spurted
thick ropes of creamy juice over the same pools already clot-
ting on the flat belly.

"By the gods, I fucking missed you!" Too good to stand, he
wrapped his arms around the angular frame, relishing the
sperm that clung to both their skins. "Though I do wish you
weren't so thin—"

"I've been eating like a horse lately," Chris was quick to
point out. "Just to regain all that I've lost."

"I'm sorry, Angel." Unable to resist the tide of emotions
strangling him, he crushed him under his more massive
weight and a ferocious kiss. "I should've never left you—"

"Oh, I always felt you very close, lover." Chris snuggled
against his chest. "Thanks to your nightly visits, the energy
touching and all."

"That energy business was never close enough for my

taste," He had to admit wryly. "It only increased my longing to have you in the flesh." The sake of truth, along with his aching heart, required him to be completely honest. "'Cause I should've never asked you—"

"Hush, lover." Two slender fingers pressed on his lips. "You are the leader now." There was such a note of respect and pride that Duncan had to catch his breath. "You're entitled to ask anyone whatever is necessary to keep our world safe."

"Not if it means losing you." His heart so heavy, he squashed him in a smothering embrace. "Never if it means sacrificing you." Pulling slightly back, he gazed in the arresting blue-gray depths. "I love you too damn much, Christopher Templeton, to make it without you. These past months at the Hall, I realized that you are the reason I live and breathe every day. That without you, my life has no meaning. Even if I am the leader now, it means nothing if you're not there to share it alongside me."

"Is that why you had to thank me so publicly?" The angel beamed one of his most enchanting smiles.

"Yeah, I had to shout it out." He raked a hand through the thick blond hair. "'Cause I could've never done it without you." Of this, he had no doubt. "If you hadn't healed everyone and erased their memories, things today would be far worse. Which is why I'm most grateful and had to say so to the High Council." His mind replayed part of his earnest declaration. "Now, everyone thinks I was thanking you—"

"While, in fact, you were saying how much you love me," Chris beat him to the chase.

"Exactly." He grinned at this amazing intuition of his lover. "I was too anguished to keep silent about it." The unfathomable pain of having almost lost what he most loved in the world had not abated yet, ready to strike at him had he only allowed it. "Had to tell it also to your father's face." He chuckled, remembering James's expression. "He was so worried about you that it was heartbreaking. I first set his fears to rest, then blurted out everything I feel about you." Just having the precious body within his arms lessened the impact of those hurtful memories.

"Sounds to me like a breach in that etiquette he loves so much." Chris chortled amused, probably imagining James Templeton's reactions.

"Worse than that." He had to set things into perspective. "He must've thought me mad. There we were, with all chaos broken loose, and all I could think about was you, all I could talk about was how much I love you."

"Is that why you didn't speak a word about her during that same speech?" The stillness of the lithe body and the note of concern were so unusual that he immediately pricked up his ears. "Even if she's the reason I'm alive and well now?"

"If I didn't, it's only because there was no time . . ." Since Chris had not been there, he left it vague on purpose. "To explain her connection to me." Which was still unclear as far as he was concerned. "Or her role—"

"Don't give me that!" Indignant blue-gray eyes nailed him to his responsibilities. "Don't tell me you couldn't come up with a plausible connection to you and to the events that happened—"

"Do we have to talk about this right now?" Pulling away, he sat on the couch, irritated with the turn of the conversation.

No, irritated with himself, mostly.

"Yes, we do." Jumping down from the table, Chris sank on the plush cushion next to him. "Since she's become the ghost of herself." The strain in his voice revealed how much it crushed him to confess as much. "I think it's your fault—"

"What do you mean, the *ghost of herself?*" Silencing his conscience's loud rebuke, he preferred to address one problem at a time.

"I mean, wait 'till you see her." From his aggressive tone, it was kind of obvious that something was eating him when it came to Ylianor. "'Cause if you think I'm thin, it's nothing if compared to her." He took a deep breath. "I only noticed it when we were on the road together and . . ." *It shocked me!*

Since he did not utter it, Duncan read it from the troubled expression crossing the beautiful face.

"Didn't you see her after you recovered?" His question aimed at assessing the situation.

"No, I didn't." Impossible to miss the regretful note in Chris's grave tone. "Not out of any ungratefulness," he added with a softer note.

"You mean, you didn't even bother to thank her for what she must've done for you?" Even if he had not been present, he could safely guess that she would have followed his request regardless of the costs involved.

No, make that his order to look after the angel even if it killed her.

"It's not like you think," Chris rebuffed on the defensive. "I know you asked her to take care of me, and she did. Servants told me she spent every day and every night by my bedside while I was unconscious." His slight pause seemed like a way to get his facts in order. "To the point that she practically didn't eat or sleep for weeks." He hung his head as though the sadness for her ordeal weighed him down. "But I didn't want her to get any wise ideas about what had happened," his voice hardened. "I didn't want her to think that it had changed things between us."

Which for the record, they had.

Or why else would he feel angry at the way he had treated her?

"I avoided her, even if servants told me she enquired after me every day." The thin lips twisted in a snarl. "I wanted to see if she could take it."

"And could she?" Kind of obvious, this had been a way to test her.

"Aye, she definitely could." Which still disconcerted his angel, given the begrudged admiration dripping from his words. "'Cause she never once bothered me. Never forced my hand with those silly excuses women often use to get their way." Evidently, he could not get over it. "She kept away, went out to help with the reconstruction effort, working every day alongside one team or another." There was a slight hesitation before he continued, "But she got tired," his voice was so low. It was more of a whisper. "Very tired."

The well of sorrow hitting Duncan clenched his stomach in a fierce knot.

"When we set off for Black Rose, I couldn't believe my eyes." Pulling himself together, the angel stared at an invisible point in midair. "But I was so impatient to see you that I didn't care. I pushed her so hard that she'd collapse every night before she got the chance to eat dinner," he huffed. "I'm still wondering how she managed to keep going with the little food she ate." He shook his head as though to clear it from some unwanted memory. "But when I offered to help her, to heal some of her fatigue, Her Ladyship refused and closed me out," he scoffed. "Like I wasn't good enough for the likes of her or something."

Small wonder, the healer in Chris would be furious. That constant pushing him away was still driving him so crazy he could not hide it.

"The worst part was waking up at night 'cause she screamed, terrified." Calming down, he edged closer as though he did not want Duncan to miss his next words.

"Terrified of what?" He could not help wondering.

"Who knows?" Chris growled. "And who cares? Her Stubbornness refused to talk about it." He shrugged as if to stress that it was not his problem.

Which did not fool Duncan one bit, for he read the worry beneath the pretense.

"I'm sure that didn't stop you from trying to guess anyway." He showered him with a most winning smile to convince him to spill his guts.

"Well . . ." Mollified, Chris fell for it. "I think she was having some kind of nightmare." His lips pursed. "And that blasted pyramid had something to do with it." His gaze turned accusatory. "But you would've known all about this if you'd have bothered to check on her —"

"All right, all right." He held up a hand to block the protests. "If you must know, I kind of kept away from our channel." The excuse sounded lame even to his own ears.

"Meaning, you kept it shut?" A flash of understanding lit the intriguing eyes.

"Meaning, I had no time for it," he muttered uneasily.

"Why do I sense that there's more to this than what you're telling?" Clearly not fooled, Chris raised the stakes.

Which left him no choice except to come clean, regardless of all his qualms.

"I had to close the damn channel!" Duncan lashed out impatiently. "Keeping it open was proving to be too difficult." *Foo distracting, mostly.* "She was just one more complication I had no time for." *No wish for, either.* "It's been a relief to be free again, without her constant presence in my head and —"

"Bullshit!" Chris retorted in annoyance. "As if you could ever be free of her!" He bent to murmur in his ear, "You fucking missed her." His raspy breath tickled. "Not just in your head." Grabbing Duncan's not-so-limp piece, he squeezed it. "In your bed, mostly." Stroking it made it as stiff as it had been just minutes before. "And this last attempt at freedom is useless." Dipping, he sucked the entire extended length to the root before returning his gaze squarely on Duncan's face. "'Cause she's in your blood, whether you like it or not." The jerking on his cock became more decisive. "She's a part of you, and you've known it from the start, though I couldn't understand it at first."

If he kept up the steady rhythm, Duncan would soon have to forego any form of conversation.

"That's why she's going to get a share of your father's inheritance, isn't she?" Chris added. "Even if it means challenging mommy dearest."

"How do you know I agreed to grant my father's adoption clause?" Stunned, he snapped his attention back on the conversation. "I only made up my mind a few days ago."

"Lover, I think I know you enough to make an educated guess about what goes on in that fertile mind of yours," the angel sniggered, cupping his face with both palms. "Two things strike me most about you lately. The first is that your feelings about her are changing, and you owe it all to Cecilia's Game." His breath played on Duncan's face. "That made you accept the fact she belongs to you like you had perceived from the first moment you met her. That she is yours, in a way no other person will ever be." He let go of his face. "Not even me."

It was kind of evident such awareness still stung him like crazy.

"Only natural, you couldn't refuse your father's plea." With an effort, he regained a measure of restraint on himself. "'Cause you feel exactly the same way he did about her."

Impressed, Duncan shifted to a side, unwilling to acknowledge that he was right. "What's the second reason, according to Lord I-Know-It-All?"

"A convenient one, I'm sure," Chris smirked in smug satisfaction.

This was sheer unbelievable!

The astonishing creature had no trouble determining that he was right, no matter the blatant lack of confirmation.

"Now that you're leader, you'll need as much support in the High Council as you can get." The way he was tackling the issue, Duncan could tell he had it all figured out. "Since your father's seat is still vacant, what better way to fill it than with a new Caldwell?"

Right again, so I thank the gods you can't guess at my third reason. "My dear angel, you and this formidable insight of yours never cease to amaze me." As a reward, he kissed him hard and fierce, going for the bruised lips, the tongue sweeps and all the other trimmings. "But she's not the only one I'm considering as a fitting member of the council."

"You mean . . ." It took a mere second for his angel to connect the dots. "My father would be willing to leave his council seat to me?"

"*Willing* might not be the exact definition of his state of mind." He beamed, remembering James's reservations. "Let's say he's thinking of retiring, and I've already informed him I'll accept only you as his replacement. Since I'm the leader, I have the final say on what member of the Templeton family gets that council seat." Playfully pinning Chris to the couch, he rubbed the swollen stick on his crotch, not surprised to find that equipment as engorged as his. "But we can talk about it later."

"Couldn't agree more, lover." Begging for another round, the angel rotated his hips and provoked the intoxicating sex he was such a master in delivering. "Considering the eternity we spent apart—"

"Actually, it was just a couple of months." He laughed, relieved that it had not been longer.

"An eternity, like I said." Undeterred, Chris arched up and spread his legs until his asshole nudged the tip of his erection. "We've got to make up for all the lost time."

"Yeah." Shoving, he impaled the whole of his thickness deep inside the fiery sheath, waiting for the stuffing in avid trepidation.

The angel adjusted his position to facilitate the slide to his guts.

"If it means locking you up here." It was so good to have the scorching fleshy walls wrapping him on all sides again that he feared he would lose it before he had the chance to do any serious ramming. "Which, considering how my mother has been treating you, wouldn't be such a bad idea."

"Oh, don't be so hard on her." Apparently afraid of the same thing, Chris did not rush to escalate the beat. "She hasn't been doing anything worse than usual."

Of course, this was just a mouthwatering preliminary, designed to spin things out of any boundaries.

Picking up the tempo, he cracked that intoxicating ass with his first blows alone.

"You know how she is." Nothing Chris had trouble handling. "How she doesn't want to have anything to do with Ylianor." Simply widened the backside channel to fit more of his pounding stiffness. "That's why she invited only me to dinner."

He plunged to the hilt. His balls almost following, carried as they were by his brutal impacts.

"But it didn't feel right somehow." The note of tenderness was too pungent to miss.

"Getting a soft spot for the princess, eh?" He whistled appreciatively, slowing down to peer in the blue-gray eyes. "I'd have never guessed, Angel."

Actually, he had. Only, he did not want Chris to know that he was one step ahead. The future of their relationship hinged on a fragile balance that Duncan himself had already placed in jeopardy. No need to pull back now, not when his gut instinct screamed that the sole way forward for the three of them was together. Which meant that he would have to beg, grovel if necessary, for his princess's forgiveness, if it was the last thing he did.

"I'm not!" An adorable red blush spread all over the handsome face. "Or maybe, I am." He shook his head as though he could not make up his mind. "After everything she has done for me, I can't treat her like a mere servant, like your mother pretends."

"Particularly since she did a splendid job of taking care of you." A more forceful banging of the fabulous ass drove him wild. "You've recovered all your energy."

"I've also gained some more." A conceited snarl curved the thin lips. "Can't you tell?" To stress his point, he raised his hips to respond to the tempo's upbeat.

"Not until I've split you in two." Hoarse breath coming short, he knew he could not sustain the pumping for much longer.

The burning on the tip of the fat crown confirmed he would soon lose it.

"Hurry, lover." Circling his neck, Chris brought him down. "'Cause I'm about to unload it all." The attack on his lips was the beginning of the end.

Friction at an all-time high, he slammed into the buttery rear, stretching it to the limit. What about his tongue suffocating Chris from the repeated lurches to his throat and beyond?

Possession his goal, he wanted to brand the angel as his own. Not just for the present. For all the future that they would spend together at the Hall.

Being his phase mate, Chris would be at the first step of the ladder, just one below him.

Hence, the need to prove his mastery over the remarkable creature that no one would ever be able to control.

Except for him.

The mere thought of it would have made him come, had Chris not beaten him to it, discharging all over his belly.

No more reason to delay the inevitable, he reclined and convulsed, banging his semen so far up it choked his angel.

CHAPTER FORTY-FIVE

"Now, I'm hungry for food." With satisfaction gleaming in the blue-gray eyes, Chris rolled aside. "Can we have something to eat, or has your mother closed the kitchen?"

"I believe we can arrange something." Reaching over, Duncan could not believe how good it felt to be reunited with the man whose love and fire were such an integral part of him.

"I told Reginald to set the table downstairs." Affectionately, he raked his fingers through the thick blond hair.

"Well, what are we waiting for?" Jumping out of bed, Chris grabbed his pants and pulled on the first leg. "Let's go."

"Are you sure you're up to it?" Duncan teased. "I wouldn't want embarrassing scenes downstairs."

"As if you'd mind some action at the dinner table." The angel's grin was a sight for sore eyes, considering how impossibly gorgeous and boyish it made him look.

"Hey, you should show more respect to your leader." Half-dressed himself, he made it sound like he was offended for real. "I'm an important man now."

"Pardon me, Leader, I almost forgot." The angel bowed in mock deference. "Good thing, High Council Leaders are my fucking specialty," he taunted further. "'Cause they can't get enough of my ass." A broad beam split his handsome face. "You must be . . ." He creased his forehead in make-believe concentration. "Hem . . . the third, perhaps?" The arresting gaze sparked in mischief. "No, wait. You must be number four or—"

"Oh, shut up!" Laughing hard, he threw a pillow at him.

"Just kidding, lover." Ducking, Chris avoided the hit. "You've kept me so busy with your welcome that I didn't get the chance to ask you." Now earnest, the blue-gray gaze fixed him in open admiration and pride. "But you must tell me all about it." Fully clothed, he went to the door. "Shall we?"

"Absolutely." He moved forward.

But he had to stop in his tracks, for a sense of sadness and despair sliced his stomach in two.

Knowing where it came from, did not lessen the impact or the pain.

"Let's call the princess." The strangled voice did not sound like him at all.

The conscience he had managed to ignore during the awesome sex with the angel began tormenting him again. He could just hope that his decision about the will would make up for the anguish he had inflicted.

Since it was neither the time nor the place to discuss this, he forced himself to finish on a lighter tone, "She might be hungry, too."

"I wouldn't count on it." There was a resigned tone in his lover's contention that he did not like at all. "As I told you, she ate practically nothing during the entire trip."

"Well, it won't hurt to try." Stifling his remorse was not easy. "If she hasn't gone to sleep already."

"She doesn't know you're back, eh?" Spinning around, Chris confronted him, studying his face intently.

"I didn't tell her," he was quick to explain. "I wanted to be alone with you first."

"I'm touched, lover." Chris's fondling of his crotch proved how grateful he was until the exaggerated response convinced him to drop his too-eager paw and take a step out in the hallway. "All right, I'll check if she's here." Turning the handle, he unlocked the door and exited.

A few steps to the right, the push of another door left ajar and a cursory glance were enough to determine that she was not.

"Seems like this shutting off works both ways." The angel chuckled as he gestured inside Ylianor's empty room. "If you want her, open communications."

Princess, where are you? Heading for the stairs, he began descending. *I'm back, and I'm hungry. Will you join us in the dining room?*

A cold desolate silence was his reply. Something he was not ready for, which tightened his stomach into a throbbing pulp.

When he thought he could not take it anymore, her soft voice echoed in his head, *I'll be right there.*

He had no time to recover.

Standing tall and respectful at the bottom of the stairs, Reginald was waiting for him. "Missus Peacock fixed you dinner, sir." Moving aside, the butler made way for him and Chris. "Shall I bring it over?"

"Yes, thank you." He inclined his head.

"If you'll excuse me, I'll be right back." Edging toward the kitchen, Reginald started his retreat.

"Just one more thing." He halted his rush. "Do you know where Ylianor is?"

"I believe I saw her in the stables." The butler's assured tone sanctioned no errors.

"Figures," Chris snickered as soon as Reginald was out of the way. "She must have known you were back all along."

Following Duncan, he entered the dining room. "Either because she saw Fuzeon." He sat down at the table. "Or because your communications weren't as broken down as you thought."

"Either way, she also knew precisely what I wanted to do first." Which perhaps, was not such a good thing in hindsight.

As if it takes any Virt to guess your priority, she scoffed in his head.

A soft knock and she walked inside.

"Princess . . ." Words utterly failed him. His blood turned cold. All he could do was perch there and stare wide-eyed at Ylianor.

No, not Ylianor.

What had remained of her!

She had lost so much weight that she resembled the ghost of herself like Chris had observed. Her attractive face was ashen. Her green eyes had grown hauntingly huge, double their original size. Her frame so skinny, he could practically see through her.

Sprinting up, he hugged her slowly, fearful of breaking her frail body. Pulling her close, he felt her bones digging into him.

All of them!

Yet, the worst of it was spotting that bottomless well of distress, more similar to the desolate void he had sensed in Virtus, and realizing that she was drowning in it.

"Princess." He caressed her face lovingly. "What's wrong?"

"Nothing." Abrupt and short, she tensed in his arms as though she would rather fight than tell him anything.

"Angel." Peering over his shoulder, he caught the blue-gray gaze. "You didn't tell me she looks like a corpse." He drew back to look her over again.

"I told you she hardly ate anything while we were on the road," Chris retorted.

"It's nothing, really." Disentangling from him, she took a seat. "Blue Oasis's air didn't agree with me." Obstinately proud, she raised her chin, defying him to call her bluff. "I may have overworked myself in the reconstruction effort. That's all." By the way her face hardened, he knew she would not tolerate further inquiries on a subject she considered closed. "How was your trip?"

"I almost exhausted poor Fuzeon in my rush to hurry back." Wondering how he could make her loosen up, he reached her at the table.

"I know," she confirmed. "Fuzeon is none too happy with how you treated him."

Another knock and a delegation came inside the room. The cook, butler and housekeeper carried trays of food. Reginald and Missus Merryweather served it to him and Chris. But when it came to Ylianor, they stopped, embarrassed.

Not Anne Peacock.

Completely unperturbed and without the slightest hesitation, she piled high Ylianor's plate with a selection of everything that was in the trays. "My prince, look how thin my poor lamb is." Unaffected by the overabundance, she kept dishing out more food. "I hold you personally responsible for it." As if she had not given enough, she placed a few more morsels on the already tall heap. "I hope you're going to look after her now that you're back."

"Anne!" Reginald intervened, shocked. "You can't talk to our leader like that."

"No, Reginald, she's right." He had to admit he had failed Ylianor in every way possible. "I should've taken better care of her."

"Yes, sir." Face set in a mulish pose, the cook nodded emphatically. "You should've."

"Anne, stop it." Flummoxed, Alicia Merryweather could barely contain her disapproval. "The prince is probably tired and in no mood to listen to your complaints." She moved as if she wanted to drive the woman out of the room. "You can't talk to the High Council Leader in that way."

"Leader, my hoofs!" Unruffled, Anne brushed off Alicia, returning to his side. "He'll always be little Duncan to me, running around Black Rose, making one mischief after another and chasing my little lamb until she was too tired to resist him."

"Anne!" The butler's jarred tone rose higher, "Please, behave yourself!"

"It's quite all right, Reginald." His hearty laughter filled the room.

"She's perfectly right, on both counts." He intercepted the cook's gaze. "Now, it'll be up to us to make your little lamb eats enough. You know how stubborn she can be."

"Yes, sir, and not only with food," Anne agreed wholeheartedly.

"Anne!" Ylianor became purple. "Please."

While Chris burst out laughing.

"It's the truth, pet." Unconcerned, the woman gripped the princess's shoulder. "Why hide it?" She swung back to him. "You know, sir, she's just like her mother. Never followed sound advice, not even if it could've saved her." A twinge of regret veiled her round eyes. "Too impulsive for her own good."

"You knew her mother well?" Of course, she did. It was one of the things he had learned from David during the briefing that had filled his memory's inconsistencies. "Didn't you?"

"Very well, indeed, Prince." Anne smiled so sweetly. For sure, their bond had been very tight, like the one between phase mates. "That's why I brought her to Black Rose for the first time." She furrowed her brow as though trying to put her facts in order. "When you were born, we needed extra staff due to the celebration and all, so I told Mary Jane to come lend a hand. She had no experience, but I thought it wouldn't matter. We both thought it would just be temporary." She shrugged imperceptibly. "Well, never were we more wrong, and she ended up staying here for the rest of her life. That's why I feel responsible for everything that happened to her, including her daughter."

"You took care of her after Mary Jane died." Very interested, he leaned forward on the table. "Right?"

"No, sir." Anne shook her head forcefully. "Your father, the gods bless him, never abandoned this child. When he died, my family and I were happy to take over and care for my pet." Again, she squeezed Ylianor's shoulder. "Because I love her, and I owe it to her mother."

"I'm glad she has at least a true friend at Black Rose." He reclined on his chair. "You know, Anne, things are about to change for your pet." Shifting his focus, he made it a point to fix Reginald and Alicia in turn. "So, she'll need all the friends she has."

The cook's chubby face lit up in understanding. "You mean, to guard her against your mother's—"

"Prince, please excuse Anne." Exasperated, Missus Merryweather cut in angrily. "This is none of our business and—"

"It will be." Dry and terse, he wanted to dispel any doubts and protect the princess as much as possible. "To all effects and purposes, Ylianor is a member of the Caldwell family." His pause was a strategic one. "I expect you, as well as my mother, to treat her accordingly. Is that clear?"

"Of course, sir." Beaming proudly, Anne hugged Ylianor, who disappeared inside the plump figure unfolding her. "That's wonderful, pet. I'm so glad for you!"

The woman's genuine affection and loyalty were not in question.

Alicia Merryweather's were.

Just watching her, he was reminded of David's suspicions, which still rang as true now as when he had first uttered them. Alicia would have carried out Sophia Caldwell's plan to harm Ylianor, which in turn had coerced him and the angel into bringing her along on their fateful trip to the Hall.

"Missus Merryweather." He caught her unblinking stare and held it. "Have I made myself clear?"

That Alicia Merryweather was appalled seemed sort of a given. Being a stickler for class distinctions, the mere thought of a servant becoming a noble was untenable, if not downright preposterous. Her horror-stricken expression spoke volumes and confirmed his worst fears. "Well, Missus Merryweather?" He insisted mercilessly.

"Hem . . ." She swallowed hard. "Yes, Prince, you have."

"All right." Of course, Duncan had no illusions about her acquiescence.

Alicia Merryweather would never accept the princess's new status.

He only hoped he had put some sense into her. "You can go." His gaze broadened to include Reginald and Anne. "All of you."

After an exaggerated bow, the trio left the room, taking away the empty trays.

"It's not going to be easy," Chris observed once they were by themselves. "Since the problem isn't only your mother."

"I concur." How could he not? "But I have to start somewhere. I can hardly wait to tell Mother of the will. That'll be a fight—"

"I don't want it," Ylianor cut in coldly.

"What?" Uncertain he had heard correctly, his attention was on her.

"I said, *I don't want it!*" Holding up her chin in defiance, she blazed with rage. "You can keep your inheritance, your name and your insufferable family. I don't want anything from you or the Caldwell, not even their detestable name."

Dumbfounded, he could not believe his ears. "Now, we're not good enough for you?" He regarded her coldly, his icy tone slicing the dense atmosphere.

"No, you're not," she spat vehemently. "Seeing how you treat me."

"How I treat you?" The fact she was right did not authorize

her to throw his generosity back at him. "I know I've been absent—"

"Ha! That's an understatement!" Ylianor spat furiously. "You and your damn ambivalence, letting me in just to shove me out the moment I'm not convenient anymore. You consider me a worthless nothing that you can take or leave whenever you feel like it!" She screamed, "I don't want to be your sister, your slave or anything else in your miserable life! I hate you, your name, your family, your intolerable lover and anything even remotely connected to you!"

Furious, she got to her feet and ran from the room, leaving him stunned and alone with Chris.

If you want to read more about Cecilia Hurst's Game of
Masters and Slaves,
Don't miss

Not in the Game
Deleted Scenes from The Game
Virtus Saga Plus

When Prince Duncan Caldwell has to enter Cecilia Hurst's
Game of Masters and Slaves, he already knows he'll have to
play Master if he intends to retrieve the pyramid Cecilia stole
from the sacred Nephis Valley. And his choice for a slave can
only be Ylianor Meyer, however fiercely Lord Christopher
Templeton resents her and her overpowering erotic intrusion
in a trip that should've been his and Duncan's alone. No,
make that in a love that should've been his and Duncan's
alone!

Such is the new setting of the Virtus Saga, where nothing
is what it seems. Not since soul-mates Prince Duncan Caldwell and Lord Christopher Templeton share a love that is unrivaled, until that fateful knock on Ylianor Meyer's dilapidated shack changes everything forever.

This book doesn't simply pick up right where Book 1 Virtus Sex leaves off. This book explodes it all—the lust and the
leadership, but also the estrangement and the chaos. Mostly
the unique connection laced with a load of jealousy and violence that is unknown to their world. Because this isn't just
another erotic dark fantasy series. This is the making of a trio.
The story of three remarkable characters that have to overcome their uncontrollable lust to face the truth about themselves and their planet, in order to defeat the darkness about
to devour them. To be as one whilst three! That's their real

challenge. Because, if they can't learn to share power and love in equal measures, how will they be able to ensure their world's survival?

NEXT BOOK IN THE VIRTUS SAGA SERIES

The Festival
Virtus Saga, Book 3

When Ylianor Meyer throws in Prince Duncan Caldwell's face his generous offer to adopt her into the Caldwell family, she has only one thought in mind — to get as far away from the stunningly gorgeous dark-haired prince and his equally striking blond-haired lover, Lord Christopher Templeton before she falls in love with them harder than she already is. Before she becomes their slave for real and surrenders to both without any shame. For each is a master in his own standing: one for pleasure, the other for pain.

Such is the new setting of the Virtus Saga, where nothing is as it seems. Not the world, since its all-pervading sex drive hides a scary lack of violence. Not the people, since soul mates Prince Duncan Caldwell and Lord Christopher Templeton share a love that is unrivaled until that fateful knock on Ylianor Meyer's dilapidated shack.

This book picks up right where Virtus Game, Book 2, leaves off and extends love and passion into torrid sex and bloody nightmares. It's a unique connection, laced with jealousy and violence that are unknown to their world. This is not just another erotic dark fantasy series. This is the making of a trio. Of three remarkable characters that must overcome their uncontrollable lust to face the truth about themselves and their planet if they want to defeat the darkness about to devour them. To be as one whilst three! To share power and love in equal measures. This is their real challenge, the lesson they must learn. Otherwise, how will their world survive?

ABOUT THE VIRTUS SAGA

Erotic Dark Fantasy Paranormal Romance Series that Explores the Dark and Light Sides of Power and Love between Three People.

The Making of a Trio: The Virtus Saga shows how power and love can be equally shared!

Now completed, Laura Tolomei's erotic dark fantasy series is continuing to receive critical acclaims. The concept of a world free of violence attracts readers. The fiery MM and MMF sex keep them hooked to every page. The titles say it all. Book 1 Virtus Sex, book 2 Virtus Game, book 3 The Festival, book 4 The Leader, book 5 The Pledge, book 6 The Heat, book 7 The Princess, Book 8 The Lord and a special Not I The Game, Deleted Scenes from The Game—they all drip passion and lust woven inside an imaginary frame ruled by magical powers, divided between good and evil and struggling to survive.

The way it all starts and progresses, nothing is as it seems. Soul-mates Prince Duncan Caldwell and Lord Christopher Templeton share a love that is unrivaled until Duncan takes shelter in Ylianor Meyer's dilapidated shack. Ylianor has always loved Duncan, and while Duncan is attracted to her, she remains a servant—okay to bed, but not acceptable consort material. Unwilling to accept it, Ylianor vows she will do anything, even come head to head with his insufferable lover, to stay at his side.

But there is more going on than either of the three realize. Lord Arthur Fairchild, Leader of the High Council, knows his planet Sendar is doomed unless the predestined Hero steps in and blocks the darkness threatening to take over. Even if one person alone fits the bill, Arthur does the unthinkable—not only does he summon the Hero, but the Hero's consorts as well. Sendar needs these three special people to become fully aware of their powers and learn how to use them together. Sendar needs these three special people to work together above and beyond their personal issues. Sendar needs these three special people to become one whilst being three to make it through the difficult times ahead. If they do not, the Virtus that hold all of Sendar's secrets could destroy them all.

The Virtus Saga Books:
Virtus Sex, The Sex: Author's Cut, Book 1
Completely revised, this edition of the original publication Virtus, The Sex, is doubled in size and has many newly added scenes.
Novel—LGBT, ménage, M/M gay, dark fantasy, paranormal, romance, series—April 5 2019, eXtasy Books.

The Sex, Book 1
Novel—LGBT, ménage, M/M gay, dark fantasy, paranormal, romance, series—March 15 2010, eXtasy Books.

Virtus Game, The Game: Author's Cut, Book 2
Completely revised, this edition of the original publication Virtus, The Sex, is doubled in size and has many newly added scenes.
Novel—LGBT, ménage, M/M gay, multiple partners, dark fantasy, paranormal, romance, series.

Not In The Game, Deleted Scenes from The Game Book 2
Novel—LGBT, ménage, M/M gay, multiple partners, dark fantasy, paranormal, series—April 6 2018, eXtasy Books.

The Game, Book 2
Novel—LGBT, ménage, M/M gay, multiple partners, dark

fantasy, paranormal, romance, series—May 15 2010, eXtasy Books.

The Festival, Book 3
Novel—BDSM, LGBT, LGBT, ménage, M/M gay, dark fantasy, horror paranormal, romance, series—July 15 2010, eXtasy Books.

The Leader, Book 4
Novel—LGBT, LGBT, ménage, M/M gay, dark fantasy, paranormal, romance, series—February 1 2012, eXtasy Books.

The Pledge, Book 5
Novel—LGBT, ménage, M/M gay, multi-partner, dark fantasy, paranormal, romance, series—September 1 2012, eXtasy Books.

The Heat, Book 6
Novel—LGBT, ménage, M/M gay, dark fantasy, paranormal, romance, series—November 15 2012, eXtasy Books.

The Princess, Book 7
Novel—BDSM, LGBT, ménage, M/M gay, dark fantasy, paranormal, romance, series—September 15 2014, eXtasy Books.

The Lord, Book 8
Novel—BDSM, LGBT, ménage, M/M gay, multiple partners, dark fantasy, paranormal, romance, series—October 1 2014, eXtasy Books.

For more info, check out the Virtus Saga official pages: www.lauratolomei.com.

ABOUT THE AUTHOR

Born in Italy, Laura Tolomei lives in Alicante, Spain, and is the author of 28+ books in her very particular and unique genre—Erotic Romance with an Edge. She has been traveling the globe since age five and has no intention of quitting. After having been an avid reader her entire life, she decided at age forty to write her own stories—the erotic romances with an edge that's her trademark—and has not looked back since. Writing novels that are on the boundary of accepted conventions is her trademark, and she guarantees an erotic earthquake with each book! Among others, they include the scorching dark fantasy Virtus Saga books, all eight of them, along with the kindred spirits of both the ReScue and the Soulmate Series, not to mention her horror novels along with a few historical ones.

For more info, check out Laura's website:
www.lallagatta.com
www.lauratolomei.com